BOOKS BY WILLIAM WISER

The Circle Tour   1988

The Crazy Years   1983

Ballads, Blues, and Swansongs   1982

Disappearances   1980

The Wolf Is Not Native to the South of France   1978

K   1971

The
Circle Tour

The
Circle Tour

WILLIAM WISER

Atheneum
NEW YORK
1988

The author gratefully acknowledges the support
of grants from the National Endowment for the
Arts and from the Guggenheim Foundation, which
helped him complete this novel.

This is a work of fiction. Names, characters,
places, and incidents are either the product of the author's
imagination or are used fictitiously. Any resemblance to
actual events or persons, living or dead, is entirely
` coincidental.

Atheneum
Macmillan Publishing Company
866 Third Avenue, New York, N.Y. 10022
Collier Macmillan Canada, Inc.

Library of Congress Cataloging-in-Publication Data
Wiser, William.
    The circle tour.
    I. Title.
PS3573.I87C57   1988   813'.54   87-30710
ISBN 0-689-11928-3

10 9 8 7 6 5 4 3 2 1
PRINTED IN THE UNITED STATES OF AMERICA

FOR *Michelle*

Contents

Case Histories

1

MOVING ON, according to the Poet, was the American way. ("Where to?" was no longer an acceptable question.) At Highway 27 we could turn south to Homestead and Key West, or follow Snapper Canal through the northern reaches of the Everglades to the shores of Lake Okeechobee at last. If either direction should lead to detour or dead end, so be it.

The ravaged sky had cleared of all but trailing veils of cloud across most of a full moon—more illumination than we needed or I wanted—a phosphorescent light that turned the landscape surreal.

Beside me on the backseat lay a frightened child wrapped in a blanket. Lee Ann might have slept this long way from Miami Beach, but I knew her heart beat in time to the taxi meter and her eyes were squeezed tight in pretense. She had seen too much to sleep.

As our cab navigated the Tamiami Trail past turpentine pines and shut filling stations, I saw a single lit-up enterprise called BAIT where the turnoff would have to be. A one-legged attendant with a crutch and a flashlight was hopping through the shadows to an outside phone booth. You could hear the phone ringing all the way to the road.

A telephone booth at night, illuminated by a flashlight beam, reminded me of a hospital where I worked long before this fateful moving on. *Poet, don't take me back to that time—I'm as sane as you ever were or I'll ever be.* That was when I paid strict attention to telephones and bathrobes and locked doors, a place where I concerned myself with such commonplace mysteries as a missing letter

3

from the Scrabble set or a pair of dice stolen from the games closet in the Dayroom.

I found the missing Monopoly dice and the letter *X* from the Scrabble set in the Poet's bathrobe pocket. He had hidden the dice to get back at Mrs. Kakafroni (our flautist, who believed a worm was consuming the musical notes in the chambers of her heart) for not selling him Mediterranean Avenue.

Our patients refused to play Scrabble with the Poet: they said he made up words. He did. Also, his game of Monopoly was unorthodox and disruptive. If the Poet himself did not land on Mediterranean Avenue, he would go to any expense ("It's only play money, Investors") to wheedle that insignificant piece of real estate—along with its counterpart, Baltic Avenue—from the original owner. Then he would place a hotel on Mediterranean and refuse to roll the dice when his turn came around.

"Why do you play Monopoly if you don't want to take your turn?"

"I've had my turn, Critic. Now I intend to rest on my laurels."

The Poet called me Critic. I was the arbiter of games at the Sans Souci; I decided which TV programs the patients might safely watch and when the set must be turned off at night. Patients came to me for playing cards, chessboards, and to be instructed in the rules of bridge and canasta and mah jong. I pronounced on the winning order of hands in poker, and decided if a Scrabble word was legitimate or not. (There was only one dictionary on 3, in the Nurses Station, kept out of reach of the patients.) Besides being monitor of the television set, I also provided books and magazines for the few who read—librarian-bookseller still, but librarian to the insane—and jigsaw and crossword puzzles for the fewer still who had the courage to work at puzzles.

It was I who reminded the Poet when he was scheduled for a shower, inquired about his bowel movements, and asked him not to circulate in the Dayroom in his bathrobe.

"Who's circulating?"

"This is a mixed floor. It makes some of the female patients uneasy."

"Who's flashing the ladies? I've got my Fruit of the Looms on underneath."

"Sorry." I tilted my head in the direction of his room.

"Don't be sorry," said he. "Never apologize. What would we do without you? It's you critics who steer us poets straight. Otherwise we wouldn't know what rules to play by, when to titillate the ladies and when not. It's the critic's job to teach the rest of us right from wrong—right?"

He went along with me quietly enough, his voice low and apparently under control—but you never knew what levels of rage lay behind a patient's offhand sarcasms. However, the Poet was passive enough to pass for one of ours, on the third floor, known informally as Passive City. On 4 and 5 the patients were segregated, male and female, to reduce the occasion and excuse for violence. But 3 was a mixed ward, where the patients were almost indistinguishable, in both manner and dress, from their visiting relatives.

"Hang around while I change." He did not look me in the eye when he said this, but at the nameplate attached to my shirt pocket, possibly reading the title Critic there. "You can check me for scars."

He was referring obliquely to the evening he was admitted to the Sans Souci. Originally he had been taken to Mt. Sinai, in Miami Beach, then brought to the Sans Souci in a police ambulance, his hair and beard still wet. (Resuscitation was an Emergency Room procedure; we had no such facilities. The patient was then returned to his police escort since Mt. Sinai had no psychiatric division, and no formal admission could be authorized.) I was on Admissions duty at the Sans Souci when the Poet was brought in.

"Gandhi," he replied, when I asked him his name. "Gandhi, with an *h*. Pray for me. I'm Hindu to the core and our local Muslims don't dig the way I partitioned India."

He did resemble a thin brown Gandhi, a bearded one, with his prominent skull and hunger-sunken eyes. He was wrapped in a blanket Mt. Sinai had provided (but requested that we return), and shoes without socks. Eventually he told me his real name, and I recognized it, though I was not at the time a great reader of modern poetry. This was a name that appeared regularly on lists of the twelve—or twenty?—front-runners in the literary sweepstakes, yet never at the head of the list. (I stocked a volume of his *Selected Poems* at a bookstore I once owned—but I did not read the poems, or sell the book. When I later told him about my failed bookstore, the confession sealed a bond between us: partly because the enterprise had been a bookstore, partly because it was a failure.)

When he gave his address as "the cosmos" I did not immediately write it on his chart; I assumed he was being facetious.

"The Cosmos Motel, in Fort Lauderdale. I kid you not."

He sloshed along beside me in his wet shoes and blanket to the shower room.

"A shower? I just had a bath in Biscayne Bay."

The Poet had been rescued by the Coast Guard when he attempted suicide by leaping from a tour boat near the Venetian Causeway.

"I'm afraid a shower is required. On admission."

"You're afraid? I'm the one who should be afraid. Listen, you know about the Nazis inviting the likes of me to take a shower. You end up a bar of soap for somebody else's shower. What is this place, anyway? Who asked to be admitted? The whole scenario was a brainstorm of the police department. Or the SS. I saw your initials carved in coral rock on the gatepost."

"That stands for Sans Souci."

"Sans Souci. Great. You know what that means in French?"

"It means 'without care.' "

"A likely story. You know French?"

"My mother was French."

"Mine was Russian but I don't know the language."

"Anyway. That's what I've been told."

"Believe everything you've been told and you'll end up taking a shower when a Nazi asks you to."

In my three years at the Sans Souci I had pieced together a working personality of patience and forbearance. Bruno, on the fourth floor, or Max, on 5, would have applied a rabbit punch, jabbed the Poet in the kidneys with a clipboard, then stuffed him into a straightjacket. I was no Nazi, I waited.

"You're right," he said. "It does mean 'without care.' "

I adjusted the temperature of the water flowing from the shower head, and asked the Poet to disrobe.

"With you watching? Why can't that pretty nurse do this job?"

"Miss Ryan supervises the female admissions, I do the men."

"Why not the other way around?"

"Patients might get. The wrong idea."

"Or the right idea."

But he let the blanket fall from his pathetically thin body, stepped out of his shoes and stood naked in the rising steam, the palms of his hands turned outward to show he had nothing to hide.

"What're you writing down—a poem?"

"I have to note any scars or identifying marks."

"The scars don't show. They're all on the inside."

In the matter of scars: my wife Valerie wore a large wristwatch with a wide band to hide the stippled marks on her wrist made by a razor blade.

My body, like the Poet's, bore no noticeable scars worth recording.

Not long before the Poet was admitted to the Sans Souci, I supervised the Admissions shower for a patient with a small scar on his abdomen, on the opposite side from an appendectomy scar. I asked him if he had undergone a hernia operation, and he explained that his wife had stabbed him there with a fish knife. A patient does not always tell the literal truth about such things, but later Dr. Krauskopf confirmed the patient's story, so I entered the information on his chart.

The patient was separated from his Swiss wife, and one night had abducted their small son and brought him to the United States. Eventually his wife recovered the boy through legal means; her husband had been briefly imprisoned. He was suffering from acute depression.

I did not know whether the wife stabbed her husband before or after the kidnapping.

Patients tended to confide in me (Miss Ryan attributed their trust to my innocent eyes and hesitant speech), but I seldom learned much more of a life than the episodes of a patient's case history. I wanted to ask Swanson about the incident with the fish knife, but one afternoon at Recreational Therapy the patient walked off the hospital grounds and was never seen again.

2

"YOU WERE conceived on the shores of Lake Okeechobee," my father wrote in that first of many letters with no return address. Since his letters were all that I knew of my father, the declaration of my conception was a statement to stir a young man's heart—I was just old enough to know what he was talking about. Even if he had not repeated the phrase in letters to follow, that first revelation would forever jingle its way to the surface of my mind. When the Poet began to ask me about myself and my origins—apparently in exchange for information about his own history—I was not being facetious when I said I was conceived on the shores of Lake Okeechobee.

"That's the first poetic line I've heard out of you, Critic."

I did not tell him that the poetry was my father's.

"Before the evening was out," my father wrote, "I had taken your beloved Mother under my wing."

My mother read this letter at the same time as I did, and said, "That is his story."

My mother and father did meet on the shores of Lake Okee-chobee in Lakeport, Florida, during the great land boom of the 1920s, but I was never to have my mother's version of this encounter and courtship. "Your father," she would begin, then say no more.

My father's letters bore the postmarks of cities all over the United States—and once from Canada—but never a specific return address. I have the letters still—they are, as I have said, all I have of my father. In letter after letter he urged me to live every day as if it were my last on earth—that may have been how he lived his. Gradually he invoked an inventory of pieties he had acquired late in life, and was still collecting, such as "Straight is the gate," and "We may not pass this way again." He had come to a belief in God during his middle years; rather, a belief in some obscure deity or variation of providence that rewarded a man in his next life for having been good to his mother in this one. "Cherish your beloved Mother, Son, as I did mine." Something to do with my birth had made a believer of him: "I remember the miraculous convolutions of your ears as a newborn babe and it dawned on me that there is more to this life than meets the eye." The style of this one-way correspondence could accommodate a phrase like "bridging the empty chasm between Father and Son before the sands of time run out," as well as an admonition on the usefulness of reading my Bible daily, as he did, and adherence to the Ten Commandments, especially the injunction to honor thy father and thy mother.

In the beginning (the first letter came winging out of the blue when I was thirteen) I thought my father was exceptionally devoted to me, if somewhat hipped on religion. He was neither, according to my mother's meager documentation. He was a crook through and through, she blurted out in one of her rare confidences, angered by a reference in one of his letters to another woman's well-turned ankle and swanlike neck. I could believe in his dishonesty, for subsequent letters confessed to "misdemeanors aplenty," misdemeanors he described in a mixture of pride and regret.

His favorite scam was promoting electric organs and speaker systems designed for churches and funeral parlors. He would collect a substantial down payment from Negro ministers or morticians ("the Colored are often operating sub rosa themselves, so not as likely to call the police") then skip town before delivery date. He operated under a variety of names along the small-town circuit from Cincinnati to Omaha, and he was still in the sales-without-merchandise business even as he wrote advising me to read the Bible every day, and observe the Ten Commandments.

I was born at Bethesda Maternity Hospital in Cincinnati, Ohio, during the Depression years—surname, according to my birth certificate, White; given name, Frank. White was not necessarily my father's name, but he was using the name White when my mother knew him. They were never married. My father left my mother— ostensibly to go on-the-road promoting—soon after my birth, to return sporadically to Cincinnati, and to her side, until some time between my third and fourth years when he abandoned her for all time. Before the age of five I was placed in The Children's Home in Latonia, Kentucky. This was not an orphanage, but a crèche, as my mother called it in her occasional French, a boarding-nursery for the children of working mothers. I sometimes stayed with my mother at a rooming house on Pike Street, in Covington, but mostly I lived at The Children's Home during the years I attended elementary school. After the day at school I would return to my Home, the first of several institutions that would shelter me, or that I would be drawn to.

At intervals my mother would come for me; I would spend a weekend or holiday with her. I was agitated and elated when she appeared, and inconsolably downcast when she brought me back, but I cannot say that life at The Children's Home was tragic, or even depressing. However, I sadly wanted a family of my own. I was surrounded with children of my own age, older and younger than I, but I yearned for legitimate brothers and sisters instead of playmates. Most of all, I would like to have had a father.

(At this point the Poet chimed in: "From the sound of that father of yours, you were better off without.")

My father fell in step with Destiny (his word) and ran off with a woman he had met at Latonia Race Track. For a few years he sent occasional money for my upkeep ("That is his story," said my mother) and kept up a postcard correspondence with my mother. The letters to me did not begin until I was in high school. As for the woman he met at Latonia Race Track, he wrote: "Mea Culpa, I admit, but I could never resist a well-turned ankle and a swanlike neck."

"Your father," said my mother.

During the early years at The Children's Home I developed a speech impediment: a deliberately acquired lisp at first, then a troubling stutter. By the time I reached adolescence I had managed, by pausing for breath every few words, to express myself without the damnable stammer. But my speech had always been slow and broken, with what some listeners consider thoughtful deliberation. (I discussed this speech disability with Dr. K when I applied for the job at the Sans Souci—he saw no difficulty in my general ability to express myself, but was intrigued by the origins of the impediment and my "compensatory cover by self-cure." I need not have brought up the problem—an example of my scrupulous honesty at the time, or of my self-conscious sincerity—for Dr. K, like most everyone else, thought that I spoke with thoughtful deliberation.) I became a fanatic bookworm from the time I learned to read, and between books was a rather idle-minded dreamer. When my yearning for a brother or sister (preferably both) was intense, I considered the possibility that I might have a secret half-brother or half-sister somewhere on my father's clandestine route from Cincinnati to Omaha. When I suggested this to my mother, she sharply replied, "Not possible,"—which only inspired another daydream, that the man from whom she received postcards from Midwestern cities, and whose (false?) name appeared on my birth certificate, was not my father at all.

I never told Dr. K about my father.

("A good thing you didn't," said the Poet.)

When my father left her, my mother went to work for an exclusive women's fashion shop in Cincinnati. The store thought it chic to hire a Frenchwoman to sell clothes to matrons in the Midwest. My mother spoke with an accent charming to American ears, though I never heard her speak a complete sentence in French. She may have sung lullabies to me in her native tongue, I would not remember. Except for the accent, she seemed to have eliminated every trace of France in her background. Only the notation on my birth certificate remained: *Mother's birthplace*—Béziers, France.

It was my mother's idea that I save my father's letters. I do not know, or remember, why she suggested this; perhaps she meant me to retain the letters as black-and-white reminders of the counterfeit life, my father's sly mea culpas as alternate Ten Commandments—since she made no other gesture toward my moral upbringing. I am still uncertain how she felt about him—or how she felt about me. I believe she would have stayed with him, for all his fraudulent enterprises, if he had not left her—but she would not have wanted me to follow in his errant footsteps. She was very likely imbued with the cynicism of the French: most men, she might have reasoned, were cheats and frauds by nature, it was the way of the world, *rien à faire*, but her son should at least be made to realize when he was cheating or being fraudulent. The letters were living testimony, a swindler's self-serving confession of constant deceit.

Otherwise my mother did not impose upon me the guilt-and-thrift attitudes of the middle-class French. She saw to my material well-being—clothes, food and housing (however institutional)—within the limits drawn by the Depression years, and from a little distance.

I was a bright enough but inattentive student through the lower grades and into high school. The speech impediment was no apparent handicap. Often enough my name appeared on one Honor Roll or the other—often enough to assure me few friends. I turned to books, not to better my grades but because I was an obsessed reader—especially of the imaginary, but I would read anything (a telephone directory, if nothing else). A passion for reading and an inaptitude for sports marked me early as a misfit, set me slightly apart in school playgrounds or at The Children's Home.

At seventeen I joined the Navy through a procedure known as Minority Enlistment, meant to provide career opportunity for under-age young men with no prospects or resources—exactly my status. The enlistment papers required the signed permission of both parents, if living. There may have been a way around this stipulation, especially in the case of an illegitimate birth, but my mother did not choose to bypass the signature requirement. She managed to get in touch with my father by way of a letter to his former business associate, Dr. Breathwaite.

My father replied—not to her letter, but to me—somewhat dismayed to know my mother had, all along, kept up this indirect line to his secret life, and that his whereabouts had often been known to her. But he did oblige with the necessary signature. He carelessly signed his current pseudonym—Whitehead, by this time—but the Navy ignored the discrepancy, or preferred not to notice, happy enough to acquire a new recruit.

"Choose your chums with care! I myself fell in with a worldly-wise crowd when younger and have spent a lifetime trying to undo the damage." (I was aboard ship when this letter was forwarded by a circuitous route of APO numbers.) "Try to associate with the officer class instead of your ordinary (or 'ablebodied' as the Navy calls them) seamen. Son, it would break your old Dad's heart to know you had succumbed to tattoos. Think! You will have to live with that dragon or mermaid on your arm for the rest of your life! As for female companionship, there is penicillin now, I know, but you could be allergic, like me."

A young man aware of my mother's wishes—a good boy, a dutiful son?—I had every intention of moving in the opposite direction of my father's wayward path. We were nothing alike, as far as I could make out from his letters, except for an addiction to words: I was a compulsive reader, but not compelled to read the New Testament, or work crossword puzzles, as he did. In the Navy I started out as a Yeoman striker on the USS *Okaloosa* (an Indian name that reminded me of Okeechobee, and my spurious origins), then became ship's Librarian on the aircraft carrier *Intrepid*. There was nothing intrepid about my naval career and I was never tempted to acquire a tattoo.

Unlike my father, I came to Miami by accident, age twenty-one, having been discharged at the naval base in Key West when my enlistment was up. Miami was the next inevitable stopping place for an ex-sailor moving north out of the Florida Keys—an unconsciously ironic choice for a son determined to avoid the way stations of his father's crooked circuit.

My father had been here before me. Miami was a speculator's paradise when my father arrived by Seaboard Railway with the battered Gladstone bag mentioned in his letters (proud of this carpetbagger's trophy, he carried everything he owned in it)—and with a forged railroad pass. The Florida land boom of the 1920s was the perfect setting for a small-time confidence man inspired by big-money schemes.

When I became a psychiatric aide at the Sans Souci, I did not know that my father, who called himself Dr. White in his day, was co-founder of the first psychiatric unit south of Pennsylvania, right here on the shores of Dade County's gold coast.

(It occurred to me in the telling that here was a remarkable piece of happenstance: the son replacing the father in the field of mental health. The Poet was unimpressed by this coincidence. And he considered my motives for "treading water" in Miami altogether tame and pedestrian compared to the dash and swagger of my father's enterprise.)

"So you faded," suggested the Poet, "and he flourished."

My choice of a profession, what little choice I had, was, I would like to believe, partly altruistic. My father and his partner, Dr. Breathwaite, were frauds. They called themselves alienists just as that term, and psycho-analysis (before the hyphen was dropped), came into vogue. The Breathwaite Institute did become successful in its day, treating wealthy eccentrics and neurotics ("We sent the indigent and basket cases back North, like returned parcels, or damaged goods") by means of laudanum and other opiates. "I for once was the silent partner, preferring to operate sub rosa, while Breathwaite enjoyed the limelight." My father, as Dr. White, did Freudian interpretations of patients' dreams.

("Dreams?" repeated the Poet. This was rich, this was worthy of an insight. "That institute of theirs and the Sans Souci are the same place. The dreams, the opiates. You with Dr. K as the front man, the stark-raving confined to the attic, Father and Sonny working a similar swindle, con artists both.")

That was the trouble with telling the Poet anything personal— and with going back over my father's letters:

"Ah sweet mystery of Life. If only we could untangle the meaning of dreams we could win every toss of the dice and know Fate inside out.

"The rich, my Boy, do not dream the same dreams as you and me."

3

"MY OLD MAN was a grubworm to that highflier of yours," was the way the Poet put it. "But you yourself and Poppa Gold were careless bankrupts both. Everything my father had he put into wire recorders when the whole technological world knew tape was what was coming. Sound-on-Wire had a certain sound to it, *n'est-ce pas?* (Speaking of sound, it occurs to me your old Dad could have sold *mine* one of those fictitious sound systems of his, the sound of silence.) Poppa's next downfall was just as typical, he collected the two cents he got back on the dollar and invested in the Davy Crockett craze, a warehouse full of coonskin caps and plastic jackets with the fringe on the sleeves some sharpie like your father sold him sixty minutes after the craze that swept the Midwest died swiftly in the East. What would your father have done? Burn down the warehouse for the insurance at least, but not my father. The only thing he had in common with your father was he had a wife and kid, too, he left behind. This is the land, my boy, where when things go crash in the night you pick up your marbles and move on. No marbles, but he still had his degree in Accounting, right? And people trusted him, like they do you. But did Poppa stick his head in the sand the way you did? The man kissed his wife and budding-poet son farewell and headed west, to Salt Lake City. Whatever possessed him, what prospects were publicized in some company prospectus, we'll never know—but my father, a Jew, the Mormons' Gentile, took off for Utah to become CPA to the Latter-Day Saints. Let my father be a lesson to you."

My own father was lesson enough.

For six torpid weeks of that Miami summer—weeks of unrelenting heat and mosquitos, a fresh-water shortage, smothered nights and dead days—I had access to the Poet's medical records, I helped compose his chart. During our nightly conversations, that obscure chart lay unmentioned between us: I was obliged to record whatever the patient told me of any significance, and I was the judge of what was significant. He was unaware, or pretended to be unaware, that our talks were clinical interviews. Apparently (in the beginning) the advantage was mine. Officially I kept watch and could, at the same time, satisfy a personal curiosity. But he was the articulate one,

assured of the common leniency extended to drunks and the demented, and just beyond his barrage of wise-talking insult he slyly
applied a superior third degree.

"Give me the word on marriage again," he might say. Or another
time he would ask: "What was the one thing that made her unique in
all the world?"

He was referring to my wife. Until then I had always kept my
home life separate from the lives of those under my evening's care,
and, while on duty, kept my thoughts to myself. (I kept those thoughts
to myself off duty, too.) But this shrewd would-be suicide knew how to
draw me out.

The questions were the same he would have asked himself,
which seemed to him to justify the interrogation. My motives for
answering were more obscure.

"Don't flatter yourself your life is so unique it'll turn up in one of
my poems." He said this to me after I had spilled more than I
intended, and he still asked for more. "You're only the least asinine
of the inmates in this Garden of Aphasia."

And yet I continued to confide in him. His insults I considered
only a neurotic's subterfuge: he genuinely needed and wanted to
know. The immediate rationale behind my eager response was that I
must expose my own case history in order to get at his. (He would
sometimes interrupt with, "Who's the cuckoo here?") Like Dr. K and
Miss Ryan, I was supposed to be a professional listener; but
self-disclosure on the part of the professional was an unheard-of
precedent, this was an innovation of my own.

When he wasn't playing Scrabble or Monopoly, the Poet played
a little game with me, a game called quid pro quo.

Confession was never part of the strategy on the Disturbed Wards of 4
and 5. On the upper floors (where I had once worked) there were no
such inhibitions as the Poet's for self-containment or reserve. Except
for the catatonics, in the precincts of 4 and 5 the disturbed shouted
and screamed their lives at you: a cacophony of more lies and truth, at
the highest decibel level, than a conscientious attendant could take
in. (That was why I was transferred to 3.)

Ward 3 was only two levels from terra firma, that much closer to
discharge and rehabilitation. Our Passive City was the next thing to
the real-time world, a sanctuary for middle-aged schizophrenics and
the elderly depressed, where certain subtleties were still tacitly
intact. Perhaps only a thin membrane of definition or diagnosis

separated the world of the clinically miserable from the normally
miserable beyond these walls. At the Sans Souci there was even a
class system in effect: the quietly insane on 3 were separated from the
shrieking maniacs above by a soundproof elevator shaft. Our elite, on
the third floor, was a small and exclusive contingent of psychoneu-
rotics who had settled into their disorders as if into an unhappy
marriage.

4

ONLY A NET of gauze separated me from my wife. This transparent length of mosquito netting bisected our living area and neatly
separated the sleeping spaces. The apartment—where we lived
apart—was no larger than a semiprivate at the Sans Souci, with
screens on the windows almost as thick as the hospital screens. The
kitchen was set off from the living room/bedroom by a counter; the
only true separation was the bathroom cubicle, with a door that
locked. This arrangement was known as an Efficiency.

I explained to the Poet that Valerie was subject to rashes,
allergies, sunburn—this was true. She had delicate almost translucent skin that insects seemed drawn to and punctured with
abandon. (Or was it the quality of the blood these parasites found so
special, slightly medicinal from the tranquilizers?) Her thighs and the
insides of her arms were imprinted with a visible network of blue
veins; the skin seemed to glow under a certain light and gave off a
sweetish odor at night. Nights were the vulnerable time. The insect
world came alive after dark: at night—that close to Biscayne Bay, or
when the wind was from the Everglades—mosquitos plagued our
junglelike neighborhood.

We kept a collection of salves and lotions in the bathroom, for
Valerie's skin would become infected; she scratched at insect bites
until they bled. Her skin's sensitivity was a chronic disorder and
apparently untreatable. She was careful never to eat bananas after
reading in a women's magazine that the oil of bananas attracted

certain insects. Had she ever eaten bananas? Anyway, an article in *McCall's* confirmed her distaste for that fruit.

My wife ate little enough of any food. As an adolescent she had been hospitalized for anorexia nervosa, and her attitude toward food had been capricious ever since. I did not offer a physical description of my wife to the Poet. He would have been interested, especially to know that Valerie was a beauty in her hollow-cheeked ethereal way. She was thin-boned and small, even childlike in her proportions, but sensual (when she had been conscious of herself in that way) in her movements, in her dreamy detachment. The Poet would have raised a salacious eyebrow to hear this, or wrung his hands in mock frustration. He sometimes did impersonations of T. S. Eliot or Groucho Marx.

She kept the television set on her side of the curtain.

"It's the same room. Really—but divided. By this ridiculous curtain."

"If it's ridiculous, why have it?"

Since I worked nights, there was no reason why Valerie should not take the television on her side of the divided apartment. Even when I was home I would not have wanted to watch the television screen: I was a reader still, and exposed to enough of the tube at the Sans Souci.

But Valerie would watch anything. I think I understood her passive attachment to shallow cowboys and glib show-biz clowns: they, and the private detectives with their blank and virile expressions, were as far removed from our bisected Efficiency as Valerie's imagination could travel. Whatever excitement she felt when homicide squad cars careened through the streets of L. A. or Honolulu, she hid behind a blank expression of her own, as if she had learnt it from the detectives themselves. In the same stark expressionless way she watched wrestling matches and listened to political appeals. Dispassionately she followed the evening news, however grim or tragic, carried over from noon.

"My wife once had a sense of humor," I told the Poet.

"Of course she did," said he. "She married you, didn't she?"

If Valerie still had a sense of humor she kept it like all else to herself. During the TV reruns of old Laurel and Hardy films she did not laugh; she sat as impassive as Buster Keaton would have sat, or as sad as Chaplin—she preferred, I think, the silent screen in response to her own silence—through the most outrageous efforts of either comedian. A child herself, she could still tune in to those children's matinees contrived by Walt Disney and Tex Avery: she studied the exaggerated schemes of talking animals without a smile, yet she watched with passionate intensity. The only affect she ever showed, or sign she allowed herself in front of the screen, was an occasional empathetic tilt of her head during a commercial when a model tossed her iridescent hair into the wind after a shampoo, any brand. Now my wife wore her hair short, but even when her hair had been long and thick and glistening, I do not remember her tossing it, in that way, into the wind.

Mornings defeated her altogether. We both slept as late as possible to put off the daily encounter with tropical heat, or simply to postpone our daylight lives. We left our separate beds at longish intervals: I usually got up first while Valerie remained entwined in her sheet (head under the pillow if a mosquito had got in), shallow breathing but otherwise lifeless. At first I used to fear she had died of asphyxiation beneath the pillow but discovered she still breathed, as cats do, as if drawing air from some invisible source. She lay silent to allow me the maximum solitude in the neutral areas of bath and kitchen before the coffee began to percolate. Often I did not even hear her leave the bed, so guarded were her maneuvers. An hour might pass before our careful circlings intersected in that limited space: even then our eyes did not meet. Valerie's eyes would be swollen, her face drained, her movements lethargic from last night's narcosis. As if taking our cue from Genesis, we looked upon one another, after the Fall, only when we were clothed.

I returned home from work shortly after midnight, Valerie already wound into her sheet, entranced by the tube. She was too absorbed in the flickering spectacle cast by the miniature screen to be alarmed by a door that opened and closed. She did not acknowledge my presence. If we spoke at all I might ask her to turn down the sound of thundering hoofbeats or screaming sirens, the only request I made of her those nights.

On my night off I sometimes secretly watched her undress behind the net, her flesh alternately illuminated and shadowed by the television screen, the light that most flattered her narrow proportions.

"What is this?" the Poet asked at this point, "some new kind of perversion."

She was lovely still, perhaps all the more so through the seductive folds of a gauze curtain. The soft glow from the tube highlighted her flesh and form in the way of lamplight or candle flame, the light of another age. For a moment she was restored to me intact (though I did not tell the Poet this), as desirable as ever.

"If we're working symbols here," he said, "what about the curtain as extended hymen?"

Soberly I replied, "I'm not working symbols."

"Whose idea was this lightweight Iron Curtain?"

"Hers. No, mine."

In truth, I had forgotten—but I remembered we had hung the mosquito net together.

5

AFTER A THREE-DAY PERIOD of observation, including Rorschach tests and the Wechsler-Bellevue—"I passed," he confided to me—the Poet was diagnosed as Depressive Reaction and placed on drug therapy. Dr. K warned the staff of the patient's impulsive tendency to self-destruction; Miss Ryan wrote SUICIDAL in red on the Poet's chart.

"Just like Alcatraz," said he when I collected his pathetic arsenal. I kept the Poet's razor, his penknife and nail file in a locked chest marked SHARPS.

Because of his adverse effect on other patients (we had a minor flood on 3 when he told Mr. Marcus, a compulsive-obsessive who thought voices came through the water taps, that he would hear the voices more clearly if he left the faucets running), the Poet was assigned a private room at the far end of the East-West wing—though he would have preferred, he said, the North-South wing so as to be in magnetic harmony with the earth's polar axis. He had a view of Biscayne Bay where he had made his suicide attempt, and the hospital parking lot: "The doctors all drive Volvos, wouldn't you know?" At first he accepted what he called his confinement-by-chloroform with the dazed resignation of the drugged, but his wit and whimsy surfaced soon enough.

"How long, legally or otherwise, can the Warden keep me in a helpless state of *sans souci?*"

Dr. Krauskopf was known as Dr. K among the patients and staff, but the Poet referred to him as the Warden, or Freud's Afterbirth.

"These things take time."

"Is that a song by Cole Porter?"

"We've been trying to locate a relative, or someone responsible."

"To sign me in here, or sign me out? Why not allow me to decide if I want to be without care, or with. Irresponsible me. That's another song by Cole Porter."

"Have you talked with Miss Pike?"

"The one with the mustache? Hardly my type. I never talk to those butch nurses on the day shift."

"Miss Pike is a psychiatric social worker."

"The one with the little gold pen attached to her gross titties by an elastic? Yeah, Miss Lonelyhearts put the thumbscrews to me. She caught me trying to write something down and tried to snatch it, thought it was my vital statistics. It was a poem. I tore it up and swallowed the pieces before her horrified eyes. The woman is a menace."

"She's trying to help."

"Let her help the needy. She probably failed as a female samurai but with pull could make it as the muscle half of a CIA interrogation team. Anyway, I'm saving my body for Miss Ryan and my bons mots for you."

"Isn't there somebody? In your family—"

"*Personne.* That's French for nobody—and also means somebody, just to confuse you students of French. I'm an orphan, a widower, an exile, a monk. Siblings, none. No next of kin since Keats died."

His sly hyperactivity was suspect. Behind the soundproof glass of the Nurses Station, Miss Ryan expressed the opinion that the Poet's behavior pattern was not compatible with the heavy dosage of tranquilizers she administered nightly. "He's too frisky, for one thing, and too fresh. And does he verbalize." She passed the Poet's chart for me to fill in. "If I wrote everything he says to me on his chart, it would take all night." She smiled, thinking of the things he said to her. "You have to keep a straight face, some of the things he says. Who's Anna L. Plurabelle?"

"Why do you ask?"

"That's what he calls me, and his Irish Grushenka. Who's Molly Bloom?"

"Characters. In novels."

"*He's* a character in a novel, if you ask me. He's got all these names for me. Rima the bird girl and Madame Butterfly."

"Better than his names for me, and Dr. K."

"God, does he verbalize. I mean, nonstop. Fifty milligrams of Librium doesn't faze him. I'm supposed to be his belly-bah dorment—what's that?"

"Sleeping Beauty."

"I mean, you really have to keep a straight face. How old is he, anyway?"

"Fifty-eight. On his chart."

"He never makes a pass exactly. Not overt, so far, anyway. He just verbalizes."

The Poet passed in the corridor, saw us nodding over a chart (his, if he had known), fluffed his beard and blew an exaggerated kiss to Miss Ryan.

Dr. K increased the Librium to three times daily, then PRN (per R.N., administer when necessary) every four to six hours. "If this keeps up—" (after the flood, after the Poet shouted, "Hitler lives!" at Lights Out) "—we'll have to resort to Thorazine."

"Or a straightjacket," said Miss Ryan, at staff conference; but Dr. K gave her a professional frown. The Sans Souci was proud of its record on the limited use of restraints.

To me, Dr. K suggested a room search, and advised that I make the inspection while the Poet was present—"to avoid paranoid accusations."

The Poet's room, like Valerie's half of our Efficiency, was suggestive of inviolate space, redolent of personal odors (Valerie's insect spray and nail polish remover, the Poet's Brut and nicotine) and invested with exceptionally individual auras. On a shelf beside his bed the Poet kept the five volumes of his work, the centerpiece was his *Selected Poems.* The books were published by a reputable New York house better known for textbooks and best-selling fiction than for collections of verse—but the Poet, with two distinguished awards in his dossier and the praise of Robert Lowell gracing the Introduction to his first volume—had been added to the publisher's list for reasons more to do with prestige than profit.

In an attaché case—among the literary journals, *Thesaurus,* legal pads (with illegible scribblings in green ink)—I came across the clipping from *The New York Review of Books* the Poet had passed to me several nights ago with the comment: "In case you proles think I'm play-pretending poet here, like Ballantine playing doctor." The clipping was of several columns of a lengthy review—quite favorable, even enthusiastic—of the Poet's *Selected Poems.* I had read the review in the Nurses Station after Lights Out, and was impressed: I even read the poems the reviewer quoted to inform the argument of his long and thorough assessment. The poems escaped me. I could not discover the significance behind the display of words or get at the heart of "the shock effect of these revelations in juxtaposition" any more than I could grasp the essence of the Poet himself. (Though I was briefly tempted to use the reviewer's term, "major poet," instead of "pt." in my own review in the Poet's chart that night.)

I also found a dozen books of matches inscribed with the crest of the Cosmos Motel. Matches were forbidden to patients, as the Poet well knew.

"I hate to ask you KGB thugs every time I want a light." He tightened his sash, shrugged, and surrendered to the philistines. "As a matter of fact, the poems you so cavalierly manhandled are more inflammatory than the matches."

I confiscated the matches without comment.

When I moved to the bed he tried to distract me with a vaudeville soft-shoe in his floppy slippers. "Cold," he advised, then danced to the window and shouted through the security screen: "Help! I've been kidnapped by a bankrupt bookseller!" I ran my hand beneath his mattress—"Cold, cold, cold"—but then I removed a Cigarillo tin, and he felt obliged to murmur, "Now you're getting warm."

The tin was full of the capsules Miss Ryan had dispensed to him for the last two weeks: a secret stash of multicolored pills, unswallowed.

"I was saving them for a rainy day." He looked out through the security screen as if for rain.

Before I finished searching the bed, I came across a Kodachrome snapshot under his pillow. It was a photograph of a girl in her twenties wearing jeans with a dark green sweater, a strand of her long hair blown across her face the way Valerie would have wanted her own hair to blow, if her hair had been long. The girl stood in semiprofile beside a tan-and-white horse, her hand resting on the animal's neck. On the back of the snapshot was written, in the Poet's green ink: "*All in green went my love riding . . .*"

"Please put that back." His voice had lost its playful mockery.

He was right: I should not have picked up his personal memento or examined it so indiscreetly. I replaced the photograph, face down, beneath the Poet's pillow.

"You get in touch with my wife," he said, "and I'll slit your throat."

Not all his remarks were playful insults. But his razor, as I said, was locked in a box marked SHARPS.

I stepped carefully through the evidence of my wife's disorderly state of mind: the remains of a peanut butter sandwich on the floor, nibbled with small neat cat-bites at the crust; her wristwatch too heavy for the thin wrist, removed, set at some hour special to her (behind time, or far ahead) and placed in one shoe, the shoe for some reason—or none—perched on the television set. The telephone was on her side of the room: she had left the receiver only half-cradled and it hummed to itself till I set it right. Valerie spoke seldom enough, and when she did speak it was into a telephone, to me or to Miss Pike.

It was midafternoon nap time, her release from daylight, the only time I stared openly into her face. A ruby-colored teardrop of dried blood clung to her cheek where she had scratched an insect bite or scraped at a blemish (real or imagined) until it bled. In the subdued light through slits in the Venetian blind her eyelids were the same pale green as the underside of leaves and her features not altogether swollen out of recognition. She wore no makeup now, but I remembered her from an earlier time when she did. She was the girl, twenty-three, who came quietly into the Just Books to ask for a copy of *Middlemarch*, the most unexpected request in my brief career as bookseller.

I ordered the book for her, and by the time it came (and I presented it to her as a gift) we had slept together in her lemon-colored room in Coconut Grove. I told the Poet about *Middlemarch* and about the lemon-colored room, and for once he made no comment, snide or otherwise.

An early endeavor of mine was to try to know Valerie by the books she read; I persisted in my faulty analysis by attempting to measure her decline of spirit by the gradual lowering shifts in her literary interests. (During Valerie's internship at University of Miami, she may have been just as misled in theory by trying to diagnose a psyche by comparing the drawings and paintings of her child patients.) The bookshelves in the room-with-garden in Coconut Grove contained psychology texts, books on art and art therapy, contemporary novels (Pulitzer winners, if not Nobels), several nineteenth-century classics, principally Dickens, whose abused children would naturally arouse her sympathies.

Valerie had finished with Piaget and Gesell by the time I knew her: presumably she had completed her textbook studies in child psychology and passed her exams in the history of art, for those titles were left on the shelves untouched. Soon the novels—and her *Oxford Book of English Verse*—went unread as well. It would have been flattering if only partly true to believe that her interest in me interfered with that first passion for reading. But the reading may have been a forced passion: I was a temporary distraction from books, but a distraction only.

When we were married she was reading mysteries and novels of espionage that were likely to become movies, and by the time we moved to the Efficiency beside the Seaboard tracks she took up women's novels of romantic intrigue at castles in Cornwall. Eventually this energy flagged altogether, even a lightweight gothic romance became too heavy to hold. She flipped distractedly through magazines that explained sex and slimming and salad making, each issue concluding with This Month's Horoscope. Her eyes were held more often by illustrations and advertisements than by the text of a story or article. Finally she was reading the inside pages of the *Miami Herald* only, and the schedule of programs in *TV Guide*. The fold of Kleenex that marked her place in *Middlemarch* never moved past the Preface.

Before I left for work I collected the bread crusts, placed her shoes together on the floor, and arranged three capsules on the night table: red, white and blue. The pills would be gone when I got back. I had appointed myself the priest of her Communion, though never present to place the host upon her tongue.

"Exercise reasonable caution," Dr. K advised me, "but demonstrate a certain amount of trust." (Dr. White and Dr. Breathwaite might have said the same.)

Valerie's father confessor was Dr. K, who treated her at weekly sessions of analysis on an outpatient basis—not at the Sans Souci, but at his private office in Sunny Isles. Because of our professional connection, and because he knew how little I earned as a psychiatric aide, Dr. K's fee for individual therapy in Valerie's case was only half the going rate.

Since we did not own a car—neither Valerie nor I could drive, and the Sans Souci was within walking distance—Miss Pike came regularly in her vintage Oldsmobile to drive Valerie to Sunny Isles. Valerie would go anywhere with Miss Pike. Only Miss Pike had ever been able to lure Valerie into our scrappy back garden, hidden from the Seaboard Railway tracks by a ragged hedge of oleander. This small opening into nature was a threatening universe inhabited by red ants, scorpions, lizards, spiders. This was a surreal jungle to Valerie, a domain of menace, yet she would venture outside, at least to the back steps, wearing her gogglelike sunglasses to drink iced tea with Miss Pike. Otherwise she preferred her own disordered garden, inside, or to languish in an enchanted sleep.

For whatever practical measures I followed, it would seem I took no substantial role in the attempt at her rehabilitation. Her damaged psyche was treated by others, though I may have been responsible for the damage. (The Poet noted my "it would seem" and "may have been" in this part of my confession.) I too was a professional in the field of mental health, albeit at the lowest professional level. As husband to the patient I was prone to misread her state and symptoms. The married are too close to analyze and diagnose one another—even if a curtain of gauze hangs between them. Ironically, I knew very little of Valerie's parents beyond a photograph of the two together looking in opposite directions, or of her past, except for the case of anorexia when she was in her teens: I assumed Dr. K now knew all. If it was possible to be jealous, I might have been jealous of Miss Pike and Dr. K.

My search of Valerie's side of our apartment was less thorough than a room search at the Sans Souci. What was I looking for? I felt more of an intruder in her secret space between thick screens and drawn blinds and the thin veil that brushed my face like cobwebs when I passed through. Even the air was different on her side. Her odor was special, not unpleasant, mingled with melon, apple, yogurt. There was almost always the lingering smell of nail polish remover. I never saw her paint her nails (she did not use cosmetics, but she did use nail polish), and only knew from the smell when she had removed the colorless lacquer. One hand, with its scarred wrist, lay outside the sheet like a broken wing.

Bread crusts, melon rind, apple core, yogurt container and spoon I carried into the kitchenette: compulsive-obsessive was one of the Poet's diagnoses of my behavior patterns.

"What about the wristwatch?" he asked.

"I took it out of her shoe, set it for the correct time, and placed it beside her pills on the night table."

"Then you threw out the bread crusts, apple core, yogurt container, and you washed the spoon."

"Right."

"Then you took a piss and shaved for work."

I shaved with a Schick electric. It was, after all, the blade from my old safety razor that left the scar on Valerie's wrist.

*   *   *

"Did you know you wind your wristwatch the same time every evening?"

The Poet watched me closely enough to keep a chart on my routine. True, after Miss Ryan and I served the patients their evening meal, I regularly telephoned Valerie: that was when I wound my watch.

"Valerie?"

"Yes."

"Did you take your patriotic pills?"

The pills were the colors of the American flag—this was perhaps the last joke between my wife and me.

"Yes."

"Eat anything?"

"Captain Crunch. I ate some Captain Crunch with milk."

"There's tuna salad in the refrigerator."

"I gave it to the cat."

We had no cat. I could picture Valerie doodling on the blotter as she waited for the call to end. But what stage of panic would have displaced the fretfulness had I not called at all? The little stick figures she scrawled—balloon heads and pretzel fingers—resembled the children's drawings taped to the wall on her side of the room. We had no children. Valerie's brief period of employment was as an art therapist at the Dade Institute for Exceptional Children. She saved the crayon drawings and muddy watercolors from that time. When the children's artwork was in place, on exhibit, the room became a gothic kindergarten: these were not the classic house-and-flowers with glowing sun—there was a distinct impression of nightmare to the show, an almost deliberate distortion painfully rendered. The colors were brooding, mostly black.

When the heat dried out the Scotch tape and a drawing fell to the floor, Valerie made no attempt to restore the souvenir to its place on the wall. I did this for her. A drawing or watercolor lying on the floor might bear the imprint of her dusty indifferent footprint. Her children, once fallen, fell to oblivion.

"Feel O.K.?"

"Feeling groovy."

"Fine. That's the way to feel."

"The way to feel is with your fingers."

When I stepped out of the third-floor telephone booth, the Poet was hovering near enough to have heard my side of the conversation.

Mr. Davidoff was waiting outside to see if I locked the booth door. I did. Patients were allowed to make telephone calls only by permission of Dr. Krauskopf. This was to prevent our unhappy charges from broadcasting their rage or anguish to the outside world. If Mr. Davidoff could have had access to a telephone, he would immediately call his broker (any Miami brokerage house, at random) to accuse the customer's man who answered of having been responsible for his ruin. He would have worked himself into a fever of accusatory rage. Otherwise, Mr. Davidoff was the mildest of patients, correctly attired and correctly behaved, the gentleman among us. He wore tailored suits complete with vest, necktie, cuff links; he called me sir and bowed ever so slightly, in the European manner, to Miss Ryan. Perhaps he had been ruined by some unscrupulous or indifferent financial institution. Meanwhile I was obliged to accept Mr. Davidoff on the terms stated in his chart: Paranoid Personality.

At the far end of the corridor, Mr. Davidoff was joined by Mr. Ballantine, who requested that we call him Dr. Ballantine. The two men fell into a huddle of agitated discourse—but no statement that could be overheard, no remark audible enough to be recorded on their charts.

As an idle consideration, what if Mr. Ballantine really were Dr. Ballantine, disbarred from medical practice because of his ex-wife's exaggerated accusations in domestic relations court—as Mr. Ballantine claimed, and had convinced several of the female patients (who now came to him with their sinuses and lower back pain)? Access to the telephone would have given him no more than the opportunity to call the AMA and clear his name.

Then we would have to believe that Miss Frith really did hold extended discourse with emissaries from the planet Neptune and that Mr. Marcus could confirm the connection with outer space by the messages he received through the plumbing. The Poet's word on Miss Frith and Mr. Marcus was this: "Society could use some advice from outer space."

As for the Poet, he was making as wide a circle as the corridor allowed around Davidoff & Ballantine, as he called them, "the last vaudeville act." He was headed for the Dayroom in his floppy slippers, hoping to bully his way into a game of bridge. (The bridge players avoided playing cards with the Poet: his sarcasms and asides spoiled the game for them.) I would have to direct him back to his room to change from the Japanese kimono to more appropriate attire.

"You and your outdated dress code. How do you know I don't have a tux on underneath?"

What if the Poet had intended his leap from the tour boat as a gesture only and not an attempt at suicide? From four in the afternoon until midnight at the Sans Souci, I could not permit myself to ask what-if.

6

"YOU WANT to know why I jumped? I was seasick, that's all. A case of *mal de mer*—with just a *soupçon* of *mal de siècle*. Can you commit a man to Bedlam because he was considerate enough of his shipmates not to vomit veal scallopini all over them? The Circle Tour, it was called—how could I resist? Captain Alighieri at the helm, with his lady friend Beatrice flipping the snap-tops on the Budweisers for him, and feeding him potato chips so he didn't have to take his tattooed paws off the wheel. The boat had a glass bottom you were supposed to watch the fishies through, but the glass needed a window-washing and I had lost a contact lens in a bowl of minestrone, so all I saw were the barnacle-encrusted beer cans embedded in the sludge where Ali had tossed them overboard on previous tours—also the reflection of a ghastly green satanic visage (my own, as it turned out) floating through the subaqueous slime. Beatrice did the tourist spiel through the jeweled phallus of a microphone strung around her delicate neck: 'Now passing Indian Creek Golf Course to starboard, folks, where famed pirate Bluebeard buried nine wives and came within a stroke of having a stroke at the tenth hole.' The folks she referred to were yours truly, and the Dowds: Horace, age sixty-eight, three years retired from Akron Innertube, accompanied by Horabelle (Horace in drag) with a black umbrella resting on her puce bermudas like a coffin on a trestle. A discreet committee of thunderheads had gathered on the eastern horizon to threaten our circular itinerary with the wrath of God, but I personally would have welcomed the downpour, or any heavenly intervention from on high—baptism, bird shit, what-have-you?—if that's what On High had in store for us. 'Why,' I asked Madame Dowd in all innocence, 'would anybody bring an umbrella to paradise?' Her scowl would have kept sharks at bay and her spouse raised his fishing rod as if to horsewhip me with it. Listen to the witnesses and I'll come out looking like a lunatic from the moment I stepped aboard—but when did poets ever appear sane to your everyday inner-tube executive and wife?—and consider if you will the sanity of blowing forty-five years into inner tubes so you can travel with Horabelle Dowd and her umbrella to Florida. Who's the lunatic here? And tell me, is it a criminally insane offense to fall in love with a hand holding a can of Budweiser if the hand reminds you of a teenybopper's hand you once embraced? I wanted it to be *me* instead of Captain Neanderthal receiving a flaky potato chip on the tongue and thus entitled to lick the salt from those delectable fingers. My so-called psychiatrist (may he wipe his ass on his license-to-practice) is trying to convince me I was 'acting out' my nymphet wife's betrayal of me by rejecting my fellow passengers on the good ship *Abandon Hope.* As a doctor, Dr. K would not qualify as a horse doctor in the Dry Tortugas. The truth is, I secretly lusted for a taste of our divine hostess's salted pinkies—but try telling that to our resident quack from Vienna. Meanwhile Horace was trying to fish over the side of the boat but all he caught was the other side of the boat, and his wife (who truly resembled J. Edgar Hoover) was offering me vitamin B out of her beach bag for my 'nerves.' (You're yawning behind that hand, Critic.) True, the scene was *boring*, as my students used to say about poetry, college, life. My adrenaline wasn't even up. But I allowed impulse to override common sense. (That's how I got married, by the way.) I snatched Mrs. Dowd's umbrella, aimed it at Alighieri, then leaned into Bea's cleavage and shouted into her mike: 'Remain in your places, everybody—this is a hijack. Above all, don't panic. Captain, take this tub to St. Tropez!' Ali's knotted brow looked like a pile of anchor chain, but Beatrice, I will always believe, was secretly smiling, if only in her soul. I mean, here was destiny's tot, surrounded by hostiles on a glass boat circling Miami Beach, only an umbrella to defend myself—what would *you* do? I jumped."

For the first time in the Poet's presence, I smiled—an unprofessional lapse on my part.

The smile gave me away. If my style had been to wait it out—no style at all—until he told all, his was to coopt me by appealing to our common sense of the ridiculous. My passkey to Passive City lost all significance. Whatever further authority I might pretend to exercise had been undermined by that unguarded smile. In one careless moment of natural rapport, the Poet and I became friends, an impossible conspiracy between keeper and kept.

"Tell me the truth, Critic. Didn't you, all your life, want to go to the South of France?"

"My mother came from there."

"You didn't answer my question. Listen, like me, you came to Florida as a cut-rate substitute for the real thing, for the great escape to Mediterranean Avenue."

He took my silence for an affirmative reply.

"Unhappily married, right?"

I was no longer smiling.

"Same miserable hang-ups, both of us—so how come you can tell me when to take a shower, and I can't even light my own cigarettes?"

"I didn't jump overboard."

"That may be your problem."

7

MY PULSE did not flutter at the sight of Béziers, my mother's birthplace, on my own birth certificate: I had not been nourished on the American nostalgia for France, as perhaps the Poet had been. My horizons were circumscribed. While I was in the Navy, my ship traveled from Norfolk, Virginia, to islands in the Caribbean that have now become package-tour resorts with names like Paradise Beach and Treasure Bay, but these excursions did not make a traveler of me.

It was the Poet's dream to go to France, not mine. (As a substitute for Paris he had once spent a day and night in New Orleans, drunk a Ramos gin fizz, had his pockets picked, "And I didn't even get a poem out of it.")

If I had wanted to travel anywhere it would have been to go West some day. The notion was too vague to be considered a dream, but the West meant unencumbered space and the possibilities that emptiness suggested. Since the Poet had taught at universities in the Western states, he could afford to raise one ironic eyebrow when I mentioned new starts in open places. ("Don't take these urges too seriously, Critic. Do I have to prove to you the world is round? Go far enough west and you'll only end up in the East.") Anyway, I could not visualize Valerie against that vast backdrop, or solve the logistics of getting her there.

Nor could I picture myself in France. But whenever I confessed to such limitations of imagination, the Poet would outline little squares in the air, square after square.

Not even the other American nostalgia, for Ireland, informed my sentiments, but I could understand Miss Ryan's attachment to the land of her blood and history—though she had never been there.

"I don't know," she told me, "but I've got this spooky idea I did live there before. Do you believe in transmigration?"

"I. Don't know."

"There was that woman Bridey Murphy that went back in time to her earlier selves."

"I think. There was some dispute over the Bridey Murphy thing. But I didn't read the book."

"They always dispute anything extrasensory or extraterrestrial. It goes against the Church. But let me tell you something that happened when you were on Admissions last night and I was up on 6 with two floors to supervise for RecTherapy. The Greek had to go to the bathroom and me with thirty-some-odd patients to try to teach square dancing to when all of a sudden in the middle of a square dance this voice said to me: *Check the bathroom.* Out of the blue, I swear—I could hear it as plain as you hearing me say it now. *Check the bathroom.* So I left everybody doing do-se-do and went in the bathroom and there was Kakafroni with her head stuck in a basin of water. I swear, it's on her chart. She filled up a basin full of water and tried to drown herself in it. If it wasn't for that voice she might have got away with doing away with herself. (I didn't put anything about voices on her chart, you know how they are here.) But how do you explain a voice out of the blue saying, 'Check the bathroom'?"

"Yes. That happens. To me too."

"But don't you think it's spooky?"

"It is."

Miss Ryan was born in one of the Carolinas; but her grandfather had come over to America from Cork, and it was his wish that his Appalachian granddaughter be named Medbh. Thus, from a generation's remove, Medbh Ryan was bequeathed a sense of place she could only know by hand-me-down.

Her favorite music was country music out of Nashville. There may have been some connection between those plaintive poor-white blues and the sad ballads the Irish sang. In the quiet hours on 3 when patients slept or tried to sleep, Miss Ryan attached a pair of earphones to either side of her hairnet, the flex-band tucked neatly under her nurse's cap, and tuned in the Grand Ole Opry while I listened alone to the murmur and sigh crackling through the intercom. The Poet considered the Nashville sound "shit-kicking music," but Miss Ryan did not suffer in his estimation because of her musical taste. Her face and hands and elegant legs were attraction enough to sustain his admiration. The only disappointment he expressed in his favorite nurse—who had taken her degree in Nursing at St. Elizabeth's Hospital in Washington, D.C.—was that she had never made the acquaintance of that hospital's most famous patient.

After the Poet's odd displeasure over this, she asked me, "Who's Ezra Pound"

"A poet."

"How was I supposed to know one crazy poet from another?"

"He was a controversial figure. He made anti-American broadcasts for Mussolini. During World War II. He was tried for treason by the U.S. Government and pleaded insanity and was committed to St. Elizabeth's."

There was a pause in the hermetic silence of the Nurses Station while Miss Ryan and I thought over insanity as a plea.

"He may not even have been in my wing."

"I think you would have known him. If he had been. Anyway, you know our poet—he probably thinks you should have transferred to Ezra Pound's wing."

"Some days you know he's got to be playing possum, and some days I swear he's loony as a coon."

"They said the same thing. About Ezra Pound."

In the Poet's chart Miss Ryan wrote: "Hostile w/nurse not knowing E. Pound when nurse wkd St. E. Hosp. Wash."

When I took the chart from her, a slight charge of static electricity passed through the metal clipboard from her hand to mine. There was a time when that invisible spark between us could have been of some significance, at the beginning, when Miss Ryan and I exchanged banal reckonings until midnight, aware on both sides that our casual remarks could lead to something, so careful of what we did

not say we were saying it. In the soundproof booth, out of earshot of
our patients, Miss Ryan began to call me Frank instead of the
professionally correct Mr. White. She had a seductive way of saying
my name with her Southern accent as if there were two syllables to it.

Miss Ryan had always wanted to work in Pediatrics. "I adore
babies—before they grow up and go mental." Her misfortune was to
have started out in Geriatrics at Walter Reed. " 'Old soldiers never
die' is right." She switched to psychiatric nursing as a way out of
Geriatrics, and had come to believe the mentally ill were wayward
children—or retarded, like Cookie, newly transferred to 3 from
another floor, a hydrocephalic adolescent. They *all* had water on the
brain, as far as Miss Ryan could determine, or had regressed to a
stage of teenage delinquency. "You can only humor them so far before
they start trying to pull something." Her attitude was flip and
disengaged. "Believe me, Frank, cool is the only way to play it to
keep from going around the bend yourself." The one exception to her
experience was the Poet, the only patient her philosophy did not
accommodate. "You couldn't classify him if you tried." At intervals
during his confinement at the Sans Souci, Miss Ryan considered the
Poet a prodigy, a satyr, a dude, a real case.

Those late evenings when the Nurses Station stood alight like an
all-night diner at the crossroads of the NS and EW corridors, Miss
Ryan and I sat side by side shuffling clipboards, recording bowel
movements and blood pressure, inscribing our arcane data and
gossipy observations in the charts. "Does anybody ever read this
stuff?" asked Miss Ryan. I had asked the same question two nights
ago, and she had asked me the time before. When she was not
listening to country music through her earphones, Miss Ryan and I
were on the same approximate frequency.

Miss Ryan was a trophy behind glass, a golden-crested prize the
male patients took note of no matter how disordered their minds. The
opportunity had been there for me to make her a prize of my own. In
this way station at the apex of an L-shaped space of confinement, we
shared a narrow intimacy with no curtain between us. I was charmed
by her; I was attracted, like the Poet, by her face and form. Miss Ryan
and I were Twins, born under the sign of Gemini (she informed me)
two days apart. "Is that good?" I asked. "It's good if you believe in
horoscopes." I delighted in what I took to be a sleepy innocence
disguised by a crisp white uniform. Her speech was slow but her
gestures swift and sharp, her expression animated. Those first nights
her trim winged cap and efficient white shoes, the buttoned-in bosom,

made me want to know her with her shoes off, buttons unbuttoned, her hair down. Leave it to the Poet to ask as crudely as he could, nudging me with an elbow and tilting his head in Miss Ryan's direction: "Are you getting any of that?"

On her twenty-third birthday—and again, on my thirty-eighth, two nights later—Miss Ryan broke out the medicinal brandy from the drug safe.

"The inventory is so messed up we could drink the whole bottle and nobody know the difference. A junkie would go ape to see how slack our medication registry is. Half the staff on the day shift don't even sign for medications. You can go to jail for having your drug inventory not add up."

We toasted slack inventories and advancing age with Styrofoam cups, but not fingers, touching. At first I felt too self-consciously onstage under the fluorescent lights of our exposed guard post: there was an imaginary audience out there in the two darkened aisles, Fire Exit signs glowing at opposite ends of the theater. (This was a year before the Poet came, so who could be out there watching?) The birthday celebrations were testament to the fifteen years, and two days, between us. I was as awkward in this circumstance as if I were eighteen instead of thirty-eight. I pretended to myself (there was no pretense on Miss Ryan's side) that I was more seriously married then I was, more affectionately attached to Valerie than I supposed. I assumed a pose of honorable intent, while the birthday girl awaited a kiss. On the night of her birthday Miss Ryan impatiently pressed her lips to my forehead in a swift passing party gesture; I returned the kiss to her forehead two nights later. Was her given name so unpronounceable that I must continue to call her Miss Ryan? I avoided using her name at all, so as not to engage the implications of using Medbh.

In the weeks that followed, the signals grew fainter. (We were both more careful to handle the clipboards by the insulated edge when passing them across the desk, to eliminate the little shock of electricity.) More and more often Miss Ryan tuned into Nashville or I escaped the pressures of proximity by double-checking the Fire Exit doors and making excessive rounds after Lights Out. We did not celebrate our twenty-fourth and thirty-ninth birthdays that next year's phase of Gemini. The initial onset of need or desire diminished to routine companionship the way it was meant to, in Passive City.

Miss Ryan and I remained friends and colleagues in a way that would have set the Poet to drawing squares in the air. We conversed in hospital jargon about the patients' states of mind with no hint or reference to our own. When the charts were done and Miss Ryan retired to Nashville, I was left alone to listen to the restlessly distressing broadcasts over the intercom. We were a seasoned team, Miss Ryan and I, and she, the supervisor, trusted me to deal with any crisis that came through the audit system. The asthmatic snoring would be Cookie's and the strangled sobs Miss Frith's. Davidoff & Ballantine whispered together in their sleepless conspiracies. Father Day, a lapsed priest who asked to be called Mr. Day, counted aloud in his sleep, perhaps to keep from murmuring the prayers that went with the beads coiled beneath his pillow. The occasional notes of a clandestine flute came from Mrs. Kakafroni's room; Mr. Thermax howled aloud in nightmare, Mr. Marcus kept the water taps running.

In no time the Poet had caught on that the patients' rooms were wired. His way of jamming the airwaves was to stand on a chair and shout quips and slogans and fragments of verse into the scalloped light fixture where a monitoring device had been planted. "Demented of the wards, unite! You have nothing to lose but your brains." "Our softsoap is ninety-nine and forty-four one-hundredths percent pure, so keep it clean in there, Critic, and take that paw off Miss Ryan's knee." He might recite long passages from *Paradise Lost* into our pipeline. Once when Dr. K stopped off at the Nurses Station on 3 after making his rounds, the Poet's voice came through the intercom with the cry: "There is light at the end of the tunnel, folks, but Krauskopf keeps putting it out."

The relief nurse, Miss Johns, stepped off the elevator at two minutes before midnight; she carried a shopping bag of knitting to see her through the long night. My relief had called in to say he would be late, and I had called Valerie to tell her the same. Miss Ryan lowered her earphones and let them dangle around her long white neck like a doctor's stethoscope. She was listening for her boyfriend's motorcycle.

JayCee was from North (or South) Carolina too. By the time Miss Ryan had turned over her key to the drug safe to Miss Johns, JayCee was revving the motor of his Harley-D in the parking lot, impatiently pawing the ground in front of the Sans Souci. Miss Ryan accomplished her transformation into Cinderella in the Staff Room where she changed into leggy jeans and a loose blouse, her corn-colored hair hanging long and loose, released from the strict hairnet she wore on duty. JayCee's hair was the same color as hers, a gold earring in one of his ears, right now hidden under the crash helmet. He carried a spare helmet for Miss Ryan slung from the motorbike's handlebar.

From the Nurses Station I could see down into the parking lot illuminated against car theft by carbon lights: in a moment Miss Ryan appeared in the light. Laterally I could see the window of the Poet's room at the far end of the L, his shadow in profile. He too was watching as JayCee tossed the helmet to the girl under the arc lights: she caught it, then held the headpiece a moment as she might have held JayCee himself. It was too dark to see the Poet's expression— could he see mine?—as we watched Miss Ryan place the plastic skull over her own, then tuck her cornsilk tresses into it. Miss Ryan mounted the saddle behind JayCee and embraced his studded leather belt. From our separate cells the Poet and I watched together as the matched pair below, conjoined belly to back, were abruptly launched into what was left of the night, bound for the juke joints of Little River in a swirl of exhaust fumes and an explosion of sparks.

In their wake, a fugue from Mrs. Kakafroni's flute wafted through the security screens and left me with the last decision of the night: should I interrupt the musical offering or wait for my replacement to show up and lock Mrs. Kakafroni's flute in the box marked SHARPS?

8

OUT OF his own bitter wisdom the Poet informed me: "There's always another man."

These nights he was constantly at my elbow explaining the odds on life and love. He was a gambler, he said, but I would not have known it from his Monopoly game. Like the serpent, he hinted at infinite possibility if I would chance it, learn to hang loose and live.

"You have to operate as if you're the last man on earth even if she told you that was the man she wouldn't marry. The only question mark in the Garden of Eden is Eve. She's waiting to be invented, all you have to do is lend a rib. Of course, there's always another man. That's the part that was censored in Genesis. Until he shows up you can at least live. Listen, take it from one who knows, a loser, sure, but the world well lost, the women in our lives are the only poems left."

He was following me down the NS corridor to check, after I checked, the Fire Exits.

"You keep these doors *locked?* What happens if there's a fire?"

"I unlock them."

"What if you're asleep on the job, or drunk, or making out with Miss Ryan on the Dayroom couch? Our lives, so to speak, hang by your key chain."

On the way back, as I checked the door to the telephone booth, Mr. Davidoff hovered not far away, waiting to check the door after me.

"You think," said the Poet, "you're here to save my life. What would you say if I said I'm here to save yours?"

"I'd say *merci.*"

"Don't be sarcastic, it's not your style. Tell me, what's with these calls to your wife?"

"I prefer not to."

"Not to call or not to tell me?"

When I did not answer, the Poet said, "Don't worry, Critic. It won't go on your chart."

Does he verbalize, was Miss Ryan's word. *If I put everything he says to me on his chart I'd be writing all night.*

As I wheeled the dinner cart down the EW corridor, the Poet, keeping almost desperate step with me, began to reflect aloud on a French poet he had translated from a stray volume found at a garage sale.

"I paid two bits for that cycle of insights, love poems addressed to a transvestite tightrope walker, I kid you not, by a nobody who signed himself Gabriel. 1890–1949."

I was not too distracted to calculate Gabriel's age when he died, the same age the Poet was now, according to his chart.

"Gabriel L'Homme. Ever heard of him?—of course not. Completely forgotten. As forgotten as I'll be ten minutes after I turn in my chips."

Please note, was noted on the chart, *any reference to death, dying or the dead.* SUICIDAL was written in red across the top of the empty page of the Poet's case history.

"I'd like to. Read the poems."

"No you wouldn't."

"Your translation, that is."

"No you wouldn't."

He was right, I wouldn't. I was asking out of institutional diplomacy and he was telling me not to be a hypocrite.

"The poems are too painful for a mind as innocent as yours."

"Maybe you're right."

"Don't patronize me, Critic."

When the Poet turned hostile, my strategy was to concede and remain silent. I concentrated on pushing the stainless steel coffin of food in the direction of the dining room.

"Anyway," he persisted, "I burnt them."

"Your poems?"

"His. My translations are safe in a safe-deposit in Santa Fe along with a lapsed life insurance policy and a notice of Denial of Tenure. Who's the immortal here, a maggoty French faggot or me?"

"I thought you said you'd be forgotten in ten minutes."

"By you critics, yes."

"Have you written? Some poems. Lately."

"In this environment? You think I'm crazy?"

"Just asking."

"Don't ask."

I pushed on. By steering the dinner cart steadily to its destination, I hoped to steer the Poet to a spirit of tranquility, but his fevered thoughts continued to spill over.

"So I burnt them. A desecration, you say?"

I had said nothing.

"The letters yes. Maybe. Yes, a desecration to burn her letters in the same bonfire. But that's another story. Letters, poems, this is getting personal—but the letters were to me, weren't they? the poems to somebody else. As for L'Homme's odious odes they deserved to be burnt, to make way for the phoenix, my translation, names changed to protect the innocent. Who needs to know how a hard-on like L'Homme fell for an American cowboy named Vander Clyde? L'Homme was a nobody, *personne*—or a poet, which is the same thing—but who, you ask, is Vander Clyde?" I had not asked. "A simplehearted or simpleminded star of the golden West who fled Texas in the Twenties and turned in his lasso for a tightrope. In Paris, if you can believe it. Picture if you will, if your imagination can surmount these walls, if your stunted mind can travel from these mundane shores—picture this calloused galoot named Clyde retired from the rodeo circuit turning up as the sensation of gay Paree—and I use the word 'gay' in the figurative as well as literal sense. His show-biz name was Barbette and for his act at the Cirque Médrano and the Folies Bergères he was a she, wearing thirty pounds of ostrich feathers and a loaded bra—thirty pounds of *feathers*, Critic, if your mind is still traveling. The costume included a quaint G-string of sequins to disguise the family jewels. (No inane regulations about bathrobes in Dayrooms in Paris, Mon Ami.) He or she or whatever the appropriate pronoun danced the high wire daintily flipping open and shut (like my case, according to Krauskopf) a frilly *parapluie*—umbrella to you—until the orchestra swelled to its ultimate da-dum of a denouement when Kewpie doll shed the feathers and showed who she really was." The Poet was blocking my way into the dining room now, but I patiently awaited the end to his story while the patients' dinners cooled. "Guess who fell in love with this queen-of-the-rodeo-from-Round-Rock-Texas-in-feathers?"

"The poet you translated."

"I already *told* you that. L'Homme, yes, but who *else?* Didn't I tell you there's always another man? Even when they're all men."

"I can't imagine. Who else. Excuse me but Miranda's waiting for these trays."

Miranda's dark face scowled behind the counter of the dutch door to the kitchen. She loathed the patients and feared the Poet and kept the upper half of the dutch door bolted before and after the evening meal.

"Give up? O.K. It was Cocteau."

"O.K."

"When he saw Barbette defeathered at the Casino de Paris, Jean Cocteau fell in love with him. You know who Cocteau was?"

"I think so. I think I saw a film of his."

"You think. You think, therefore you are. Yes, Critic, he made films. He was a surrealist, a drug addict and a queer. Actually he was a poet, a poet, a poet."

He stepped aside then, but fluffed his beard at Miranda and gave the bird to me.

"Poems, letters." The Poet was still at it. Behind a barrage of indignation, nastiness and wheedling, the Poet had a message for me I was not receiving. He sought me out immediately after dinner, walked beside me on any pretext, placed himself constantly in my path. "She couldn't write a poem if you spelled one out for her, but *letters*, those letters."

I assumed he was desperate to tell about the girl in the photograph who had been his wife.

"Once she said if children commit adultery shouldn't it be called infantry? How could I help falling in love with her?"

If I questioned him about her he replied with a question about me or my wife or my relationship with Miss Ryan.

"Tell me the truth, Critic, are you getting any of that?"

So I let him ramble and probe and spout riddles.

"Only seventeen people could relate to L'Homme in any one century anyway, so I burnt his stuff to spare the rest of you the embarrassment." When he noticed my distracted eye, he assumed an attitude of outrage. "Hey, who's important here? The patient you're supposed to be tuned in to, or Lady Macbeth down the hall?"

My concern was now with Mrs. Minor standing at the door to her room wringing her hands: a scream hovered behind her eyes. Mrs. Minor was a forty-year-old widow obsessed with sanitation and tidal waves, especially during her menstrual period. As it turned out, Miss Ryan had observed the patient's distress at the same moment, and quickly went to her.

"If I can engage your flighty attention span once again."

I turned back to the Poet.

"To get back to art now that Mrs. Melodrama has been taken to her padded cell (believe me, there's no poetry there), consider these bad poems and sad letters burning in the same flame. The letters from a tender bud of a teenybopper to her degenerate professor and the poems of a degenerate Frog to his tenderfoot tightrope walker— consider, who out of seventeen people in any one century would have the flair and daring to put two and two together and come up with a masterpiece?"

He meant himself, and needed no confirmation from me concerning his genius.

"There was the same strain of heartbreak running through both declarations of love. As for the poems, I could—without being queer myself, mind—actually in some surreal way identify with the man, L'Homme, the ruined poet that is, *not* the transvestite please, who by the way fell off his tightrope finally, feathers and all, broke his hip and limped back to Round Rock to die. (By then Cocteau had taken up with a baby-faced novelist named Radiguet—didn't I tell you there's always another man?) Are you listening? Listen, don't go writing in my chart tonight that patient-manifests-latent-homosexual-overtones because if I identify with a fellow poet it's an aesthetic empathy, not a Freudian fixation or a gay latency or whatever you Critics arrive at when you arrive at an assumption."

What would I write in the Poet's chart tonight?

"Whatever you do don't tell K it was L'Homme's reflection I saw mirrored in the glass bottom of a tour boat before I abandoned ship or Dr. Sauerkraut will go into labor pains and give birth to a theory. Symbolic, yes. I grant you the recurrent motif. But I see L'Homme as more spiritual father than literary doppelganger, so don't pass the information to the authorities or they'll put me in a padded category. You can tell K my real father was a tired accountant keeping score for the Saints, a baseball team in Salt Lake City. While his wayward son was wasting time reading *The Waste Land*."

Miss Ryan passed us with a balled-up bedspread under her arm, the chenille *S*'s stained with blood: tonight she would write *menses present* in Mrs. Minor's chart.

"Then his cells went haywire." I had to remember the Poet was now referring to his father and not the French poet. "Instead of how it is here, where you put the haywires in cells."

We were walking in the direction of the Dayroom—eyes fixed on the backs of Miss Ryan's legs, whose elegance could not be disguised by the institutional white stockings—when Cookie, the hydrocephalic adolescent, attached herself to us. She was pleading for a deck of cards: "To play rummy with."

"Go play with yourself," said the Poet, trying to shoo her away with the back of his hand—but I nodded to her and said, "Sure."

As Public Defender of Passive City, I had not only to protect Cookie from the Poet, I also had to protect the Poet from Cookie, who had swiped a pork chop from the Poet's plate that same night: "He don't need the protein like I do."

Now, after a spasm of blinking, Cookie waddled after us down the EW corridor. The Poet increased his pace, trying to outmaneuver Cookie and still keep me on his leash.

"Cocteau was the other man, do you follow me? He moved in on Barbette, L'Homme's fine-feathered friend, as soon as L'Homme's back was turned. Heartbreak I could believe—after reading the poems, bad as they were—is just as poignant gay or straight. It's a matter of translation. Betrayal is the same old betrayal, anguish is anguish, whatever flesh or feathers involved."

To the Poet's visible dismay, Mr. Marcus wandered out of the men's room and fell into step with our raggletag platoon. We paused while I zipped his fly for him and he tried to press an envelope on me, to be mailed against hospital rules. We then continued, a foursome now, to the Dayroom door.

"Can't we manage this expedition without Pumpkin Head and The Plumber tagging along?"

The Poet could identify with anguish in Paris half a century ago, but not with the anguish next door. *Believe me, there's no poetry there.* Mr. Marcus was twitching with anxiety about his letter, which must have concerned nothing less than apocalypse since it was addressed to the President of the United States. I was obliged to remind Mr. Marcus that all mail had first to pass through Dr. Krauskopf's hands.

"But Dr. Ballantine said it was all right."

"Mr. Ballantine is a patient here. Dr. Krauskopf is in charge."

More often than was tolerable I was called upon to say no. Despite my habitual warning to the Poet about proper dress in the Dayroom (he was in his kimono again), he followed me into that communal sanctuary muttering: "This thing you've picked up about time and keys and bathrobes is, you realize, anal-retentive and puts you in the same boat with us sickies."

I did not answer—nor, as I unlocked the games closet, did I make an issue of the Poet's kimono.

"So I changed Barbette into a nineteen-year-old chick who adored frisky horses and older-type poets. Poet's license. Our professor of rhyme and reason given horns by a hippie from Denver instead of L'Homme's ridiculous capitulation to Cocteau. A mundane Old World triangle neatly transposed to the New. We turn soap opera into opera proper, what Baudelaire did for Poe the other language around. Are you still with me?"

He, rather, was still with me. As I nodded I could feel his overheated breath on my ear: "Then what was my point?"

"Is this an exam?"

"A symposium."

"Art? Art. Art, I guess." I was searching the closet for cards.

"Art, Pointhead, is counterpoint to what I'm telling you. Love. Lovelovelovelove. I'm talking *love* here for the love of Christ—" his voice jerked into another register, "which even you should recognize if you could unwind your watch and commit your soul to something beyond Dayroom rules and fucking Fire Exits."

His agitation was contagious: Mr. Marcus chewed on his envelope, I was winding my watch. Suddenly the Poet fell silent, winded. Hopeless Mr. Thermax sat across from the television set staring into its dead eye, the screen not yet illuminated for the evening. He dared not shift his eyes to our disorderly ranks. His shyness was even beyond the Poet's sardonic commentary. (Mr. T, too, had been robbed of his pork chop by Cookie—but when I restored the chop to his plate he hid his face in his hands.)

The sight of Mr. Thermax with his flushed elephantine face lowered in chronic humiliation interrupted the flow of the Poet's diatribe. He stared first at Mr. Thermax, then again in slow motion at the mixed ensemble whose company he kept. Leaning back to express his revelation to the ceiling he roared: "This is impossible."

At that moment I brought forth a rummy deck. The Poet made a pass at reading my wristwatch while I offered the cards to Cookie, and in the same instant Mr. Marcus attempted to press his letter into my hand once again, a travesty of crossed wrists and cross-purposes, so that the cards were knocked to the floor in a riot of numbered hearts and spades and scattered royalty. Automatically three of us bent to recover the spill of cards, but the Poet majestically abstained. He stood upright and unmoved, no part of our comedy of errors, and intoned: "Is this mad, I ask you, or just sad?"

"You're a poet and don't know it!" said Cookie, inspired.

This was the tilting point of a drunken boat, and the Poet made his second reckless leap. He was at Cookie's fat neck in an instant: the cards exploded again in midair. The girl's thick-lidded eyes bugged open in shock, a wad of tongue slid between her lips as she gurgled and choked—the Poet's strength was in his frenzy, but that was strength enough.

I wrestled with Cookie's attacker alone—Mr. Marcus had scuttled out of harm's way and Mr. Thermax crawled even deeper inside himself—but luckily Miss Ryan had seen all from the Nurses Station, and called the fourth floor for help. Cookie was saved, my lip split by the Poet's elbow. Bruno came down from 4 to help me hold the patient while Miss Ryan injected 5 mgs. of Haldol into the Poet's sad twitching shank.

I knew now what I would write in the Poet's chart that night.

9

"WHEN DID you take your pills?"

"Didn't. The cat ate them."

I could never know who answered for her. Did she speak for herself out of her own secret moods—or was she saying what she said under the effect of pills?

"Eat anything?" I asked, knowing that the worst way to deal with anorexia was to refer insistently to food—why did I deal with her the worst way?

"I ate the cat."

She was not always flippant or hostile on the telephone. There were times when I knew she must have been waiting for me to call, desperate for the phone to ring. Often she seemed to want to crawl into the mouthpiece and reach me from inside an electronic cocoon. Sometimes she wept.

"There's meat loaf in the refrigerator."

"Evelyn came by and watched *Wanderlust* with me." Evelyn was Evelyn Pike, but I could never think of her as anyone but Miss Pike. "She fixed me a bowl of Captain Crunch and that's what I ate, with raisins."

Valerie's outlook shifted when Miss Pike came by. Miss Pike was Valerie's only friend. It would seem that Miss Pike took more pains over Valerie's state of mind than I ever did.

"How do you feel?" I asked.

That ridiculous question again. Valerie often answered, "With my fingers," but this time did not bother to answer at all. She was still distracted by the earlier pleasure of Miss Pike's visit.

Finally she whispered: "The Miami palm trees are all dying of lethal yellow."

In the background I could hear the murmur of television commentary.

"I didn't know that."

"And somebody fired shots at the Popemobile."

"I didn't know that either."

"Now you do. It's on television. I knew about the palm trees before television did. It's a secret until television tells it."

*   *   *

We kept our own secrets out of sight. Only last night when I showered late with the astringent taste on my tongue from the antiseptic Miss Ryan had applied to my split lip, I thought about Miss Ryan, Medbh.

Are you getting any of that, Critic?

Standing alone in that stall of broken tile I caressed myself in the way of an aroused adolescent or a curious child and came to terms with my physical solitude. My wife played no part in the simulated act except for the thought, as the sudsy male essence spilled into the drain tangled with Valerie's hair: the shower stall was where Valerie had slit her wrist.

Secrets. I knew nothing of Valerie's father and I had never spoken to her of mine. Surely she talked about her family and background to Dr. K—while my own case history poured into the Poet's ear. Confession here was known as therapy: our secrets spilled out to spare us the further burden of them.

My father's letters were in a safe-deposit box at Dade Federal Savings, Valerie's memories of her father were locked away from me. Why had I never asked about her father, why had I never told her about mine?

"Dear Son, wherever you may be.

"Your beloved Mother—God rest her soul—and I genuinely wish her a better life in Heaven than she ever had on this Earth, tho I know not what tales she may have told you concerning your old Dad. As a matter of fact, I turned 80 in '80. 'Warren came in with the century,' my precious Mother, and your grandmother (tho you never met her) used to say. At this late date I could turn in my chips from one minute to the next and not know what hit me. Breathwaite said I had the blood pressure of a man half my age but that was in my forties when I had half my age. Cigarettes are no help, I know, but a smoke is an oldster's sole pleasure at this stage. Your Mother always blamed me for stepping out on our union, but I reminded her that life together is a two-way street. If blame is to be placed (and I do not want to accuse a person that has passed on) people in glass houses should not throw stones. Who is responsible for this long-standing estrangement between father and son? And speaking of Breathwaite there is a mystery there between him and your Mother I will not go into, if stones must be thrown. I know not what tales she may have told you concerning Breathwaite but can imagine. But all of that is water under the bridge and a skeleton best left in its closet. If she told you I was your father in name only why not write your real so-called father to sign those papers for you to enlist at age 17? Due to your being a minor at the time. She said you were dying to enlist but there was nothing from you personally on the subject so I had to take your Mother's word for it. Mea culpa, I admit, but women are a mystery, Son, that only gets deeper the more you think you know them. I could have kicked myself for signing without a lawyer looking over my shoulder. You were supposed to be released at age 21 but that is a lifetime to a 17-year-old or someone subject to seasickness, like me.

"I hope and pray you inherited your beloved Mother's good looks, for she was a looker, I'll say that for her. But always remember you got your love of books from your old Dad. (She wrote you could read the comic strips before you ever entered kindergarten, but I doubt your Mother ever read anything but cookbooks and price tags). Your Grandmother that never laid eyes on you in her lifetime was a reader too, with a vocabulary that a college professor would be proud of, and was lying in her hammock reading a book (I forget the title, but it was a classic) when she passed away. A strange lady, granted, as people would say, but not 'dotty' as your Mother used to put it. It comes down through the generations, a love of books and an extensive vocabulary. Keep a dictionary in your suitcase as I do at all times, and a Bible.

"What I am getting at, Son, is that you have not answered a single one of my many letters sent to you out on the high seas yet. In my mind's eye I can still picture you as a tot in your first sailor suit waving to the tollbooth keeper on the Suspension Bridge across the mighty Ohio River. I have never seen a photo of you in your Naval uniform. Be that as it may, my own intention is to bridge the gap your Mother, in all innocence (let us not condemn the Dear Departed), put between father and son over the years. Fate is funny, my Boy. An atomic bomb in the hands of some insane politician (and they are all insane, if you ask me) could wipe us off the face of the earth—you, me, the State of Florida, everything—if the wrong button was pushed."

His letters were like that. My grandmother, his mother, was a Southern eccentric of which there is no equal except perhaps those aged Englishwomen shut up in drafty castles in Somerset, or confined to the final pages of Valerie's gothic romances. I owe to my father a love of books and, as far as I know, little else. With no schooling to speak of, except what he learned from my strange grandmother, my father was erudite in his way. He read biographies of famous men (then claimed to have known them personally); he worked crossword puzzles to extend his vocabulary and studied *The Wall Street Journal* to acquire the businessman's lingo. He dawdled in libraries, picked through dictionaries, memorized the Beatitudes.

Of course it was true that I had never answered any of his letters. Like Mr. Marcus, who wrote to the President, my father did not reveal the origin of his correspondence.

10

FROM THE NURSES STATION I could see a restless spark circling beneath the Fire Exit sign. It was long after Lights Out—no more than two charts to go, the buzz from the intercom reduced to a somnolent hum. The catherine wheel of light was surely a lighted Marlboro, since it circled at the Poet's end of the EW corridor. I had not lit the cigarette for him. Perhaps Miss Ryan had provided a light, but I did not ask her this. I knew he must be keeping his own matches again, a gesture of defiance directed at me, the only show of independence he could muster under the circumstances.

"Has he been swallowing his medication?" I asked.

"I probe his mouth with a tongue depressor to make sure. Last time he started to lick my fingers."

"He has a thing. About women's fingers."

"He has a thing about women, period. Who's Annabel Lee, by the way?"

"The name of a girl. In a poem. By Poe."

It was nearly time for the midnight-to-eight shift and Miss Ryan had not done the narcotics inventory, but she added my last two charts to her stack so that I could pace with the Poet.

"The worst thing I ever did," he said, "was not thank him for doing my income tax."

Did he want to talk about his father again? There were tears in his eyes and I asked him if Mrs. Kakafroni's flute had kept him awake.

His voice was controlled but the tears flowed: "I have discovered the precise epicenter of hell."

"Miss Ryan could give you something to help you sleep."

"What Miss Ryan could provide I assume you have exclusive use of."

I waited.

"Ezra Pound knew, and now I know."

"Know what?"

"Where hell is."

I waited several heartbeats before asking, "Where is it?"

"In here." He tapped his forehead with one finger.

It was not the moment to inquire about his medication or mention matches. I tried to steer him out of the monotony of pacing clockwise and into his room, but he pointed with his cigarette at the scalloped light fixture in the ceiling, the eternal ear.

"Guilt is the Warden's cover story for all my sins of omission, or emission. When I ask him, 'Why should *I* feel guilty? she's the one who skipped out on me,' he regresses to the cocktail party pedant who paraphrases your question by way of another question: 'Zen vy do you veel guilty?' Listen, that lovely naive liar of mine told me the guy was her *brother*, hitchhiked all the way from Colorado just to visit Sis. I had a seven-to-ten graduate seminar that night and like an idiot laid thirty bucks on them, my blessing, to go to a disco together. I never saw her again. Turns out the hitchhiker was some apprentice guru she was once at a be-in in Denver with—no relation whatsoever, except sexual. (I could tell you about the private eye, a gorilla in a white suit I hired, who found out all this for me, but that's another story.)"

Women, my father wrote, *are to be trusted about as far as I can toss a boxcar. Your beloved Mother claimed to be French but she could have been Canadian, for all anybody knew, or from the Louisiana bayou.*

"Truth may be beauty, *mon ami*, but beauty is not truth. My beard for example she declared was adorable during our whirlwind courtship turned out to be 'flaky' on the honeymoon and made me look ancient so would I shave it off? O.K. I take into consideration her grotesque childhood, trundled from barracks to barracks by Major-Daddy Warmonger, surrounded by slavering GIs all her tender young Army life. (Mommy went AWOL when the kid was still in kindergarten.) Picture her in her first bikini, already overripe at fourteen, enticing whole platoons for fatigue duty in Major-Daddy's backyard during sunbath afternoons, trim hedges for a better look, mow her lawn for her, apply Lan-o-Tan if necessary. Put yourself in my place.

A pedagogue's wet dream transfers from Camp Pendleton to Pendennis College and asks the Poet in Residence to look at some 'little things' of hers after class. I looked. That extracurricular peek cost me tenure. (I'm not saying she wasn't worth it.) (I was never too happy in the halls of ivy anyway: Ezra Pound lasted less than a semester—what does a poet want with all that Blue Cross and bullshit?) The Committee on Promotions referred to the episode as 'unwarranted involvement with the student body.' Who warrants these things? I read her puerile poetry, got involved with her student body, and fell in love with her—in that order. Guilt does not appear on the indictment, Critic. Anguish, yes."

The question to answer at the Sans Souci was, had anguish alone swept this man over the side of a tour boat, and was the Poet deranged in a way the profession considered clinical? Miss Ryan probed his mouth with a tongue depressor to make certain he really did swallow his bedtime capsules. Would that I had probed past his madcap monologues, listened for the ventriloquist behind his verbal high jinks.

"Ve vill now discuss anguish as a vay of life." His impersonation of Dr. K included an Eastern European accent the doctor did not have, then he would stroke his beard in imitation—but Dr. K's pink chin was clean-shaven.

Lately our exchange had been lopsided: the Poet revealed only what he thought would be good for me to know while asking in detail about my father, about my wife. "What the hell is a patriotic pill," was the first thing he said to me when I stepped out of the phone booth one night. At that time I may have been evasive or tried to change the subject, but eventually I confessed to my own guilt and anguish along the milestones of a sterile marriage. I succumbed to what I considered his wit and wisdom, his charm. Institutional protocol had broken down. The Poet had acquired access to my case history: the roles of patient and attendant were reversed.

"You mean to say your wife and I lie on K's same couch?"

"She goes to him. Yes. Once a week."

"My next interrogation by K I'll sniff the premises for your wife's perfume."

"She doesn't wear perfume."

"It figures."

Suddenly I was back at the Efficiency with Valerie asleep on the other side of the net. I could smell nail polish remover and citronella—or maybe it was the mosquito-spray plane that had just passed over the Sans Souci parking lot.

"The confessional was invented in the Middle Ages," the Poet informed me. "Before that you went to your local soothsayer who figured your fate through a mess of owl's entrails. Then came the age of anxiety and Siggy updated all this with a couch. Now the spawn of Father Divine solve our lives and loves for us for fifty bucks an hour. I'll take the owl's entrails any day. How come you let your wife's psyche be tampered with by this clown?"

"It helps. Or the drugs do. I think. I know that she comes back, a little. For a little while. After she's been to him."

"Back from where?"

"From the epicenter." I tapped my forehead the way the Poet had done.

For a moment this silenced him. Then he asked, "What do you do about your own case?"

"What case?"

"Don't tell me you consider yourself sane. You and Horace Dowd. Square, yes—" he made the sign of the square and said— "you probably even dream in black and white. But don't confuse acceptance with sanity."

"I didn't slit my wrist."

The Poet's forehead became corrugated: "She did that? She tried?"

"Yes."

"Don't we all?" He flashed his goofy yellow grin.

"Not all," I said. "Maybe the ones who haven't have to stand by the ones who have."

"You think you've been appointed to save your wife's life? Talk about guilt. Ever occur to you, Critic, you may be more your wife's problem than she is yours?"

"I can't take that chance."

"Spoken by a true critic," he sighed. But he had brightened, relieved to know he was not alone at the epicenter.

"I don't know. About anything, I don't believe in cure. I don't think we get over. Whatever went wrong."

" 'The best lack all conviction,' whatever that says for you. Meanwhile you leave your hamster's cage only to tiptoe in here at night to commit the slowest suicide of all."

"I do. What I have to do."

"Take flutes away from old ladies, play parlor games with the crazies."

"That's what I do, I can live with it."

"I can tell from your wrists." He nodded his shaggy head in resignation. Suddenly, as if to discover how many games I did know how to play, he asked me if I had ever been to Calder, a Miami racetrack.

"I'm not much into gambling."

"Of course not," said he. "What critic ever played it any other way but safe?" He stubbed out the first cigarette, half smoked, then brought another out of his kimono pocket: I lit it for him, officially. By this time Miss Johns had arrived for the shift change at midnight, so the Poet drew me into his room, knowing the intercom would be turned down while Miss Ryan briefed the relief nurse.

"Ever hear of a horse named Naiad?"

"Afraid not."

"Don't be afraid. You wouldn't have."

Then why ask? I wondered, but allowed the Poet his moment: his hands trembled; he was excited, but the excitement was under control. At least his visage had been cleared of tears.

After Lights Out an automatic control switch reduced the intensity of ward lights to a minimum. The Poet had got around this measure by removing the shade from the lamp on his night table and replacing the bulb with a 100-watt bulb stolen from the Dayroom. He now put on a pair of owlish horn-rims and fumbled under the bed for his attaché case.

"I assume you know what a naiad is?"

"Some kind of water nymph."

"Bravo. There's hope for you on the intellectual level if not the emotional. But no such nymphs exist in the polluted tidepools of this place. Miami's naiads, assuming there ever were any, would have evolved into the professional variety complete with coin slots where once a softer slot engaged our fancy—so the term has fallen into disuse. Except by a racehorse owner trying to come up with a cute name for a fast filly, first time out. You know what a villanelle is?"

"Some kind of poem?"

"Bravo encore. Your erudition floors me." He got up off the floor and placed his attaché case on the bed. "But not very likely would you have sullied your scientific mind with a villanelle entitled 'Naiad' written by the most important unknown poet of this century, about a naiad in the flesh."

He was about to show me his poem, I assumed, as he fumbled among the literary quarterlies in the attaché case—but he produced instead a racing form. There were column-lists of the next day's horses, their sires and dams and case histories: one, with the name Naiad, encircled by a magic marker.

"By the way—not relevant, but worthy of note—a poet named Gabriel L'Homme also wrote an ode to a naiad of his own (the word's the same in French, only with an *e* that makes it feminine, but his was not) called *"Naïade,"* nothing to compare with the American. The naiad I wrote about is named for the state she was born in, the virgin state, many states removed from the state I knew her in, called Ginny for short by her Daddykins, by all who knew her, as if she went with tonic, or was tonic. Tonic and intoxicant both."

He ran on, spilling over in this way; but unlike most of the babble I listened to in this tower, his could be interpreted eventually. Did he refer to his child-wife? He did.

"Since you know my wife by photographic reproduction only and not by the other means of reproduction, the one in the biblical sense, and since you know not the poem nor do you follow the ponies, you could not have discerned fate's negligent irony in running my runaway naiad in the seventh race at Calder tomorrow."

My father spoiled the term "fate" for me. No, I could not see the irony here.

From between the pages of his *Selected Poems* he drew forth a dozen twenty-dollar bills. I had not thought to examine the volume when I searched his room: patients were not permitted to keep money or valuables in their possession.

"It's only play money, *mon ami*."

His eyes were larger than life behind the glasses, he showed his yellow teeth: he was on a manic high and I could have attempted to restrain the exuberance but tears might follow as soon as the fever cooled. He needed a co-conspirator. I neither agreed nor disagreed to become his silent partner. My passive acquiescence meant only that I would rock no boats.

"Funny thing happened to me on the way to the madhouse, the taxi driver that drove me to that tour boat believed in transmigration of souls. In a way he reminded me of you, he kept leaning out the window telling everybody else how to drive. All the way from Fort Lauderdale he bent my ear about souls being Hollanderized like fur coats and put back into circulation. But only related souls, from something he called the celestial soul bank. Actually I was interested. I kept recalculating his tip the more insights he offered. If a mink coat can be renewed, why not a used-up soul? (The Warden should have talked with this cabbie before signing on with Freud.) So

I asked him what he wanted to come back as and he said as a passenger instead of a driver. I told him I intended to be in the driver's seat next time around."

"What," asked I, "would I come back as?"

He winked as he placed the sheaf of twenties in my hand.

11

"SHE'S RELAXED with you," was the one sincere compliment I could always pay Miss Pike. "She feels. Better."

Whenever I spoke with Miss Pike I wanted to offer her the same assurances I automatically dispensed to patients—like Miss Ryan with her medications—to get them through the night.

The trinkets jiggled from Miss Pike's ears as she nodded. "I'll take her to Crandon Park," she proposed. "We can do Piggly Wiggly on the way back."

Piggly Wiggly was a supermarket at the Miami end of the MacArthur Causeway. For Valerie, the aisles of Piggly Wiggly promised enchanted distraction.

"She trusts you," I went on. "She feels. Safe."

"We have this ongoing one-to-one."

She was incapable of a smile, and her eyes gave no clue, but I knew the prospect of this outing pleased her. For all Miss Pike's professional engagement with psychiatric social work, she was as removed from the real-time world as was Valerie. The only photograph on her desk was oddly enough of Dr. K—no trace of family, if she had any. To identify herself (to herself, it would seem, since her name was also on the office door), she kept a brass plaque on the desk that said Ms. Pike.

"I only need," I explained, "the afternoon."

"No problem."

She had learned the reassuring No Problem from Dr. K, but she had not picked up the professional smile that went with it. In the photograph Dr. K might have been saying No Problem alongside hers, for his mouth was open: he had the look of someone who knew something the rest of us would never comprehend, and whatever he knew there was No Problem to it. He looked out at us and smiled upon our enterprise.

"Dr. K," I reminded her, "stresses stability. And security. She can't take surprises. You're the only person she."

"We relate well," she finished for me. The mannikins at her earlobes danced in agreement.

Miss Pike did relate well to Valerie, but apparently to no one else. Patients shrunk from her bulldoze approach. Her relentless sense of dedication antagonized the staff—unfairly, it seemed to me. "I try to meet people halfway" was her poignant strategy as she waited hopelessly, by herself, at the halfway point.

"Well," I said. "Thanks."

I was always thanking her. Those first months I worked at the Sans Souci I thanked her excessively for getting me the job. (It was Miss Pike who knew of the opening for a psychiatric aide: she told Valerie, who told me.) I now thanked her by way of ending our conference.

"I try," she said, "to be supportive without being too directive or prescriptive, and she relates to that approach."

I remembered seeing Miss Pike help Valerie assemble the pieces of a jigsaw puzzle: the delight was on Miss Pike's face, as much as she could show delight through the heavy makeup, without a smile. Miss Pike's voice rose an excited decibel when she suggested they watch *Wanderlust* on TV together or when Miss Pike read aloud the instructions for a cake mix, with Valerie her mildly interested audience of one.

At noon Miss Pike's outsized Oldsmobile would bear these two truants across the Rickenbacker Causeway to the Crandon Park Zoo. There Valerie would linger before her caged favorites, the birds, especially a formal family of penguins so out of place in Miami. They both agreed the great horned owl resembled Dr. K.

(Once I had returned from an afternoon's liberty to find Valerie and Miss Pike cutting out paper dolls: Valerie was using the scissors with a concentrated intensity she rendered only to cartoons on television. Miss Pike was a radiantly animated child. I had caught sight of them through the front window, then diplomatically withdrew. I went for half an hour's stroll and returned only when Miss Pike was due to take her leave, the paper dolls hidden away.)

As they drove back to Biscayne Boulevard in the aged black hearse Miss Pike steered with such uptight competence, the two could anticipate, at least, their pushcart tour of Piggly Wiggly, accompanied by Muzak, before the hollow return.

I passed the shopping list and four tens to Miss Pike. She in turn, with a request of her own, handed an envelope across the desk to me.

"When he sees it's been opened he'll turn hostile." Miss Pike blinked, as if the Poet had swung at her. "He turns hostile the minute I come on the floor."

The envelope had been neatly slit open, the message surely scrutinized by Dr. Krauskopf and herself, then replaced. Inside the envelope was another letter, also opened (and another envelope inside that one?). The outside envelope was addressed to I.M. Gold at an Alabama address, forwarded to the Cosmos Motel, then sent on to the Sans Souci.

"We have to examine all correspondence, for their own good. He might listen to you, he won't me."

I responded to the appeal in Miss Pike's eyes. Would I give him the letter? No problem.

12

THE TRACK had fallen under a spell since the Daily Double. Idling in the concrete labyrinth beneath the stands, solitaries mumbled to themselves as if stumbling along the corridors of Passive City after Shock. One defeated fan thrust a tout sheet at me, another made a gift to me of his untouched hot dog. They tasted their graphite pencil points for luck and precision, circling the quaint names of starting three-year-olds. They glanced only in swift takes at the tote board in the infield oval where the statistics from two previous races still lingered in lights. Or they paid rapt homage to the underground video screens flashing a pattern of digits to the initiated.

I made my puzzled way through the maze, confounded by the mathematics and codes. The Poet could have deciphered this numerical display, and his accountant-father come to some conclusion over totals. My own father would have found the scene familiar and the numbers comforting: he had been an habitué of the old Latonia

Race Track in its day, and there had met the woman "with trim ankles and skin like peaches and cream" for whom he left my mother. When that racecourse was obliterated to make way for an oil refinery, the change, my father wrote, effectively eliminated the sporting element in northern Kentucky, and killed off the town of Latonia in one blow.

There was nothing to be nostalgic about at Calder. The pit beneath the grandstand was animated, but practically devoid of women—at least the kind my father was attracted to: "with hair the color God gave it and skin untreated by chemical means." Calder was an up-to-date racing enterprise, strictly business, and its women appeared to be part of the bargain.

Outside, along the coliseum ramps, the students of Equus were so engaged in the painful research of a racing form, or deep into self-addressed monologues, it took minutes for anyone to realize a patron of the track was thrashing in a fit at the bottom of an escalator. I ran to him.

An epileptic writhed on the cement floor, snorting forth a spray of saliva and blood. A crowd gathered, no one offered help beyond the advice on several sides to grab his tongue. The spectators, their faces twitching, were as helpless as the epileptic under siege.

Finally a security guard with two paramedics came to my aid. Somebody said I could have been sued for moving him, and I said I worked at a hospital. The four of us maneuvered the heaving victim onto a canvas stretcher while the escalator continued its relentless descent, spewing torn and discarded betting tickets at my feet. I was shaken. What kind of omen was this?

At the catering stand I swilled an icy tasteless beer to recover from the drama at the foot of the escalator. I drank too fast, then foolishly ordered another to occupy the time between races. I had no intention of taking part in the grim ritual at Calder until my own appointed moment of truth: the seventh race.

"Don't for the love of God get shut out," was the Poet's warning, and that seemed to be the watchword of every bettor in sight. I might have been watching a silent film that jerked into fast forward at post time: stunned humankind milled around me in disembodied animation. The frenzy reached its peak just at the buzzer that signaled absolute paralysis of all tote machines. After that there was only the suspense of the race itself to be endured.

I was to place our bet immediately after the classic bugle notes struck the summer air—taps, or reveille?—to allow for a secure interval before the final buzzer sounded. I had been warned, I had been rehearsed. "The amount, count it (count it *before*), the horse's *number*—not, despite the beauty of it, the name—and then the winning words: 'to win.' "

This incantation the Poet repeated to me twice I now recited to myself with one more beer.

"Say it," said the Poet, "as if it were a charm, or a prayer. (Don't you goyim pray your heads off when you want something enough?) Make yourself into a believer, for my sake at least. For Christ sake concentrate. Say it: amount, the horse's *number*, 'to win,' say it like the bugle notes still hanging in the air, loud and clear. And don't forget to check the numbers on the tickets he issues. Remember, there's magic at work here."

Standing next to me, his beer untouched and going flat, was a slight flyweight of a man who could only have been a jockey (at liberty for the afternoon, or disbarred for some conspiracy?) agonizing over a dope sheet pressed to his red-haired girlfriend's breasts. She towered over her miniature lover by a full head, her breasts at the level of his narrow eyes, an ample bookrack for his reading. Her face was turned my way, with an expression of insufferable indifference, until our eyes met and she was startled out of her revery. She broke contact with my stare so swiftly it must have hurt her neck. My eyes had become restless in this setting, I was being rude. I searched for thoughts in the steel girders overhead, waiting for the afternoon to end. Another misplaced princess caught my eye, this one unaffected by anyone's stare: she was being delicately careful of her pleated skirt as she folded herself prettily into a crouch to pick up scattered pari-mutuel tickets in the sad hope of something worth saving in that hasty discard.

A stag line of old men hovered near the cashiers' windows. The Poet had prepared me for them; he called them the Ten-Percenters, oldsters past the age of sixty-five, living out their Social Security years. At that age they were absolved from income tax, and for a gratuity would cash the winning tickets of a younger bettor. Any winning sum above $1,000 was subject to an automatic twenty percent withholding fee: by paying ten percent to a Ten-Percenter the holder of a winning ticket still came out ahead. "At Calder, Critic, even the IRS has to take its chances."

I fixed an eye on one of these: his lively eyebrows bristled like underbrush, his long grey locks grown yellow at the ends. He must have been about my father's age: for a moment it occurred to me he could, for all I knew, be my father. But the style was all wrong, his costume was contrary to the way I saw my father dressed. The jeans were those of a teenager, he wore a baseball cap with ventilating holes; the folded upper half of a pair of Social Security spectacles peeked out of the pocket of his polo shirt. From beneath the tangled brows he returned my stare and almost imperceptibly nodded yes.

The old man might have known a winner when he saw one, or he had the faith of poets. There were bound to be winners among us, but the look of a winner would be the least obvious of all. Still, the old-timer had responded to my uncool stare: he knew something.

The seventh race was called "The Last Home," like a sad game of hide-and-seek. (I thought of The Children's Home in Latonia, a first home instead of last.) "For Fillies Two Years Old Which Have Never Won a Race Other than Maiden or Claiming." Naiad was number 3, surely a lucky slot unless the numbered floors of an insane asylum came to mind. Sal Barcelona was up, at a weight of 114 lbs. I tried to see the portents in these printed statistics, but was not gifted for this.

A snappy anthem rang out over the public address: my heart swelled, not with the purity of the bugle call but in a panic remembering the Poet's words. *Pick a window with a short line, and don't get shut out.* A shambling stumblebum suddenly drew erect at the bugle's signal as if responding to a local patriotism. Bewitched, I followed the stumbler to the nearest cashier's window.

No line was shorter: only the tentlike *cubaverra* of the stumblebum ahead of me, giving off an odor of the hundred days he must have lived in it. I knew him. He was a small-time South Beach gangster who was once a patient at the Sans Souci: Paranoia was the diagnosis; he was convinced a squad of hit men were out to murder him for a treachery committed in Chicago in 1929. "There's a c-c-contract out on me," he informed us, and this entitled him to a sequence of seventeen shock treatments paid for by Dade County.

Sam had been a sparring partner to champions, his brains scrambled by the machine-gun blows to the head. He was on Welfare, he sold neckties out of a shoe box on Collins Avenue, he walked dogs for pocket money. In the Fifties he had wrestled under the name Uncle Sam until he was enjoined by the American Legion not to wear our nation's flag as a cape in the wrestling arena.

"No Trifecta this race, Sam," the cashier said to him, then leaned past Sam's bulk to give me a knowing tilt of his head:

everybody knew Uncle Sam. Even the brutal Miami Beach police permitted Sam to peddle his neckties in hotel driveways.

"Then do-do-do me a Perfecta. I'm going to wheel it. How much to-to wheel me number three-three-three, with every other horse?"

Number three, Sam too had a thing for naiads. The coincidence would have jolted a genuine gambler's faith: nothing an incipient ruin like Sam might propose could possibly come out right. I thought about changing lines, for luck. What would the Poet have done? But suddenly Sam swung around to me and winked in inexplicable complicity: "We all be-be-be winners by and by," as if he had rehearsed the line. It would have been insulting to walk away after Sam's assurances: I was committed to a punch-drunk's destiny.

"Luck, Sam," I said.

"Luck, yourself." The way Sam mumbled, it could have been an obscenity.

Sam could not have remembered me—could he remember anyone since 1929?—the aide who accompanied him to EST (I worked the day shift at the time) and waited with him in the Recovery Room until the effects of an electrified seizure had worn off. Dr. Lazar, the EST technician, assaulted Sam's cortex in the same brutal way his brain had taken its beating in the boxing ring. I would then lead him back to 3, trying to pace my own steps to his stumble. When he remembered anything, he remembered the grapefruit juice he drank before EST or remembered lighting Al Capone's cigars for him or sparring with Tony Galenta.

"I was a Go-Go-Golden Gloves back then. I wrestled p-p-prime time on TV."

As Sam paid for his wager in crumpled singles and an assortment of coins, the Ten Percenters nudged one another, winked and whispered together, deciding the outcome among them. After Sam collected his string of tickets, I moved into the vacancy.

"Three hundred seventy-five dollars on number three, to win."

The Poet would have approved of my performance. As I walked away with the receipt for a piece of folly, I tried to see the poetry of it, or the humor.

The Grandstand East was a hall of mirrors, tinted glass against the glare, so I strolled outside to take my place among the railbirds scattered at the periphery of the racecourse. For no other reason than our having been together at the same window (he could not have remembered me from earlier than that), Sam shambled up beside me. Just as mysteriously, the Ten Percenter with the shaggy eyebrows broke ranks, trailed Sam and me, then took up watch on my right, like a second bodyguard. It would seem the Poet had choreographed this unlikely formation: fate or destiny had again come into play—or the three cold beers had benumbed my senses.

The jockeys appeared to be suspended over their flat saddles like puppets, doll-like except for their criminal faces, almost dainty in silk and leather. I watched to see if Sal Barcelona on 3 was less of a broken-nosed desperado than the rest: he was smaller only, as was his sidewise cantering mount. I tried to catch Naiad's eye—the horse, after all, was the protagonist in our plot—but that sleek prima donna dodged eye contact. Nor would the jockey look my way: performers can have no connection with the crowd before performing. By the time the horses reached the starting gate, I came to the conclusion that the only true nobility in this spill of horseflesh and humankind were the prancing beasts themselves.

A buzzer rattled the unearthly calm. In simultaneous advance, the hooved contenders exploded out of their slots. They might have been the tin horses of a children's game set off in tandem: a carrousel where no horse, for all his straining forward, could outrun another. I could make nothing out of the confused cluster of animals and men, so I turned to the tote board and watched instead the mounts outlined in light bulbs, their numbers shifting in place.

The tumult all around did not penetrate the religious contemplation of our unique trio. It seemed we three knew a secret, even if a different secret each.

13

IN THE DAYROOM a repairman had dismantled the television set, its secret side for the first time revealed. His rough hand was plunged among the intestinal tubes and wires while frightened Miss Frith stood by, watching in anguish as if the operation were being performed, without anaesthesia, on herself. Cookie, of the fierce need for protein, and hefty Mrs. Concannon, denied a diet of prunes, danced together to the distant sound of Mrs. Kakafroni's flute a loveless lesbian waltz. Nowhere was the Poet badgering the team of Davidoff & Ballantine, being spendthrift at Monopoly or making Scrabble miserable for his fellow patients.

Even before checking the Fire Doors (an example of how negligent I had become) or greeting Miss Ryan in the Nurses Station, I hurried down the EW corridor with the money wadded inside my shirt. I had already debated the ethic of whose trust was being betrayed: Dr. K's edict about safekeeping, or the Poet's need for exploit—and had come to no conclusion except to place my money on the Poet. (I had won only half as much as the Poet, having only half his faith in precognition.) By now the only sure thing I knew was the sum of our winnings.

Mr. Davidoff was secretly trying the locked door to the telephone booth. At my approach he guiltily dropped his hand, burnt by my gaze (indifferent and distracted as that gaze was), then tucked the offending hand inside his immaculate jacket in a lunatic pose of joke and cartoon, a form of salute, which I good-naturedly returned by raising two fingers like a papal blessing meant to wish him well.

At the Poet's door I collected myself, took a breath, felt again for the money, suppressed a fatuous smile. I sensed his death before I entered. (The dead—contrary to scientific proof—do give off an aura.) The corpse was strung up in the bathroom: with the sash to his kimono he had hung himself from the shower head, and now dangled there in the gruesome rigidity that follows the cessation of all vital functions.

He had managed to conceal one last book of matches from his careless guardian, for the washbasin contained the ashes of papers he had destroyed, perhaps a photograph among them. The note he left was addressed to me: "Finish my poem for me, Critic."

Underground

1

WHILE I SLEPT Lake Okeechobee went by in the night, not even a dream of it to remember. At La Belle a character in a white suit boarded the bus bearing his ticket in a plastic briefcase. Something about this hairless latecomer spooked me: the collection of ball-points that embellished his jacket pocket was a harmless enough sign, but then I recalled a line from the Poet: "I could tell you about the private eye, a gorilla in a white suit I hired . . ." The gorilla could barely keep his balance down the aisle as the bus got under way. As fate would have it, this disaster sat down beside me.

"No smoking," I warned him.

"I just hold it," he wheezed. Saliva gathered at the corners of his mouth when he spoke; the fat thighs in white duck spread to my side of the seat.

He began by a candid report on himself: he seemed prepared, with all those pens, to sign autographs or write out a subpoena. At first I no more trusted his story than I believed in those odd pink eyes—why should he, without the least apology or by-your-leave, offer up the history of his life? As soon as he suggested what he did for a living, I was afflicted by portents. The Poet would have come up with a nasty name for him—the Foetus, perhaps—but I thought of him as the Skip Tracer.

Next he showed me a Tallahassee newspaper photo of himself and the governor of Florida (they looked alike in their total baldness) blatantly ignoring one another as they shook hands for the camera.

"I received a state citation." He did not say what for.

My uneasy lack of response did not discourage him. He dug a gun permit out of his briefcase, but fortunately not the pistol that went with it. I nodded. He then produced a pilot's license. "Hobby of mine—pleasure, not business. I'm the owner of a sassy little Piper Cub that'll take me anywheres on this planet. Business, I take the bus and make out a voucher for air fare." He caressed his unlit cigarette suggestively. "I got me a friend in Accounting. Bring my apprehendeds back by air, though. Listen, I nail five out of seven my outfit sends me after, that's all the company cares about. For the last six years I have maintained highest company average of any agent on the books. So don't go asking me for plane tickets and restaurant receipts. I eat at Dunkin' Donuts and collect for four-star dinners at the best in town. Just remember, ones I nab the client gets eighty-some percent convictions. Don't go running no expense account audits on your number one."

I did not grace this philosophy with a second nod. The Greyhound air conditioning had reached my stomach; I knew before he asked he would ask: "Where you from."

"The shores," I said, "of Lake Okeechobee."

I sat regretting that I had answered at all, while he was put to a reflective moment of silence by my answer. The culpability I felt was out of proportion to the threat, but his presence—gun permit, percentage of convictions—suggested some ultimate incrimination.

"The problem with the world today is all these different credit cards everybody carries."

I had changed our winnings into traveler's checks. This meant, I now realized, I would be leaving a trail of signed American Express checks for agents like this foetus to follow.

"I'll tell you something." He unlaced his desert boots and made himself at home. "Talk about your prodigal son, the prodigal daughter is more like it. Teenage runaways are nine out of ten times female. A boy, hell, he just naturally leaves home and nobody thinks twice about it. I done it myself, fifteen, quit school, left home—you think the FBI was notified, or my hometown police? I was on my own, nobody gave a shit, that's where the Bible gets it ass-backwards. Their daddy's not killing fatted calfs for some delinquent boy come home. I never saw my old man's face from age fifteen on. My sister, she only got as far as the next town with some fucker she took off with and my dad had the two of them in jail by nightfall of the day she left home. You lose sight of your little girl you turn over every stone in Kingdom Come to get her back. I'll tell you something else, there's

girls I traced you wouldn't want them back, you wouldn't recognize
them. It's no paradise out there."

Out There was the surreal topography of turpentine pines he
indicated with his fist turned into a pistol—but all that flat emptiness
falling away forever was what I had opted for. The contemplation of
infinity always made my head swim. Meanwhile, what came between
me and my escape route was his fat hairless reflection in the bus
window.

"You want to know where nine out of ten embezzlers turn up?
You find them at the races. I closed out more company fraud cases at
the racetrack than anywheres else."

Nothing was more calculated to feed my unease than talk of
racetracks. This surely was the figure behind the pay window when
the Ten Percenter cashed in for me, fat face hidden beneath an
eyeshade. I took a swift confirming look at him while he explained the
statistics on runaways, and not runaway horses: "More'n seventy-five
percent takes French leave, you'll pardon the expression, is the
girlies—but it's the men I go out for. Domestic Court cases you get
ten times the money to bring back Mr. Alimony in handcuffs than
bring a female to heel."

That must have been when I decided to grow a beard. I saw
myself with a beard, I started growing a beard that very instant. He
was grubbing through his plastic briefcase for a warrant for my return
to Miami, but all he came up with was a meal voucher in time for the
rest stop at a café called Arcadia.

I made straight for the men's room, not so much to relieve my
bladder as to retire to a booth with a door that locked where I could
consider my situation out of sight. In blessed privacy I studied the
basic anatomies rendered by a transient graffiti artist—no help. Nor
did the crude accompanying poetry afford distraction. I pulled the
chain and got the Poet's words crashing down with the flush: *Flee this
place, you pudding*. He was always saying I was denied the knowledge
of good and evil in Passive City. *Your trouble*, he said. He was always
telling me my trouble.

No hospital smell here to overcome the all-too-human stench:
you had your nose rubbed into the reality of right now. Is this what
you meant, Poet? On the way out there was the choice of condoms or
chewing gum from the same dispenser.

I retreated by way of the screen door behind the dining area,
where the Greyhound exhaust lay heavy in the stagnant air. I boarded
the empty bus and took the Poet's attaché case from the rack where I

had stashed it. As I stepped out again I took oblique notice of the foetus-face behind the café window, his cigarette now cockily alight, easing along the self-service counter past a cache of glazed doughnuts.

An assortment of mostly tourist-tagged autos spun along the sunbaked highway. I watched the traffic apathetically—puzzling out the attitudes of drivers, considering the romance of license plates— then, on an impulse, made a fist with my thumb pointed north.

Travel light was the Poet's way, and my father's. All I carried was the stolen attaché case (who would miss it, the owner deceased?). My father traveled with the original Gladstone bag his precious mother had given him: "Empty, and with no other impedimenta than that which I picked up en route." I had left my electric razor at home—you can't go home again just to collect your Schick and toothbrush. (What if your wife should look up, for once, as you came out of the bathroom?) My farewell shave was accomplished with the Poet's razor, in the Staffroom on 3, borrowed from the SHARPS box. I carried a lightweight chino jacket I hoped was waterproof—no matter what or where, I was bound to be rained on. The traveler's checks were in the inside pocket of the chino jacket. In the attaché case I carried assorted mementos, including two packets of letters my father had written to me over the years. And a book of matches from the Cosmos Motel. ("Suicide? Don't make me laugh, Critic. I've only got my *Selected* out. No poet commits suicide until he's published his *Complete*.") I had a not-at-this-address in Alabama and a mother's address in Manhattan. I carried a birth certificate to prove who I was, and an Honorable Discharge from the U.S. Navy—but no document with a box to check for Married or Divorced, no license to fly.

A Seminole in a furniture-moving van told me he had run over a coral snake just two seconds before picking me up: "Was that serpent a metaphor for original sin or did I merely save your ass from getting bit?"

"Maybe both."

"An equivocator. Just who I needed to talk to next."

Stenciled upside-down on the inside-out brim of his Navy white hat was the name *William Fremont*. He wore the brim so low over his forehead that a union button pinned to the *o* in *Fremont* was like a cyclops eye to steer by. His tribal name was Billy Birdsong.

"My people call me Billy. White man with forked tongue calls me Fre."

An elaborate manipulation of gears and fancy footwork got the moving van moving again.

I did not offer a name of my own and he was unfazed by the discourtesy. We perched high and mighty on our diesel thrones behind a sign that said NO RIDERS in reverse. It was Billy's rig, but the insurance company made him make this unfriendly declaration.

The cab was air-conditioned. There was a bed built into the cubby behind our heads, Sony-Hitachi speakers at the head and foot of it like bookends. Part of the dashboard complications were buttons and switches to a tape deck and amplifier: there was a CB microphone and a radio tuner on my side of the dash. Billy lowered the sound on a tape playing guitar, so we could talk. "Bach," he said, "Segovia at the guitar." Below the dash was a rack of tapes: baroque music mostly, and a section devoted to the plays of Shakespeare, BBC productions. Indeed, there was poetry on the open road, as I had been advised by the Poet, but who would have thought a Native American teamster would be its oracle?

With Segovia playing background music, Billy launched a story that continued for the next many miles of highway. The nautical details of his tale were out of place on this landlocked expressway: the only water to appear to us during his sea story was the odd occasional tide pool that, by the time we plunged into it, turned out to be a mirage.

"The USS *Narcissus* was guarding our farflung Mediterranean frontier from the insidious incursions of godless Communism and I was her scout, Sonarman First Class halfbreed Fremont, sir, listening for kerplunks in the watery depths that might mean Russky subs with their evil torpedoes aimed at the tender underbelly of our proud land."

Surely the Poet was inventing these people and arranging, in his own mysterious way, for me to meet them. Billy was not so much a lapsed Seminole as a dusky exotic out of a ballad being composed at the moment. He wore a crow-black ponytail. Out of habit I checked his wrist for scars, none: an attempt at a tattoo was only a faint heart of darkness on his forearm. I might have known he had been in the Navy, from the white hat, from the way he invited me to climb aboard—but no guarantee who's who these days, the way we deck ourselves out, or run on. Especially if the Poet was making all of this up.

"Before I retired from the Naval service of my country (and it is my country, in some half-remembered but unrecorded way), I played guitar." He was telling the same story, but this was a new tack. "Not an instrument your Native American is generally known to play. (Tom-tom is what that is.) My first love was harpsichord, but that's an instrument that won't fit easy in a wigwam. So I became a guitar player. Played for the crew at Happy Hour and for the officers in the wardroom in my spare time when not listening for kerplunks in the watery depths. One night's liberty in Villefranche-sur-Mer I was urged by the gentry to play Native American music for a Frog party aboard their yacht—the *Pequod* or *Le Vaisseau Fantôme* (I forget which)—anchored off the hibiscus gardens of Cap Ferrat." The Poet had to be in on this, at least the French part. "Ghostly white sixty-footer with a crew of nine not counting hired garçons serving hors d'oeuvres under a candy-striped canvas rigged over the fantail. Three noble masts spiked against the *azur* of the Côte d'Azur, but their sails were secured; diesel power, all you wanted—but she wasn't going anywhere. A beauty, a worthy vessel. Beauties and worthies with all the travel potential in the world, fated to stand fast. Cinderella liberty is all that's allowed in foreign ports, but it was only a shadow after ten and the Shore Patrol made Villefranche miserable by outnumbering Native Americans nine to one, so I said to the gentry—to a white man decked out in white linen, in particular— *pourquoi pas?*"

I felt suddenly I was at sea, with all of a midwatch before me to listen to this man's story.

"From the slipperiness of the decks there must have been hors d'oeuvres and whatnot consumed since before sundown. You had to watch where you stepped not to slide on a turd of pâté or in a pool of vomit—that kind of party, the burnt-down butt end of it. A lull in the festivities had somewhat paralyzed the afterdecks. Zenith was reached an hour ago, but people still swilled and chattered to their wits' end since it was too early to quit. And more champagne left than anybody wanted to think about. That was where I came in. I was the mysterious stranger meant to turn the tide, give the party a second breath. (If you're looking for a moral to this story, it's our times, our instant heroes.) I was the entertainment, destined to bring the dead to life. Time was when the public turned to presidents and pirates to recharge the batteries, now it's rock stars and dope dealers."

He had wanted to travel to the South of France, wanted to be at the party aboard the *Pequod*, but he lay in his shroud-pac in the Morgue at the Sans Souci, no relative to claim the remains: "No next of kin since Keats died."

"White Suit introduced me as an original, which I am, while I tuned up listening for stray kerplunks in the bass line. I played "Tennessee Waltz" at some joker's request, to warm up with, then "Money Talks" (it sings, it dances) to remind White Suit to remind the gentry that a white hat would be passed at the finale and gratuities would not be taken amiss. Finally I riffed through my personal repertoire. A thing came over me. Not gradual, just a quick click at the place where the spine joins the skull. Halfway into "Peace Pipe Dreams" I was standing there under the candy-striped canvas, but not there—you know what I mean? Moved. By the last note and the word 'smoke' I was moved off to one side slightly elevated from where I generally stood."

"You mean you stepped outside yourself?"

"Verily. That happen to you too?"

"At a racetrack. Once."

"Then you recognize the spiritual nature to our humble fumblings down here. Loading furniture, listening for kerplunks, playing guitar or trying to find a place to park—you might when you least expect have a run of Nirvana. You dig?"

"Yes."

"Crowd caught on with a click of their own. Sloshed as they were, and the state I was in, I could objectify such flyspeck phenomena as a deck ape peeping out a porthole with tears in his eyes. Here was higher manifestation than that which is manifested on a day-to-day basis. A fateful happenstance. I had got these lost souls tangled up in my guitar strings. Irresistible force meets immovable object and transcendence takes place. Even the waiters paid attention, as if getting paid to. White Suit was in seventh heaven. A pair of lesbians making love in a lifeboat peeked out from under canvas to compare notes. This was Ultimate City we had sailed to, still at anchor with the sails secured.

"Irony of it was it wasn't me that scored the celestial heights one stardusted night off the mustard-colored ramparts of Villefranche. (You could see Corsica from the crow's nest, but from where I stood you could see farther than that.) My twin—and I do not lay the word 'art' on some innocent hitchhiker lightly—my twin the artist stepped in at the moment of truth and relieved me of duty. Whoever the mysterious dude was—my own ghost, an invisible musical genius, the fabulous Other—he took over. Twin Billy was the one strumming my guitar and growling out the homemade lyrics word for word. I do scat instead of vocal, so did he. But this I can testify was an identical different Birdsong in the spotlight and not yours truly that was originally introduced."

I wanted to ask where a person goes from the celestial heights, but he was into another dimension, remembering. Then he was back on terra firma again, shifting gears preparatory to navigating an unexpected cloverleaf that came up out of nowhere.

"You want to go to Bradenton?" he asked me, but before I could say no he said, "Fine. You'd have to back out the wrong-way lane at the Bradenton exit and go back to Go. You want to go to Wauchula, Bowling Green, Winter Haven?"

Which reminded me, where *was* I headed?

"You can't get there from here. Engineer of this fuck-up was named Dodgson, I swear. I read all about the scandal in the Tampa papers, Dodgson & Associates is an out-of-state outfit that pulled the same scam in Maryland. Lowest bid on the contract and the highest bribes, neither Dodgson nor his associates knows a highway from a hole in the ground, they subcontracted the construction and retired to Las Vegas under another name. It's not just the signs and arrows either, which you can always change, but the whole entire layout. Nobody goes anywhere on this pretzel." Billy was chuckling over the puzzle of a cloverleaf: "But you have to hand it to Dodgson for brass."

On at least three of the ramps roadworks were under way to untangle the twisted misleadings of the interchange. Hard hats dangled from bosun's chairs painting out the lane indications. Billy double-clutched us to one side of a stalled line of cars onto what looked like hot coals, then we rumbled into a poured-concrete gallery beneath Dodgson's chaos. Pumping the air brakes, Billy brought the monster van to a dead stop in this underground maze of concrete buttresses. With the engine off, the sound of pneumatic drills and the honking of tangled frustrated traffic was only a distant echo topside.

"This end of Florida," Billy informed me, "is a pinball game. You ricochet off rebound bumpers if you play by the rules. Injun know." He tapped a finger over one ear at the brim of his white hat. "Best way to play white man's game is first go down the rabbit hole."

That was the answer to the question I had not got around to asking.

2

"Piss call," called Billy, and we dropped out of opposite sides of the cab to relieve ourselves down under. The stanchions we watered were spray-painted with graffiti of no greater literary worth than at the Arcadia Café: *Pussy Is Better than Hamburger* and *Jesus recycles people.*

"Know what I'd write if I had a spray can handy?" Billy asked. "I'd write what the painter wrote on his gatepost in Tahiti. 'Where do we come from?—' "

" 'Who are we?' " I went on, zippering up. " 'Where are we going?' "

"What about that? Should have known you'd know the lyrics to the song of Tahiti. Only Gauguin wrote it in French. I figured you for a literary dude, there's that crease between your eyes that comes from reading the footnotes."

"Tax attorneys get the same crease, from fine print."

He was itching to ask me the same three questions, but kept his cool down here on the cool underside of Dodgson's folly. Then we took tea, of all things, in the back of the moving van, on furniture covered with pads and dust sheets, with the van doors propped open for light and ventilation. Tea was Fortnum & Mason's Earl Grey—this Seminole took his tea seriously—boiled up on a camper's gas ring. The cups were bone china, and whether they were Billy's or belonged to the owner of the furniture, I never knew. From where we sat on a sofa trussed up like a cadaver with rope and canvas there was a tunnel-vision view of an auto graveyard: a crane took shape in the distance, a praying mantis with a smashed car body in its magnetized claw.

"A car," said Billy, "that didn't make it through its designated lane. Dodgson's got half interest in the auto-wrecking business."

"O.K.," I said, warmed by the tea. "Yes. I'm a reader. Of books."

"Remember, I'm not asking."

"I was in the Navy, like you."

"Figures."

"Do sailors have creases, too? O.K., I started up a bookstore. I read the books instead of selling them. Worked at a clinic."

"I know what kind of clinic."

"Right. What other kind is there anymore? For the disturbed."

"There's cancer."

"This was a clinic for the mentally ill."

"Remember, I'm not asking."

"Anyway, I'm telling. I was what they called a psychiatric aide. There was a poet there."

"Always a poet."

"We had this thing going. Not what you think."

"How do you know what I think?"

"He was an influence."

"Good or bad? I hear no evil."

"He talked me out of the life. The rut. I was in."

"And that's why you're on the road."

"Right."

"What happened to your poet?"

"That's another story."

"Fair enough," said Billy. "I'll tell you the rest of mine."

He was off again to the Mediterranean.

"White Suit made a pass at my ass, naturally. I was the star of stars, and he wanted a piece of me. I politely removed his hand from my manhood saying, 'I prefer not to.' He was a literary dude too, like you and me. Turned out he was English, not French after all, but spoke French to fox the Frogs."

"This poet. He spoke French too."

"Don't they all. Anyway I was too high that night—and not on firewater—to think straight. He said he was going to put me in a book. Sounded like a flower he was going to press between the pages. That's the new pitch, instead of putting us innocents into the movies. Hey, you're not a writer yourself, by any chance? You're not by any chance writing me down in your head to put into a book?"

"Not by any chance."

"Well that's what White Suit did. Couldn't shake that ghost-writer our whole shakedown cruise. Wherever the *Narcissus* sailed, HMS *Pinafore* was there before us: Genoa, Brindisi, *Rhodes* for the love of the Great White Father. (Greece, everything's dead white so he blended right in, but I recognized the creep from his shadow.) I drank an ouzo with him and told him to lay off, he was taking notes."

"How did your music go? With all this."

"Music? Wardroom concerts, hey." His hey was a form of punctuation, his war cry. "Happy Hour. No, I was never going to be great again, great as that night when the champagne was running.

After scoring that high, the life of a drone was too sorry a scene to maintain. Music, hey. I sold my guitar, the guitar I bought in Barcelona, to some fucker on our sister ship the USS *Sisyphus*, a great guitar, too, and he got it for peanuts."

The tea had turned tepid in our cool cement burrow on the underside of the action. Billy's hat brim had slipped so far down over his black eyes I thought he might be asleep. We sat that way awhile with our tea down to the dregs. Was that a grand piano under canvas?—I was trying to guess pieces of furniture from the shapes under the padding. Then Billy roused himself.

"Remember, I'm not asking questions. Only one, any driver asks a passenger."

"Where am I going?"

"Something like that."

"Alabama, I guess."

"Your guess as good as mine."

"Yes. Alabama."

"With a banjo on your knee? Looks more like an attaché case."

I drummed a little tune on the attaché case: "I'm trying to locate. Somebody."

"Naturally." He flicked his ponytail at a host of imaginary flies. "Nonetheless this here load goes to Tarpon Springs."

"If she's not there, she might be in Texas."

"They do end up in Texas. Or Vegas, or L.A."

"She was married. To the poet I mentioned."

"Hey, I hear no evil." He put his teacup down to cover his ears. "You don't sound too sure, son, of your eventual intentions."

"Not yet, no."

"Then come to Tarpon Springs with Billy Birdsong. I'll allow you to help me unload. You got a congenial face despite the worried eyes. I dig that crease."

"Thanks, but just take me as close as you can to Tampa."

"Help me unload in Tarpon Springs and I'll pay way above minimum."

"Thanks. But I'll take a bus in Tampa. To Tallahassee."

"Why not Sarasota, the clown's town? I thought you were going to Alabama."

"I am. I'm going to. Go there."

"Something wicked this way comes," said Billy, as an aqua-colored Cadillac eased down the rabbit hole. "I thought only Native Americans knew this lonesome trail."

The car rumbled past us and parked two car lengths from the van, blocking out view of the auto graveyard. The passengers seemed unaware of our presence; their conversation rose above the echo of traffic and trip-hammers:

"They were burning rotten grapefruits the other side of the river."

"It's in the *car* I'm telling you," said she, on that hysterical note necessary to convince her dense spouse.

("Shit," said Billy, "I thought this was the one true getaway from that kind of mankind.")

"Maybe I run over a skunk when we took the Tamiami Trail."

"I-have-smelled-it-since-Miami-Beach."

The Cadillac bore Michigan plates, but these were no doubt the Dowds (I remembered them from another tour) and Mrs. Dowd was telling her husband she had no intention of driving into Flint with the car smelling to high heaven.

Horace wearily left the wheel, and once outside the car's air conditioning was instantly attacked by gnats. A winged halo above his sunburnt pate, he squatted—oblivious of witnesses drinking tea in the back of a moving van—to inspect each tire in turn. Mrs. Dowd was puzzling out the message on a concrete stanchion—*Pussy Is Better than Hamburger*—fanning herself furiously with a road map.

Mr. Dowd came around to the trunk where a bumper sticker invited us to SEE THE PARROT JUNGLE. His wife's car door was open now, one fat doll's leg adangle outside: "It's in *here* someplace." She slipped off a plastic glass slipper and sniffed at the sole.

As soon as he opened the trunk Horace staggered back, struck.
"My God."

His wife scrambled out of the car and was immediately beside him, one foot barefoot, the road map to her nose.

"What's in there?" she screamed.

"My God it's a dead dog."

The odor fanned out as far as our tea table, no escape from the heavy sickening waves of putrefaction. Billy jettisoned the tea and we joined the horror show. The rotting creature was lodged between his golf clubs and her Amelia Earhart suitcase, its spaniel's ears draped over a tire jack. The eyes were open staring my way, the teeth bared grotesquely.

Mrs. Dowd wept. She tried to balance herself on one shod foot and shield her tears behind the roap map—weeping not for the deceased animal, but for her suitcase and his golf bag—while her stunned husband wondered aloud how the darned thing got in there in the first place. Our unexpected presence neither alarmed nor relieved the Dowds. Billy addressed me, sotto voce: "First a deadly viper, now a dead pooch—what do these signs signify?"

After Billy pried the corpse free from the Dowds' Caddy with their jack handle and I tried to calm down the wife by telling her she could swab the trunk out with disinfectant, we retired to our own untainted vehicle. Billy made subterranean echos slamming the van doors shut. Back in the driver's seat, he played the instrument panel like a pipe organ, the motor working up steam. We rolled past the Dowds, he with his arm around her trembling shoulders, car doors hanging open like broken wings, a dead dog staring us out.

The rig carried us into a shaft of dizzying sunlight out the end of a tunnel marked NO EXIT, then into a confusion of indications: oblique and curved arrows turning back on themselves, signals that belayed signals fifty feet later, NO LEFT or NO RIGHT, arrows with serpentine tails trailing into broken white lines that became solid again out of pure caprice, short-circuited lanes intersecting at SQUEEZE LEFT and an unfinished piece of roadwork beneath a tattered banderole announcing *Gateway to God's Country* that led, according to Billy, to the polluted Raccoon River, plugged at its source with peach fuzz from a canning factory.

With the Dowds and a dead dog beneath the misbegotten cloverleaf to stern, we broke for the indeterminate horizon at the edge of a griddle.

"How come another bus?" asked Billy, reminded of my request. "Looked like you were allergic to buses from the way you jumped ship from that Greyhound in Arcadia."

"Just that one. That bus."

"Willy Blake warns that the road through hell is the straight road. So take a detour. Come on to Tarpon Springs with me."

Dante's hell came in circles. Straight is the gate. What had Billy put in that tea?

"Thanks, but my course is set."

We passed tokens of the sorrows of travel: a turtle smashed flat, and several crushed heads of lettuce lost from a truck gardener's truck. A hedge of oleander made a pink divider between eastbound and westbound traffic and reminded me of our own oleander hedge hiding the Seaboard Railway tracks. Billy called it dogbane and said Seminoles made poultices from the petals. One of its paler blossoms, like a child's deflated balloon, turned out to be, on passing, a latex tube limp with love's labor's lost.

"I could show you a good time in Tarpon Springs. Not just gay bars either."

"Thanks. I'll get out at Tampa."

"I bypass Tampa." Was there an edge of contention in his voice? "For a rig this big Tampa's worse than Dodgson's cloverleaf. You can watch the Greeks dive for sponges in Tarpon Springs. Greeks go both ways, and there's Greek girls—if that's your thing—that do belly dances."

With patients who had become intractable I waited out the episode in silence. I did the same with Billy. I was beginning to realize that my new sense of independence was only relative to influence and happenstance. Billy was behind the wheel.

I was now wondering about a strange rise at the horizon, a hill that grew steeper, loomed larger as we approached. The peak was surely the highest elevation in all of Florida. We were close enough to be overcome by some incredible perfume this phenomenon exuded, and then I made out a building huddled against the lower slope that identified itself as a frozen orange juice plant. A funnel piped through the roof spewed forth the pulp and peel that made this mountain out of a molehill.

"Fooled you, didn't it?" said Billy, in a better mood. "Like that paleface in a white suit fooled me with his French. You would have thought he was an impresario and all he was was a writer of books."

"Did he ever write about you?"

"The noble savage is always showing up in people's books. I wouldn't read it if he did write me up. I quit reading when I quit the Navy, now I listen to tapes for the true shit. Read? I'm too busy pulling myself up by my bootstraps the way the Great White Father in the White House enjoins us to. In the Navy I made First Class but never went up for Chief because people been calling me Chief all my life, now I'm trying for Redskin of the Year on the cover of *Time*. Can't afford to lose my bearings reading books about me, I keep my eye peeled for true north instead of magnetic." Billy pushed the white hat off the bridge of his fierce nose and unbuttoned his shirt flap in the draft, showing more and more of himself as we cruised along. There was even a streak of grey in his ponytail. He showed his teeth, but the smile was benign. "It's all maya, man, like a mountain made out of orange pulp. How do you know anything I'm telling you is the straight case? I've told more sea stories in my time than true ones. What's your story, for instance? Man traveling without a background is highly suspect on the open road. You sure you're not wanted somewhere?"

"Not that I know of."

"Haven't I seen your picture in the post offices of America?"

I could feel my beard growing.

"Not mine, not yet."

He took me into Tampa anyway, right through midtown traffic to the Trailways station. From a great height Billy handed me down my chino jacket and attaché case.

"I dig you right well, is why I asked you to Tarpon Springs. 'We that are young shall never see so much nor live so long.' " A nickel flipped from Billy to me, and I caught it the way a bellboy would. His picture was on it, he said, and he warned me not to take any wooden ones. "Forget my insistence, fella, but that's only when I dig somebody and want the sentiment reciprocated. How do we know if we pass this way again?"

My "so long" would only have been an echo of his (and Shakespeare's), so I said "Adieu" to make it official, and tickle him.

3

THE POET'S LINE: "eyes wide as oysters, hair down to here," was a promise to me, so naturally I would sit beside the prettiest girl on the bus. I still toyed with notions of prophecy and programming.

She wore no makeup; she was dressed in a pink suit too hot for the season, a little girl's color, all innocence and Easter Sunday, an Alice-in-Wonderland pink ribbon wound through the invisible net that kept her tresses intact. She paid no notice of me: her knuckles had whitened with the bus's sudden acceleration and her small hands gripped the armrests as if we had become airborne. Trailways etiquette permitted at least an opening moronic remark about the heat, but as soon as I said it the air conditioning hummed on, rendering my inanity superfluous. Her veiled eyes were fixed in all modesty or panic on the seat in front of her. She was too shy or frightened or indignant to reply.

It was not conversation I sought—I had overdosed on talk with Indian Billy—but mere physical recognition, as if she knew the poem too and knew we would meet on this bus. Strange how aroused I could become by this girl's mute presence. Her silence in fact was a blessing. Words would have spoiled it. There was this mystery to contemplate at leisure: girl on a bus in a rose-colored suit, who are you?

Another ploy was to pretend to sleep and allow my weary head to drift by inches onto her shoulder. Even her annoyance would be a kind of beginning, but she made no protest—so no apology neces- sary—even as my ear pressed against a pastel lapel. She seemed altogether unaware or indifferent to the obvious pressure against her breast, a stranger's breath upon her bosom. So comforting was this passive acceptance of herself as my pillow, I truly slept.

There was nothing erotic to my dream, no symbols Dr. K could have interpreted psychosexually. I traveled aboard a trawler on the Gulf, fearful of a crew of sponge divers who tried to rob me of my money. I awoke with my hand clutching my hip pocket (but the traveler's checks were in my jacket pocket) and the other hand a brazen fist thrust into the girl's lap. Oddly enough my demure neighbor still stared fixedly out the window despite the crude intrusion. She was out there with the immobile cattle and darkening garlands of Spanish moss, intent—desperately so—on whatever she perceived in the middle distance. I detached myself from her with an embarrassed murmur of apology. I do not think she heard.

What *had* the Poet meant? Whatever it was he was hinting at, this encounter was no part of it. Anyway, my attitude had shifted and was no hornier than the dream: I meant to climb innocently into her mind, to think what she might think of me as an incipient prowler into her space. Was I, to her, the intruder the Skip Tracer had been to me or White Suit to Indian Billy?

As the landscape gracefully darkened, the Spanish moss went into shadow and the cattle disappeared—but the girl remained transfixed. The words to a pop song popped into my mind: "How far do you run when you run out on someone after someone ran out on you?" Trailways flicked switches and the bus interior was suddenly alight: not even this abrupt transition touched her.

There's girls I traced you wouldn't want them back.

At the Sans Souci I would have tenderly taken her wrist and felt for a pulse. "Pt. does not verbalize" would appear on her chart. With only one side of her face to go by, I looked for tears. I could only wonder what potion labeled DRINK ME had transported her to the suburbs of Catatonia. I knew I was in no way a spark in her outer darkness, in no sense could I become a chapter in her fate.

4

"ARE YOU GOLD?"

"A yellow-fanged Doberman thrust its muzzle between the Major's legs and clawed frantically against the linoleum. The beast was trying to crash through the screen door at my throat.

"I'm a friend." I-am-a-friend, present tense—though the Poet was of the past.

"I won't invite you in." The Major was trying to shout above the animal's relentless outrage. "Killer'd eat you for lunch. Why don't you people shave?" He appeared to be counting the bristles in my beard.

The beginning beard would put anybody off, especially a military man and his paranoid watchdog. Behind the ten-day growth of bristle I could be a deserter (I was), or a Communist, a spy, a poet.

"Come around," he commanded, "to the side of the house."

A severe-looking woman in a butcher's apron appeared behind the Major. She reminded me of a prison matron I had met at Miami's unemployment bureau. She helped the Major drag the dog away from his sentry post, then the Major met me at a side door. Over his shoulder I saw a stuffed falcon on a perch in the kitchen, but realized the bird was alive when I saw newspapers spread beneath the perch to catch the droppings.

Before the woman could close the door behind the Major, hell's own hound leaped through.

My breath caught. Convinced I was the object of the animal's frenzy, I shrank inside myself awaiting the fangs—but the beast flashed past me to a hurricane fence between properties. There, frustrated by the barrier, he vented his savagery through steel mesh at spectators lounging beside their cars parked opposite the so-called House of Death next door.

"Damn you!" raged the Major, whether damning the watchdog or the woman who had allowed his escape, I did not know.

Lithe and awkward as the dog, the Major loped to the fence to drag the Doberman from his vicious sport. Since the Major, U.S. Army, retired, wore semi-uniform (suntans without insignia, combat boots, a Marine Corps cap of faded camouflage) one of the spectators called out: "Are you a cop?"

"Damn you!" It was clear the Major was damning the rubber-
necks now.

"Fuck you too soldier," cracked back at him.

The Major did an instant about-face showing his and the dog's
rear to the street crowd. To me he called out: "We can't talk in this
atmosphere."

The underground shelter was fully electrified, alarmingly so: at first I
was blinded by the extravagant illumination. The generator hummed
nervously all during our sojourn. When my eyes adjusted to the
terrible light, I could make out supermarket shelves of canned fruit
and beans and vegetable soup, packets of dried foodstuff, K
rations—brand names outboard, compulsively aligned. There was a
miniature refrigerator and a stainless-steel sink. A two-burner hot
stainless-steel plate was set upon the refrigerator: next to it, a
camper's gas ring in case the generator failed.

I turned to the Major's bookshelves: a set of *Reader's Digest*
condensed best-sellers (as many as four to a volume), the collection
bookended by The Holy Bible and *The Last Whole Earth Catalogue*.
On another shelf was a two-volume work by Clausewitz, a biography
of "Ike," *The Joy of Cooking*, a series of foreign languages made easy,
The Diaries of Count Ciano, stacks of *American Legion Magazine*,
Looking Out for Number 1, and a spiral-bound treatise on septic
tanks.

"I get my best ideas down here," confessed the Major.

The dog had scrambled down the earthen stairs behind us, and
the Major clutched the dog's studded collar until the animal could
grow accustomed to so alien a presence as mine.

To one side of the shelves was a steel desk with swivel chair.
Here, evidently, the Major recorded his ideas on the heavy upright
Underwood. The ideas were then inserted in the folder bearing the
title "Straight Talk from a Forgotten American."

There were two framed pictures on the desk: one, of a
narrow-jawed young soldier, a son, surely, who had followed in his
father's footsteps. The other was an enlarged photograph of a girl in
her twenties standing beside a horse, a long strand of hair blown
across her face. The Poet would not have looked at the book titles
first, as I had done—he would have fixed miserably on the second
photograph.

The Major let go of the dog and sat down at his desk. No word
about where I was to sit, if I was to sit, so I stood at attention while the

Doberman brusquely inspected my crotch. The Major was fingering the keys of the Underwood as if about to tap out a letter to either his son or daughter, a restless eye moving from one photograph to the other—then abruptly he rummaged in a desk drawer where he kept typewriter ribbons, rubber bands and a .45 army pistol.

"I also maintain an M-1, an AK-47, tear gas ejectors and a substantial supply of ammunition for every weapon on the premises." He had swiveled around to show me the pistol but did not bother to display the rest of his arsenal. "A standard .38—which the Missus is well-versed in—I keep at the house. She is just as handy with a shotgun, and we've got two of them. For when the sirens go."

The Major showed a portion of his dental plate, a grim smile warning me of sirens, while the dog, satisfied that I carried no weapons of my own, retired and spread himself across the earthen floor.

"Yes and here is exactly where you'll find me. When the sirens go."

He meant here in the mine shaft, or whatever this excavation had been. From the Spartan evidence, I would find him alone. There was one of everything, but only one: one "Camp Pendleton" coffee mug, one baby-blue toothbrush, one desk, one chair, one towel, one Oriental backscratcher, one brass ashtray, and a narrow single bunk bed—for number 1.

"Let me ask you something," began the Major as I sat warily and uninvited on a crate that possibly contained hand grenades. (The only other place to sit was the Army cot, its khaki coverlet folded rigidly for inspection, a surface I dared not disturb.) "Why the beard?"

"Mine, you mean, or your son-in-law's?"

He meant both: "What are you people trying to prove?"

I could tell the Major that Abraham Lincoln wore a beard—or, to keep it military, General Grant. The truth was too flippant to tell. I carried no shaving gear, and since leaving my wife I could not look into mirrors.

"The character next door, naturally he had a beard."

The man next door was being held in the Montgomery County jail pending trial for the murder of two teenage runaways, both male. The bodies had been dug up from beneath the lawn adjoining the Major's putting green.

Although I had heard the story from the cabbie who had brought me here, the Major could not resist a lurid review of the crime.

"Exactly next door to me." He flushed, outraged anew. There

was something gruesomely humiliating about the massacre perpetrated by a civilian on his own turf. "The very damned house next
door."

Without the cabbie's warning ("Rosedale Drive? You a cop, you
from the newspapers?") I might have rung the doorbell to the House of
Death. Only the Major's fence and a flag and a Disney lawn ornament
distinguished number 46 from 48: the dun-colored bungalows were
otherwise identical.

"Homicide had every intention of plowing up my lawn too, but I
got a restraining order." Since the first body had been unearthed
slightly to the Major's side of the property line, this legal counterof-
fensive was called for. "Clothing was not yet totally deteriorated, I
have not seen so ghastly a sight since Okinawa. They had to identify
the victim by his dental work. The boy probably had a beard too, but
the face was gone."

In the past ten days, both the Major and I had stared into the
face of death.

"Picked them up in his pickup, the pervert, then picked them
off at his pleasure." The Major caressed the .45 with such passion I
feared it would go off in the direction of my own hateful facial hair.
"Jap sniper has more moral backbone than that degenerate creep."

Thought of the perverted drama just next door set the Major's leg
to quivering, as if he were about to dash forward—but run where in
this narrow burrow? The spasmodic tic was taken up by the
Doberman—man and dog regulated at the same internal pitch and
rhythm—the dog's hind leg began to vibrate until spastic paw met
cocked ear and he could scratch his demon's head in relief.

My own relief came when the Major's leg was stilled and the
pistol safely deposited in his lap. Then the dog slumped at ease, head
resting on his slender paws, the reflection of his master in a golden
eye. My breath came easier as the Major brought a humidor out of the
desk drawer and his hair-trigger restlessness was engaged by clipping
the end of a cigar with a device attached to his cluttered key chain. I
was thinking of the Poet's shifts and tics, the nail-biting beard-
brushing mannerisms—my compulsive watch winding (I no longer
wore the watch on my wrist but carried it in my shirt pocket where it
ticked somewhere in the vicinity of my heart)—our symptoms of
agitation in confined spaces.

"I assume the Jew wants something of me."

He did not offer a cigar to his son-in-law's emissary, why should
he? He disliked me on sight but so craved an audience he could not

send me away. And for all his dismissal of a despised son-in-law, his curiosity was aroused.

"So what does he want?"

He lit the Dutch Master with a kitchen match that left a lingering sulphuric reminder of some satanic presence at these depths, though I discovered nothing conclusively diabolic about the Major. He was a bully and a threat, in the way of his killer dog, but he was humanly foolish too, behind the Groucho Marx cigar and his bald dome gleaming under the overbright light.

"He wants, he would like." The Poet wanted nothing now, but I did not tell the Major that his son-in-law was dead. "He would like to get in touch. With her."

Only what the living wanted was at issue.

"Money? That's what Jews are after. He always thought he could get something out of me through her." He entertained his grim smile again. "Now he thinks he can get something out of her through me."

The Major inhaled with great deliberation, then exhaled with an expression of extreme distaste, as if the cigar as well as son-in-law offended him. An effective smoke screen soon obscured his freckled face yet brought his daughter's photographic image into clearer focus. The daughter in no way resembled her father (as he so clearly resembled his watchdog), and I wondered—as I always had when comparing my wife's visage to her father's photograph—where do these ethereal beauties come from, parented by such imperfect specimens as Valerie's father and Major Ward?

"Money, well, yes." I invented my cover story as I went along. "But the other way around." Nothing I could tell this man would be good news or bad: he had written off his son-in-law from the beginning, and had perhaps by now disowned his daughter. I would not add the Poet's death to the indifferent body count next door. "He wants to send money. To her, through me."

The cigar came to halt before it could reach the Major's lips. He might have wanted to ask the sum, but said instead: "Am I supposed to believe this?"

"Up to you. I'm trying to locate her. For him."

The ventilation system was not yet in operation (the project delayed by the discovery of a corpse where the air shaft was to have been), and even though the Major had left the shelter door ajar, we were soon coughing in tandem. The major's cough was seriously symptomatic and possibly chronic. As he coughed, the Major rapped his fist against his chest in an ecclesiastical gesture of mea culpa, though this was a man unburdened by guilt or given to admission of weakness. He then confessed breathlessly to emphysema, but he did not extinguish his cigar.

During one of his manic monologues, the Poet convinced me that humankind cannot resist self-torture or, this tendency extended, self-destruction: I was the perfect example of his theory. (So was he.) By persisting in a dead-end marriage and enduring a nowhere job I was a clinical case of masochistic behavior and should be the patient at the Sans Souci, not he.

Here was the Major, further proof of the Poet's thesis; not that he should be hospitalized—or should he? He had dug himself a grave, and here he was in it. This was not only a tomb but a gas chamber. When the sirens sounded, yes, you would find him here alone with his tics and traumas and hypertension, the forgotten American, suffering the special sealed-in agony of slow death while the rest of us, yes, would also be consumed, but swiftly consumed in the first searing flash. The persistent glow of the Major's cigar was merely a reminder of how much longer he would burn.

"He confessed to both crimes," the Major coughed out, "no more, no less." He had returned to the subject of his neighbor's villainy. "And that was what won me my restraining order. The police, of course, and the local yokels are still praying for a bonanza. A few more cadavers to his credit and the pervert will become a nationwide celebrity. Like the creep in Texas, or that spic in California."

He watched me narrowly—and the dog either coughed or growled—as I left the grenade case to move closer to the stairwell for air. The Major tensed, the dog hunched himself upright, as if to prevent imminent escape. I stood frozen, merely sniffing for the surface. Both watchers relaxed, then dog and master settled back into the hazy blue funk.

By now the Major sensed my reluctance to linger in his private asylum. He deposited the .45 in its desk drawer, then went to fumbling in another drawer, a drawer with no weapon in it.

"Except for the idiot beard, you have the earmarks of an honest man." The Major granted me that, then grunted, "On the other hand, so did my neighbor."

He did not immediately find what he was looking for. He glanced at his daughter's photograph and tried a drawer at the other end of the desk.

"She could," he said aloud, not necessarily to me, "say exactly what was on her mind, age two. Eight years old she had her own pony she handled like an eighteen-year-old. Never spanked her her whole life, never needed to. A beauty from the start. Highly strung, like the thoroughbred she was, but smart as a whip, independent, knew what she wanted and wanted only the best, and deserved it. And got it, as long as I was around." He spoke of her in the past tense, the way I spoke of the Poet in the present. "Impossible to believe she would do what she did. Unless under hypnosis, under the influence of drugs. They all smoke pot or snort cocaine these days. A generation of the damned." His words, in their way, had the same dry rhetorical ring of my father's letters. "A type named Gold, for the love of God. She even went through a Hebrew wedding, the kind where the kike steps on a wineglass to crush the bride's spirit." His tongue darted forth, a viper's gesture, to disengage bits of tobacco from his lips; his eyes ranged the supermarket shelves of instant tea, instant coffee, instant soup—here where instant was meaningless. "I put her through college. She had a charge account at Nieman-Marcus. Gave her a horse—she sold the horse, for him, I guess, for money. She's still got the RV I bought her, paid for out of an Army pension with her mother's alimony to pay and a second wife to support." He scribbled a line on his notepad of ideas, an address copied from an envelope in the drawer. As he turned back to me with storklike fragility, the menace in his eyes and brows faded to despair at the leaky corners of his graven lips. "How many shekels does he bestow upon her? Never mind. You want to know something? These people—" he was staring at the name and address, but I could assume I was one of these people "—are of the number who led our youth downhill. They are why we lost Vietnam. Deadbeats and hopheads and perverts have breached our defenses, they buy and sell a girl like her. While the once mighty American republic turns its back. Be that as it may, here's where her last escort worked. Some beer tavern in Texas. A guitar player this time."

If the Major's ramrod right arm could tremble, it trembled as he passed the scribbled dispatch to me. I folded the notesheet into my jacket pocket, with the traveler's checks. In exchange I thought to offer information about the Poet.

"He's in a hospital. In Miami."

"His whereabouts are of no concern to me."

Actually I was rehearsing lies suitable for the future. I went on, relentlessly, despite his disinterest. (What he truly would want to know I would not tell him. His son-in-law lay unclaimed in a hospital morgue, zipped into a plastic shroud-pac Miss Ryan and I had grappled with together.) I closed with a superfluous line of sancti- mony: "I made a promise. To do this, for him. And for her."

"I washed my hands of her and him both, the day he stepped on that wineglass." The Major dusted his trembling hands, then leaned back in the swivel chair, apparently comforted. "She's as dead to me as my son, killed in action, September, 1967."

I had the address, I had received a confidence, I was free to go. But I could not resist a parting salvo: "Tell me, sir." (He was welcome now to the sir.) "Would you consider, would you want. If she should, so to speak, come crawling back?"

The freckles paled. I had touched nerve, I had gone too far. At first it was like watching a boulder crack, but then the visage was solid rockface again, instantly. The Doberman lurched into his attack crouch, but the Major cooly caught the dog by the collar and held him at bay. I took it the Major was counting to ten, so I hastened up the earthen stairs before my legs turned to water or the pistol went off.

5

AT THE SURFACE, I was trembling, but from relief. Meanwhile it had rained. I sucked at the damp earth smell rinsed by nature's own sweet fallout. The Major's putting green glistened, the Disney dwarf supporting a birdbath grinned at me. For a moment I was the Poet, convinced the universe could be restored by something as reasonable as rainfall.

The Butcher eyed me suspiciously, watching from her sentry box behind the screen door, the immobile falcon watching with her. She was folding the American flag she had rescued from the wet. Other eyes besides hers and the falcon's watched from across the hurricane fence. The curious were still out there, but safe inside their automobiles, out of the rain.

I had best hit the road. There was a chill in the air, and I responded to it with a shiver, but the only remaining sense of menace was the sight of an auto tire swaying suggestively from the hangman's tree next door—and the clouds beyond, piled up like skulls.

An antique station wagon eased up beside me, the window rolled down on her side. A farm couple, they could take me as far as Mobile. I had just emerged from underground, I must know something—what news from the tomb?

"A friend," I said to myself, but aloud.

The station wagon lurched forward.

"Not here," I explained. "A friend of mine died. In a hospital."

They would take me to Mobile anyway. I crawled in among the Styrofoam egg cartons in the backseat; the station wagon smelled of chicken shit. The woman kept twisting her beak my way, the wattle of her throat very like a hen's.

"My husband, he's got us a theory."

"Murders," said he, "is all the same. The Kennedys too, exact same thing."

I had trained myself at the Sans Souci not to take theories too seriously. The chicken farmers spent summer nights sitting out. They kept a pair of binoculars on the back porch, watching for flying saucers.

From Mobile I took a train and slept deadweight across the state of Mississippi to the port city of New Orleans.

The Poet had been to New Orleans before me and had left no trace. The rooming house was opposite the docks, redolent of the funky odors of dead flowers and banana rot. "They put chicory in their coffee," my father wrote, "and bury their dead aboveground." My father had contracted malaria in New Orleans: here was where he and Dr. Breathwaite opened their clinic for the private treatment of tabes dorsalis.

"From the dread spirochete *Treponema pallidum*, commonly known as the Neapolitan disease ('Big Al' Capone, a Neapolitan, died of it) or familiarly called the French pox. Its better-known name comes down to us from the afflicted shepherd Syphilus, from the Latin poem so entitled, written by Fracastoro in the latter part of the fifteenth century."

My father was a crossword puzzle fan, where such arcane data came in handy.

"Tabes dorsalis, or, in other words, 'a wasting away.' It will make its first appearance innocently enough, and just as innocently disappear. Undercover, as it were. The unsuspecting victim breathes a sigh of relief, thinks he may have had but a touch of gonorrhea, commonly known as 'the clap.' The years come and go, his youthful indiscretion has slipped his mind. (Son, I hope and pray you consult your Navy medic after each and every escapade ashore!) Meanwhile the apparently dormant but insidious spirochete has been running the gamut of our daydreamer's spinal column. Like a termite, gnawing away in its own good time, from the coccygeal nerve to the medulla oblongata in the brain.

"First symptoms: loss of weight, slight weakness in the ankles and/or wrists—seemingly harmless enough. Gradually you discover you cannot walk a chalk line anymore, and chalk it up to age, or too many beers at the tavern. Anorexia is next (loss of appetite, to the layman) plus a puzzling numbness in the lower parts. When the eyesight dims to the point of near-blindness, the poor bugger begins to suspect something's up. ('Big Al' was no better off than a Bowery bum when his medulla oblongata went haywire.) Too late, of course. Sensorimotor deterioration of the arms and legs—locomotor ataxia— has reached the point of no return. I have known piano players to lose control of their fingers in the middle of a concert, and tap dancers to unknowingly tap right off the stage."

Breathwaite and my father dreamed up a cure called Serum X—mercury arsenic, bismuth and coloring, in proportions my father no longer remembered, "but ten years ahead of its time. Then, darn it, Ehrlich the German grabbed the headlines when he won himself a Nobel Prize for Salvarsan (nothing more than your basic arsphe- namine, Doc Breathwaite's same Serum X, give or take an ingredient) but Ehrlich had the PR boys behind him, calling his stuff '606'—a catchy trademark if there ever was one, and one that naturally cornered the market."

The long-dead poet Fracastoro, not the recently dead Poet, haunted my encounter with the girl at a bar where the men wore seersucker and open shirts under a ceiling fan with atmospheric cobwebs trailing from the blades. Her eyes were set too close for poetry. Her hand, in a conjurer's distracting gesture, swept peanuts from the dish on the bar in front of me while her other hand touched my thigh with professional delicacy. I shifted my khaki jacket out of reach: the traveler's checks were in the pocket. She could have been the girl from the bus to Tallahassee, minus the hair ribbon and catatonic stare—anyway, not the girl the Poet promised. Nonetheless I bought her a suspect margarita, thoughts of tabes dorsalis prevent- ing further purchase.

My landlady with the bandaged hands, burnt at the kitchen range, informed me that Lafcadio Hearn had slept in the very room where I was to sleep.

"Little short fellow." She spoke as if she had known Mr. Hearn personally, though this was a New Orleans of another age. "He had inferiorities about his size and went to live in Japan amongst littler people."

She lingered at the doorway to my room, looking me over through thick glasses whose lower crescents magnified her catfish eyes. There was a volume of Hearn's Japanese ghost stories on the night table between twin beds: I did not read the stories, but ghosts populated my dreams.

A cabbie told me next day: "Trouble with women, there's always another man."

The Poet's very words. Even the tonsure was the same: bald spot no bigger than a silver dollar at the back of his Afro. (I had trimmed the Poet's manic overgrowth only two days before his death.)

"Could you use a woman?"

"Trouble is, the other man."

"I got a young fox for you, she's independent."

I tossed Indian Billy's nickel, pretending I was playing fate against free will. I caught it, slapped it on my wrist heads up. Fate decided against lingering in New Orleans, as maybe it had for Lafcadio Hearn.

The Major's information was dead on: Lawrence Priest worked in Austin, Texas, at a bar called The Screaming Eagle. He said I could call him Larry. But he was not the guitar player the Major referred to, only a mail drop.

"Never played guitar but I could've been a hundred other things. Could've inherited my Daddy's filling station, for starters." He pointed to the shadowy outline of a piston and pump, the university's very own oil well, still in operation. With great verve and criminal indifference, Lawrence burnt up the after-dark avenue called the Drag giving me a tourist-guide rundown on the sights. Mostly he talked about himself. "Started out PreLaw but there's a type of law-school hustler I could never hack, so I switched majors to BusEd where the hustling was ten times worse. Finally said fuck this and dropped out." An armored vault of a building he called the HRC—no windows, only slits for riflemen—was where the University of Texas guarded its rare collection of personal letters of famous poets. Ghostly streamers of toilet paper dangled from the limbs of live oaks along fraternity row. "Only thing I did at UT I was proud of I was in a MassCom motion picture for about five minutes, only they didn't give me any lines to say. After I dropped out of school I drove a shuttle bus, did auto bodies, took wedding pictures, read meters. The dust from them wire sanders on auto-body repair can mess up your lungs for life or I'd still be doing that for my Daddy, good money. I never stick to any one ambition. The man that never fitted in, I guess you would say. Could have been a rock-and-roll arranger, hot-rod race driver, stunt man, pro football—you name it. My trouble, my Daddy never offered me the right incentives. Kept telling me, 'It ain't what you know, it's who you know.' I was going to study refrigeration by mail and every time one of my lessons came he said, 'It ain't what you know, it's who you know.' Hear that fifteen times a day it gets old."

We passed a stark orange tower eerily lit, the famous tower.

"Yeah, that's where the dude picked off eighteen people on account of he never got along with his Daddy, there's a lesson there."

"I was told you play guitar?"

"Me? Not me. My buddy does. Pilot, he gets a lot of practice down in Chihuahua." Lawrence's beard was as short and ragged as mine because he had been down to Chihuahua State to visit a buddy of his in prison for possession of narcotics and you did not cross the Mexican border with a beard anymore, or long hair. "I took him some bucks and a carton of Luckies. In the Third World cigarettes are the same as money." He offered me a cigarette.

"Thanks. I don't smoke."

"You clean? My buddy he carried his cargo in a case like that. You carry your shit in there by any chance?"

"No, no shit."

"I still haven't figured you out yet—if you're a cop or dealer or a dropout like I am, or what."

"I'm a friend."

"You better be, you want to hassle Ginny."

"No hassle. I've got a message, for her."

"Ginny. Met her on a Friday the thirteenth and that little lady spelt bad luck for me from then on. Tell you something, in the sack she's your ever-loving buddy—but that's the only place. What message, who from?"

"Her husband."

"No shit? I never knew she was married. I got a message for her myself. Tell her to go fuck herself."

He intended to tell her so himself, for he was taking me straight to her. He wanted to see her face when she saw him again. Lawrence had known Ginny when she worked as a vocalist at The Screaming Eagle during Happy Hour. "She sure looks great under lights and cute as hell holding a microphone, but she was headed exactly nowheres in Country and Western. I could've told her she didn't have the heart for Country and Western, but she never asked me. Country and Western is all heart." He knew where she parked her RV ("She lives in that mother") but she would be working at the Riviera Nites at this hour. Lawrence had borrowed the relief bartender's Dodge pickup to take me there. "Gin don't like her life interfered with. You better be who you say you are, you want to talk with her."

"I am."

"I used to have my hair down to here." He reached backwards to touch a shoulder blade. "But you don't cross the border with long hair anymore." His yellow hair was growing back spikily except for a shaved patch on the top of his head where a wound had healed, still cross-hatched with stitch marks. "When I had my hair down to here, and a beard, Ginny thought I looked like Jesus Christ. A lot of people said that, that's how I got that part in a student movie. Only I didn't have any lines. The reason Gin and me got it on in the first place was me looking like Jesus. She's into a religious fixation."

"I heard she was with a guitar player, lately."

"That's Pilot, not me—only he's in jail in Chihuahua. Me, I had every potential career under the sun *except* guitar. Worked in a window shade factory when I was fifteen, boring holes in the ends of window shade rollers. Handled a bulldozer, sold beer at rodeos, sheared sheep. I was apprentice dentist to a horse dentist on Lyndon Johnson's ranch. (Horses get cavities too, you'd be surprised.) That's how I met Gin. Gin's horse had a rotten tooth I took out. I told her I could get her an audition at The Screaming Eagle, just to get next to her. Too bad I never noticed it was Friday the thirteenth."

We skidded into a vast parking lot, spaces mostly taken. We got out and walked past a parked car with mud-splattered doors and a FOR SALE sign on the rear window: two large bare male feet portruded from an open window; I could see a girl inside, the back of her halter, leaning over the man—who was invisible, except for his feet—feeding, teasing, caressing him.

"I'll introduce you," Lawrence offered. "That'll needle her ass. I want to see her face when she sees me again." He was grinning all over himself at the prospect of seeing Ginny's face. "She had a shiner when we split, my compliments."

Her father said: I never spanked her. Never needed to.

"That's not half the shit she handed me. She brained me with a bottle once." Sentimentally he fingered the bald place in his convict's haircut. "Broke a Perrier bottle right over my head." He was still grinning, goofily amused.

Inside the Riviera Nites (a stucco warehouse with the twinkling neon announcement: GIRLS) the sledgehammer harmonies of disco reverberated just this side of the tolerance threshold. I was at first bedazzled by the gyrating illumination, though not blinded by it as I had been by the Major's fluorescent trench works. Here was no confined space like his (except for restrooms labled *Cowboys* and *Cowgirls*), only a Western dance hall flooded with colored light and charged with sound. Lawrence, a familiar to these waters, swam ahead of me through oceanic depths of shifting liquid light to an empty cabaret table still wet from our predecessors' drinks. Immediately a loose-hipped cowgirl in fringed leather miniskirt broke through the ranks of musclebound bouncers lounging in the vicinity of the service bar: she made for us, tapping her hip with a tray the size of a tambourine. At our table she threw back her head and bathed her pretty face in the lights: no, she was not Ginny.

After the waitress skipped lightheartedly away with our order for beers, a disembodied voice interrupted the disco beat: "Allllrighty you he-men hunkered down out there in paradise, the ladies love you, men is what they dance for, so rear up and make their ever-loving acquaintance."

The voice referred to a bevy of topless dancers with green eyelids and vivid lips performing solitary turns from a series of individual platform stages. They could be perceived as mirror images distorted in movement by a flow of colored strobes until each in turn took center stage under a probing white-hot spot that revealed individual coloring and slight variation in the shapes of breasts. The minicostumes were fins of sequins.

The ritual was this: the featured dancer shed fins and gills and the last vestige of modesty but for a spangled garland over the pubic hair as she found herself hooked on sound and caught in the net of light. She writhed and twisted to the beat until an angler from the crowd drew near, then another. As many as half a dozen men might sidle up to her during that run, two or more at a time, until the solo ended and another wriggling prize was washed to center stage in her wake. The voice from the DJ's glass pilot booth urged he-men hunkered down out here to brazen up to the edge of any chosen spotlight, as one by one the luminous shapes broke the surface of subaqueous light, to feed whichever naiad caught his fancy.

A figure in lariat necktie and checkered shirt (or did the lights checker the shirt for him?) was now at ringside, immobile, holding a crisply folded bill as stiff and upright as a hard-on, the gratuity aimed deliberately at the dancer's spangled centerpiece. She would be drawn to it by tradition or instinct, her G-string soon snapping at the bait in swift piranha nibbles. According to the exotic rites established here, a client was permitted this proximity to the performer of his choice by way of fastening, with all delicacy and restraint, a flap of paper money to the hipline of a G-string. Meanwhile a stag line of bouncers shuffled moodily in place, cracking knuckles and flexing their triceps, observing the action through shifting currents of color to make certain only banknotes came in contact with female flesh.

"That little lady is something else."

"What else?" I asked him.

"You got to know her to know that." One hand slid down the cool sweaty side of his beer bottle.

"Is that Ginny?"

"The one," said he, tilting his bottle toward center stage, "with all the money on her ass."

As he said it, I watched the long hair whip across her face in response to drumbeat (instead of wind). Of course, thought I: the same otherworldly attitude as in the photo, her vagabond gaze then as now fixed on the middle distance. She was alone with herself staring through the patron's noose of a necktie to distant corners of the cow palace: pool tables at the outer rim where players stretched alongside like swimmers at the edge of green baize pools, and beyond that periphery to shadowy solitaries grappling with video games. Even as Checkered Shirt tagged her with a piece of green, Ginny smoothly removed herself from further intimacy with no more than a final flip tilt of her pelvis by way of thanks. Nor did she acknowledge the admirer at the opposite side of the stage, as he too tagged her, this time on the starboard hip. Her disengaged attitude bespoke tribute as her due. If I was to approach her, I should approach with a folded traveler's check.

Cooly she skipped downward to a platform closer to our table, but her eyes swept past us. I was keyed to her presence—Lawrence grinned and stared beside me—but Ginny was carelessly elsewhere. Other men moved out of shadow and stood beside her dais until they too could affix their folded banknotes to this slippery purchase. At length, from a third and distant platform, she retired from sight, an abbreviated skirt of green strung alongside her nether parts.

But Ginny had indeed seen us—or spotted Lawrence, whom she knew—for she soon reappeared in casual waitress attire to intercept our waitress with the tambourine tray. She took the tray with its second round of beers and brought it to us.

"Have yourself a brew with us, Gin."

She ignored the grinning Lawrence and addressed me with a ferocity entirely unexpected: "Are you a lawyer?"

I could have been anyone. Because of the false prop (she did not recognize the Poet's attaché case) I was lawyer, dealer, businessman, cop.

"He's no lawyer," said Lawrence.

"I asked him." She refused to acknowledge Lawrence's presence.

"No," I said. "I'm not."

She sat down then. There was a fourth chair at our table, empty, and I could not resist the sensation that came over me: the Poet was sitting there, just as I was, watching Ginny's small agitated hands.

"Who are you then?"

It was a good question.

"He's a friend of your husband's," said Lawrence, spilling the greatest joke ever told.

"I asked *him*."

She still would not turn in Lawrence's direction, but her nostrils flared. Something in her fierce regard confirmed what Lawrence had described as a streak of violence.

"I'm just a friend. Of your husband."

"What makes you think we're still married?"

"I know he thinks you are."

"You can tell him from me I filed for divorce."

All of this made Lawrence into a grinning clown, he was so extraordinarily happy.

"Is it final?"

"It will be. And I don't want any hassles from him over it. I couldn't locate him at his college so my lawyer put a To Whom It May Concern in the papers. That's legal notice in Texas, whether the party reads it or not. Are you sure you're not his lawyer or something? I don't want him hassling me over this. If he sent you to try and stop me he's wasting his time and your breath."

Now was the moment of truth, if I were willing to reveal it. I could have informed Ginny that the divorce was as final as it would ever be. But my character had suffered a sea change, so I stalled. I could no more tell her what she needed to hear than announce that her husband sat there in the fourth empty chair.

"I'm no lawyer. He didn't send me. For that. I just came."

"Came for what?"

Men did not make a pilgrimage to this shrine for nothing. I thought for a moment what I might say—lying had become second nature since my session with the Major—then sweated out a line ex tempore: "He just wanted to know. About you, where you were. If you were all right."

It sounded so true Ginny visibly softened and shifted her focus to the empty chair. But Lawrence could no longer hold back a cackle of laughter. I had been sent on the most ridiculous errand imaginable. If only he had known my actual destination (or if I had known), the laughter would have been just as appropriate.

Ginny turned on him and snapped, "What are *you* doing here, you moron? This man and me are talking business, you just hit the road, you."

Despite the solid blast of disco, a tuned-in bouncer the size of Uncle Sam, the gangster at the racetrack, caught the pitch of Ginny's voice or sensed the tension at our table. He was suddenly among us.

"You having trouble with these people, Gin?"

"Nothing I can't handle, Leo."

The frustrated giant faded back into shadow and Ginny's mood shifted again. Her whiplash manner had evaporated instantly: as the wicked smile swam close, I considered her complicated nature.

"Leo represents something I haven't figured out yet." Even Lawrence was allowed now in her confidence. "That old boy has been in and out of hospitals all his life." His case history was also the same as Uncle Sam's. "Prince will hire just about anybody for their muscle as long as they don't have known police records. I thought Leo must be queer at first, or something—his idea of a pass is to flip his dangle out of his pants at a lady in the dressing room if he catches her alone. Unzips and stretches out all he has to offer, but no action. I mean, a lady makes a grab for his thing and he'll run off and hide. I mean, is he a case or isn't he?"

It was only fitting that a harem be watched over by eunuchs. I kept trying to work out the design of a poet's wife in this setting—no prettier, no less pretty than any other naiad under lights. What set her apart? She was as much a part of the distorted sensuality on display, yet not with it, with her moods and shifts and the infinite extension of her gaze. Dreamily she followed Leo's silhouette as the bouncer moved away, then she remembered Lawrence was with us and her voice turned sharp.

"How's your head, by the way?"

"I quit having dizzy spells."

"All you ever had was a dizzy spell, that's your nature."

To me, Lawrence said, "Didn't I tell you she was something else?"

The silken mane was in disarray from her dance, the equine eyes wide apart. Earlier I had thought of her as one of a school of fish, but she was something else in her eye and temperament, a thoroughbred.

Lawrence was telling her about his trip to Mexico: "I was down in Chihuahua. Saw Pilot in prison down there, he said to say hello."

Ginny's eyes narrowed, her tolerance had by now been used up.

Lawrence rattled right on: "I took him some cigarettes. Cigarettes are the same as money in the Third World."

"Hit the road, Larry."

"He said you were the worst news ever to cross his path, being busted included, but to say hello anyway."

"What I'm saying to you is goodbye. And I mean it."

On that exchange Lawrence decided to return to The Screaming Eagle, grinning still. He had got his wish, he had seen Ginny's face.

"Good luck, you-all."

Ginny took no notice of Lawrence's departure. "How is he?" she asked me, meaning the Poet. She really wanted to know.

I hesitated for a heartbeat. "Fine," I said. I would have to say more than that. "He was in a bad way. For a while. But he's out of it. Now."

It occurred to me as I said that, that the men in Ginny's life were casualties of one kind or another: the walking wounded, prisoners, hospital patients, the dead.

"Out of what?" She was genuinely concerned, another switch of attitude.

"He was in a hospital. For a while."

"What hospital? Where?"

"He was in a hospital, in Florida, where I was working. For a while. The kind of hospital your bouncer was in, and out of. But not for the same thing."

"Oh no," said Ginny. "Not him. But what for?"

"Depression. Depression was part of it."

"Depression?"

Truly the Poet sat at the same table with us under the same flicker-flack of kaleidoscopic light, not at all depressed, smiling upon us—or was it Lawrence's grin that lingered? But Ginny could see him too, she was staring at the Poet's chair.

"That's nothing new, depression. He's always depressed. About the state of the world or his hair falling out or a misprint in some line he wrote. Who isn't? I'm depressed myself sometimes. He's a depressing person and you can catch depression from somebody the same as you catch the measles or something. And he sure could depress a person, once he got started. He's funny, too, but you never know whether he's out to make you laugh or cry. He writes poetry, did you know? That's enough to depress anybody."

"Yes." I meant yes, I knew he wrote poetry.

"That's the way poets are, that's how everybody is, you get depressed. If every time you're on a bummer you went to a hospital you'd be in and out of hospitals like Leo. What else was he?"

She was truly concerned, and it added something to her face. It was not possible to look into those deepset eyes and make up symptoms, so I offered the truth.

"Suicidal."

The word struck at the same time as the terminal notes of a disco piece, a synchronization Ginny could respond to. Her shoulder twitched to the beat of both sounds.

"Listen," she said, after a breath, "you and me have things to talk about. Listen, I have to go back on. I'm going to do one more set and then tell Prince I'm getting my period. Then I'm going to meet you outside in the parking lot." She plucked a set of keys from the pocket of her fringed skirt and tossed them on the table, a Texas gesture of infinite trust. "You go out there and wait for me in my car and I'll be out in about twenty minutes. I drive a maroon Toyota with an anti-nuke bumper sticker, probably the only Toyota parked out there, at least the only one with that same bumper sticker."

The Poet and I rose at the same instant, but I was the one with the keys.

6

AT THE HOLLOW of her throat dangled a tiny gold cross, a gift, she told me, from the Poet. When the Poet stood naked under the shower at the Sans Souci, he had worn a miniature Star of David around his neck—a gift, I wondered, from Ginny? Under the deceptive lighting of the Riviera Nites the cross had been invisible, but this close I took note of it.

We were in her narrow bed together, a space the size of a bunk in an officer's stateroom or the sleeping cubby in the back of Indian Billy's moving van. Ginny's rig—not an RV as Lawrence had called it, but a separate trailer bullet-shaped and painted silver set upon a foundation of cinder blocks: its trade name was Tradewinds. The trailer was parked in a ragged fringe of woods beside the golf course. Across the road was an all-night Safeway drawing bats and luna moths to its neon, but no customers. There was little traffic at this hour, and the silence was otherworldly after the din at the dance hall. Her face and breasts and the little cross were illuminated by the soft glow of a gooseneck reading lamp. She had removed most of the stage makeup; her lips were pale, but her eyes were made large by the remaining traces of mascara, the lids still faintly blue as if bruised. The careless mask-edge of makeup below her chin suggested a small girl who had got into her mother's cosmetic case. From time to time she put her small fist to a cat's yawn, but she was very much awake and nervously animated. The Poet was nowhere in sight.

"This poet named Pound got fired the same way, he was a professor too. Ever hear of him? For balling some girl in his room and it got around."

"Ezra Pound."

"Yeah and he went to Europe and was honored until he stopped writing poems and wrote propaganda for Mussolini. He read propaganda on the radio and they tried him for treason. It takes all kinds."

Pound had fled to Mediterranean Avenue, but the Poet had chosen the Cosmos Motel.

"O.K. he crucified me and I crucified him." She brought the little cross to her lower lip to taste it, or kiss it. "It goes back and forth, that's what a relationship ends up being. I was naive at that age, who isn't? Like my own mother at that age, she got the bright idea she'd marry an Army man. Me with a poet. Was I naive. Not that the whole production was a downer, I was the subject of poems, and he once told me I was myth made flesh, no kidding. And you sweat a lot of insight out of a mistake like that. Maybe the insight alone was worth the hassle. I was his muse, he even said it in French. *Ma muse m'amuse.* That kind of talk, especially in French, can go to your head, eighteen years old. What a relationship. The whole concept was too far out to believe, but since him I can size a person up a whole lot better and decide whether its going to be a hassle or not. By the way, don't think just because we screwed it's a relationship."

I did not think anything beyond listening to her bewildering case history and the pop philosophy a Riviera dancing girl was trying out on me in the middle of the night.

"Your karma can go haywire in some previous incarnation. In many ways he's a very spiritual person, without knowing it. I don't know, I know I'll never forget him. (That's all he needs to hear to try and contest the divorce, so whatever you do don't tell him that.) Live and learn is what it's all about, and don't make the same mistake your next relationship. Like my father, he's a very conservative person and my motivation I admit may have been to give him a heart attack by getting married to a Jew. An older man, my own father's age—and a poet. Take India, they betroth girls that are still children to already mature men. How old are you, by the way? Never mind, age is irrelevant, it's all maya and deceptive. Maybe I've got this thing, speak of motivation, about beards. Larry had a beard too, I can't see what else I could have seen in that screwball, till he shaved it off to go down to Mexico. So did Pilot. If you believe in horoscopes it's like getting your stars crossed but he used to say—or was it Pound?—the fault lies not in our stars but ourselves, and that's the truth. He's Taurus and I'm Pisces, what a combination, but I didn't know what he was when I met him. At eighteen, who knows their ass from a hole in the ground? I was a veritable virgin in his poetry class. I don't know what he told you but I was. Technically I lost it riding Rascal my horse but actually he received my cherry on a silver platter."

Ginny kept cigarettes and a Bic lighter under the pillow with her diaphragm. Of the diaphragm she said: "I don't know why I keep this thing, I had my tubes tied. Sentimental, I guess."

She did not offer me a cigarette—it was a Ward family failing—so I was not obliged to tell her I did not smoke, but I did.

"Believers don't smoke either. I was in a cult something like the Moonies called True Believers, the only difference was there wasn't any father figure like Moon to bow down to. I didn't drop out till my brother got drafted. That was when I smoked my first cigarette." She lit a cigarette with the throwaway lighter, smoked—her nostrils flared when she inhaled—and was silent, looking out the screened window of the Tradewinds to the supermarket lights across the road. She turned back to me holding her hand out flat, palm down, and at first I thought she wanted me to take her hand, or take her pulse—but the glowing cigarette was inserted between two fingers.

"This is the first time I ever talked about my brother my hand didn't shake."

True, her hand with the cigarette sprouting between two fingers gave no hint of inner turmoil.

"Neal. My hands used to shake like crazy every time his name got mentioned. Whenever I thought about him I could literally see his face."

Neal was the brother who was killed in Vietnam, at a place called Hamburger Hill. Do we only see the faces of our dead? I could not with any success make Valerie's face materialize, but I could conjure up the Poet's face at will.

Ginny was looking across the narrow living space to the opposite wall where I thought she might have kept a photograph of Neal like the one Major Ward kept in his underground shelter. But there was no picture or souvenir of her brother anywhere in sight. In fact, there was no attempt at décor inside the trailer—Ginny was her own décor—except for a single Walt Disney figurine, a twin to the dwarf that supported Major Ward's birdbath, set upon the bookshelf. She was not looking at the figurine nor at the book spines of her science fiction collection; her eyes were glazed over and her expression remote—it was the expression she wore under the dance hall lights, and in no way allowed for penetration into her secret space.

"At this point in time I'm where I can realize Neal's karma was just part of the eternal design. He didn't have to die, but I can accept the inevitability of it. It was his choice to venture forth, he didn't even have to go into the Army because the temple in Denver is registered with the Council of Churches. Believers can conscientiously object if drafted—they maintain nonprofit tax-exempt status and special postal rates and all, right up to the Attorney General. But not Neal. He went anyway—and not just because of Dad. Dad would have had a stroke if his son refused to fight Communism before it ended up in our own backyard, but that's not why Neal went. He had to, it was written. Deep down Neal loved his country as much as the next person. We were a very close family at one time. And totally patriotic, till Mom copped out. You had to know Neal to know why he went. The Believers were stunned, believe me. The temple held a marathon love-prayer one whole weekend for Neal's redemption but they lost out to the Army. Neal said he heard the call. I dropped out of the Believers and went to college. If a woman drops out it's just one less weaker vessel according to them, and that much more room in the communal bathroom—but if a male Believer defects it's the same as Satan pulling the strings. They stop pronouncing his rebirth name and refer to him as the Departed, it's depressing. If he left any clothes behind or a razor or something personal the Believers burn it, except the razor which they destroy, or bury, or whatever. Then they scatter the ashes like it's the person himself deceased which was ironical because of Neal actually getting killed. In Vietnam. When I saw them burning Neal's sweater in the stove in the communal kitchen I freaked out. I knitted that sweater. It was only through Neal I was a Believer in the first place. I never believed as truly as he did, who knows their ass from a hole in the ground at eighteen? But I believed in him, and that's how I got hooked. Neal was something, believe me. I was still at the age where the only way I could conceive of myself was through a man's conception of me. In the Believers, if you were a woman, forget it. Even if you were the Virgin Mary you couldn't be among the Chosen, but they still make you sell their magazine and cook rice. Believers don't even bother to brainwash women. They consider them basically unclean so you can imagine with that and how totally conservative they are about meat and sex and cigarettes how high the dropout rate for women is. I only believed as long as I did because of Neal. It wasn't even the Cong that killed him but some Marine, if you can believe the irony. Dad would never accept this, but what does he know about the endless wheel of becoming?"

She fanned the nicotine fumes from our immediate vicinity and stared through the dispersed cloud at perhaps a vision of the endless wheel. In the silence I wondered if she expected me to comment. As she smoked, and the nostrils of her doll's nose flared, I had a vision of my own. I saw Ginny as a budding adolescent (younger than in the photograph with the horse), then as a child, an infant, a fetus, an embryo, a shadow behind an X-ray screen, a microdot in the void—all of this with my eyes closed.

"Hey. Are you conked out on me?"

I opened my eyes. I then tried to imagine her missing mother's face from the daughter's delicate and flawless features. A beauty, her father had insisted, *a beauty from the start*. The strange eyes not to my taste—or had my taste altered with the Poet's promise of eyes wide as oysters? But she was a beauty, "lovely in her bones." I must decide if I would watch her even more closely than this—the perfect skin, her measurements ideal—to discover what beyond her wanton ways a poet saw in her.

"One thing I learned from experience—from marriage and religion and everything else—is that what looks weird at first or turns out a bummer in the end, you can just blow it off, your essential oneness stays untouched and the cosmic flow just flows on. Things aren't actually weird or warped or cool or anything, they just *are*. My peacenik brother killed in a war. And me being the wife of a known poet."

I could not tell her the word was widow, not wife.

"My name in the Believers was Hope. Funny, I haven't thought about my rebirth name since I dropped out. When I dropped out I lost eleven pounds in ten days, you wouldn't have recognized me. All I did was cry. Then I wrote poems, in his class, in college, and that was what saved me from a total nervous breakdown over Neal being killed. Poetry, you can let it all hang out. It's like meditation, where you make it with your innermost self. All of a sudden I saw my own potential. I stopped crying, I stopped doing dope.

"In class he called me Miss Ward like anybody and I called him Professor Gold. Some students called him Dr. Gold because he's a doctor of letters. Then when I came to conference he called me Virginia and later Ginny and finally Gin. The first time we made it was on a couch in his office in Pennybaker Hall. His beard smelled like nicotine. I was hooked, on cigarettes. Then poetry, then him. My name in the Believers made him laugh, Hope. He called me Fanny. He had a million names for me like Lolita and Lady Chatterley and Lilith—and that's just the *L*'s. At first I thought he called me Sister Carrie because the Believers had practically made a nun out of me but she was a character in a book that ruined another character named Hurstwood. I didn't exactly ruin him but I lost him his job in Utah. He was the poet in residence before I came along. Then, he said, I made him the poet in prurience. 'Ruin me,' he used to say when he wanted to ball. Destruction is a real turn-on, I mean the concept that I could ruin his career for love literally gave me goose pimples. You actually do ruin each other, back and forth—that's exactly what a relationship is. How does he look? He's got the world's worst case of insomnia, he could never sleep. Do you think I really ruined him? Is that why he's in that kind of hospital?"

"He's out now. His behavior was, well. Bizarre."

"Frankly, he's a bizarre person."

"Well. He's out of it."

"Not him. He's too bizarre to suddenly just become normal. He'll have a relapse or something."

I could think of no lie to insert here.

"Poets are naturally bizarre or they wouldn't be poets and let their careers be ruined for love. It's not normal but it's—nice."

"Yes."

"Do you think it would shock him too much to receive divorce papers in the mail?"

"That. I don't know."

Before she slept—like Sheherazade, guiltless and purged after a night of narrative—Ginny reminded me not to be deceived by superficial phenomena. It was all maya. As she drifted off she said, "Goodnight, Neal." This brought her sharply awake again.

"Did I say Neal? God, what a Freudian slip. I'm not into incest, believe me, but I really would like to call you Neal. I wonder what my brother would have looked like with a beard. You don't actually look anything like him, but you're a terrific listener like Neal was."

"Do you want me to call you Hope?"

"God no."

7

EXCEPT FOR a trio of golfers wearing cowboy boots and sunglasses and denim shirts with embroidery, Austin that early could have been Sunday anyplace, not necessarily west. Last night's smoke-eyed patrons of the Riviera were today working off hangovers aboard battery-powered golf carts buzzing down the fairways, sidecars of iced Coors riding shotgun, for a hair of the dog.

I surveyed this emerald realm from the little caboose step-down at the back door of Ginny's Tradewinds. In the parking lot for the golf course were station wagons with gun racks and bumper stickers about where to go if you didn't like it here. The sprinklers must have been on all night: the turf was a moist mint green, the color of money. The dust of Austin had settled, you could breathe—that was why the ranchers were out. Those gallant cinematic horsemen from my childhood matinees in Latonia returned to me—still trying on a hell-for-leather look of cowpokes whose nobler feelings were locked inside—riding electric carts and chasing golf balls in the suburbs of Texas.

Before stepping outdoors to urinate into the dew with some discretion, I had awakened to the mystery of an unfamiliar bedmate. (My wife, if she slept, slept somewhere beyond the horizon, late, Eastern standard time.) This was a poet's widow I had slept with or been bedded by, no curtain between us. I rejoiced in the exceptional luck to have won this willing flesh. I remembered how sinuously athletic and coldly competent she had been with me in the night, for *the ladies love you,* I remembered, *men is what they dance for.* And I had made her ever-loving acquaintance.

For all my part of the exercise, I might as well have been serviced by an avid sister of the streets in New Orleans. But I rejoiced, I had scored.

The Tradewinds was parked in a vague overgrown terrain dotted at the edges with Coors cans and Diet Pepsi empties; the official parking lot was on the green side of a chain-link fence. I walked the ragged strip of woods bordering the undulating dreamlike greens of a golf course, a circular hike to loosen a love cramp, a walk on the wild side to clear my head. I would have liked to order my thoughts, perhaps in the way of Major Ward who filed his best ideas in folders. I stumbled over nothing new in that respect.

I did come across an occasional discarded condom to remind me of man's inexorable fate—and my own—and once, a stray golf ball planted in the undergrowth like an Easter egg. I collected it. The golf ball would join the five-cent piece Billy had flipped me, and my father's letters, in the Poet's attaché case. I was in need of touchstones and souvenirs. Also, I came across a five-dollar bill (a fin, my father used to call them, the price of a liter of the embalming fluid he sold) that had somehow got itself planted in the hollow of a tree. This thing with trees, my druid status of mind—but I could not resist the thought of that inverted crotch shaped like a dancer standing on her head, the money as obscenely situated as the same banknote tucked inside a G-string. *Things aren't weird, they just are.* I reached into the hollow and pulled out the five, then tucked it into my pocket as if I had won a bet with Mother Nature.

Don't for a minute think she's just another dumb broad, Critic.

Like Lawrence, I think. She's something else.

—or some gabbily naive know-all with a brother fixation.

She's a fateful happenstance, she's an alternate universe, she's Sheherazade.

The dawn patrol of golfers drove on in search of challenge in the shape of holes while I, the ambulant philosopher, kept my eye peeled for doughnuts and took the opposite way. I would have to decide my next direction or go with Ginny's flow for a time yet.

After traveling full circle around the golf course and safely back to Safeway, I noticed last night's shift of starlings had been relieved by a morning watch of scavenger crows prospecting the dumpster bins alongside a loading platform. An antediluvian pickup was parked beside the ramp: two clerks from the storehouse behind the supermarket trundled crates of spoiled grapefruit and far-gone bananas into the back of the truck. *Andy* was spelled out in runny purple paint on the cab door. Andy himself sat behind the wheel in overalls and railroad cap—a black man confined to his obesity, unable or unwilling to unwedge himself from the driver's seat and see to the loading of rusted celeries and black avocados and battered loaves of bread. Before Andy could rouse himself from a seeming fixed lethargy, his truck sucked up the surplus of the seventh day.

When the last loaf was loaded, the pickup got under way, discordant harmonium of gears and exhaust: immediately the rust spots on the fenders took flight. What I had taken for rust stains had all along been ochre-colored butterflies attracted, no doubt, to the vehicle's storehouse of odors. Here was the maya Ginny warned me about, the deceptive way of the world. A working poet would have found a way to integrate this spectacle into the universal panorama, but no poet appeared in the vicinity of our golf course. I accepted the moment's magic for its significance to me only: the divided mind of a moment before became a determination. The thoughts I had entertained along the circumference of a golf course, like resident butterflies, were dispersed in an instant. Even Andy recognized my enlightenment. I would, like him, scavenge the same territory.

Why not hang in with the Major's daughter for a time, study her fix on the cosmos? Andy's dead stare through a cracked windshield came alive as he spun the pickup in my direction and saw me in my moment of sartori. He seemed to know I would stay on as Candide and cultivate Ginny's garden.

He smiled a caricature smile, waved one elephantine arm and winked—not at the clerks, in gratitude, but at me, in conspiracy.

8

GINNY READ only science fiction, wrote only poetry.

"All I read before him was Kahlil Gibran and *Christian Concepts*. Handmaidens had to sell their quota of *Christian Concepts* while all the Apostles had to do was mimeograph it. My brother was an Apostle. You felt like a streetwalker. The technique was to love-bomb innocent pedestrians, especially men, into opting for Jesus Christ by buying our magazine. If they bought one you tried to lure them out of Satan's domain into ours, without actually putting out—if they were men—which, when you come to think of it, is the same technique at Riviera Nites." After a while there was a way of listening without listening. "It was a gimmick like everything else, like advertising or politics. I dropped out. The void isn't half as empty as people suppose, even the Prophets profited from their drift through outer darkness. I went with opposing flows for a long time trying to heal the hole Neal's nothingness left in my life. The true way takes forever. You can't, I found out, just accept the first guru type that comes along and points out the path. That's a one-way street, believe me. I mean, if all the signposts have been erected by the Devil, how do you know which traffic cop to trust? The scales on my eyes were slow to fall, but when they fell—*brother*. Is there, by any chance, some vodka left in that jug?"

The Smirnoff came in liter jugs from the shelves of Safeway (except Sunday morning, when the shelves were roped off by the Blue Laws) and we sipped at it—mine on the rocks, hers diluted by lemon-flavored soda pop—she more thirstily due to the night's dehydrating efforts under hot lights. We dined on delivered pizzas (Duane, the delivery boy, was in love with her) and the good Colonel's counterfeit chicken. There was no call for me to prepare meals for Ginny, who did not eat meals, as I had for Valerie, who did not eat meals either. We defrosted frozen tacos or popped papier-mâché chicken parts into the microwave. While the cubed cheese and tomato paste of ersatz Italian fare liquefied in the oven we sat on Ginny's yoga mat drinking Russian vodka made in Hartford, Connecticut.

She kept me as one would keep a pet or souvenir. Nothing hung between us in those shipshape narrow spaces except an occasional silence of a contemplative ten minutes while Ginny meditated on her prayer mat. Otherwise she was obsessively verbal: she even chatted from the chemical commode, the toilet door ajar. She attended my needs as a nurse would—her own needs were other than those of the workaday flesh. (Whatever release she sought was anyway beyond my poor powers.) We dressed only when the cranky air conditioning worked; we slept naked, a lover's sandwich, in the cramped bed pressed so close I could not tell if it was her stomach that rumbled from the frozen dinners or mine. Cohabitation took place spontaneously but mechanically as between windup toys their synchronized motors purring. In some sticky kind of confined freedom we navigated the constricted passageways of the Tradewinds with our bare moist parts brushing stainless steel or each other's bare moist parts. How the Poet must have relished Ginny's easy streak of affectionate disregard, her indifference to decorum (forbidden bathrobes in dull Dayrooms of repressive institutions), her frank immodesty and permanent display.

"Face it, life's screwed up. And lonely. That's how the Believers can come on to you with jasmine tea and homemade cookies and reap converts right off the streets. They prey on loners, then pray over them. Talk about white slavery. When you wake up after the brainwash you're signed on for a sixteen-hour day of heavy meditation and cruise duty and KP and your own personal bodyguard to keep you in line. Actually the First Believer is some Korean in Seattle many times a millionaire on account of all these drones out working the streets for him. So all you've evolved into is a remote-controlled robot making big bucks for Big Daddy.

"At least the Bahais I almost joined don't push the commune bit and bodyguards and one bathroom but deep down, when I was halfway converted, I realized my old complexes about a militaristic father were pushing me into it, because the Bahais are so pacifist, so I backed out."

The fringe religions had left their mark on her but in strangely contrary ways. The thing about bathrooms she resolved with her own personal flair. She showered with no shower curtain between us. (Where, I was too lazy to ask, did the water come from, where did it drain?) She did her meditation in the lotus, in the nude—as free with the sight of her flesh as the use of it. As for peace, the Tradewinds was the epicenter of tranquility. I was never witness to the tantrums she was famous for, the wild bucking mustang that threw dudes like me for a loop—I rode the saddle too passively for tantrums.

"Then there was this Hare Krishna I met who looked a lot like

Neal. The exact same eyes and real intense, except the Hare Krishna's hair was shaved. But again, it's all so self-conscious it's almost mainstream, like the chants and cymbals and going barefoot."

From these snatches of case history I could assume she collected strays like me. I was this season's trophy. In question was how long I could share a trailer with her and enjoy the dubious blessing of being Neal. A week was infinity to her, the time we had been together. As with religions, less depended upon doctrine than her own quicksilver temperament.

As for me, I had undergone decided alteration. First, the beard rendered me unrecognizable, even to myself. Sloth and detachment brought on pouches beneath my eyes, I took on a tube of flesh around the waist. I lost track of time, time lost track of me. The extent of my reading, like Valerie's, had been reduced to the *TV Guide*. Walks took me to the laundromat and supermarket and once as far as a prefabricated mosque where the faithful from the Middle East (who came to Texas to study oil technology) lined up their shoes at the door before prayer, a tall pair of cowboy boots among them.

Those boots were the same snakeskin pair Lawrence had worn. And I remembered the familiar borrowed Dodge pickup I kept seeing parked beside the laundromat. Suddenly all my fat complacencies were scattered and the old paranoia took over. Did Lawrence take some interest in my movements? Could he be patrolling from a laundromat parking lot, mounting surveillance from a neighborhood mosque?

Late, late, long after "The Star-Spangled Banner" faded into vacancy on the tiny portable TV—the set a gift from a forgotten lover, a miniature replica of the console model at the Sans Souci—I would listen for her Toyota to rumble contentedly into its home port of a rustic parking slot marked off by Perrier and Sprite cases between the trees. For several uneasy seconds after the purring motor fell silent, I strained to hear the sound of voices. (By the second week it dawned on me I could not maintain exclusive rights in this partnership.) Someday, or rather night—as inevitable as the message in the music she danced to—she would be escorted home by a newfound stray.

"At first I had trouble reconciling his seventeen Cadillacs. The First Believer, I'm talking about. It was the kingdom-on-this-earth aspect all over again—he publishes his own books and owns his own record company and he's a maniac for direct mail. Like, how do you relate an Elvis Presley hang-up like collecting Cadillacs with the godhead? Believe me, a host of temporal doubts nagged at my consciousness, but that's merely the way on the way to enlightenment. Not the First Believer's idea of enlightenment but mine. Cadillacs are only so much maya unless you're actually driving one.

"I was at this session trying to concentrate on nothingness with naturally a shitload of irrelevant clutter you have to clear from your frequency if you want to tune to the essential being when one thought took over that wiped me out in the middle of the First Believer's holy *om*. The FB was making a personal contact tour of our temple in Denver—and the man, I mean, had charisma, you had to give him that, and eyes, granted, his eyes saw right into a person's solar plexus—but looking into his eyes was when this one thought hit me that literally wiped me out. What blew my mind out of all time and dimension was like a voice that said out loud to me: 'You're your own salvation yourself.' That was it. That's what I was seeking, that was the answer all along! No ashram, no tent city in Seattle or retreat to retreat to (like my Dad in a bomb shelter) because I dwelt in the temple of my own being and no quota sales of brownies door to door or peddle magazines in the streets about concepts or trying to love-bomb innocent bystanders or brainwash them with what Believers believe in and explain what the chants and mantras meant or why the men have to shave their head and everybody accepts crowded oneness with your so-called soul partners in damp leaky bathrooms always out of toilet paper. Forget it. You're your own concept. You can chant *om* in your own private bath and it comes out the same. Hope. Even my husband had names for me like Lolita and Lilith when I was essentially me from the beginning and the only way to reach selfhood was to revert to my original identity. Henceforth, brother, I went back to being Virginia Regina Ward with total control over this little lady's soul and ever since I let it all hang out, screw Lilith and Hope both."

Her enlightenment included me, for immediately as if to demonstrate satori in person, she was out of her blouse and I unhooked her bra for her and helped her peel down her skin-fit jeans. She took me on, or rather under—something she called the spinning top, out of the Kama Sutra—I but a piece of cartilage appended to her spin. All I need do was receive her blessing and express my delight.

9

THE TELEPHONE BOOTH across the street was just far enough to feed my new uneasiness: was that Lawrence Priest inside with legs so long he could prop one foot on the narrow shelf while he dialed? The distance was too deceptive and the grin hidden by the telephone for positive identification. I could not see the pile of coins for the foot, so I was left wondering if the unidentified watcher was dialing Miami, if he had quarters enough to call my wife.

Of course not. He unhinged his flexible insect leg and hung up. When he came out of the booth he was wearing a Safeway apron, a clerk working the night shift calling home.

But such sights nagged at me, like the one misty morning I thought I made out not Andy's swayback pickup across the street, but Lawrence's—gun rack and all. I got up and went over there and it was Andy's. He was making his collection just as I arrived; we knew one another now: he could overcome his ponderous lethargy to rub a peephole in the dust on his windshield, then slowly lift a hand with the pink center showing in a gesture of recognition. I waved back. That was how we shared the thin side of a morning.

I then carried our plastic DisposAll bag of chicken bones and pizza crusts (a prop, my cover story, in case Andy had been Lawrence Priest) to Safeway's waiting dumpster. The frozen dinners had come from the supermarket in the first place. Andy and I were but links in the perpetual chain of replacement, which somewhat resembled the digestive system itself.

Now that I was up, and Safeway open—open twenty-four consecutive hours, in fact—I might as well shop for the frozen pizzas of the future, for however long my future with Ginny would endure. The glass front doors were propped open with burlap sacks of potatoes so that Safeway might hyperventilate last night's air conditioning; I entered through this exhale. There was a spectacular choice of daisy chain chariots inserted one into the other as if alternating male and female. I chose the one detached shopping cart, shunning the daisy chain. Choices: here was where Valerie had been happiest, permitted the exuberance of choice a fairy tale offered. (Why did I think of Valerie in the past tense and the Poet forever in the present?) I was the only customer on tour, not counting the Poet.

Aisle clerks crouched at the lowest possible gaps in the display pyramids. I thought of the Major stocking every available space in preparation for the Day. (The supermarket was illuminated in the same hallucinatory way as Major Ward's fallout shelter.) A yawning butcher shuffled and dealt packets of prime ribs into a sarcophagus of slaughtered beef. We did not dine on these cuts: I was offered Ginny's own prime ribs and succulent tenderloins. But we did eat pizzas, so I flipped a frozen wheel of dough into the cart. I chose a brand of Florida orange juice diluted from concentrate to dilute the vodka we drank and provide the vitamin C necessary to our exertions. For me alone the lone cashier could rehearse her first have-a-good-day of the day.

Some puckish architect with a sense of authenticity had allowed a pecan tree to grow up as nature intended through the center of the store. This too might have made Valerie happy—it only made the Poet smirk.

Other mornings when I was awake at first light, to brood over choices, I might make a tour of the dew-laden golf links while Ginny slept wrapped in her innocence until noon. There was too much time to brood, being housebound to Sheherazade. Ginny's demands were reasonable enough: she asked only that I sleep and feed and listen. The leash she held me to was extensive, my services minimal. Any duties I performed were those of volunteer: on Fridays (this one was a thirteenth) I chose to serve her by an excursion to the Tarrytown laundromat.

Vast trees of impeccable pedigree shaded my way. My spirits were high on this easy tour. Lawn sprinklers regulated by an invisible timing device tossed jeweled droplets in my path. The curbs were crimpled like piecrust to accommodate bicycle lanes, but I crossed little traffic of any kind except a familiar jogger I called Jogger, straining at a tighter leash than mine. The only other soul I encountered regularly was a citizen pitching a solitary game of horseshoes, a man who would have asked me to pitch with him but for my beard. I avoided the popular lakeshore at the end of Endfield, not yet ready to contemplate a body of water that might remind me of Biscayne Bay.

I needed these surburban spaces to think in. I had come across letters to the Poet in Ginny's care.

I made pilgrim's progress through an environment of lazy reassurance, a neighborhood of churches. The titles of next Sunday's sermons were displayed on outdoor bulletin boards, injunctions to Do Right that my father might have written. Sunday morn I could see the worshippers easing out of their polished limousines—everything gleaming: teeth and glasses and watchbands—carrying Bibles edged in gilt that caught fire from the relentless Texas sun.

But the all-night laundry was another kind of space, a rite that perfectly concentrated the mind. The laundromat was even better than a golf course for working out the human dilemma.

Ginny's delicate intimate wear was entrusted to a fastidious Vietnamese establishment—perhaps in defiance of her father's ideas about dealing with the enemy—but sheets and towels and aerobic warm-up togs traveled along with my rough wardrobe in one bundle. The laundromat shared drive-in space with a bank and a taco takeout service. Only a Big Boy and the laundromat were open that early, attracting the detritus, myself included, of the night before. Galoots whose cars or girls had quit on them hours ago came here for the cigarette machines and pay phones. Their phone calls were never answered. The good old boys lingered through half-a-pack on the wooden benches opposite the vibrating dryers—for where else can you go with your car shot or your girl gone in Austin at sunup?

I took my ease at this way station, comforted in knowing no Skip Tracer would come here at this hour to launder his soiled white working clothes, and convinced it was too early for Lawrence to spy on me from the parking lot.

Girls with a time clock waiting ran their waitress uniforms through a cycle and drank the day's first Coke with crushed ice. Somebody's transistor played "Settle In, Sister." Nobody—not even I—used the waiting time to read except for a taxi driver who pulled up front with an *Off Duty* sign on to join us after the night's drunk run, with an *Austin Statesman* to relieve his mind.

"I find out as much from driving people around as what's in the paper."

"If that ain't the truth," said a working girl in short shorts, "and politics are the same." I recognized her. She was a cashier at Safeway. She had a bruise on her thigh from pushing the cash drawer shut. The cabbie left his newspaper behind, but I was disconnected from news of the world. I had become a closet reader of letters left about in a careless hiding place.

Jogger came by with his plastic flight bag full of sweat socks and jockstraps he dumped, still running in place, into a machine, then timed himself to the cycle and jogged on. Across the parking lot a family of four came out of the Big Boy together: they had identical wickedly tiny red eyes and were nibbling toothpicks as a team, right down to the freckled overfed youngest, maybe five years, who at nineteen would take over his Daddy's used-car lot for him. They opened four simultaneous car doors still picking their teeth.

I had once considered buying an automobile of my own, the great American means of moving on. I did not have a license to drive. And there was this letter addressed to the Poet that made me think of moving farther on than even a souped-up Thunderbird would take me.

Meanwhile I watched the water ballet of laundry through a porthole, in Technicolor—never a colorfast disaster despite mixing my dun-colored drabs with Ginny's bright-dyed exotica. Her sheets were the same lavender tint as her stationery. And the stains were the same rusted Rorschach of menstrual blood as Miss Frith's hospital sheets, and Valerie's, which I also laundered in the long ago. Ginny put towels down when we made it in bed, so these were stained with baby oil and our commingled juices. Her makeup sometimes came off on a pillowcase and was hard to wash out.

Twenty minutes of tumble-dry kept the machine's vibrations going go-go-go. Go-go-go was always a possibility. I got more of an answer to my dilemma from a dryer than the forsaken galoot got when he tried his number again. Musically the dime came back like the refrain in a Nashville ballad. My dryer quivered to a dead stop and I was ready to retreat from the visible universe of Tarrytown into the immobile fastness of a mobile home.

At home there was this sleeping beauty wrapped corpselike in her winding sheet. I hovered over her with a mug of instant coffee—the coffee was for her, but she did not awake to its aroma and I did not venture a kiss—and studied her pristine otherworldliness. The detached strand of cotton-candy hair that lay across a lavender pillow slip was lifeless, the hair ends having lost all of last night's electricity, but she lived—oh, how she lived. Ginny emanated waves of kinetic life force even when she slept.

Eyes wide as oysters (closed, waxen now), _hair down to here._

"Eyes, Son," my father used to push the homily, "are the mirrors of the soul." If so, said the Poet in another mood, the genitals are its implements. An image continued on through the kindergarten lyrics of a pop song called "Mechanical Doll": _Eyes that sweetly open and close, who's got the key that winds my baby up?_

Dr. K had once discussed a patient at staff conference: a girl afflicted with seventeen distinct and alternately demanding personalities. Ginny had solved that schism by being her own concept. Nevertheless she played at several separate roles. My favorite was the double-jointed gymnast who coiled herself around my excitement. She scored a discharge into her sheath every time, without a tremor of pleasure for herself. Hers was exceptional sexual expertise, and I was grateful for the hospitable access to her soft parts—but she granted no admission past that heated threshold. Her caresses were on impulse only, but she offered every thought in her head. To her I communicated nothing and committed myself only to her offerings. Ginny spoke of divorce proceedings and the law's delay, while I remained silently corrupt, passively conniving. I kept from her the knowledge of her widowed state, and felt no guilt.

In pursuit of that private heart—I quote the Poet not the disco lyrics—*open only to you.* Do not count on the promises of poets. Ginny closed her eyes during intercourse so that she might imagine any ghost of the past entering her. The private heart she opened was in another place, and open to the public.

In a little while she would be up and into her rituals—meanwhile the coffee grew cold—and she wanted me there for them, for she talked ceaselessly even during yoga. With her hair in a handkerchief, and the pale unpainted face blanked out behind granny glasses—she wore contact lenses when she danced or did aerobics—she counted the greenbacks given her the night before. She kept the thick bundle of banknotes flat under the paperweight of a cold steam iron, destined for deposit later in the day: "The IRS is going to wake up and tax gratuities one of these days, and I want to be in a different business or another country when they do."

She was her own housekeeper and grimly kept her doll's house dust-free in dusty Austin. The Tradewinds exuded a lingering odor of furniture polish, insect spray and lemon-scented cleanser. DisposAll bags of garbage were kept nestled in the refrigerator so as not to attract the Kafkaesque cockroaches of Texas—her one great dread and the ultimate threat to her peace of mind. In the same refrigerated vault she stored a mayonnaise jar of marijuana, the lid pierced to keep the grass from wilting. Despite a certain disorder of mind, her living quarters were uncluttered: the few possessions out of sight, the extensive wardrobe neatly closeted. The science fiction collection was arranged alphabetically by author. Like the jar of pot, she kept herself and her space as cool and moist as the climate and unreliable air conditioning allowed.

Her small hands were clutched in a baby's fist-balls when she slept, the one uptight part of her anatomy. The double-jointed fingers were folded out of sight—I recalled the landlady's bandaged mitts in New Orleans and the tense knuckles of a sweet young thing holding the armrests of a bus seat and thought of the hand holding a can of Budweiser and a milk-white hand dispensing pills, all of them the Hand, the one that held the bridle in the photograph and last night grasped my implement with the tenderest intent. Her mouth (the mouth had accomplished the next stage of intention) came open to expose the cinematic teeth and kitten's curled tongue in a yawn. At the same time the little fists that in a dream grabbed at a gratuity or swung on the guy who got too close, the fists opened from buds into blossoms and bent backwards at the wrists in a stretch of luxurious abandon. Instantly the eyes popped open like a mechanical doll's.

"Morning, Neal-baby."

She bounced up and out of sleep ready to inaugurate the day with a preliminary layer of makeup. This was only the ritual touch to total metamorphosis into the ultimate stage version of herself: nothing overly vivid would appear in the blandness of expression until a sumi brush painted her features in place backstage. An empty but angelic face took on only the halftones of what she was to become tonight at the Riviera Nites. She sprinkled her face with Maidenfair moisturizer in the bathroom, then applied pinkish foundation mask with swabs of cotton and Kleenex. Cotton balls and stained wads of Kleenex accumulated in the DisposAll bag at her ankle. The mirror was encircled with Hollywood light bulbs, and she sat before it in a director's canvas chair that could be folded away to make passage to the shower. (I sometimes looked into that Cinderella mirror myself— the Dorian Gray mirror in my case—checking the bloodshot state of my eyes and soul, the progression of the beard that transfigured my demeanor.) She frowned professionally at herself and applied a tad of orange to the pink. The unfinished effect of Ginny's first-stage makeup was that of a faded summer tan, or a beginning blush. This was Ginny in reverse: her face the negative of the photograph I had seen before I had seen her in the flesh.

As for perfecting the outward texture of her physical self, Ginny was a faithful patron of the Body Shoppe, an institution devoted to health and beauty tucked under the Mo-Pac overpass at Enfield. The Body Shoppe was as devoted to Ginny's skin as the Van Thuoy Cleaners to her silken underwear. At the Body Shoppe she was massaged and molded by rubber discs and firm fingers, the length of her legs waxed and the fine hair depilated, the peach fuzz removed from her forearms and the pubic hair shaved and coiffed into a lower visible triangle to accommodate the G-string. The rough calloused elbows and heels were sanded softly to the baby layer below, but Ginny performed her own pedicure at home, cheek resting on knee, the toenail snips clicking like dice until finally she applied the colorless lacquer to the nails. "I can't stand somebody to fuss with my feet," she said, as if offering instruction about foreplay, protective swabs of cotton wedged between the perfect toes. Nor would she expose herself to ultraviolet in the Body Shoppe's solarium: "You worry what those rays are doing to a person's genes in the next generation," and because Prince, manager of the Riviera, preferred light-skinned lovelies over dark.

As she sat back semisatisfied at her dressing table—spooning a lemon-flavored yogurt, with a Kleenex under her chin—I considered the blemishes. Without mascara to enlarge her eyes, Ginny acquired a mean-spirited aspect that made me think my father's old saw might bear some relevance. When her face was only half-painted, the eyes lost all candor and appeared to squint as wickedly as those narrow-eyed people coming out of Big Boy. I had occasion to see the poison rise to her eyes when, with a science fiction paperback, she smashed an invading cockroach, and once at the Riviera when she dealt with Lawrence Priest—but on no occasion so far had she flashed this venom in my direction. (I imagined, when I read through her mail, how she might react if she caught me at it.)

Her long hair successfully hid the tiny ears the Poet referred to as mother-of-pearl, but the ears lacked lobes, and to Ginny this was an unfortunate defect best kept out of sight.

Ginny drew her lips back with the littlest finger to be certain the teeth were as photogenically aligned as ever and the gums had not overnight lost their poster pink. (The ghost of a poet was watching her at this, weeping.) By now her delicately airbrushed face had taken on all the definition daylight allowed, the final expression to be applied backstage at the Riviera, and the hair-brushed hair gift-wrapped in a silken Valentine motif. A perfume whose label promised Je Reviens was her personal musk, to offset any lingering whiff of nicotine—she stubbed her cigarette into the yogurt container, the last she would smoke until the small hours—and she applied the scent to her wrists, armpits and the insides of her thighs.

Dressed finally in tight denim and loose silk, she assembled her bundle of banknotes for deposit in the Tarrytown branch of First

Texas, dark glasses against the fierce light, and her free-form handbag with the can of Mace in it against rapists. She kissed me swiftly between the eyebrows and did her little disco step to the door.

"*Ciao*, Neal-baby," she called out to her house husband as she set the Toyota into orbit.

10

"As soon as Mrs. G went out to Park-n-Market to purchase a six-pack of Budweiser (for your old Dad's personal consumption, she drank Coke only) I took the trouble to take stock of her flatware. Son, hers is the finest set of sterling silver money can buy, and this little lady, widowed as she was, had taken an uncommon liking to me. Each piece right down to the pickle forks is inscribed with a fancy *G* for Greenleaf, her deceased husband's family name, handed down—name and sterling both—from generation unto generation all the way back to the *Mayflower*, or at least Paul Revere, who was a top-notch silversmith before he warned the populace the British were coming. I could have been a crook for all Mrs. G knew, with a truck parked around the corner."

I padded through the Tradewinds walking barefoot in my father's footsteps. My bated breath began to show on the frostbitten air, I was chilled to the heart, so I turned off Ginny's defective air conditioning. My father's warnings to me against his life of illegality and guile had been but trumpetings of pride and triumph all along.

Behind a Masonite panel above the miniature refrigerator was a network of pigeonholes and miniature drawers housing a lifetime of memorabilia. The unit might at one time have been a sewing cabinet, for *Singer* was printed across the frame at the top. There were even thimbles and thread in one drawer, but no needles—though who would expect Ginny to engage in needlework? I discerned nothing noticeably secret about this stash; the panel door had no lock, and I felt only fleeting twinges of criminal guilt pawing through Ginny's personal notes and accumulations.

Here was the receipt for the sale of a horse named Rascal, and there an instruction booklet for playing electric guitar. She kept supermarket margarine coupons (9¢ Off Regular Price!) and unpaid parking tickets from as far away as Santa Fe and a printout of her college grades: B in Poetry 110.

Most of my findings were banal enough to spare my conscience any dark reflection. She collected recipes for complicated quiches and unlikely lemon desserts—Ginny, who had never troubled to fry an egg. She, or someone, had typed the lyrics to a Nashville anthem: *Christ Jesus, the Greatest Cowboy of Them All.* I could hardly accuse myself of strip-search and violation. But one collection of letters was kept in a locked jewel box: the key was in the lock, I naturally turned the key. The letters were from Neal, the real one, letters inviolate, so I only read one.

"Hope, I saw something two days ago that turned my stomach." (He spared her the details.) "Some days I believe I'm losing my faith in human nature. Or losing my mind, one."

I was startled by a sharp tap on the metal siding outside. I put Neal's letters back and closed the panel; I put on my socks for some reason, to answer the knock.

It was Ginny's postman with his tricycle pushcart of mail. He wore regulation light blue-grey shorts and short sleeves with the P.O. coat of arms, an expression of surprise under the pith helmet—the helmet his own idea: against regulations, against the brutal sun.

"Ginny home?"

We blinked at one another. He knew her first name, he had hoped to make delivery in person. His bare bowed knees were sunburnt above the knee socks and he had women's breasts pushing at the P.O. pockets—certainly more belly than Ginny would have put up with: a middle-aged messenger bringing mail to the door of an Occupant Unknown at an illegitimate address. Even the Civil Service subscribed to her vibes.

"She's at work."

Uneasily, against every instinct, he handed me the three envelopes. I thanked him and he tipped his ridiculous helmet. Nothing to fear from this bearded intruder: these letters were but bills from B&D Sportswear and the Body Shoppe. The third was a printed brochure from the Chamber of Commerce in Anchorage, Alaska— Anchorage, Alaska? I rolled the letters into a twist that fitted into the handle of the vodka jug, so as not to forget to give them to Ginny tonight.

Then back to the hardcore correspondence behind the panel.

There were letters to the Poet, and from him. The letters addressed to I.M. Gold had been forwarded from Washington State, New Mexico, Colorado—and lately from Major Ward's address in Alabama. Envelopes with cellophane windows that were obviously bills were inscribed in Ginny's schoolgirl script: RETURN TO SENDER/ ADDRESS UNKNOWN. She had not bothered to return these to her devoted postman or place them in a mailbox.

The letters from the Poet to her were typed. She kept them in an open drawer in no particular order, in their original envelopes. The envelopes were addressed to her in care of her father on Rosedale Drive, and like the letters from my father to me they bore no return address.

"—admit admit admit admit you received whatever euphoria- -kicks, that is—in this life from YOURS TRULY. (And remember please please please the fucking *mileposts*.)"

In another drawer, scattered amongst her Safeway premium stamps and entreaties from *Time* and *Newsweek* to renew, she kept, of all things, a document from Brandeis attesting to her husband's Mastery of the Arts as well as the Poet's birth certificate.

"O.K. then think ye back on me with tenderness *quand même*. None of your Cracker prejudice, no postmortems—and you may find cause for rejoicing. Don't tell me there's no inkling left of those tickle-lickle times. Consider the oldie but goddamn goldie who first turned you on. (We do *not* count your apprentice years of dry-fucking off-duty soldiers in the back seats of Army jeeps.) You it was who tendered the endearment to your beloved That Night: 'Jesus honey how sweetly you're hung.' "

There were no poems from him to her, but one from her to him, a second draft, for the original title *Birthday* had been inked out with a Magic Marker and revised to *Your Birthday*.

> On your birthday, Sweetheart,
> Candles glowing on the cake
> Reflect back at me from your wise eyes,
> My private heart is yours alone.
> We traveled the endless highways of love
> Together, and our love will go on
> As the years fly by.
> VIRGINIA REGINA WARD

She kept a spiral notebook instead of a diary, entitled EVENTS (the equivalent of her father's STRAIGHT TALK), to chronicle the highlights of her life: first kiss, first spotted sheets, number of copies of *Christian Concepts* sold the day she was given the rebirth name Hope, first cigarette. She did not lie about the events in EVENTS, and confessed in its pages that the first time she went "all the way" was with a boy named Boyce, and not the Poet.

There were letters from her divorce lawyer and letters from The King's University in Belfast to the Poet, concerning an application he had submitted, a residency he sought.

They were married in Salt Lake City by a Justice of the Peace, Virginia R. Ward and I.M. Gold (he never used his given name, whatever it was). Ginny kept the marriage certificate with the letters from her attorney-at-law.

As for Events to come, I had no precognizance, but playfully and carelessly I began to practice the Poet's signature.

11

IF LAFCADIO HEARN could opt for Japan, why not a poet for Northern Ireland? I was disconnected from the world and its news but knew about Belfast and that astronauts with names like Buzz and Buster were commuting almost monthly to the moon. ("The moon," wrote my father, "makes me seasick to think about it. Whatever you do don't let the Navy put you in their astronautical program and ship you into space.") Was Northern Ireland anything like the moon: a place of desolation and dust?

A man named Bannister was writing letters from Belfast in the name of the Arts Council of County Down.

Meanwhile the Poet had written Ginny: "What's with Vegas all of a sudden, why these bitter tidings from the desert? This independent bit is only another phase, believe me. So you need a personal Cloud 9 all your own. Try to recall how beclouded you were in your independence—and *grief*—when we met. I dried your tears on my beard, I put my manhood in your hand to keep your hand from shaking. That was the bad time, remember?, after Haiku or wherever it was you lost a brother. I was the only soulmate in this galaxy who could listen, really listen. Then came Cloud 9, with room on it for the two of us."

Ginny also saved her father's letters.

"Smarten up my girl, it's later than you think. I tried to make a lady of you though you grew up without a mother to point out the fine points and tell you what's what. Whatever happened to the All-American girl who fell in love with the All-American boy? I kick myself when I think how many chances you had to wed an officer and a gentleman." Threaded through his letter was the same case my father made for filial devotion. "It was no picnic for a soldier to try and serve as father and mother both. Don't forget the pony I gave you when you were eight."

At the other end of the trailer a husband and wife conferred on daylight television, their foreheads touching in public intimacy. She chewed at a thumbnail, he tried to show manly support in their crisis of choice. It was a game show called *Giveaway* and there was either a set of mixing bowls or a brand-new Pontiac behind the golden curtain. The husband and wife were completely unstrung by greed.

The Poet was fourteen years my senior, we looked nothing alike. Did the Arts Council of County Down have only his application and poetry to go by?

Ginny's stationery was lavender-scented as well as colored, and embossed with a darker violet *V*. On impulse I took a sheet of stationery and with Valerie's Mechano ball-point (a choice of four colored inks on the push-button shaft) I wrote under the *V*, "Dear Valerie,".

Dear Valerie, dear God.

I tore the sheet into the smallest possible lavender bits and watched them flutter into a DisposAll with her Tampax and our watermelon rinds. There was a knock at the back door, tentative enough to be less of a jolt than yesterday's: I closed the Singer files with greater sangfroid, and did not put on my socks.

Out back the heat struck with brutal midday force—Indian Summer, Billy Birdsong would have called it—where a quartet of astronauts (they were that clean-cut and eager-looking) stood among the Sprite and Perrier crates. They might have been a matching set of Ginny's admirers come to pay court, they resembled for all the world a Christian rock group called Forgive and Forget. All four were dressed alike in seersucker and electric-blue ties and carried a Bible each, so they must have been Mormons or Jehovah's Witnesses, but I first thought of them as God's spies. The elder, with greying sideburns, was the one to speak.

"Sir, if you could grant us a single moment of your time, there's a message for you of utmost importance. We stopped by your home previously and had an interesting discussion with Mrs. Gold on that occasion." He had her name written down in his Bible.

"She's at work." I was feeling the heat, and a sense of oppression I felt when the Big Boy family got into their car still picking their teeth.

"Well now that we've talked with your wife and she showed so much interest in our message we wonder if you might want to hear something that may not save your life, but will surely save your soul."

"She tells me everything. I may have already received your message."

"Sir, that may well be but I would appreciate a single moment of your time to elaborate on what we discussed with the Missus." There was nothing Texas in his intonations, which may have been a liability. "On that occasion as I recall we discussed Hebrews 11:16." The man with the grey sideburns opened to a marker in his Bible and began to read: " 'But now they desire a better *country*, that is an heavenly—' "

"You'll have to excuse me, folks." It looked like a long passage from the deep breath the elder took before reading. "I was in the middle of something."

The three younger men closed ranks, and I felt outnumbered and vaguely threatened while the elder went right on reading:

" '—wherefore God is not ashamed to be called their God: for he hath prepared for them a city.' "

What saved me was the arrival of Lawrence Priest, backing a pickup, uninvited, into Ginny's parking slot. I might have been uneasy to see him show up—"For the wicked flee when none pursueth,"—but he was grinning, and got out of his pickup without reaching for the gun rack.

"Now where, sir, in that passage can we examine our own selves?"

Lawrence loped over to our outdoor revival and called out to one of the younger Witnesses: "Je-sus Christ, Wayne—is that you?"

Wayne was the tallest of the four, with an animated Adam's apple: he flushed, and agreed, saying, "Sure is."

"What the fuck happened to your hair?"

"Cut it."

The elder was still trying to discuss Hebrews 11:16 but Lawrence had engaged Wayne in a side discussion of when they worked together as bus drivers on the UT shuttle. Meanwhile a golfer in a motorized cart drove over out of curiosity, it seemed, but he was really trying to recover his golf ball that had rolled under the relentless water-spray of a greens sprinkler.

"Another comfort of those who travel," said the elder, to the golfer now, who appeared to be the only one listening, "is taken from the Book of Ruth, Chapter Two."

While Wayne was passing church literature to Lawrence, I managed to back off.

" 'Why have I found grace in thine eyes, that thou shouldest take knowledge of me, seeing I *am* a stranger?' "

"I'm afraid I was in the middle of something," I said.

Don't be afraid, said the Poet. The trouble was, Lawrence Priest followed me into the trailer.

"Ginny gone?" he asked.

Invariably they sniffed for a trace of Ginny.

"She's at work."

"How she treating you?" He was grinning all over Kingdom Come, but I suspected him of espionage. He was pretending that my shack-up with Ginny was the greatest joke yet, but he could have been looking out for Pilot's interests, or his own.

"She's treating me. Fine."

"Does she tell you you're a good listener?"

"As a matter of fact, I am. A good listener."

"More power to you, Ace."

The grin could stretch no farther without splitting his lip. I thought he meant to pass the church literature on to me, but it was a letter he handed me. Ginny still got mail in care of The Screaming Eagle. She had mail drops all over Austin.

"It's for her ex," said Lawrence.

"She's still married."

"That's right, you told me." I thought he would laugh outright. "And you're a buddy of his, so might as well give it to you, to forward back."

It was the letter I was waiting for.

"Not you, Neal." Ginny sat on the yoga pad of foam rubber saying over and over, "Not you," to reassure me. She was a little high on the hash she had sprinkled on the pizza we were eating. "The Neals in my life I truly bless. It's the other sons of bitches I've had it up to here with, it's the studs I'm talking about."

Her long bare limbs beneath the baby-doll nightie were twisted into the lotus, a Riviera ashtray at the apex of her suggestive angles. I was taking it easy on the hashish, and was casually aroused.

"Not him, either. I look at my husband from a whole new perspective. Now that he's out of my life. And I'm into my own selfhood." High, she was not much altered from her customary state, except for the repetition. "And not you, Neal."

There was a heat wave on, and the air conditioning would only work on high. The walls of the Tradewinds were sweating, and Ginny in her nightie gave an unconscious shiver so I put my chino jacket over her shoulders.

"Not you, Neal, it's the studs I'm talking about. I've had it with the sons of bitches imploring you to do something for them for your own good. Looking out for my best interests with their eyes on my boobs." Her boobs, for the moment, were covered by the draped sleeves of my chino jacket. "And no more motherfucking father figures—not you, Neal, you're an older-type person but nothing like my father that's reverted to the stone age and lives in a cave, you really live in the real world but his mind's down a mine shaft. He keeps saying come before it's too late just so he won't be alone for the apocalypse. So what if we don't have nuclear parity with Russia? All Dad reads is Revelations and *Army Times*, let him go read the Bhagavad Gita for a change or the Kama Sutra to get some perspective." She smiled serenely at the thought of her father reading the Kama Sutra, and flicked ash into the place between her lotus petals. "Neal and me were ten years apart so you wonder about my parents' sex life between when Neal was born and I was. He'd be about your age—my brother, I mean, not Dad—if he hadn't got fragged in Pleiku or somewhere."

She was humming "Over the Rainbow" behind her smoke screen, then went into a lower-keyed reverie, talking more to herself than to me: "What they think and what I am is nobody's business but I sure would like to give Prince someday and the bouncers a piece of my mind. And the studs, *and* the bitches in the dressing room a certain type that says I ball everybody and their brother, who cares what they think? What they can't swallow is me being a totally private person and not the nympho they think. If I do consent to ball a certain individual that's between me and the individual and not the whole dressing room and Prince."

Her words were bitter but came out in little puffs of smoke, mixed with bile: there was saliva at the corners of her mouth. Or she might be hungry again, so I took the remains of our pizza from the microwave.

"Basically I'm more of an animal lover than human, I've had it with men. Not you, Neal, you're different. You're cool. If this rig wasn't so small I'd keep a dog like Dad's only I wouldn't call him Killer. I'll tell you something." Now she was talking to me, directly into my eyes. "Men. I never get off on a man, ever. Don't take it personal, Honeybun, but I just don't. Ever. I never come, no matter what. Men take it personal if they think they didn't push the right buttons so I fake it. My trouble is I'm too conditioned to the phony way men try to turn you on to be turned on. You don't, and I respect you and truly dig you for not turning phony on me, but by now I'm too conditioned to the phony sons of bitches. I think if I ever did actually meet Neal's actual twin on the street I'd literally cream my jeans— but men in general. Don't talk to me about men."

She might have been saying it was politic to let sexual nature take its course—or something. To illustrate the point or having become heated by her own politics she obliterated, between her legs, the half-smoked cigarette and then shook off my jacket and squirmed out of her nightie—without my help, without my asking.

I undressed and took my place beside her on the yoga pad. Naked, together we shared a pizza slice spiced with hash, alternating bites, as intimate as Ginny permitted in the way of foreplay. (Meaning to keep my head, I nibbled at the portions least spiked—would the Poet deplore my timid choice of oregano over hash?) Her breasts were small but carried genuine weight, and she allowed them to be weighed and fondled by my free hand. Thus her nipples were anointed with olive oil from the pizza while she applied baby oil to the dry fissure between dancer's legs. Her nipples, as she warned, remained indifferent to a man's touch.

When the moment seemed appropriate—to Ginny—we tasted the tomato paste on each other's lips and she casually fingered my cock. We buckled into place at her instigation: she swung her legs open, gracefully—all such gestures Ginny performed with grace— and guided me between them. We were lubricated into position in the classic missionary, her ankles locked at the small of my back to keep us there. Before we got into our rhythm, or hers, Ginny flung an arm to the transistor behind her head to turn the music up.

We rocked through a run-through performance that may have been fevered on my part—my perspiring stomach suctioned to her cooler anatomy—but as far as my partner was concerned, the usual dry run. She no longer bothered to pretend to a turn-on, which was honorable of her, or negligent. She had lapsed into her disco trance: her eyes were open wide, as wide as they would go, but from the expression in them she was in touch not with the earth turning but the universe. She had set herself on automatic pilot, the exercise accomplished in less time than it took to eat pizza.

Immediately she was searching for her cigarettes and lighter and experienced a slight tremor (not from ecstasy), so I again put my chino jacket over her shoulders, for I realized she was too high to know how cold she was.

"My next life," she said, "I intend to be in the saddle. Instead of being saddled myself. Marriage. You're just a handmaiden all over again catering to male expectations whether you love the joker or not. Not you, Neal—husbands I mean, and studs. Believe me, I've had it with the male race. As soon as I get this divorce out of the way, I'm going to get me another horse like Rascal."

Now was the time to divulge the great secret that she was free, but she might have brained me with that heavy brass ashtray for not telling her before. Instead, I fixed her a vodka and Sprite.

"I swear I'm going to get out of show business and into something legitimate."

She might go to Southern California, she knew people in Malibu. There was a chance to do hosiery ads with an outfit in L.A., she said, as she stretched one perfect gam at me, her toes fluffing my beard. Or Las Vegas. But she had already been to Vegas, the raw side of show business, and that was for the birds. She might go back to Denver.

"I could finish my M.A. at DU if I wanted one, Denver's got it all over Austin for lifestyle. The climate for one thing, and no roaches. I could switch my major from English to MassCom, or Philosophy. One thing about the U.S.A. you've got every opportunity in the books. If you play your cards right. I could even teach. If he could teach, anybody can."

The important thing to learn from Ginny was how to have it up to here, then so jauntily move out from under. The go-go-go girl did not ask me my plans.

"Nobody in Denver would know if I once danced topless in Austin or not, I dance under another name. If they did and tried to deny me tenure like they did him I could prove it was prejudice. Affirmative Action would just love to get their hands on a case like mine."

Another place she could go was Alaska, if she could get Gas to fix the pistons on her Toyota. (Gas was a heartstruck teenage swain who provided free gas, telling her her smile was her credit card.) She would have to sell the Tradewinds because a Toyota could not haul a trailer that size up the AlCan Highway.

Words of Indian Billy came back to me: beauties and worthies with all the travel potential in the world, fated to stand fast.

"Alaska's no colder than Washington State was and there's twenty guys to every woman."

Mobility in any direction was eminently possible for Ginny: men served her, men eased her way. Monsieur Perrier was a married man with half-interest in a bottling plant who supplied her with Perrier by the case. "He delivers it to the door and has never got a foot inside or as much as a handshake."

An electrical engineer she called Sparks had engineered the clandestine power line running from the Tradewinds to the golf pro's shop, electrical current courtesy of Lake Austin Country Club, and all he ever prevailed upon her to play was an occasional nine holes with him—"Daddy taught me how to play when I was little"—with not a ghost of a chance for a one-to-one plug-in after the game: "Except for his golf game, Sparks comes on too heavy."

A man named Sprite left a crate of that beverage every week, in competition with Monsieur Perrier. Sprite had proposed to her three times. ("Marriage?" was my naive question.) "I told him I was still married to my original husband, but he wouldn't believe me."

Like Andy, Ginny was sustained by left-handed benevolence, and she flourished on the local overflow.

"He tried to talk me into enlisting in NASA—my father, I mean, not my ex—and be the first lady astronaut." High she was, but never uncoordinated: she rolled onto her back with lazy abandon and began doing bicycle pumps in the air. "I laughed in his face." The drunken boat rocked with her olympiad and I removed myself and drink safely out of range of her kicking spree. "My ex said." She was a bit breathless all the same. "There's no depth in outer space." Privates and poets, bouncers and bartenders did their pitiful best to best her while she high-kicked higher than everyman's head. "But he meant." She meant the Poet. "Reading science fiction so much."

The view I had of her moist cleft between the pumping thighs was uninspiring, especially since the liquid essence I had spilled there was spilling into the little thicket of pubic hair, so I turned in the direction of the Walt Disney bookends.

Even Lawrence, badly beaned, was back. He had brought her a gift carton of cigarettes "the same as currency in the Third World" when he brought her mail. No man would leave this little lady in the lurch, only in good hands—a multitude of hands.

When her legs at last returned to earth and I had moved the spilled ashtray elsewhere, she drew me to her and placed my head at the heart, sticky as it was, of her lotus fold. I could feel her heartbeat against my ear, not in the customary place but through her solar plexus. I was imagining a poet's troubled head lying in that place in his time.

In the night, as we slept under the chenille spread (the runaway air-conditioner was still unstrung: turn it off and we would turn to butter) I thought I felt her manicured fingernail scratch and flutter across my buttocks, but in a moment she threw off the thin coverlet and yelped aloud. She was not a screamer. A water roach had crawled in with us, drawn to the smell of postcoital spill. We were suddenly up, lights on, and in an instant I had cornered the creature where it scuttled along the window screen and impaled it on the straw spikes of the same whisk broom we swept up cigarette ashes with.

Back in bed, reheating one another beneath the chenille, she murmured, "You're an officer and a gentleman."

"I never even made third class. In the Navy."

"You're first class," she said. "With me." She was asleep the instant she said it.

I took longer to return to the comfort of slumber. For a long stretch of the early morning hours I was bedeviled by episodes that had only got started and episodes that had not started yet.

What does a Poet in Residence *do?*

I contemplated the endless wheel of becoming and wondered what would become of the freckled kid with mean eyes coming out of Big Boy with his family: would he really become his father in fifteen years or would the Major have his Day before? How long oh Lord would I remain a substitute sibling to this child of impulse, nurtured by her pizzas and pizzazz? (Was she a mystery worth solving at length, or was she simply something else?)

And another unfinished episode: did the couple on *Giveaway* really go for the Big Chance, and if they did did they get the mixing bowls or the Pontiac?

"Don't tell *me* our landscape together was all flats and hollows and empty parkings lots. Remember that cemetery in Salt Lake City and what we did between the tombs? We brought the dead to life. Then we *flew* and we both knew it, over celestial terrain. Even if you don't know it now. Now you're talking bad dreams, you're bitching in the wilderness because *you are alone.*"

It was the time of night I called the Reading Hour, and I was in the middle of my research, savoring the Poet's lyric sarcasms, when the Toyota purred into place early. When the sound of its fine-tuned motor died, I heard voices, two. It was fated to be.

There was barely time to stuff the letters back into their slots before Ginny burst into her mobile home escorting a slim young man with a battered guitar. He was wearing outsize pants that appeared to be gunnysacks sewn together and a denim shirt with the sleeves sliced away at the shoulders. On his shaved head was a dust-colored railroad cap like Andy's.

"It's like the greatest imaginable coincidence of a lifetime." Ginny was as aglow as she could get. "That both you boys made miraculous escapes from intolerable conditions and walked out of places that were putting you down."

His eyes were so deep in their sockets they seemed bruised: the intensity of his stare reminded me of my landlady in New Orleans. He greeted me with a shy but suspicious con's smile, but there was nothing criminal about him I could swear to.

"Neal, I want you to meet Pilot."

He offered a rock-hard hand. As Pilot and I shook hands I needed to ask no more questions. The way Ginny devoured his broken profile informed me fully about the workings of time.

12

I COULD still ponder what might await me at some distance.

There was a flight to Salt Lake City where the Poet's father was buried, and one to Cincinnati where my mother died. But I would not go back to cities of the dead. Ginny's favorite place for starting over was Denver, the Mile-High City—all the more reason not to go there.

The cab driver who drove me to the airport looked nothing like the Poet (how could he? he was black) but voiced a sentiment the Poet might have uttered.

"What Austin needs is not more skyscrapers but a first-class racetrack for us sporting people."

13

PASSENGERS on the New York flight by way of Dallas–Fort Worth wore identical polo shirts with CCAA embroidered on the left breasts instead of alligators. It was a charter flight, or a conspiracy, but I wangled my way aboard.

There were moments during that first lap I thought I must have gone against the gods to fly east instead of west, the crowd so rowdy and out of tune to my mood. I might have traveled to the Great Salt Lake to confer with polygamous visionaries who cultivated fierce beards and abided by the word of an angel. I would never stroll the campus of Pendennis College in Santa Fe where Ginny collected all those recipes and wrote her first poems and her husband was denied tenure. Farther west was Olympia State (Ginny kept a photo of the peninsula extending into Puget Sound: another campus, but pine-clad and green green green—where the Poet took his Ph.D.) but now— seat-belted into place with the frolicking CCAA bound east—I would never explore those western possibilities.

The CC of CCAA was Corpus Christi and I at first assumed the congregation was headed for the Holy Land—but no. They were a sporting crowd as eager and disorderly as a crew of sailors out for fun in a foreign port. The stewardesses could not cope, and at first refused to serve before-dinner drinks. The Athletic Association made paper airplanes of the Emergency Instructions in their seat pockets, and set them flying across the aisles inside the belly of the mother plane. The film was in black and white, and featured blacks, so they threw cocktail peanuts at the movie screen. When the scowling flight captain made an appearance meant to impose a modicum of discipline (a flying Captain Alighieri of the Circle Tour), they sang "Big Boy" at him with insultingly salacious verses of their own.

"What do you think," asked my inebriated seatmate, "about Kansas's chances?"

I sensed the Poet's presence in the empty seat between us, insisting that poets do not follow football.

"I'm afraid I don't follow. Football."

My reply was so hilariously original it was broadcast from one CCAA to another and my seatmate, in honor of my wit, grandly paid for both our vodka-tonics procured from the stewardess's pushcart.

New York City was the Poet's birthplace, and I carried the document that proclaimed the event. (Ginny would never miss so obscure a souvenir as an ex-husband's birth certificate, but she would miss the two hundred and fifty in fifties I lifted from between the pages of her *Stranger in a Strange Land*.) I had entered my true state of marginality, I accepted its implications and its consequences.

It may have been for my marginal sense I chose a nostalgic pile of brownstone to dwell in called the Chelsea Hotel, where the bronze plaque out front commemorated the sojourns of such predecessors as Brendan Behan, Dylan Thomas and Thomas Wolfe. It was that kind of hotel.

The rooms were narrow condemned-cells with high ceilings and antique baths—or mine was. The drains were occupied by resident cockroaches, a pygmy species compared to those Ginny so loathed, and through the pipes the strangled sounds of other rooms resounded: the ghosts of poets and playwrights still suffering private dreads and delirium tremens. My walls were thin enough to broadcast the presence of a tubercular next door. The Poet may have objected to these accommodations, for he appeared nowhere on the premises.

That first overcast afternoon I took a Circle Line boat tour of Manhattan that sailed both the Hudson and East rivers and enjoyed the view of the city known as fabulous from the vicinity of Ellis Island. Unlike the Poet, I returned from my excursion intact.

A set of photographs were issued me by a shady operator off Times Square, a snapshot artist who specialized in I.D. Examining my glossy face under I.D.'s faulty light fixture—an unshaded bulb dangled from torn nerves and cartilage overhead—I hardly knew myself from a Wanted poster in a post office. The Post Office, in fact, was altogether obliging about my application, and accepted both photographs and birth certificate (and twenty-five dollars) as bona fide. I would receive my passport through the mails, in the name of Gold—I was known as Gold at the Chelsea, a sparkling name for my dark purposes.

I had twice attempted a "Dear Valerie" on Hotel Chelsea stationery, and now tried a "Dear Ginny."

"Dear Ginny," pause. "When I was in Austin."

When I was in Austin. Is that, asked the Poet, a song by Tennessee Ernie Ford?

"When I was in Austin."

I would finish the letter later. I would finish the letter after a pastrami sandwich in the Blarney Stone on 23rd. In the men's room of that establishment I was aware that the urine passed through my penis with a sharp and unnatural sting; my shorts were stained with some foul discharge. I had slept with contagion and suffered its aftermath. Damn-oh-damn.

"A lesson I learned early in life, Son, is there's no such thing as a free ride."

Depressed I was, but so fascinated by my putrescence I lingered over it until a patron of the Blarney Stone glanced at me askance, and winked.

It cost me less than fifty of the two hundred fifty I lifted from Ginny to be treated for the clap at the outpatient clinic of St. Vincent's, the hospital where Dylan Thomas died from acute insult to the brain.

Endings: I never wrote past "When I was in Austin," but I was, in two weeks, cured of the clap and received a passport through the mail.

I baffled my way through a nightmare of tunnels, stranger in a strange land, hurtling from station to station in graffiti-painted trains for a final errand, a last plunge underground. The décor inside the cars and out was a chaotic appliqué of names and initials: this was how the insulted and injured signed themselves. Their name was legion, but I abstained. I had taken the precaution of signing myself Gold in the Hotel Chelsea register of guests.

As bearer of bad tidings I would be unwelcome, even abused— but as my father wrote, there's no free ride. At least I would clear the air with the Poet's mother, confide my secret to the one person most concerned. I would render a strict account to the accountant's widow of her son's last days, dissembling only over the word suicide. I would like to have kept myself out of it, anonymous. But there was no free ride.

I successfully changed trains at 14th Street, moving from one moral position to another.

I could hardly announce, Behold, I am your son now. Just render the facts of the matter: a death notice in the statistical terms of a birth certificate. Suicide was the word to forswear.

I emerged from the elaborate labyrinth at Astor Place.

"Hey, Man." Man was the panhandler's name for me. "Got any change you can spare?"

I had only fifties in my pocket, and a five-cent piece given to me by a Seminole on the move. (The panhandler had an open cut on his forehead where Lawrence the bartender bore a similar gash.) I turned my empty jacket pockets inside out to prove the absence of change, and out came the golf ball. The panhandler slapped the ridiculous artifact from my hand, and with a fierce what-the-fuck kicked it into the street. The golf ball bounced and rolled along the gutter pursued by a small girl on a single roller skate, but too late, for the ball rolled down a sewer before dark-skinned Alice could scoop it up. There went my last souvenir—the clap had been cured—to remember Texas by.

I crossed St. Mark's Place referring to a city map and the return address on a letter Miss Pike had passed to me. ("So she wants Out, get *Out*. Divorce is not Fatal and it is not your Shiksa that upsets me as much as your Attitude." The Poet's mother, he informed me, was illiterate—at least in English—and was obliged to employ a commercial scribe to write letters for her. I wondered if the sentiments, like the capital letters, were hers or the ghostwriter's.) The Poet told me he had once seen W.H. Auden, his face like the bottom of an old tennis shoe, pushing a baby stroller full of groceries along St. Mark's Place. There were no baby carriages along that Polish-flavored street, nor any plaque commemorating Auden's passage from the Bowery to Second Avenue.

At Tompkins Square I was swept into the branch library on a tide of excited schoolchildren just released from the local P.S. The building smelled of books and humankind; I inhaled deeply of it, strangely moved. (Yes, my Just Books had been a misbegotten stunt anticipating all the wrong responses to the printed word, a deserved failure.) Here was a citadel of books, a last outpost. Even Mrs. Gold could take profit here: there were shelves of books in Russian as well as in Spanish, Polish and French.

What a civilized assortment and an epicenter of calm (even despite the thunder of kiddies charging up the stairs to the Children's Room)—if anywhere in this world of premiums and printouts *The Selected Poems of I.M. Gold* were to be found, it was here. And, after all, this was his old neighborhood.

At the Reference Desk an intense young woman sat reading *Consumer Report:* a citadel of that, too.

"Are you Irish?"

It was a foolish question, even though the nameplate on the desk said "Mrs. O'Leary."

"No," she said. She put *Consumer Report* into a desk drawer, exchanging her reading glasses for a pair she looked at the world through, then folded her hands in prayer.

"Sorry. I'm going to Ireland. I just thought."

"If it's Mrs. O'Leary you want, she's on her tea break." I suddenly expected Mrs. O'Leary to materialize, looking exactly like Miss Ryan of the Sans Souci—but no. "She's not Irish either. It's her husband's name, and he's English."

"Oh."

I tried to think of something enlightening to say. The woman sat praying for me to go to Ireland, immediately.

"Where is your poetry section?"

"Which poet?"

I started to say Gold, but it was like giving something away to reveal my rebirth name, so I said, "Auden."

She unfolded her hands long enough to point in the direction of the 800s, saying, "He's English," meaning Auden, in the English section.

At Auden's slot I idly fingered *The Age of Anxiety* waiting for the reference librarian to change her glasses and sink back into *Consumer Report.* A shelf away I found two copies of I.M. Gold's *Selected Poems.* Why two? I wondered. But of course this was his old neighborhood.

Perhaps I just wanted to see if the Poet's picture appeared on the dust jacket, but there were only quotes and blurbs—Robert Lowell's, among them—and no photograph to distinguish Gold from fool's Gold.

I was standing close enough to the checkout desk to hear one clerk say to another: "I've had it with computer dates. I answered an ad in *New York Review of Books* that said a DJM, 5′ 11″ looking for bright swinging stable SJF under thirty, send photo, and I did, and he didn't even answer."

For several idle moments I lingered under the nineteenth-century dome donated by Astors and Mellons contemplating the extraordinary racial mix of readers. I felt a sense of safety and daring at the same time. Why this book, this place, this time? I could not put the book back.

At the charge desk the two girls, black and white, continued trading courtship sagas.

"Remember that Egyptian guy with all the overdues I let him get away with? I didn't charge him any fines. Now, well, I'm dating him."

"Is he straight? I worked at a branch in the Village and I swear the only straight that came in the place the whole time was a delivery boy from Gristede's."

This was New York. In the Reference Room a scattering of winos dozed and dried out over volumes from the *Encyclopaedia Britannica*. And I had not even ventured into the city's upper reaches past Times Square.

A reader with a face like a potato under her babushka waited patiently to check out a novel by Joseph Conrad, in Polish, translated from the English. The black and white clerks seemed not to notice she was there.

Of late I lived by my father's twisted code: I now considered myself guiltless for walking away with one of the two mint copies of verse by I.M. Gold, because there were two. The sentry at the Reference Desk was otherwise engaged, being chattily relieved by the real Mrs. O'Leary, who appeared to be Italian. With the reckless awareness I may have been watched, I waded through the incoming tide of schoolchildren on the blind side of the charge desk. In a moment I was safely outside, possessed of my contraband volume of verse.

The Poet's mother had come home to the Lower East Side of New York after her husband's death in Salt Lake City—her domicile was the original address on the Poet's birth certificate, only three blocks from Tompkins Square. It was a derelict neighborhood of mostly vacant tenements exhaling the stale immigrant breath of another century. Originally Ukranian and Jewish, the mix was now Puerto Rican and Black, and this population too was dropping away: the city was emptied of humankind as I traveled east.

This was true marginal country—and I should have felt at home—but a strange land where a stranger might end up as broken and abused as the telephone booth I passed, beaten to death, castrated (a torn wire dangled where the receiver had been ripped out), evidence that you did not call out from no-man's-land for help.

On a site destined for excavation a sinister dwelling huddled between a building just leveled and another with windows streaked by white crosses, like bandaged eyes, the first stage of imminent demolition. The sealed front door of the building to be torn down still bore a Fallout Shelter notice.

Out of the window of this one intact tenement a dark arm—male or female, I could not distinguish—protruded actively: the mysterious hand threw chicken entrails to a tribe of fierce interbred cats stalking through the splintered beams and burnt black skeletons of last year's Christmas trees poking up through the rubble next door. I waited at a distance through this savage ritual. When the last string of intestines hit the gutter and the jungle cats retreated to battle over their slippery largesse, I began a reconnaissance of the building. I ventured across the street to pass through a miasma of cat into the pillaged foyer of pried-open mailboxes.

With not the least expectation that the buzzer system worked I nevertheless pressed the button opposite the names in pencil: Gold-WILLERT. Immediately a window shot open overhead.

"What's that? Who down there?"

Hoping not to be struck in the face by chicken slime, I stepped outside the foyer to look up. I encountered a scowling black face four stories above. A little boy, beside his angry mother, was jubilant to see a human face on the abandoned sidewalk.

"I'm looking for Mrs. Sophie Gold."

"Ain't here."

"When will she be back?"

"She won't be back, she moved. I got the place now. What is this?"

The little boy balanced a bottle of sudsy water on the sill and dipped a wire lorgnette into the mix to make airy bubbles streaming through the upper atmosphere.

"Moved? Where to?"

"What're you, a cop or something?"

"I'm a friend. I knew her son."

"She went to Florida."

"Where in Florida?"

"Who knows? Never knew the lady. Miami, someplace. People move, they move."

I was reluctant to let it end there. The black face still scowled down at me.

"I wonder. Does she know? Her son is dead."

"How'm I supposed to know? Never knew the lady."

The window slammed down like a shot, cutting off the source of bubbles, the last of which drifted mournfully in the direction of the East River, as if mother and son had gone under, the bubbles a last trace of their surfacing.

Poet's Corner

1

ON THE FLIGHT from New York to London I sat next to a nervous grandmother with a grandson's photograph around her neck like a holy relic. She eyed my beard fearfully.

"You don't smoke do you?"

"I gave up smoking," I said, aware of who I was. My old self would have said, No I don't.

"I'm allergic," she said. "Excuse me for saying it but you look like the kind of person that smokes."

"This is a nonsmoking section." With a gesture of my hand to the neighboring seats I assured the grandmother we were all non-smokers here.

"You never know," she said. Then a new worry occurred to her: "You're not a hijacker, are you?"

"No I'm not."

My old self showed her how to lower the back of her seat, as I might have done with a patient at the Sans Souci, and she uneasily assumed that position. But she was up again with a bounce reciting previous air tragedies she had seen on TV: the plane that skidded into the Potomac, the midair collision over the Canaries.

My reassurances came to naught when she saw I was ordering vodka from the stewardess. She nervously fingered the photograph and was unhappy in flight.

"Say," she remembered suddenly, "did you hear about that casket that fell out of an airplane onto somebody's greenhouse?"

* * *

"Would debarking passengers who have had any contact with poetry please report to Immigration at the air terminal building."

Poetry? The air pressure had gone to my hearing or they were on to me already.

Like those subway passengers in New York, in our collective guilt or fear of contagion we avoided one another's eyes. Who among us had come into contact with poetry? As we filed forth onto the tarmac, into the soft black rain of Aldergrove, I shoved the suspect collection of poems inside my jacket.

Everything else that represented my newly invented life had been taken from me at Heathrow-London before I was allowed to board the shuttle flight to Belfast. The ancient Gladstone bag I had found at the Salvation Army outpost in lower Manhattan, a portable Remington typewriter I bought myself in London (a prop, a cover story), the ditty bag with borrowed (now useless) razor, and the attaché case with my father's letters—all had been confiscated by Security, sealed into separate plastic bags and dispatched to the belly of the plane by conveyor belt.

During the intimate body search at Heathrow the *Selected Poems* and an Indian nickel had been discovered on my person, but briskly returned to me. I could carry one book, but one only, aboard the aircraft—after the volume was flipped open and dangled by its spine for whatever piece of armament might fall out. *Those poems you so cavalierly manhandled.* The bully boy of an officer showed no evidence of humor, so this was not the occasion to play Oscar Wilde and declare I had only my genius to declare.

Anyway, I was already suspect because of the American coin. What was a Yank doing on a night flight to Belfast with a £ key on his typewriter and a five-cent piece in his pocket?

At Aldergrove a woman in the crowd held aloft a notice scrawled in her own lipstick: *Prof.* GOLD. The D in GOLD had run off the edge of the cardboard. I took a breath, set my jaw and went straight to her.

"Professor?"

"Gold," rolled off my tongue.

"Singh," she sang and revealed her specialty: "Ulster dialects."

She placed a dark hand in mine. Despite the Western tailored suit in wool, and the study of dialects, her scent was redolent of the East. The lacquer on her fingernails perfectly matched the carmine lipstick. A foreign warmth in this cold place: the white teeth and innocent whites of her eyes in the dark setting of her face made me immediately aware—how had I got to this, so soon, in my daring?—of an erotic possibility, white on black.

There was an element of surprise in the air, but she allowed only her great puzzled eyes to show it. I swam in those liquid eyes, and at the same time wondered if she carried a photograph in her handbag. After the first hesitant question—"Professor?"—she had covered with a jeweled smile, I knew all was well, I was in.

When I mentioned the bizarre announcement on the plane, she said, "The stewardess must surely have meant poultry." She spelled the word poultry for me in her crisp English, then announced, "I've read your poems."

For a moment I saw the Poet lounging under a warning notice not to leave luggage unattended. Did she read the dirty ones? he was wondering. She made no further literary comment but that, while her Eastern eyes tried to bore into the skull of the man she assumed had written the poems.

I lowered my head in modesty.

To break the spell, she appropriated my American dollars and carried them to the Currency Exchange. I studied her perfect legs as she walked away, and went a bit dizzy from speculation. Is this the occasion, is she the one? I turned back to where the Poet had been standing, but that unreliable shade had faded, and in his place a middle-aged woman I had seen on the plane (who was definitely not the one) was assembling an incredible inventory of baggage, each one stickered with a maple-leaf logo of Canada.

The exotic Dr. Singh returned with a packet of sterling notes. I had expected to see the multicolored portrait of the Queen on them, but they were the bland local currency issued by Ulster Bank Limited.

As she drew me to the carrousel I could indulge the thought of her dark hand in mine under far less formal circumstances. I savored the suggestion of her hips beneath the woolen skirt and fell under the sway of that sway. I tried to imagine the effect of a visiting American, not so inconsequential at that—a poet, one that glittered like gold—placed in her care. Did she ever wear native dress in this rude climate? I imagined how she would slink beside me in a sari, if she chose to slink beside me.

They cared about titles over here, and my title bore a certain cachet. Distinguished Poet in Residence—it said so in a letter from a man named Bannister. My conniving extended to whatever treasure this title might attract. Then my poor bags came trundling around the carrousel horseshoe wrapped in their plastic shroud-pacs.

She assessed my meager dowry and commented: "You must buy a brolly straight off." A brolly was an umbrella.

Of course. I intended to place myself in her dark capable hands, be embraced by her and comforted. The sight of my belongings had unnerved me. I needed to be restored to the state of confidence I was in when winked at by a fat black scavenger in a rusted truck.

The barricaded airport might have been designed by an architect of penitentiaries. Barbed wire was strung along the outer limits of the parking lot, a persistent rain blew through the brutal searchlights. Farther along this moonscape in the beam of arc lights I saw what must have been control towers manned by machine gunners.

Her car was a Mini, to suit her demure and miniature self. We folded ourselves into her toy and adjusted our separate centers of gravity. It was like being safely packed inside an egg. Close as convention allowed, I was enveloped in her aura and attached to her hip. Her exotic scent was all the more overpowering in our confinement, her bared knees occupied my thoughts. We set off with a jerk of misapplied gears and a musical "Sorry."

She drove on the wrong side of the road until I realized the left was the right side here. Her windshield wipers went on being frantic, but I at last relaxed. In the heart of the hostile black void I could make out the ghostly shapes of sheep, where sheep may safely graze, behind barbed wire. Dr. Singh was giving me charming instruction in the pronunciation of the word eight.

"Pronounced h'eight, the person is probably Catholic."

"Hate?"

"No, h'eight. H'it is the Protestant way of saying eight. Or a variation that sounds more like aight."

"They both sound like hate."

"But not at all." Her heart would verily break to make me understand. "You don't hear the difference?"

"The hate of one sounds like the hate of the other. To me."

"It's the aspiration of the letter *h*." Little she knew of my own aspirations. "*H'eight*. Or as the Protestants say, h'it. The closest a Protestant comes to the Catholic h'eight is aight."

Ulster dialects were her world and she wanted more than anything in that world to instruct me properly. Her perseverance was endearing, I could have kissed her for it. But not yet. The car was brought to a stop at a roadblock.

Dr. Singh made her way warily over the corrugated treads to the metal gate where a young soldier with a rifle awaited us. The soldier thrust his cocky wet beret into her window, and she showed him some papers from the glove compartment. I was obliged to produce my passport. The soldier touched fingers to his eyebrow in a slack salute and allowed the barricade gate to be raised. As good as Gold, I had been accepted: the salute was my welcome to Northern Ireland.

2

WE ENTERED the city alongside a river she named the Lagan past the shadows of cranes and warehouses, the Queen's Bridge, then the Royal Courts of Justice and finally past the Queen herself guarding the floodlit City Hall, Victoria, formidable in stone but deceptively thin. A convoy of armored Army trucks slowed us at Donegall Square and a patrol of foot soldiers surrounded the Royal Courts. My fear of being shot by a sniper—or exposed as a counterfeit—was eventually dispelled by my beautiful chauffeur's complete aplomb and dispassionate lecture.

"People in Belfast have an ear for accents, especially in the ghettos."

"Is this a ghetto?" I asked, for we had left City Hall behind and the streets had turned mean, though too dark to read the graffiti.

"This," she said, "is City Centre."

O-apostrophe was generally a Catholic surname. From the first word out of a stranger's mouth—stranger to that ghetto, that is—he was known for what school he had attended, what church, what part of the city he was from. O'whatever was mostly Catholic and Mc's Protestant, but not always.

"Micks?"

"M-c. Like McDonnell and McDonald of Scots origin."

I was not as dense as I pretended, or as interested, but wanted to keep the reassuring chat alive. She had a passion for explaining and I was delighted to play dumb. All down Great Victoria Street she differentiated for me the Conleys with single consonants from the Connellys with two *l*'s and two *n*'s and the Connallys with an *a*. As she went on about the significance of names I felt warm and secure and removed from my swindle.

"Dunne with an *e* is Catholic, without, Protestant—but not always."

How could I keep from falling in love with her?

When we passed the brooding outbuildings of the King's University she made the cryptic announcement that we were expected at the belly.

The Belly she referred to was the Bellingham Park Hotel. There we stood in a downpour while a security guard frisked me for explosive devices. The volume of poems was still inside my khaki jacket. When the guard enbraced my waistline and ran his hands along the insides of my thighs, I naturally wondered how they went about searching the women. He merely glanced into Dr. Singh's handbag, but even that brisk invasion of privacy was one I would like to have performed myself, to see if she might be carrying a poet's photograph, or some biographical scrap about Gold, in there.

The glassed-in foyer could be observed from the front desk: we lingered in that locked passageway until a desk clerk was convinced we could be safely buzzer-released into the lobby. Dr. Singh collected my room key and—oh promising omen—kept it in her hand. The aged hall porter attended to my embarrassment of luggage, first stripping the shabby collection of its plastic epidermis provided by BA.

Originally I was to have been installed in the Staff Common Room on the university campus, but there had lately been a bomb threat against the Common Room, so my reservation had been transferred to this secure hostel. Now. Would she hand me the key to my exile in solitary or accompany me to the very door and perhaps beyond? The moment of truth was postponed: she kept the key and warmed my heart with the offer of a drink.

Then she added, "The poets are waiting to meet you."

"Poets. What poets?"

"The Ulster poets."

Was I supposed to know them? I thought I was the poet here. My expression must have collapsed as thoroughly as my hopes, and I feared she would take offense. But talking to poets—so soon. What if someone asked are-you-Gold?

"Are you cold?"

"Not really. Someone just walked on my grave."

"Is that an Americanism?" She collected such expressions. "Here we say a goose has."

"Has what?"

"Has walked on one's grave. You're not too fagged?" Fagged meant tired and fags were cigarettes here.

"Not really." I had learned to say not-really in London.

"They are keen to meet you."

I had also learned to say by-all-means when I meant the opposite, so I said, "By all means."

Her enticing hips moved ahead of me, and I concentrated on that sensual essential as I was drawn into a strangely noisesome but soundproof lounge beyond the lobby. Remember the title, remember the cachet. I would be reserved with the poets and play to Dr. Singh, which is surely the way the Poet would have played it. En route I managed to squirm out of my wet jacket with the *Selected Poems* still enveloped in its folds.

The beige windowless padded cell was so much like the Dayroom at the Sans Souci I looked for the television set—and there was one, but not the same model. Also, an open log fire crackled in a spacious grate where the games closet would have been. The flames reflected in the faces of those assembled to welcome me to Belfast. They were burnished faces for the most part, with expectant eyebrows: were Irish faces scarlet by nature or by drink? Or they may have been embarrassed to meet a water-soaked Yank and have to host another poet, an imposter at that.

To my great relief there was a tendency here to smile through the awkwardness, or make a joke of it.

"Somebody b'god get Gold a drink."

The poets looked no more like poets than I did. Not even the Poet looked like a poet, unless Gandhi looked like a poet. Anyway, what did a poet look like?

Pairs of low round tables were pulled together in figure eights laden with sturdy pint glasses of dark ale and delicate sherry glasses of white wine.

"Gold b'god should be given a drink."

"The man hasn't had his hand shook. He hasn't sat down yet."

Through the cigarette fumes and across the debris of drink we extended our hands as Dr. Singh presented her damp Yank to the smiles and eyebrows. Several of the younger poets, consigned to students' tables, stood formally to receive my hand, shyly, but with frank blank stares and a touch of awe, as they might have received a monsignor. Without a hope of tagging the parade of names to a circle of faces, I concentrated on large and small hands. I avoided the eyes altogether. I made quick takes of a few passing faces, especially the women—I thought the women might be more indulgent than the men and easily won over. Or did I mean duped?

The names Dr. Singh had trained me in were there: Dunn—with or without an *e* I had no way of knowing—and a Mac- or a McDonald along with a Donald, given name, or Ronald, from Donegal. I would never have known Dr. McDonald from Donald O'Donegal except that McDonald had a bristling military mustache and spoke an incomprehensible Scots while O'Donegal carried an Irish harp case with his poems in it, and had no mustache. At one of the students' tables was McDonald's son Donalbain from *Macbeth* and at the next table a cast of Lords, Gentlemen, Officers, Soldiers, Murderers, Attendants and Messengers from the same play.

A red-bearded Michael, or McMichael, gently asked, "What will you have, Professor?"

"He'll have a drink," said a drunk, "for the love o'god."

I got through the last of the hands and names and made a mental note about wrists. Hands—no matter what the size or force, male or female—appeared to be attached to the same wrist, the universal poet's wrist. During the round of pallid handshakes I determined that the wrist was not limp, certainly not limp—a true poet had taught this poet that much. My own wrist was as thin and weak as any here—a promising sign?—but my premature theory of poets and wrists collapsed with the knowledge that many of those here were members of the English Department, critics not poets.

I was placed at the center table between two of the women, poets or critics or both, merry Mary of English and Deirdre O'Dear or O'Dare, the latter something of a dumpling, the former with features as sharp as blade. How wise and considerate of the Committee to dispatch their glamorous Indian princess to meet me at Aldergrove instead of married Mary (her husband was Rupert Bannister, of the Arts Council correspondence) or plumpish stumpy Deirdre, whose resemblance to Cookie of the Sans Souci was unearthly and disturbing.

Dr. Singh sat opposite me, preoccupied and out of touch. Someone asked her, "What does he drink?"

To survive here, it occurred to me, I need only drink with them.

"Whatever," I said uncertainly.

"A whatever-and-water," a wag said. They were not above putting me down but I trusted they would not put me out.

"Get the man b'god a whiskey and water."

I sat not in the place of honor (that would have been, as far as I was concerned, beside Dr. Singh) but two places away, for a place was left empty, in memoriam, for the Old Poet, my predecessor, who had dropped dead strolling through the rose trellises in the Botanic Gardens six months ago.

When I dared take a sidelong assessment of faces I could find no hint of suspicion or trace of outrage. Only a polite puzzlement, perhaps, in certain eyes as they tried to place a few of the mug shots of poets they had considered for this post. But all in all the gathering seemed glad enough to have me. I was hostage to their need for a poet-passenger to deplane in Ulster's alien territory.

"And with ice," said a bard with a bird's chirp. He had been to America—he showed a Massachusetts driver's licence to prove it—where one and all, he declared, took ice in their drinks.

"Not ice," said Deirdre with a shudder. "Can you not see the poor man is chilled to the bone." Her way of saying man and bone came very close to rhyme.

"A hot Powers wouldn't hurt him any," proposed Mary.

"A hot Powers wouldn't hurt anybody."

A man with long wet mustaches attached to his sideburns asked me if I knew John Powers or Paddy? Jameson's or Bushmills? But these were just names without faces.

"A hot Bush would put him right."

"Get the man b'god a Bush and be done with it."

"Indeed," said Deirdre, "a Bush. A wee Bush will put him right."

"Not so wee as all that," said the wag. "Everything's bigger in the States."

"And a lager on the side," said the bard from Massachusetts. In America one and all drank a chaser.

Dr. Singh gently translated into Cambridge English: "They are proposing a Bushmills whiskey with a lager chaser."

"Lovely," said I addressing her rather than the question. Lovely was the term I learned in London pubs, all the barmaids used it.

Dr. Singh would have a white wine. O'Donegal left his harp case of poems behind and went off with a wet tray to fetch a fresh round.

"He's a lovely man," said Mary, and somebody said, "With the women."

The talk was about O'Donegal the instant he was out of earshot.

"Don't be telling that about him."

"He's a lovely voice."

The talk was about O'Donegal's wicked ways with women, but not in so many words. The word bounced back to me when Dr. Singh asked if I sang.

"Afraid not."

There was truly nothing to fear but fear itself this night so fearful in its anticipation.

I gathered that O'Donegal had got a girl with child in Donegal and not married her.

"Shush, enough of that."

Bedchamber Music was the shameless name of his poems about her. He sang from the poems accompanied by his dulcimer.

"Off-key," said the wag, "off-color."

"Enough of that now."

"No poetry," said Mary. "Remember, we said no poetry."

"With the poor man just off the plane," said Deirdre.

Arts Council politely asked, "What do you think of our emerald isle?"

"Man just got here for the love o'god."

"Lovely." I tried to remember some evidence of loveliness as I bathed my gaze in Dr. Singh—but she was foreign to this isle, as I was. "There were sheep," I said. "Grazing. The other side of the barbed wire."

"That was Provos," said the wag, "cleverly disguised as sheep."

"No politics," whispered McMichael.

"There's a nice metaphor there," said Ian or Liam, a student poet.

"Lovely," said Mary.

"What's metaphoric about Provos?"

"Sheep, I mean," said Liam. "And barbed wire."

"No poetry please, we're Irish."

"Some of us."

"No politics," said McMichael, this time darkly.

The man with the Massachusetts driver's license was telling about '66 when he was burnt out in Belfast—and was himself burnt out as a poet—he fled to Dedham where they executed those anarchist fellows and he had a wee nervous breakdown at Massachusetts General—and was himself electrocuted. The Americans offered thirty-six shock treatments all in a row and asked not a penny's recompense. For he was indigent and a poet.

"Dunn writes confessional verse," explained the lawyer-poet Bannister.

"Could have had your thirty-six at Purdysburg, and no charge either."

"Och there's always a charge to shock treatment."

"An electrical one."

"But the Americans," chirped Dunn. "Oh, the Americans." He was all sentiment and nostalgia for the States. "In America they do it up brown. And there there's no National Health."

I did not know if I was being put down or set up, but the drinks had come.

"Let up, let up," said Bannister the barrister, his beer mug a gavel. "Man hasn't yet tasted the water of life."

My drink was a handsome shot of amber (no ice) in a stemmed glass, then a half-pint of lager beside it, to quench the fire of the first.

Dr. McDonald said something unintelligible and Arts Council translated, his pint aloft: "To our right honorable guest."

"Hear, hear!"

Glasses went up and I wondered if I was being put down.

"Our Poet in Residence, long may he reside."

"*Distinguished* Poet in Residence," Bannister amended.

The humor here was deceptive, if I was being put down. Impossible to assess the mockery of their remarks, all was said in dead earnest and never a smile as a giveaway.

"Hear, hear!"

"*Slíante.*"

"*Slíante.*"

"Health."

"Cheers," said Dr. Singh, tilting her glass in my direction but not close enough to meet the Bush I tilted toward her.

Arts Council had wet the tips of his mustaches in Guinness, and continued his citation.

"Here's a man comes to us in pristine innocence. Not knowing one side from the other, Catholic from Protestant—"

"Sheep from Provos."

"—think of the great good fortune *not to know.*"

Nor to know, they in their pristine innocence, a fabricated poet from the real thing.

"Hear, hear."

"Nobody to ask the man 'who are you?' or to bloody well care."

"—a man, a poet—a *distinguished* poet—comes to our province—"

"Country!"

"—under no cloud, no cloud such as we've known."

"And squat beneath in squalor."

"Let up, let up," cried the lawyer-poet calling the company to order.

Although Arts Council had more to say on the subject of my innocence and good fortune, it was evident to all that he was incautiously stoned and might say damaging things—or rile O'Reilly the wag into saying them. To cover, the conversation broke into separate clusters of discussion, small talk about bicycle thefts and the cost of coffee and crew racing on the Lagan: nothing more controversial than a comparison of the freshness of kidneys at two competing butchers on the Stranmillis Road. October had turned warm, Mary observed, and a hot time, O'Reilly added, at the Divis Flats—but McMichael shushed him.

The Don Juan of Donegal sat the other side of Dr. Singh, but for all his reputation shrank from her and conversed with Deirdre. I counted on this as a sign he had not scored or sung with Dr. Singh. I sat warming to the fire, and drink, thinking what I might say or sing to warm her to me.

But Dr. Singh was singularly attentive to the clock above the fireplace with *Guinness Is Good for You* written across its face. She was out of touch, the other side of a curtain, cut off. With nothing more to teach me, she was lost to me. Her concentration on the clock set me to winding my wristwatch.

I was still winding, and staring into the emptiness of the Old Poet's memorial chair, when the oddly smiling Liam came between me and my ghosts and said, "I'm away, sir." Then he headed unsteadily for the gentlemen's.

When he had gone, a lecturer in English categorized Liam for me: "First Year Honors."

"Only nineteen," sighed Dr. Singh. "He'll want to talk with you."

"And talk," said O'Reilly, "and talk."

Dr. Singh gave the wag a look. But I was prepared to listen, and listen.

"Writes poetry," the lecturer with a hyphenated name warned me. He was English.

(The Irish were mostly English in the King's English Department.)

"Shake a tree in Belfast and six poets will fall out."

"Or a policeman," said the wag.

"It's a disease here," said someone, not a poet.

"Only nineteen," said Mary, back to Liam. "And drinks."

"Like a poet, like a sponge."

"Och he is a poet, and a sponge."

Dr. Singh came sharply to Liam's defense with, "Enough of that." It occurred to me that anyone who left a gathering, however convivial, was subject to trenchant review.

"And where," asked Arts Council abruptly, "might your wife be?"

All wrist movement ceased, I stopped winding my watch. I experienced a destabilizing flutter of pulse.

"Some time ago." I hesitated over whose wife I should refer to. "My wife and I." Then, in the interest of truth, and for Dr. Singh's benefit, I offered the Americanism: "My wife and I split."

Deirdre tilted her head to one side in sympathy and Mary to the other side in surprise. The students were commenting among themselves in the soft shushing sounds, all consonants, I took to be Irish. Dr. Singh was apparently unmoved.

It was not the politic time to excuse myself, but I asked directions from McMichael and learned the word loo from Dunn. Now of course I would be discussed and the gathering could decide my fate.

Music had started up in an adjoining lounge as I passed through. A rhythmic air, both plaintive and gay, reminded me of the square-dance tapes Miss Ryan used to play in Recreational Therapy. A woman fiddler was playing it while her partner was assembling parts of a flute out of an attaché case, like a plumber putting together sections of pipe. Above the music I could hear my name, the Poet's, bandied about, handed round for comment.

Arts Council was saying to Bannister, "I thought you said your man would be black."

3

"Your man would be back," was maybe what he said, not black, but if they were so far off base as to think the Poet was supposed to be black then I was in like Flynn. (So that was why they sent Dr. Singh to meet me: dusky Dr. Singh, only coffee-colored but as black as they had at hand.)

I had wanted to be alone in the loo to collect myself and consider strategies, how to approach being their poet, how to approach Dr. Singh, but the young crooked-smiling poet with hair as long as Dr. Singh's was there smiling crookedly into a urinal talking to himself, one supporting hand against the tiles and the other dreamily shaking his pizzle. The half-smile had become a full grin when I entered, a Lawrence Priest grin. He roused himself to a second introduction, Liam Sweeney, with cock adangle and hand outstretched.

I would have to learn the protocol of touch after failing in the theory of wrist. At his insistence I shook with him whose same hand had shaken a penis but I shrank from opening my own fly while he was turned to me all grin and bright-eyed and unbuttoned.

Music from the outer lounge drifted in to us through the ventilator, and a drunken voice called out from a toilet booth:

"Is that your Yank, Liam? These Yanks are all wankers, so tell him to fuck all."

"Fuck all yourself," said Liam merrily. He tried to stuff his cock back into his pants, but failed, so left it hanging loose airing in the foul air.

"Say a poem to him, Liam. Here's your chance. Recite him your bloody poem."

"Fuck off," called out Liam with dazed good nature. He gave the equivalent of a shrug, then leaned with both hands against the tiles as if under arrest and being searched.

I could see where Liam had vomited a vile spaghettilike substance into the urinal trough. The setting, the harangue from the stall, the smell—even the sad and jaunty music rattling through the ventilator—put me off my pressing intention. I was unable to relieve myself.

"All Yanks are wankers and poets the worst."

"Who's there?" I asked, meaning who was in the toilet booth.

"Call me Liam," said the voice.

"That's him," agreed Liam. "A poet, too."

"And shadow. I'm his bloody doppelganger, poet and prophet, the shadow in the stall."

"That he is," said Liam. "He tells us. What's on."

"Ask him," asked the Shadow, "What his I.M. stands for."

"What I.M.?" I answered.

"Your name," said Liam, then he answered the Shadow, "Stands for I Am."

"So am I," said the Shadow in the Stall. "Call me Liam."

"Liam's his name. Too. True. Dogs me every footstep. Mugs take him for me. Put out of pubs. On account of him. I'm barred for life from the Four-in-Hand."

"Wouldn't let the likes of you through the door of the Four-in-Hand. That's my pub. That's a Prod pub, you idjit. He means the Egg, on Eglantine."

"Barred for life," said Liam bitterly. "On account of him. Me bloody doppelganger."

"Is the Yank black, Liam? They said he was going to be black. Och, but he's white I can see through a crack in the door. And they dearly wanted black or at least a red Indian as a relief from the monotonous white poets we're up to here with already. Didn't I say he'd turn up white? The Shadow knows. All of you swore his takeoff from Blake about being black and bereav'd of light meant he was a literal black, but not the Shadow. I told you he'd turn up white, didn't I, Liam? Did I not, now?"

"That," said Liam, "you did."

"Say a poem to him, Liam. Liam rewrites the poets' poems for them, somewhat altered, under the influence. Do your Blake for him, Liam. Do your Yeats."

"Fuck off," said Liam. Then, on reflection or by reflex, Liam began to recite. He leaned over the urinal and recited to the regurgitated slime of spaghetti, his words so slurred there was no hope that I could follow.

"That's his poem," said the Shadow, "about your casket what falls off an airplane and crashes into the Palm Court in the Botanic Gardens, symbolic like. That truly happened, did it not, Liam?"

"Fuck off," Liam called out modestly, struggling to remain upright while at the same time trying to force a hand into the pocket of his jeans. "This is bloody," he said. "Awful to ask."

"Bloody awful is right," said the Shadow, "but ask he will."

I kept expecting the Shadow in the Stall to make an appearance, but nothing stirred from behind the booth door. The disembodied voice could have been a ventriloquist's trick, one Liam imitating the other, an echo shifting from shadow to substance.

"Bloody awful to ask but."

"But ask away," the Shadow advised him, and to me he sang out, "Wants you to know how piss-poor us pissed poets who pissed here are."

The Shadow spoke without the flourish of a flush or any other accompaniment. Nor were his feet visible below the stall door. My father in his letters had warned me never to sit directly on a public toilet seat but to stand and squat on the toilet-bowl rim to avoid the risk of venereal infection. Like my father, the Shadow may have been squatting there all along.

Liam managed to pull out the lining of his pocket to show me the pocket was empty. In response to this telling gesture I brought forth a clutch of fresh Ulster banknotes from my billfold, perfumed by Dr. Singh's original touch. Liam sobered on the instant. His eyes became bright and his smile heartfelt as he plucked two five-pound notes out of the lot as lightly as Dr. Singh had first taken charge of my American dollars.

The Shadow, invisible still, knew all.

"Got a bird he wants to buy a bottle for before the Off-Licence shuts."

A barmaid lowering the grille to the service bar was calling out: "Drink up, gentlemen, ladies, Time, please." She was pointedly ignored. The music played on with accelerated gaiety and the drinkers drank at deliberate leisure. Then the barmaid doused the log fire with a pitcher of melted ice cubes, and as the logs spit and hissed at her, she cried out, "Time, please."

Besides the missing place honoring the Old Poet, another place was empty too—Dr. Singh was missing. I was bereaved of light.

Sad fat Deirdre in her uncanny way was aware of my bereavement.

"Sarojinni is ringing up," she said.

Sarojinni Singh. It had taken me all this time to acquire her full and musical name.

"Ringing from your room," explained Bannister the barrister. "Not to worry. Hotel charges are reimbursed by the university."

"By Arts Council," said Arts Council, "as a matter of fact."

Bannister amended his assurances: "The English Department lays claim to you as our poet but Arts Council does as a matter of fact pay."

"Ringing her husband," said Deirdre, ruining my night.

Where was the ring if she was married?—or maybe they didn't wear rings in India and made do with those red dots on the forehead. Then where was the red dot?

"Wife," said Dunn or Dunne, "never rings me."

Dunn, explained Mary, was not married.

As if to compensate for my loss of light, Deirdre had bought me a large double whiskey at Last Call. Last Call was the equivalent of Lights Out at the Sans Souci. How many whiskeys was that since the two vodkas at Heathrow to fortify me for the ordeal and a miniature Johnny Walker in the men's room at Aldergrove? Whiskey said Deirdre was from the Irish *uisgebeatha* which meant water-of-life but hardly made up for the loss of light. It took another pitcher of ice water to obliterate the last spark of the log fire with the barmaid calling Time. That would be four whiskeys and two lagers if this double counted for two. Women here bought the drinks as well as men. Why hadn't Sarojinni bought me a drink instead of having a husband to ring, and no ring?

"Husband?" I asked.

Somebody in English said, "Dr. Singh."

"I thought she was Dr. Singh."

"So she is," said McMichael, a thought dawning in his red eyes. "She is at that. Never thought of her that way but Saro is Dr. Singh as well. We call her Saro in the department. So might you, actually, for you are, you see, attached, in a way, to English at King's."

"Under auspices," said Arts Council, "of Arts Council."

Attached in a way to Saro but not the attachment I aspired to. Saro was alone in my room attached only to a telephone. Like Valerie used to be—but I was the one who called, the husband. Did Dr. Singh the husband assure his wife all was well when she swallowed her pills and ate meat loaf instead of Captain Crunch?

"Time, gentlemen, ladies, please." The fire died its frigid death and Lights were almost Out. The man with the Massachusetts driver's license studied his stout as if the secret of the universe lurked in the dark soupy remains. The Irish students in English were discussing how hard to fry a fried egg sandwich and why the new university of Ulster was built at Coleraine instead of Derry. "Drink up now if you please."

O'Donegal had a bottle hid in his harp case for that dreadful time after Time.

"A rare pairing," said Mary, "I always thought they were both."

A man called Conley or Connelly asked, "Both what?"

"Both Hindu. Or both Pakistani, but Rupert says they're mixed."

"Like Ulster."

"No politics, please."

"That's Hindu and Pakistanis," said a student, "that's religion, not politics."

"Same thing. In Belfast."

"I thought they were deadly enemies. Like us."

"They're married, are they not?"

"Not like Catholics, now. Not like Protestants."

"Hindu, Pakistani—Taigs and Prods, it's all the same slaughter-thy-bloody-neighbor."

"We said no politics."

O'Donegal's bottle was going around.

"I never knew the difference which was which."

"Derry or Coleraine?"

"Taigs or Prods?"

"Enough of that, now."

"Singhs, I mean. Who's who, which is which?"

"He's the wog of the two."

"That'll do now."

"She's the wiggle."

"We're not like that," said Mary. "Really."

"Never mind Dunn."

"Boethius is the wog and Ulster Dialects is the wiggle."

"Shut him up, somebody."

"That's the drink speaking," said Deirdre.

"We're not like that."

"He's the bloody wog and she's the frigging wiggle."

There was a silent jostling scuffle between Bannister and Dunn, but only the Old Poet's empty chair was overturned. I passed O'Donegal's bottle to Conley.

"Hurry up please it's Time."

"There's your Yank poet turned Brit," said Conley, identifying the barmaid's plea as a line from *The Wasteland*.

"Gentlemen, ladies, Time *please*."

This time Sarojinni Singh floated back into our confusion to put a stop to the malevolent blather. Radiant Saro. Her white smile against the dark skin restored the light and brought the beige lounge back to life after a subdued mood and dead fire. Now I knew the facts of a woman who had just made love to a husband by telephone without pills or cats or Captain Crunch to discuss but a subject of such intimacy the bride needed neither ring nor red dot to signify her bliss. I stopped myself from rewinding a wristwatch already overwound. She pressed the room key still warm from her hand into mine—the last thing, alas, I wanted from her.

4

THERE WAS gunfire at first light, or backfire. I came awake staring through the open bathroom door expecting Sarojinni there in the flesh, only a bath towel or the steam of a bath between her dark flesh and mine, but the image was from another life—a loss, alas. The Belly's bath towel hung with due respect and all decorum in its place. I was remembering Ginny and wanting her to be Saro: Ginny, who used to put a bath towel down to spare the sheets—the easy display of that athletic lovely nude, and having her on the towel, had spoiled me for customary deprivation. There would never be such unrestricted access again, Belfast was the abrupt end of a free ride.

(Another loss, minor to my hungover mind, was the missing copy of *Selected Poems:* must have misplaced the volume in the bar-lounge or the loo. I would have to read that poem about the black from Blake to know what I had written.)

There was no window in the bedroom (but an extra bed): the light came from the bathroom through a barred window over the tub. Was this what freedom was like?

Enlightenment, said the Poet—he was sitting on the next bed, the declivity of the twin bed's mattress was the clue—does not translate into idle promiscuity, despite the delight of a romp with my wife. Enlightenment (he repeated) can filter through the bars of yon window sooner than from between a pair of legs, or out of a bottle.

In some ways I preferred my father's pop philosophy to the Poet's.

"What about," I wondered, "release?"

I could make out the Poet's face now, turned to the coffin-shaped bathtub. No showers in Ireland, only claw-foot tubs. No chance to hang oneself from the shower head.

"How do we know dead end?" I asked. "From the open road."

"Call it a detour, Critic—a bypass like the ones where the heart is concerned, or a transition in the form of a puzzle like the cloverleaf you scrambled through in Florida."

"Then Dr. Singh—Saro?"

If I thought he would write my poems for me, I was mistaken. As the light from the window grew stronger I saw now the next mattress had become flat, so no answer. The Poet was in the bathroom standing on the edge of the tub, calling through the bars on the window: "Help! I've been sidetracked by a bogus poet!"

Thunder answered him from outside, a disturbing rumble that throbbed with my head, like the sound of stifled explosion or the onset of earthquake. I climbed to the edge of the bathtub in the Poet's place and looked out: through the bars I watched armored lorries rumbling down the Malone Road, destination unknown.

5

"WHY SHOULD Northern Ireland? With all you poets. Need another one?"

"Need a foreign one," said Liam leading me to the outer limits of the Magic Circle. He knew a pub just past Shaftesbury Square where we could scoff an Ulster fry.

We were searched at gunpoint before we got there.

A patrol in combat boots and camouflage waylaid us on Botanic Avenue: they were running a house-to-house search for snipers. Liam was the long-haired suspect bearing manuscripts of the poems he had recited to me last night, and made to stand leaning against a bakery window as he had leaned last night against the urinal while a soldier roughly patted him down. The patter gave him his poems back.

I opened my arms with my hands out empty, nothing to hide, and was asked for I.D. I was unnerved by the businesslike way a recruit's rifle was pointed at my foot, my hand trembled as I handed him my passport.

"A Yank," he called out merrily without even looking at my name. "Nashville," he announced, to prove he knew all about America. "Elvis Presley."

We were cheerfully allowed to pass on, my passport and Liam's poems a pleasant diversion from grim duty.

"The shits," said Liam when we were released, "they're everywhere."

The pub was the Crown, heavy with landmark age, its sills atilt with antiquity and the weight of a mahogany bar and the countless kegs rolled across the broken floor tiles. One solid pub of a pub, said Liam of it, not yet blown up and rebuilt. *Odd Man Out* had been filmed at the Crown.

"The scene is where your man is bleeding to death in one of these here booths."

As we settled into the booth like odd men out, it occurred to me to wonder if this was Liam Sweeney I was with, or his Shadow, Liam Keene. Liam took a fiver from me and went to the bar for pints while the vast TV screen suspended above the entryway beamed a tennis match over the edge of our booth.

After Liam delivered our two thicknesses of Guinness, he went back for platters of Ulster fry: eggs fried solid with underdone pink bacon and sausage, soda bread fried in the resultant grease—a dish it would take the remainder of a grey day to digest.

I could have had black pudding with my fry—a sausage made of pig's blood, as Liam described it—but I declined.

Liam had a distinct smell to him now, closed in as we were in a private booth, a smell beyond the beery bar-smell and burnt edges of the eggs of an Ulster fry. He smelled of having gone unwashed and slept in his clothes for a week, a pungent pickled smell of sweet and sour. He smiled in a crooked way to keep from showing his bad teeth; his features were just short of angelic and framed by an eighteenth-century scrollwork of curls—but the crooked side of his smile verged on the sinister, and I tried to think what gave him that air of bardic innocence.

"My Da has got issued a court summons that I'm to be up before the magistrate." His look of incorruptible disbelief was dead on. "They say I kicked in a shop window and I remember no such act."

I remembered some of what was said of Liam in his absence last night: a princely drunk in the early stages, cocky by degrees and a dreadful menace by Last Call.

"Unless I was half-cut and didn't know I did it."

I tried to cheer him by saying I liked his poems.

"They say around I steal my verses but that's the envy talking. Liam says that, my bloody doppelganger, gets me barred from pubs is what he does. Couldn't write a line of what I write if he tried, the bloody Prod." Liam did not have the proper face for showing outrage. "My bloody luck to have the same face and his name."

"Maybe he kicked in the shop window."

"He might have done," said Liam, inspired. It was an easy out, but not likely to impress a magistrate. "He used to steal Fanta from that wee shop, and I got the blame for him."

I had eaten only the eggs to my Ulster fry while Liam had swiftly devoured all of his and was wiping the plate with a piece of bread. Now he poked across the booth table at the bits of sausage remaining on my plate.

Liam had been a protégé of the Old Poet, and when he spoke of his mentor, tears appeared in his eyes but his appetite was unaffected. What did a Poet in Residence do, actually? I wanted to ask. You ask, said the Poet, therefore you are.

Bannister had said something about the goodnesses I might perform, none of which were obligations. There were no responsibilities except to be—to be the Poet. If I would be good enough to grace meetings of the English Society with my presence and be so good as to attend readings of the Ulster poets and perhaps perform at a wee reading of my own. "I'm not much into reading," I told him (I meant reading aloud) and Bannister beamed at my modesty: "Splendid," he said. "Poets are always reading to us—much as we would feel deprived, we might be glad of a cease-fire."

If I would be so good as to read an occasional student poem for evaluation and any comment or help I would be good enough to offer.

"What did you think of my poems?" asked Liam, sated.

"Good." I tried to think of something good to say. "I liked the images."

"How did you like those socks standing up like badgers?"

I didn't remember reading about socks, but said, "I liked that. That was good."

"That was a true one. My socks stood up that very way, that's how ripe they were. Most times I sleep with my socks on but this bird I was with wanted me down to my birthday suit like her so next morning I saw my socks standing up like badgers and wrote it down. You will come to my reading, will you not?"

"I will."

I learned nothing from Liam about what a Poet in Residence does. Liam declared that the Old Poet had taught him nothing. His poems came to him, he said, out of the blue, you might say. Out of the blue, it seemed, came the idea to borrow another tenner from me. On second thought I was learning a little something about what a Poet in Residence does.

"You can't teach me anything," said Liam, once he had whisked the ten pounds out of sight.

"Wouldn't try," I assured him.

Liam finished his Guinness with insouciant swagger, then finished mine for me.

Outside it was drizzling and Liam would accompany me no farther, for he had pressing business elsewhere and anyway did not trust Belfast past Shaftesbury Square—being from Downpatrick, "where the mountains of Mourne sweep down to the sea"—but he was good enough to point out for me the approximate direction of City Centre, where I might buy a brolly, before he nipped into the betting parlor next door to the Crown.

Only cars making shop delivery and busses with City Centre on their route were allowed past the checkpoint gates. There were turnstiles and guarded passageways at the pedestrian barricades. At the guard post off Donegall Square I innocently queued up in the women's queue, but was swiftly dispatched to the male guard—though I would have preferred to be felt up by a woman. The elaborate preamble to entering the shopping center gave expectations of an abrupt change of climate the other side of the barrier, but it was drizzling there, too. Still, the ritual was strangely redemptive, as if passing through Confession (or taking an Admissions shower) and finding yourself cleansed and innocent and admitted to the sacred precincts.

At British Home Stores—where the new fall deadfall lock was featured, and fire-retardant blankets were On Sale—I purchased an impressive umbrella that opened like a bat's wing at the touch of a trigger, a useful weapon against the weather here. I walked with it furled, London banker style, to the bank.

Ulster Bank Limited was for some reason unguarded while all other public entrances in City Centre were manned. (On entering the department store I had been frisked by an electronic device like a coat hanger, and my furled umbrella was felt up as I left.) Apparently a bank was sacrosanct.

For me the bank was another in a series of calculated risks. Bannister had informed me that henceforth my honorarium would be paid by check, or cheque. I would need a bank account in order to acquire in-pocket money.

In imitation of Liam's confident swagger, I strode up to Reception—then my knees went weak when I saw an Indian princess at the desk. But it was not Saro. She wore a red dot between her eyes and gold earrings in her ears and was the thick reflection of Saro's thin. Still, her eyes were the same vast pools I had tumbled into a night ago. Her voice, too, carried accents of Delhi by way of Cambridge that were so evocative of Saro's intonations I could not concentrate. Then, when she drew back from her desk to take forms from a drawer, I saw that she was pregnant, and all double-sense of Reception as doppelganger was dispelled.

My hand did not even begin to tremble as I wrote beside *Next of Kin:* "none." I flourished my passport to verify the counterfeit signature: I.M. Gold. While I signed, the Indian princess idly fingered the gold ring in one ear, indifferent—as Saro was, alas—to my vibes.

I presented her with fifty pounds in her own bank's banknotes as an initial deposit, in return for a virgin book of checks, or cheques.

My father could not have performed more professionally.

I thought about my father as I walked through the arcade parallel to Boots, and out the other side on Fountain Street—the City Centre at its very center stirring at so leisurely a pace and unnaturally hushed from lack of traffic, downtown Belfast going about its slack business unconcerned and unaware of my criminal presence. Did my father, when he accomplished his synthetic deceptions, experience the same mix of guilt and elation, feel he was walking inches above the sidewalk yet wonder if he was being watched? A police helicopter buzzed and hovered overhead.

Safely through the exit turnstile I immediately triggered my umbrella open, but just as immediately the drizzle ceased.

6

MY VAGRANT COLLECTION of baggage was piled in the lobby of the Bellingham Arms Hotel watched over by Mary Bannister on one side and Deirdre of the Sorrows on the other.

"Does make you something of an orphan," said Mary, "but you're *our* orphan."

"And a distinguished one," said Deirdre.

I was being evicted.

The septuagenarian hall porter shuffled a wide path past the emplacement, wanting no part of any decrepitude other than his own while the desk clerk listened for ticking and said, "Never know what's left inside left luggage." The Poet would have said: Why do you critics persistently insist there's more to a poet's baggage than meets the eye?

"Temporarily," said Mary. She was wearing her jogging outfit with Adidas on her feet.

Deirdre wore the long sleeves that emphasized the fleshiness of her upper arms and turned her shapelessness top-heavy. Where oh where was Saro to see me through this crisis instead of these two dowdy sisters of mercy?

"Could've shared my humble digs but there's the wean." Deirdre had a wee babe at home.

We moved out together carrying my motley possessions through the security foyer while an incoming tide of journalists in denim jackets full of pockets and pipes (the newsreel cameras hoisted on their shoulders like children held aloft to watch a parade) jostled us from the opposite direction.

"The BBC has taken over the Belly for the telly," explained Dee.

"They'll back down," said Mary, meaning the hunger-strikers at the Maze and not the journalists come to attend the hunger-strikers' wake. "They'll back down, they always do."

Mary was referring to the hunger-strikers but Deirdre meant the journalists when she said, "They only come when they think the crack is good."

Crack seemed to mean ambience, for Deirdre had referred to the night at the Belly as a good crack.

One of the black taxis disgorging the BBC lingered long enough to be commandeered by Mary. The driver seemed reluctant to take on a passenger in jogging togs and Adidas but he had already been boarded by our party and my baggage bound for King's.

As we trundled down the Malone Road I studied our driver's face looking for the poet's look and listening for poetry (for this truly was bard's country, where gossip was sung, loo chat could be scanned, and cabbies spoke in iambic pentameter) but he was a thick-thumbed bullyboy with no wrist. He barely missed hitting a cat that slid across the taxi's path, saying, "Cats are slippery. If that cat had've been a dog it would've been a dead duck."

Deirdre crossed herself at the cat's crossing—a black cat, it was—but Mary paid the near-miss no mind. By such signs I was to determine who was Catholic, who was not.

My escorts took me to the row house on Fitzwilliams known as *English* and began with ModBritLit on the ground floor asking there, and at VicStudies, if anybody knew of a wee flat, a bed-sit, or a room to let. We moved up a flight to AngloSax and MidEng with no luck, and Mary began asking on every landing who might lend a sleeping bag. Beowulf of AngloSax thought McDonald's son Donalbain might know of a bed-sit on Snugville Street, but outside the Magic Circle.

"How far outside?" asked Mary.

"Off the Shankill," said Beowulf, and Deirdre winced and said, "Too far."

"What's this magic circle?" I asked.

Deirdre drew a magic circle like a communal halo over our heads, meant to encompass the campus and environs. Inside the circle I was safe, explained Mary, on neutral ground. Outside was the Outer Darkness.

"Unsafe," agreed Beowulf. "Who's to know what you are Out There, out there you must be one or the other and know which neighborhood is which."

"One or the other what?" I asked.

"Doesn't matter Out There you're our poet," said Mary.

Deirdre added, "And a distinguished one."

"Are you a Protestant poet? they'll ask, or a Catholic one?"

In a contested land of Catholic and Protestant was I the only Jew?

"You're safe here," said Beowulf, "Comparatively speaking."

Miss Chaucer of MidEng had a spare pillow to lend and thought McMichael in ElizDrama might have a sleeping bag, for he often napped between elevens and lunch. McMichael, alas, napped in his chair with a rug, though he knew of a student who camped in the Mournes who might.

Deirdre switched on the electric fire in the Old Poet's office, given over to me. The office was as narrow and high-ceilinged as the condemned cells at the Chelsea Hotel.

"Safe enough here," said Mary, but she was sharp enough to discern my dismay. Her eyes followed mine outside.

The immediate view from the office window was neutral enough and vaguely comforting, in the larger picture. The university buildings were substantial in mock gothic brickwork and appeared unlikely to be shaken by shell shock. The campus lawns were refreshingly green for the season with floral borders vividly abloom. A careful phalanx of concrete bulwarks defended the cubist Students Union from automobiles bearing explosive devices. King's Bookstore was a browser's tranquil retreat behind another rampart of gaily painted oil drums, also filled with concrete. Beyond the campus lawns loomed the impregnable modern tower of a library built to last (like the Humanities Research Centre in Austin) long past the life of its literary contents. The cocky comic-strip steeple of Wormwood Hall was tiered with repair scaffolding along its spire, like a Chinese pagoda too quaint to bomb.

But there was that scarred hole in the foreground.

"Not to worry," said Mary, "you'll have a safe bed-sit in due time."

The upper floor of the private house was so neatly gutted it was like a cutaway. Floors and ceiling hung suspended in space, the open-air orange, pink and purple walls (students had lived there, safely escaped, "at exams at the time it happened") were as gay a touch against the slate sky as the floral borders that defined the campus. With its austere Georgian front blown away, the upstairs flat was disturbingly intact, complete with plaster-dusted furniture, like a life-size section slide of the inside of a dollhouse.

Better this dreary cell, Mary and Deirdre gave me to understand, than such risky premises as the wee flat across the way.

From my office phone Mary rang up Clive Lovely, the Composer in Residence, whose wife Belle had two of everything, concerning a spare sleeping bag. There was a lovely desk I could sleep on, with a gooseneck lamp to read by before bedtime. I sat in the Old Poet's chair, afraid to desecrate his memory by swiveling in it. Desk, swivel, student's desk-chair with palette armrest for taking notes (Mary sat in it, with the telephone resting on the palette). Deirdre fussed with the electric fire. Fire regulations were posted on the door. Overhead hung a unit of dusty bookshelves stacked with "A" Level exam booklets all the way to a hole in the ceiling patched with plywood where McMichael's radiator upstairs had overheated and burnt through the floor.

Deirdre had to leave to see to her wean who was left in the care of the lady at the launderette in the Students Union. She left me with the suggestion not-to-worry, but as an afterthought added, "Best not go skylarking about campus after dark."

Meanwhile Mary had managed to contact the student who knew the student who had a sleeping bag and was dead certain, or the student was, that the bag would be delivered to English before nightfall.

With Deirdre gone, Mary could inform me, "She's a lovely person, the dear heart, but troubled."

"What troubles?" I asked.

I was Not to Know that, as yet, only that she had suffered and was an outcast and called a witch, and worse.

"The Department has adopted her, you might say. She's our mascot, so to speak. We're attached to her and she to us. She has a wee babe she can barely care for—a long story, but I'll say no more."

The hint was there that Deirdre's tale was as tragic as the blasted flat across the street. Mary herself for all her sharp looks and gossipy hints had a soft place in her soul for the Deirdres and delinquents (like Liam) who wrote poetry. She confessed to poems of her own: "Sonnets, the sonnet is my form," which I might like to peruse when I was settled.

"Settled where?"

"Not to worry."

Besides her poetry Mary had a professional life as Dr. McDonald's executive secretary at King's English Department as well as amanuensis to Rupert Bannister, her husband, who was translating *The Book of the Dun Cow* from the Gaelic.

"Rupert has no Gaelic himself, but Dee helps and I advise, and anyway it's the poetry that counts."

I might like to peruse Rupert's translation when I was settled, was Mary's suggestion, as if to settle my mind.

"By all means."

Then Mary introduced me to the Staff Room across the landing where I might brew a cup of tea beneath the melancholy gaze of a

Virginia Woolf poster, and to the bathroom next door—temporarily a stockroom for Xerox paper—with a claw-foot bathtub full of soot. The student with the sleeping bag arrived breathless from having taken three flights of stairs at a clip.

"Felim, sir," said he, pushing a lump of fleece at me. (I thought he had said "feel 'em.") Feathers were escaping through slits in the lining: white plumes lodged comically in the boy's reddish tresses.

"Felim Delaney," declared Mary, "might well be our next important Ulster poet."

For want of something to say, I said, "So you write poetry?"

"I do, sir," said Felim.

I thanked him for the loan of his sleeping bag and he immediately thrust a wad of poems at me, if I would be good enough, when I was settled, then Felim was gone in a swirl of feathers.

For a trinity of nights I slept on the Old Poet's desk top tucked into Felim's downy pocket when I would have, the gods willing, shared Saro's veils and feathers and perfume. Dr. Singh, Sarojinni's djin, was known as Boethius Singh because of his specialty in Latin Studies. My nightly prayer was that Brahma or Mohammed would recall Boethius to Utter Pradesh or utter Bangladesh and leave his wife behind to my devices.

Those nights I might lie awake for numb minutes in dumb wonder at disturbances that might have meant gunfire or fireworks or backfire from Out There. Sometimes I came awake for no reason and reached out at night for another person and my hand might set the Old Poet's swivel chair squeaking like the turn of the screw. His ghost left me otherwise in peace. Since the hunger strike I could hear or thought I heard the distant banging of garbage-can lids, ominous tom-toms that Molly the Cleaner had informed me was the traditional tattoo for trouble in the ghettos. Prisoners were starving themselves brain-damaged or to death and policemen and soldiers shot in the back while I but sneezed from the damp and suffered wet dreams from reaching out for Saro. I steered as clear of the Short Strand and the Shankhill as the hall porter of my suspect luggage, and never watched the telly at the Belly and stopped reading the Belfast *Telegraph*.

That boy Felim, so eager and smiling, and Mary so confident that they would back down. At Staff Room tea if I remarked on the whiff of tear gas as far adrift as the Botanic Gardens, Deirdre would say, "Now, now," as if soothing a wean. "That's the DDT you smell," insisted AngloSax, "the stuff they spray on the roses." At the Royal

Victoria Felim's eight-year-old brother was dying horribly of burns, but whether by accident or ambush I was Not to Know.

There were the jokes that passed over my head that set them to laughing over what I would have considered sad, a humor I would never get and directed against themselves. Me they only teased and put on with their sly straight-faced misdirection while the Big Joke, the grim one, was on them.

They wanted and needed me, I was a treat. If I no longer feared exposure, then what did I fear?

Absent-minded McMichael was mindful enough to provide me with a city map of Belfast, the areas "where sheep may safely graze" marked in green, for Neutral, or comparatively so. Miss Chaucer of MidEng offered me, to go with my bag of feathers, a pillow she had embroidered herself with the Red Hand of Ulster on one side and an Irish cross on the other. Sharp-minded Mary revised McMichael's map and lent me a plain pillowcase to cover Miss Chaucer's erratic needlework.

In one drawer of the Old Poet's desk I found a compass, of all things, which verified my suspicion that I was sleeping out of sync with the earth's polar axis. Also in the drawer was a wooden ruler with inches printed on one edge and centimeters on the other. Did the Old Poet use the ruler to measure his meter by?

I tried to make a metaphor of the ruler used to measure my troubled dreams and chronic insomnia to their fearsome Troubles paid in blood, and failed. There was no comparing us.

And there was no finding me out, I was in. In their innocence they needed me if only to nod yes to their poems.

Another desk drawer was locked and no key to it, but not-to-worry I would come across the key in due time. Mary might carry it on her compleat key ring or if not we undercover operatives always found the key to people's secrets.

7

THE FIRST HINT of sanctuary to turn up was a To Let on Chlorine Gardens that Mary discovered on a jogging tour around the Magic Circle.

"Penelope something, Number 13, across from the Science Library—a bit dizzy, from Bath, a divorcée—but you said you were divorced yourself, did you not?"

"Separated."

"Things fall apart, as the poet said. There's no divorce in the Republic, you know, you can imagine how married couples in the Republic feel when things fall apart. Six into twenty-six won't go, don't talk to me about Unification." Then she remembered she was not to talk about that. "But it's a room with a roof over your head and convenient to Science in case you fancy scienctific reading. Should do nicely till a wee flat or bed-sit turns up."

Number 13 was the unpainted half of a gingerbread house with a strip of bleak garden frontage where rosebushes rotted in the muck. Penelope met me in the vestibule wearing a torn pink wrapper and Greek sandals. Her hair, newly washed, was wound up in a turban of toweling.

"We have had mice," she said darkly, then brightened, "but no longer."

She led me into a deliciously overheated kitchen where she had been drying her hair before a gaping oven door. The cooker, she called it, and introduced us. The kitchen was papered with tourist posters of southern places: a promenade on the Riviera, Marrakesh at night, Mykonos—even Beirut, at least its beaches, before the city was blasted apart. There were also postcards from these ports of call as if to prove such places did exist, with their Kodachrome palm gardens and picturesque ruins.

Because of the excessive heat the postcards were falling from the taped places of display. I stooped to recover the latest fallen and almost keeled over with déjà vu: dear God, the drawings on Valerie's side of the room. The card was from Corsica, not Miami.

"The fridge refuses to cool the way it should." Her accent was British—Bath, I remembered. "Everything freezes except the freezer things, but a man is coming Monday."

Penelope turned her cherubic face to me and tilted her turbaned head in resignation to the failings of domestic machines and Ireland's failure to repair them. Wet blond curls hung below the toweling and her small toes peeked pinkly out the ends of her sandals. Was the hand across her breast a gesture of modesty or coy come-on? The Poet would know.

Before Penelope could lead me from the kitchen, an Athenian poster curled at one corner where its thumbtack popped out of the plaster and another postcard fluttered from the sweating wall and I heard mice scuttling behind the fridge.

At the top of a wrought-iron spiral accordion of stairs I was shown my poet's garret with camp bed under a miniature skylight obscured by soot and pigeon droppings. Penelope presented me with a mysterious electrical plug to assemble and a pen knife to work with, a trial by ordeal I miraculously accomplished to be rewarded with a glass of sherry. She managed to pour the sherry and one for herself without losing her grip on the torn pink flap at her bosom. The garret radiator opened infinite promise of electrical heat—wired now to its new outlet—but we sat waiting on the camp bed sipping our sherry in vain: no heat hummed forth despite my poet's touch at repair.

"We have a telephone." Who were we? I wondered. "But we can only for the moment ring out. The company will send their man around in due time and if he should come round while I am at King's would you be good enough to ask—this being Belfast—for identification?"

She recited the telephone number like a poem, for me to memorize, and when I could recite the numbers in perfect sequence she collected twenty pounds from me for this week's rent.

After the guided tour of the premises we were back in the kitchen where the mice gamboled behind the fridge and the postcards were falling, falling. Before I set off for my office in English to collect the sorry scraps of baggage I traveled with I watched Penelope one-handedly unwind herself from the turban round her head, the other hand still clutched to her breast. Was the dance of the seven veils meant for me? No, for she had dipped into her crouch on a prayer rug of the towel and thrust her cherub's head into the gaping oven to dry. Nothing sensual intended, she was ending it all at the very beginning in the mock-classic pose of a suicide.

8

A NURSING SISTER from the Royal Victoria Hospital with an uncanny resemblance to Miss Pike thought her poetry was too urgent.

"I'm perhaps too quick off the mark, like as if a poem was an emergency and must be attended to straightaway."

"But perhaps," I said. "A poem is. An emergency."

"What I sense in my poetry is that urgency a mother-to-be who has broke water must feel."

"I sense that. I understand. What you're saying."

"Like as if I'm about to give birth in a black taxi before we can reach Obstetrics."

A retired trades union official with a cycle of poems about shipbuilding that ran to fifteen hundred stanzas said: "I don't know where I get my ideas from."

"There's a mystery there," said I.

"How is it with you sir?"

I remembered something Liam had said, so I said, "Out of the blue."

I told Bannister his translation of *The Book of the Dun Cow* must have been difficult, his not knowing Gaelic.

"The very devil," said Bannister, and was so impressed with the difficulty he said it again. Then he said, "I may not have got the sense straight but the poetry is what counts."

Bannister had come to remind me I was not assured, by which he meant insured, since I was not a part of the social security system, and to say he would send a man around, a private assurance agent.

"Insured against what?" I asked.

"I may tackle the *Táin* next," said Bannister, inspired. "With Mary's help of course, and Dee's. You must ask Mary to show you her sonnets sometime."

The hall landing in front of my office door was like a dentist's waiting room. Sometimes there were as many as five poets waiting for me before I opened shop. There were two seminar chairs on the landing, and they were always taken, by poets writing scraps of verse on the palette-shaped armrests. Other poets sat on the steps or lounged against the balustrade or leaned against my door, waiting.

Bannister's private assurance agent came round with a briefcase full of assurance policies, but the talk turned to his verse. He wrote poetry in his spare time.

"Under another name, of course, sir, as I would not want the firm to know. We are associates of Lloyds of London."

He had been saving the labels of a product against rising damp in order to enter their contest for a free trip for two to Hawaii. He was torn between submitting a jingle or a limerick. The limerick was the catchier of the two but a jingle would be best if it had to be sung as an advert.

Mary Bannister came by in her jogger's togs with her hands behind her back.

"Rupert said you were anxious to see my sonnets."

"Sonnets, yes. You write sonnets, I hear."

"They're far too personal."

"Oh."

"I can't show them."

"To anybody?"

"Only Rupert. Rupert reads them when they're finished, but not the public. I would just die to think they were to be read by the general public."

"Oh. Well, then."

"No one but Rupert. They're not to be read by the public, mind."

I had resigned myself to not reading them, and said, "I understand."

"Promise me you'll keep them secret from the public."

I promised. Reluctantly she released them to me, sheafs of onionskin she held behind her back. I was to read them then and there, Mary standing over me watching my face for reaction, retrieving the sonnets from me sheet by sheet as soon as I finished them.

"Lovely," I said, sonnet after sonnet. There were more of them than I would have believed. "These are sonnets, all right."

"Indeed, they are," said Mary. She had colored with pleasure every time I said lovely, and now was quite flushed. "I flatter myself to say it, but the sonnet is truly my form. I can't write that personal in any other form but the sonnet."

"They are personal, all right."

She wrote them in her head while jogging and when she got to the office wrote them down.

"You're the only person besides Rupert I've revealed them to."

I tilted the wrist in recognition of the honor.

All of her sharpness had softened, and she flushed with thoughts of new sonnets she was unable to reveal. In her elation she decided to dedicate the one about the wedding of the stars to me. The stars in the poem were symbolical. Stars were the emblem of the United States, were they not? (If only the six counties were as wedded as the United States were we would not have all this dissention and bloodshed.) She would xerox a copy of "The Wedding of the Stars" with a personal dedication to me and put the sonnet in my pigeonhole.

I knew now the power of my office. I need only sit in the Old Poet's swivel chair and look poetic and nobody recognized the desecration.

Powdered widows from the Malone Road came to me, and lorry drivers from the Divis flats. The lorry driver's verses had been laboriously copied out by his wife on loose-leaf sheets with title pages as if ready for the printer. The nursing sister's poems were typed on the backs of the forms used on hospital charts, without a trace of blood.

Students mostly shoved their scraps of verse at me and quickly turned away as if they might be caught at poetry. (I was afraid of being caught not at it.) Their poems were scribbled on the flaps of envelopes or scrawled along the flyleaves of textbooks; they were written in ball-point on the reverse side of bursar's receipts or beer pads from the Egg or paper napkins from the Students Union. A young girl named Darling had penned a miniaturized sestina on the surface of a smooth stone, like a psalm written on the head of a pin.

"Use it," she offered, "as a paperweight. If it's no use in the world as a poem."

None of their poems was about the Troubles. They might write about private misfortune, or earlier troubles as far back as the Battle of the Boyne or the great potato famine, but even the nursing sister whose chart forms on the reverse side were concerned with blood and burns and missing limbs, wrote nothing about what happened Out There. The poets took pains to spare me the tragedy of the place. They tiptoed around their mystery while I, their laureate, gave nothing of mine away.

"My Da tells me either appear before the magistrate in Downpatrick on the morrow or RUC in Belfast will catch up to me and drag me off to Castlereagh where they're known to interrogate you to a bloody pulp."

There was a genuine tear in Liam's left eye, but that could have been from the cigarette smoke he blew in that direction. After all, he was only nineteen. He must find seventeen pounds for bus fare by morning or face Castlereagh and the consequences.

As one crook to another I believed him, and forked over twenty pounds. He swiftly made the banknotes disappear. In return he unscrolled a poem from his shirt pocket, and with a flourish, and my pen (which he forgot to return), dedicated the lines to me. It was the poem about the casket crashing through a greenhouse.

"I'm away," he said, like a man who could not keep magistrates waiting.

"I'm not sure. About your rhymes here. Love and shove, well, yes, but. Belfast and shellfish, I don't know."

"I see. I think I see what you mean, sir."

When Grainne was gone and no one waiting I tried the lock on the Old Poet's desk drawer with a key I had come across under the blotter. There was a citation with seal and ribbons from the Lord Mayor and a large gilded plywood key to the City of Belfast. The drawer was full of letters of condolence on the death of the Old Poet's wife, and a collection of Victorian pornography. There were notes for a final volume of poems to be called *The Last Home* and a student poem, the one about a casket crashing through a greenhouse, dedicated to the Old Poet by Liam Sweeney.

Once the November rain had washed the pigeon droppings from my skylight I could lie corpselike on my cot and make out an occasional chrome-tinted light. B'god, it was a watery sun malingering there beyond the drifting fog and monotonous slate. If a capricious sun winked at me in its camouflage of Ulster mist, there was hope of something. I was furthermore granted an occasional glimpse of seagulls winging overhead commuting from the dock spill at Belfast Lough to the dustbins of the Bellingham Arms, another hope of something, a reminder of something else. Only yesterday I had caught sight of Sarojinni Singh's red Mini winging westward on the Lisburn Road—only once, and the scarlet flash had passed by before I could lift my witless wrist to wave—but all the same, I had been shown the tailfeathers of the bird ineffable.

Through Belfast's ashen aspect there did appear the color of passion, the color of blood: there were autumn leaves in the Botanic Gardens and I waded through that mass of color—the first autumn leaves since my childhood in Latonia—coming back from the showers at PhysEd, the only showers, according to McMichael, in all Belfast. And I had the sight of red red roses blooming behind the shatterproof glass of the newly restored Palm Court. Or Gretta, the custodian at the County Down Museum, was burning leaves in a steel drum in a great display of spark and flame. I lived for color and light and clung to a bright thread of hope. Not to worry, not to abandon hope even where autumn smelled most morbidly of rot and ruin in the sunken mossy glen between the Science Library and Friar's Bush Cemetery. When I passed through the grove of dead trees that housed blasted rooks' nests I could see at the windows of the Library rose-cheeked readers browsing the stacks of books that held so much promise for students of the North to win a fellowship to MIT or discover in the card catalogue a handy handbook on plastic demolition.

But what hope was there for me? I had spoken to Saro only once since the night in the lounge at the Bellingham Arms. The word passed between us, ever so brief, at a sherry party for Miss Chaucer who had got engaged to a Burns scholar at the University of Hull. At the party Saro reigned, dispensing wine and watercress sandwiches from Dr. McDonald's sideboard while the bride-to-be stood groomless in our midst—Robbie could not attend, attending as he was to Robert Burns across the water—wringing a nervous piece of handkerchief in the style of Miss Frith during a panic seizure at the Sans Souci: Miss Chaucer was unable to express her happiness at our happiness for her.

I caught Saro—almost by the wrist, but remembered the rule of touch in time—for a single instant alone, in transit with a tray of crisps and watercress for O'Donegal, who feigned not-to-worry how beautiful the hostess was, or had been struck blind. The only word I got with her was the word that I had had no word.

"We must talk," she promised.

O'Donegal accepted a triangle of bread laced with watercress without daring to stare—while I dared, and stared—until sly Lawrence of ModBritLit cleverly absorbed her soul by being desperate to know if she had detected Celtic dialogue patterns in *Women in Love*. In cold-blooded silence I vowed to oust BritLit and Boethius both and bear Saro off to Samarkand, transport her ephemeral form to somewhere warm and removed and horizontal.

She had promised to talk.

While waiting for enlightenment, between office hours at King's I sat in the sitting room at Chlorine Gardens, half wallpapered as it was (Penelope had set the room ablaze with a careless fag). In front of the

Queen Anne window beside a faulty gas heater afflicting the atmosphere I read the pile of poems bestowed upon me. Those first lyric
tributes to William of Orange and William Butler Yeats had shaded
into darker works on Granny's wake and Uncle Todd's cancer. The
dead chill of early December brought on the thanatopsis complex in
Ulster verse. Penelope's Queen Anne window gave onto an oblique
view of the frozen grove beside the Science Library: the amputated
limbs and rotted stumps gangrenous with moss—not to speak of the
bleak abandoned birds' nests—afflicted my mood too, paralyzed all
aspirations, placed me in touch with the universal death wish.

Wednesday was the one day I must not sit among the rolls of
rose-pattern wallpaper and pots of paste and upturned buckets. That
was the day Penelope's weekly group, the Seven Sisters, met.
Wednesdays I nursed a pint of Smithwicks at the Egg or the Bot or the
Belly and read poems to the music of their jukeboxes.

Between poems my hollow existence was teased by such byplays
of conjecture as what was Penelope's sex life like and where-oh-where
was Saro?

When Sarojinni was missing for a second consecutive day at
elevenses I asked about her as innocently as I could dissimulate.

"Londonderry," said Milton (the man who taught *Paradise Lost*,
a born-again Christian), "with her tape recorder."

"Derry," added Deirdre, by way of correction.

"And will remain in Londonderry until the commencement of
next term."

"Derry," added Deirdre.

What did I care for their disputes over place names in this
empty and barren place?

Penelope's faithful cooker blew up during the bake of a steak-and-
kidney pie. The Bomb Squad came believing Provos had targeted
Chlorine Gardens: a team of hearties in umpire's chest protectors and
masks and foundry worker's gloves, as frightening as the sight of
terrorists would have been. Penelope's bangs and eyebrows were
singed, but she greeted the Bomb Squad with customary good cheer,
apologized for her cuisine, served them glasses of sherry and went
about scraping meat pie from her wall posters. The mice survived
nicely and played behind the burnt-out oven as merrily as ever.

(Our petty domestic accident occurred the same day a suitcase
at the Hotel Carrington went off killing four guests in the lobby and
maiming fourteen.)

Since the hot water pipes at the gymnasium had burst—not-to-worry, said the handball coach, shower pipes had burst before but would in due time be set right by Maintenance—I was obliged to heat a kettle of water on the gas ring at home, hoping to render a frigid inch of bath water tepid enough for a fast rinse while Penelope's assorted underthings might drip drip drip down my back.

(Through the bathroom wall to the next-door half of the gingerbread house, I heard a radio broadcasting the ambush of a British patrol outside Carrickfergus: a sergeant major and his driver had been incinerated by petrol bomb.)

The hall chimes were playing an insistent melody and I arose from my sqalid bath to answer. For some moronic reason I was cheered by the sound of chimes, aroused out of isolation. It might be Saro. Or the telephone man to repair the phone so that Saro might ring.

It was Gretta. I had hurried to the door in my British Home Stores bathrobe and barefoot for this. Gretta was one of the Seven Sisters: chopped-off straw hair and chapped ears and bones grown strangely awry. She asked what sounded like Pennybone but meant Penny-home? which is what she always asked. That was the extent of our front-door conversations except when I inquired about the weather and she was justified in uttering the single word rain.

But Gretta was useful to Penelope's disordered maintenance and domestic upkeep. Except for a barmaid who wore leather wristbands at the Elephant & Flea, Gretta possessed the only sturdy workaday wrists in the Magic Circle. She was employed as custodian at the County Down Museum, stoking its furnaces and swabbing its corridors, and part-time grounds keeper at the Botanic Gardens, the only female grounds keeper in Belfast. She now had her denim sleeves rolled for action as she shambled past me in mud-coated gum boots to wrestle with paste buckets and recalcitrant scrolls of rose-print wallpaper in the burn-scarred sitting room.

I was back splashing heroically in my bath when the chimes sounded again, Penelope had forgotten her keys and Gretta was out of earshot.

I went down to her. She was shaking her wet umbrella in the foyer, then coyly revealed that the seven Wednesday members had grown to ten.

"Since you, Professor Gold, serve as our poet laureate, we thought you might christen the Seven Sisters with a new poetical name."

"How about. Ten Sisters?"

"Poetical, I said, silly." She assumed the pose of a music-hall chorine spinning her brolly of its final droplets.

These bathrobe-raingear conversations—if I attempted to translate Penelope's playful coquetry into sexual terms—were inevitably about nothing and hopelessly led nowhere. I did however feel myself grow semitumescent inside the folds of my bathrobe.

Penelope pretended to pout at my lack of inspiration for a new poetical name, unaware of how she had inspired me elsewhere. She then passed an envelope to me—wet from the mailbox, posted from Derry/Londonderry—*poems*, tenderly signed Sarojinni Singh. My heart hammered so hard, my transport so complete, I could hardly feel Penelope tapping me playfully on the shoulder with her umbrella as if bestowing knighthood.

9

DUE TIME does by some miracle come round. Maintenance had filled the leaky hole in my office ceiling with plaster, and now I swiveled high and dry (no poets waiting on the landing, for a change) reading from the Old Poet's bruised copy of *The Pasha's Delight*, unabashed pornography, a purple Cook's Tour of Persia, when I was startled out of my erotic research and private revery. There was a chorus of shouting in counterpoint to the squeak of my swivel chair. I went to the window and looked down upon student clusters blooming against the wet shrubbery along Fitzwilliams.

The students were carrying placards or banners of bedsheets pierced with holes to let through the wind, painted in what appeared to be blood. The bloody words were streaked and blotted: from this distance, on a dark day, I could not make out what the students were marching for, or against. It was raining on their parade.

What frightened me was the far more strategic massing of the military: the Royal Ulster Constabulary wore green uniforms pregnant with flak jackets, walkie-talkies dangling at the hip. Transport trucks emptied out camouflaged attack troops positioned thickly across the evergreen campus. The patrols fanned out in disciplined menace, soldiers swiftly taking sniper positions behind parked cars and mossy elms: one soldier, just below my window, steadied his rifle on a fireplug; another was prowling the cutaway rooms of the bombed-out ruin across the street. If the panorama had not been so grim, his green camouflage against the purple wall might have been laughable.

The students seemed completely oblivious to the presence of armed opposition.

University Avenue was now blocked off with armored vehicles, so now the parade monitors formed up the raggletag cortège with handmade bullhorns of rolled pasteboard: they were to march by way of Botanic instead. Was that Liam down there? That was Liam—I thought he was in Downpatrick, or in jail—or that was his double. Oonagh was down there, and Grainne and the girl named Darling who had written a sestina on a stone. I recognized Felim, though his red hair was tucked up into a navvy's stocking cap. The students had tied white handkerchiefs around their necks, nothing to do with surrender, only in case of tear gas.

These were students I knew whose poems I read. *The Pasha's Delight* trembled in my hand.

A guerrilla squad of RUC confiscated a placard that bore some offensive slogan I could not read. The placard was given up peacefully enough, but a scuffle started when the police attempted to suppress a bedsheet for by now a milling swarm of students outnumbered the men in green. Whistles, shouts—I could not make out what was shouted—and as the mass of students pressed close, the police conceded. The green uniforms drew back and the bedsheet was hoisted anew.

The parade passed westward under my window, policed into a narrow column that was not given leeway at either edge. Slow-moving cars moved alongside the march at the pace of a funeral procession: these were newsmen and photographers, followed by the soldiers who had left their sniper positions and now infiltrated the ranks of the RUC. My last sight of Liam was of that apprentice poet pulling the world's tiniest bottle from his stained khaki rain jacket—a jacket so much like my own it could have been mine. He took a swig from the bottle then tucked it safely away.

Would they be hurt or killed? I was Not to Know. But I had drunk with them and read their poems. Three safe stories above their incendiary issues and bloody collisions I loitered in my swindler's sanctuary.

Beware, alien, of that failing of you Yanks. (It could have been the Old Poet warning me.) Don't take our Cause more seriously than we do.

Weak-kneed with fright, I locked the Old Poet's *Pasha's Delight* away.

No further than "Dear Valerie" into another letter, I answered the soft knock at my office door. It was Saro. I stepped back from her dumbstruck, for I was expecting wizened Molly who emptied wastebaskets at this time of day.

Too heart-strangled to speak, I turned away from my dream and yanked the sheet of stationery from Olympia's clutches crumpling Dear Valerie into a paper ball.

"Did I interrupt?" Her enormous eyes were wide with genuine concern. "Were you composing a poem?"

"It was. Not at all. Well."

"I am sorry if I broke into—something."

"Nothing. I've been wanting to. Talk and, well."

"Here we are," she said, and so we were.

Felim's sleeping bag lay rolled into a sausage at one end of my desk—why had I not left it conveniently open? It was closed, so I offered Saro the Old Poet's swivel chair. (My line of thought was completely unstrung: if the ghost of the Old Poet sat in the swivel, then Saro would be sitting in his lap.) But she chose to sit in the seminar chair, her lovely sculptured arm bare to the elbow extended along the armrest, her eyes looking into mine, the whites of her eyes as white as bond paper before the first muddy lines of a poem are traced across it.

She opened her silken purse—the same handbag a security guard had violated the night we met—and plunged a dark hand into its suggestive vulviform. She brought forth her latest poem, still warm from conception, and placed the page upon my Olympia, then snapped shut the purse's clitoral clasp.

My arms were crossed to hide my nervous hands, but the pose was too standoffish so I uncrossed them. I tilted forward in the swivel chair, leaning on my knees, and Saro leaned back so as not to be leaned upon.

I must read the poem while she watched. They all expected that. So I drew the sheet of paper into my lap—instead of Saro—and fixed my expression in advance. She leaned forward as I leaned back, to read me as I read. I nearly swooned from her perfume.

I had read her first poems, now this.

This is the pits, Critic, was the Poet's opinion, but I thought I saw something. Some hope. In them.

To keep the conference honest I think I said old-fashioned more than once, but what did I honestly know? You know greeting-card verse when you read it, you chiseler.

Effective I said, and once went so far as to say moving, and was not struck by lightening or turned to stone. Original, I think I said, encouraged by the rapt attention I received. For the first time in our vagrant acquaintance, Sarojinni Singh was hypnotized by my words, her splendid liquid eyes fixed on my lips.

I tried to think of something genuine to express, even the mildest reservation to counterbalance the bogus critique, but my dissembling soul was unwilling to risk it. I allowed the word romantic to sum up and hang in the air between my lips and her eyes.

She sighed and leaned back and said, "I've always loved—" and I leaned forward to be the object of that love, "Lovelace and his century."

I'll drink a tear out of thine eye, thought I, and would have. I was carried away by the moment. Even the fire regulations posted above Saro's chair became poetry. *Here we'll strip and cool our fire.*

Her arms were bare but the collar of her white blouse was too high, a tightly buttoned secret like Penelope's clutched wrapper—did she not realize how graceful her long neck was?—and she was veiled in an aura of wooly white, a cardigan draped hastily over her shoulders against the frigid transit through the corridors of English. Her dark and splendid face, with the black hair done up in combs high on the back of her neck, drew away from the white wrapping like a flower in the snow. Alas, her famous legs were encased in cinnamon-colored slacks.

"I think." She was thinking aloud, all sober gravity and high seriousness—which cost me her smile. "I think that poetry is due for a sharp turn. A turn to its inspired and illustrious origins. I think we must, all of us, go forward, if you will, by going back." Our knees nearly touched, and by going back she would be against the wall. "Back to the romantic tradition from which poetry sprang."

"I think," I said, my thoughts turning on the term romantic, "you might be right."

"All the early, if you will, nobility of spirit and, well, higher consciousness."

"You might be right. The moderns—myself included, I would

have to say—have, well. Let us down. On the higher-consciousness level."

She was no longer listening to me any more than I was listening (word for word, if you will) to her: wired as she was into her own generator, eager as I was to be wired into her.

"Our so-called enlightened age." She was playing with one empty sleeve of the cardigan and toying with my civilized restraint. "Has altogether bypassed the wellspring of expression, the poetic essence, if you will, everything that art and poetry once concerned itself with."

"Love," I ventured.

She nodded modestly as if I had found her secret out.

"Love in poetry," I continued, as our knees touched, "and in life."

I heard an automobile horn outside, but ignored it. She drew herself up at the sound and shifted her slacks to one side.

"In the seventeenth century," she began, but got no further into that licentious century, for the auto horn now blared insistently.

Damn the driver out there.

"Love," I picked up again. "The pop music of the age. Seems to have, well, taken over. In that department."

This was the first statement of mine she had registered. She frowned on my notion for a moment, then brushed it aside with her empty sleeve: "What my own poetry attempts to do is turn back to what poetry once was and is capable of being again."

The horn horned in again and I went to the window with a curse ready. There lay the empty campus vacated by its revolution, the peaceable kingdom, strangely quiescent (except for the horn) after the tumult of twenty minutes ago.

Only a red car down there to disturb tranquility—a red car I quickly recognized as Saro's own red Mini.

"Oh," I heard her say.

I was about to tell Saro I loved the line about the stars imploding and her image of flowers from Mother Nature's paint box, but I opened the window and leaned out. The little man had his head out of the car window and was banging with the flat of his hand on the horn. He had the same Gandhilike coloring as the Poet, but not the Poet's electric hair. This was my first glimpse of Boethius Singh, his little self perfectly fitted to the Mini, his rodentlike features tilted up to mine.

I heard a scuttling sound and turned just in time to see her shawl of a cardigan sweeping out the door. The door closed and she was swiftly gone.

By the time I was back at the open window, Saro skipped along the outside sidewalk to the curb, the empty arms of her cardigan flying after her. Boethius was out of the Mini now, scowling at her from his sentry post against the fender. He took her by the back of the neck, that graceful neck of hers, in the ruffian gesture of a drunk grabbing a bottle, a gesture to which Saro submitted. She lowered her head—she was taller than her brown-domed spouse—and allowed herself to be inserted into the passenger seat.

Boethius got in beside her, a small angry dog in the manger, yip-yapping something at her I could not hear. The Mini sped off in the wake of the protest march and I was left, when I closed the window, with her lingering scent and dreadful poem and the sour resentment of the displaced.

10

THE WET to my lips was too cold for a kiss and I came awake to the season's first snow blown across the skylight. The melted droplets had dribbled through a new crack in the panes, and into my beard.

In the dead cold I stumbled up to turn the camp bed once again—longitude and latitude, earth's axis, be damned. I put woolen socks on my feet and an Aran sweater over my nightshirt, then slept until daylight filtered through the coverlet of snow and I stared upward at a dead pigeon flattened against the broken pane in the skylight. My beard had frozen in the night.

Through the long winter's day I hovered miserably over my radiant glow of an office fire drinking tea with lemon Mary ferried to me from the Staff Room. My bones had turned to water, I took aspirin with the tea. When Molly came by to complain about the contents of Beowulf's wastebasket, banana peels again, and the cigarette burns on McMichael's windowsill, her mouth fell open at the sight of me.

"Och," she said, "what a turn, sir, you gave me. You're the living image of the Old One his self that sat at that desk before you."

I checked my reflection in a windowpane (I had been avoiding mirrors of late, afraid of whomever I might see in them): a ghastly aspect, true enough.

Molly fled without emptying the wastebasket, and with my double vision I thought Felim had entered, in a leather miniskirt, but it was slim boyish Fiona, who looked enough like him with the map of Ireland in freckles across her face, who had come to discuss her pets (a parakeet) and debts and triolets. Fiona would ever after be able to boast that the Poet in Residence had swooned over her poems. As soon as she said, "You're looking unwell, sir," I saw two Fionas, or Fiona plus her twin Felim, and fainted.

I came back to the world in a black taxi, Fiona on one side of me and McMichael on the other. Bannister rode shotgun beside the driver, for legal aid and moral support. From the back of his head, the driver was the Poet himself—if I could trust my instincts under such extraordinary circumstances.

My escorts extracted me from the taxi at Chlorine Gardens and delivered me—it was Wednesday—to the Seven Sisters, or ten. (There was more than one of everybody: Bannister paid off two Poets at the door to the taxi.) Deirdre, with husky Gretta's help, dragged me to the pea soup–colored sofa. An unnatural ray of sunlight—unheard of, this side of the Science Library—heightened my color and provided stage lighting to my laying out. Deirdre applied a sour-smelling washcloth to my fevered brow, with ice in it—had a sister broken an icicle from my beard, or had the fridge come at last to life?

By now the sisters, their Wednesday shattered by this alien male presence, were murmuring their goodbyes—"I'm away"—and soon I was left alone with the nursing sisters, one of each. The sitting room, though it spun, was a welcome and familiar place with its cabbage roses peeling from the wall because of the unaccustomed sun or from the force of my fever.

"A doctor," said Penelope, "has been sent for."

Was the telephone working or had a sister been sent?

Because of Deirdre's responsibilities as a mother, Penelope advised her not to be risking infection, but Deirdre hinted at having risked worse and suffered more—for the babe's sake, and her own—and would b'God attend me till the doctor came.

Gretta was another standing by, standing fast, and with her muscle, Penelope's direction and Deirdre's will, I was transported to bed—not to my monk's pallet in the attic but to Penelope's own substantial four-poster—and tucked in tenderly with Penelope's personal felt-covered hot-water bottle at my feet and Deirdre's ice cloth on my brow. I had an invalid's view of the deceased back garden and my own stark scarlet face flaming in the antique mirror on the opposite wall.

The original piece of ice had melted—nothing, of course, to be had from the defective refrigerator—so Deirdre simply wrung out the washcloth into a quaint chamber pot. I remembered with intense longing my bottle of Bushmills in the attic beneath the swayback mattress, but was too weak to ask for it.

Before Lights Out, Deirdre placed the tepid washcloth back upon my forehead where I would have given up the ghost to have Saro delicately winding my turban in place.

This much I knew—though Penelope later claimed that a three-dimensional doctor had come—during one sleepless interval a single finger of grey-green light illuminated a white-bearded uninvited guest: Dr. Breathwaite, Dr. Whitehead, Dr. K?

"Cheers," said the spirit.

The visitation did not unnerve me, my nerves had turned to water with my bones.

"Who?" I asked. "What?" I was too weak to be frightened.

"Not to worry."

This was not my father's style, I ruled Whitehead out. In the state I was in it could have been anybody—the Poet, his beard and hair bleached by the grave, or the Old Poet, his hair and beard bleached before dying.

"Not to worry. Wives wee-men, poets on the march. Remembering is the sickness, hey-diddely-do. Memory's the black hole we all tumble into, joke's on us all. Derry-derry-down and a faretheewell-o, there's their poem, the Great Joke tied all beribboned, the desire and pursuit is all."

Having delivered the garbled word, his solace in a nutshell, the shade departed by way of the window, through a subaqueous slit in the pea-green drapes and into the vacancy of Out There.

When Penelope came with a hot hot-water bottle to replace the cold she assured me, No, the doctor was not bearded and certainly had not come in through the window. Later Gretta came thumping into my sickroom with an offering of her own: the electric heater I had failed to make function. With her own thick-knuckled navvy's mitts, Gretta had pieced together plug and wire, and now plugged the apparatus into a socket with dumb triumph. Was she trying to tell me in her mute way the same as the ghost was saying: electric heaters are the source of misfortune? A working heater is a dandy symbol of imminent recovery. A little later Penelope returned and unplugged the heater, thinking the room heated enough or overheated, and carried it elsewhere. After that I was left to my plague-ridden hallucinations in peace.

In the later stages of my illness I suffered chills as well as fever, and when the plague came to the coughing stage I thought I might have contracted TB but Penelope said the doctor said no. I had the flu. Consumption was the poet's disease, influenza the Great Joke played on laymen. If my hosts had considered such matters they could have unmasked me on that theory alone—but all of Belfast, it would seem, had conspired to believe in me. Staring at my alternately pale or flushed face in the antique mirror I came to the conclusion the face I saw was perfect for deception, empty of any significant expression, unmarked by anything worth reading there.

Whatever else I would carry off from Belfast besides poems about stars and flowers and stiff socks, I would carry away the thought that Gretta was papering the walls of Penelope's sitting room still. *Memory's the black hole we all stumble into.* There are these persistent images in our archives that recur disproportionately to all others. The picture preserved forever from my hapless sojourn in Chlorine Gardens was Gretta's startled face staring at me from my camp bed through the stark white V of Penelope's opened thighs.

Truly no voyeur's impulse, or obsession to know, drove me there—I had burst into the attic room, delirious and looking only for my bottle of Bushmills under the mattress. (This immediately after staggering out of the bathroom where a debilitating cascade of diarrhea had convinced me that only a shot of Bush would put me right.) There were clues that should have informed my discretion. For one thing, the room was significantly warm; and Gretta's gum boots stood empty, upright, just beyond the open door, on either side of Penelope's torn robe lying in a puddle of pink.

It should have occurred to me (but it did not) that Penelope would be obliged to occupy my bed since I occupied hers. The two women—ripe Greek fig attached to slender leafless bough—had positioned themselves in an embrace I recalled from another world of confinement and distress, the Sans Souci, where I blundered upon Cookie and Mrs. Kakafroni lying on a pile of soiled sheets in the Laundry Room, coiled together as the ancient serpent devouring its own tail. I wanted then, I wanted now to wish them love—love by all means, by any means—love among the ruins, but Gretta's stricken eyes would not have believed my wish.

I withdrew, closing the door after me, too late.

11

THERE'S ALWAYS ANOTHER MAN, was the lesson, even when the man's a woman. Penelope and I decided together without saying so that I might be out of place in Chlorine Gardens, odd man out. So I slept another trinity of nights on my desk top before being taken in by Bridey of Irish Studies who had been driving me in her asthmatic Ford to Kelly's Out There in the Short Strand for what she called the crack and the plaintive laments sung by Tom Kelly himself, all of which put Bridey in a frame of mind to have a go with a poet. For two weeks while her parents were down south in the Republic I might share her downy Murphy bed and her slightly skeletal self, underweight and possibly anorexic, for I could never tempt her to eat but only drink at Kelly's—a disburbing replica of Valerie—until the fourth night of the fortnight when Mum and Da got back unexpectedly from Cork and I could hear the whispered interview in the vestibule: "Who's he?" A good question, one that I dared not ask myself.

The Bannisters took me in for the holidays like a misdelivered Christmas parcel. What a quarrelsome couple they were when Mary wasn't jogging and Rupert interpreting the *Táin* in his basement study. For another fortnight's reprieve I was granted half-rates on a room in the Common Room until it was needed for a visiting lecturer in the History of Science or the Science of History from Trinity College Dublin.

Outcast I was, and for all my minor trials of displacement there were those—no comparison meant, nor consolation—far worse off this bitter January, hunger artists "on the blanket" in the Maze, starving to death in the H-blocks. I was back at the office, no bars on my cell.

February turned impossibly warm for the space of three days, then came a series of remarkable reversals in wind and mood and temperature. A week's resplendent sunrises offered balmy promise that was immediately breached by thunderheads rolling in from the direction of Iceland, then the rain fiercely whipped by wind would reverse umbrellas for an hour, then a lazy sun easing into a natural setting as if only waiting there all the while—a delicious spreading sense of warmth and comfort that by noon had become hailstones. Any wonder a man turned to drink?

Another worse off for winter shelter was Liam Sweeney, at his wit's end for dossing down, according to Fiona McFee. Liam, she said, was "sleeping rough" in the Botanic Gardens.

"I thought they locked up the parks. At night, for security."

"Oh him, he goes over the wall. Regular Humpty Dumpty."

Fiona was one of the girls whose phone numbers Liam collected, but, "Never rings," she complained. Then it occurred to her, "But where's he to ring from in the Botanic Gardens?"

She was a slim boyish stark-white Kewpie in a leather skirt who waited tables at the New Abercorn and wrote poems. Fiona was best known locally for having won a free permanent wave for knowing who wrote the words and music to "Over the Rainbow" for a Downtown Radio quiz.

I pictured Liam lying on a park bench with a crown of snow on his head, but Fiona said he had found a way into the Palm Court and slept under trees imported from the tropics, the temperature kept high, appropriate to Egyptian foliage. He had smashed a shatterproof glass pane to crawl inside with the steam-heated palms.

"A great one he is for smashing glass. He's broke his arm, too. He broke into a sweet shop in Downpatrick, did you not know?" But for all his reckless criminal ways he was, Fiona sighed, feeling her prize perm, "our next great Ulster poet."

12

HAS NIGHT turned to day and the bleak morning black—what hour is this, what excuse of time to rattle a man awake? Somebody was calling Gold in the dark.

Dread dawn and we were only moments ago drinking rounds I remembered at the Elephant & Flea, the Bellingham Arms, either the Elly or the Belly maybe both. I felt for the gooseneck lamp: no clock of course in a poet's office and my watch in my pocket unwound. There was warm blood on Miss Chaucer's pillow. I was not past recall of pulling the sleeping bag up snug and so uncoordinated I punched myself in the bloody nose. Must have bled in my sleep through the night, or only moments ago it happened.

The banshee wail from somewhere down on Fitzwilliams was "Professor Gold," and there was Liam down there in the streetlight swinging his arm in a plaster cast like a cricket paddle. Said something I said I'd do it. Do what?

"My first ever. To read me verse."

Said I'd said I'd present him to the public for the first official reading of his young poet's life. The Antrim Academy was this school full of Prod teens that by rights the other Liam, Keene (and keen to read), should be reading to, but this Liam said he'd said he'd do it.

"There's blood on your mug," he called to me, so I threw the key to English to him and went to the Xerox bathroom to wash.

"Not to worry," said he when he came up to the office and saw I was staring at his arm in a plaster cast he was as proud of as a new poem. There were in fact poems written on the plaster, and telephone numbers.

I was concerned for his arm now and not my nose. Had he indeed been interrogated at Castlereagh or been hurt in the protest march?

"That march last week was a nuclear thing about not putting Yank bombs on Irish soil. You must've seen wee Keene on the march for he's the fanatical anti-nuke of the two of us, I was down in Downpatrick not Castlereagh where they nailed me—would you believe it, and me not remembering?—on that shop window thing, back the same night to celebrate getting off with a stiff sermon on abuse of drink and got pissed with the boyos and took a dare and fell off the ramp on my drinking arm."

He swung the arm about in its silken sling for me to admire and be concerned about, then rested the cast on the armrest of the seminar chair. His familiar smell had been etherized at the Royal Victoria and the only odor I caught was from the silk sling, a gift kerchief no doubt from the girl he had fallen for, for it was a girl who dared him to walk the ramp, not the boyos.

"Have you a fag now?" he asked.

"I don't smoke." He knew that. "You've got a cigarette already."

The smoker's hand trembled in the ghastly dawn.

"Only a fag end I picked up in the gentlemen's." Last night he bedded with the girl with the prizewinning perm and she had put him out at daybreak because of the talk. He had had to wash up at the public gentlemen's on Shaftesbury Square. "Tis how low you can stoop, fag ends found on the floor of a dirty loo, O lucky you not hooked on fags or fallen to the lower vices."

"I'll buy you a pack," I offered, "on the way."

"Silk Cuts," he specified, then spied the office phone. "Could I ring up a mate of mine?"

All the call boxes in the Magic Circle had been damaged by students trying to extract coins out of the slots. Students, he explained, did that at the end of the month when their grant money had run out.

He dialed, then held the receiver away from his ear as someone cursed at the other end. The telephone conversation was about drums.

"He's holding your bloody drums till he's paid so there's no use crying over spilt milk."

The mate whose drums had been confiscated was Liam also, Liam's doppleganger, the Shadow. I could hear the second Liam calling this Liam Liam from the other end, and echo of Liams back and forth—unless he was talking to himself, this Liam or the other one.

"You was an idjit to leave your bloody drums in my digs so don't go shooting blame in my direction. I thought I was doing a mate a favor to care for your gear for you and now you sound like a magistrate giving me bloody what-for. I'm the worse off, not you and your dumb drums. Been put out of my digs with an arm broke and a sore head of a hangover can be felt as far as the Mournes."

When the frustrated echo hung up on him, Liam explained to me that Muhammed the landlord of the Piss and Garlic Palace had locked him out of digs for nonpayment and locked Liam Keene's drums in till he was paid what was owed.

In the taxi to the Antrim Academy, Liam justified his broken arm and smoked up the cab with his Silk Cuts.

"I've the devil's own vertigo for such heights that would make me faint to look at in daylight but there was this dream of a woman looking on and a man's manhood was under challenge. Faint heart ne'er won fair lady, but och what we risk for the winning of them. Woke up in a ward of groaning men at the Royal Victoria, one of them shot in an ambuscade in Andersontown in the bollocks, poor sod's seedbag spilled open and curtains to his sex life. There's other and truer devotion night after night in Belfast than students pissing their grant money away in pints and taking dares at the Tinker's Dam. Woke up with the arm broke in two distinct and separate places, like north and south."

As we drew closer to the Academy and Liam's fate he confessed to stage fright.

"I'd walk that wall twice over than go through with this bloody reading."

His pale worried face was raw-shaven with bits of tissue attached to the mishaps. He wore a mangled gaudy necktie screwed at his neck like a noose—no smile for the cabbie, crooked or straight, under the circumstances. I squinted at the driver to see whose double he was, but the man was unknown to me. The only poet in the taxi was the unfortunate in the next seat.

In the waiting room to the Head's office, Liam and I were given cups of black tea by a uniformed prefect with the school crest on his jacket pocket. At least the Styrofoam cups warmed the hand that held it, and Liam had his Silk Cuts, drawing deep of a last fag before execution.

The Head, in his black robes of learning (and a piece of tissue on his chin, like Liam's) led us backstage in time for Assembly. Chairs scraped somewhere the other side of a curtain. We could hear the low resentful murmur of a captive audience herded into an unheated auditorium at an unforgivable hour. Liam was trying to scratch at a place inside his cast he could never reach; the prefect had to remind him to douse his cigarette. After that, Liam plucked at the bits of toilet paper until his visage reverted to angelic innocence. Then the curtain swept back and exposed us to the multitude.

I stepped up to the pulpit to mumble some scraps of background on the Young Poet. He was born. He attended. He began writing. I skipped over his criminal record, but otherwise brought him up to this very morning's moment, and finally said Liam Sweeney aloud to tentative and dutiful applause.

The applause did it. Weak as it was, trailing off so soon, hands clapping in unison worked the miracle in Liam. He bounced forth with more élan than the morning called for, all eagerness unleashed. In an instant he had become a true bard of Ireland: he had discovered his calling just the other side of dread. His winning smile was back, eyes flashing passion. He warmed to performing as if he had been born onstage.

First, he chatted up the girls in the front as comfortably as at a pub—for the girls were seated foremost with hockey sticks across their knees (boys huddled in the rear, they carried no weapons), four rows of blue skirts, uniform jackets with rounded buds pressing at the lapels, dark sheer stockings: a collection of fresh pubescent colleens. Liam was high at the sight and smell of them. He projected his apprentice gifts in their direction.

Liam did not recite from the page, he had brought no poems with him except those put to memory or newly penned on his plaster cast. He sang out his verses from the top of his head and it was to the girls he pitched his tuning fork, directing a lyric flow to those flower faces in the front. I gnawed distractedly at a thumbnail, carried away. The boy had his own swinging style through the echo of earlier poets (especially of the Poet), but what was it about the words that made me uneasy? What had I to be uneasy about, the sole counterfeit here?

The boys too sat in some awe of this articulate stripling, admiring, in their adolescent way—or inexplicably envious, as was I—gangling out of their jacket sleeves, mouths, as they gawked, slightly ajar.

As Liam played to the crowd, testing his depths, he grew bold enough to insert certain verses hardly appropriate to classroom sensibilities at Assembly. The line "my Everyman at the ready, my Everyman on the rise" raised more eyebrows than mine—fortunately the Head, in his robes and tassels, had retired from the auditorium early to attend to more prosaic affairs. Only the Instructor-in-Charge was at hand to monitor content. Sleek innuendos slid past him while he dozed through the recitation, or the outright references were out before he could rouse himself.

Who would have thought this daring rogue poet clamorous with phrase and gesture—his cast cracking against the edge of the pulpit for emphasis—had been all atremble seconds ago, suffering the bends and scattering nervous ash over his agitated lap?

The final poem was the one that caught me sharp, that did me in. I was too tangled in the implications to judge its worth or care if it was poetry or slander. It was my turn to be agitated. "Dark Princess."

        Dark all the way down
        To her musky black Persian purse.

The princess and her purse at the mercy of this boy's Everyman while witless unwitting Gold lounged in the Belly's lounge through the rape of his borrowed bedroom, the cavalier swive in his very bed. My nose began to bleed again: I fled Liam's stage in midapplause for the cold comfort of lavatory tile.

Downcast beyond recovery, I plodded beside the boy poet. (Liam, an invisible crown of laurel tilted over his brow, walked above the surface of the earth.) We passed a bombed-out area, or a demolition site, screened from the public by a wall of mismatched doors. *Never a door closes*, wrote my father, *but another opens*. A door had been slammed in my face and brought on nosebleed. I pressed the red-stained handkerchief to my nostrils enduring the mixed funk in silence: emotionally bankrupt but light-headedly aware of a purging. I could have thrown up back there, or fainted, but didn't. The sickness ran parallel to the last stages of hangover—bad vibes for now, but never again.

No taxis in this neighborhood, naturally—nor buses, apparently—but Liam was propelled forward on waves of applause from back there, transported by triumph, content to walk home or float. No hint of my depressed state penetrated his galling euphoria.

Saro was dead to me, about time. When once I imagined myself the gallant tearing the monkey's paw from that perfect neck, I could not displace the current image of Liam in my bed with my dream. I nursed my horror and abhorrence in secret, not a word of my hurt to the victor.

As we walked (friends, it would seem, from our ambulant proximity) I was assuming that Liam knew the city—after all, this was his country—or that he had applied his prodigious memory to the proctor's directions. But my distracted companion was too full of himself to consider true north. (He was assuming I knew.) For the first part of the hike a watery sun illuminated our circular way, but now the familiar cloud cover formed overhead and you could smell the storm being distilled at Cave Hill.

"Where are we?"

Liam heard nothing but the sound of one hand, his own, clapping.

"Where are we? I asked."

"Where?" He looked around for the first time. Then he reached into his pocket as if to pull out a map or a compass, but came up with the pack of Silk Cut.

We paused, and a pall fell. Disorientation is centered in the solar plexus, and I had a new discomfort to deal with. This was Out There.

Liam put a cigarette between his lips, then a hand to the dog's dinner of a necktie: "Down these streets," he reflected, "a man could end with his throat cut."

We were lost in the city where it was a fatal lapse to be lost.

There was an ominous absence of graffiti to confirm the worst: *Up the IRA*, at least, would have meant one thing, and *No Pope Here* another. We could have assumed protective coloring accordingly or come up with appropriate cover stories. But who would listen to stories Out Here? There was no one in sight to lie to, or surrender. Bannister had warned me about this place: the only message from behind this brick and those broken windows was shoot first—behind the hollow sockets only snipers lurked. This was the place where no birds sing.

For the first time I missed the gritty sight of military convoys rumbling down Crumlin Road. Where was Crumlin Road? I wished for tank-trucks and Land Rovers bristling with armed men, but you can never find a soldier when you need one.

"We'll nip into a pub and use the telephone."

Did he mean to ring the Confidential Number to report terror? (What number was that?) I thought tamely of calling a taxi. But there was no pub, not even the pubs snug behind barricade cages with signs in the window: REGULAR CUSTOMERS ONLY. Liam pointed the way with his cast and a cigarette between two yellow fingers, but his instincts were contrary to mine. The street he indicated was empty enough, but I saw no safety in its grim silence. The first block had been blasted to rubble, houses burnt and population displaced—the life of it too mysteriously absent. Liam surely reasoned that trouble here had expended itself beyond recall—violence had spilled over, done its devastation and moved on. But I thought I heard music, and turned the opposite way. Liam followed.

A Salvation Army band—six uniformed souls, uniforms!—was assembled two blocks away. They had the street corner all to themselves: were they only at practice? In the cockeyed way of the world there was no one to listen to them but Liam and me.

Liam was as reassured as I was by their Victorian pillbox hats and rimless glasses, but he may have sighed "Lovely" at the sight (reminded of his success) of the sexy dark stockings on the lasses. Drums and tuba, sounding brass and tambourine played "Nearer My God to Thee," the hymn the ship's band played the night the *Titanic* went down. I put money in a tambourine, saved.

After that blessing, the thump and oompah of the Salvation Army carried us down the last mean street of unkempt dollhouses with an occasional Union Jack painted vividly against drab brick or, once, a crude skull and crossbones drawn on a letter box. The echo of "Nearer My God" kept the bullets from ricocheting against the curbstones.

After the Salvation Army the only sign of life was a slattern in a window calling out to her spindly infant playing with mud in the gutter: "Crystal, get over here!"—as if our shadows passing would pollute the child. But even against the darkening sky of unwholesome cloud, I could make out the sketchy latticework of shipyard gantries. A shipyard would have to be neutral ground.

Anxiety yielded to hope around the next corner as we emerged from a tunnel of emptiness: there lay City Centre in all its worldly animation. I could have embraced the shopworn pedestrians and echoed Liam's "lovely" to the turmoil of clogged traffic.

The hayseed here was Liam, altogether innocent of the city past the perimeters of a magic circle. Only down from Downpatrick a year, he had never ventured into the business district of Belfast. It was up to me, the alien, to show him how to present himself for a search at the barricaded passageway—Liam attempted to enter the turnstile by way of the Way Out. The blind were leading the blind this day.

I recognized the sorry façade of Caesar's Palace across from the Public Library, an urban gambling casino with 2p slot machines along the wall; nothing would do Liam, gambler and poet, but to nip in and try his luck for the second time today. We found ourselves in the company of dead-eyed housewives sitting numbly at electronic Bingo while fortune's queen sat enthroned in City Centre's center reading the pips that popped up through a vacuum tube. Liam backed out again when he saw that chance was women's work, and I backed into a woman on her way in, excused myself, and thought I recognized her face from the passengers I had flown to Belfast with: a gold maple leaf in her powder-blue lapel reminded me of the Canadian maple leaves on her luggage in Aldergrove.

There was a travel agency on the next corner, and another on the next. The window displays were a patchwork of Hawaii, Marrakesh, the Bahamas—favorite hot spots such as Miami and the South of France—while here the wind was up, rain on the way.

At Fountain Street we passed through the lower bastion of City Centre's ring of barricades, beside the Linen Hall Library where I had searched in vain for the *Selected Poems of I.M. Gold*. (But did discover the bank next door where I banked his stipend.) Then I led Liam down Great Victoria past the resurrected Opera House, a baroque target for terrorists but carelessly overlooked, like the equally venerated but vulnerable Palm Court in the Botanic Gardens. We were hurrying along now ahead of the downpour, seeking the dark comfort of a pub within the Magic Circle.

In passing I pointed out the expanding bookshop where I bought secondhand paperbacks with vivid jackets to pass the reading time in grey digs (before the inevitable eviciton), but Liam—who did not read novels, and had more experience at evictions than I had—absorbed only the information that a massage parlor had occupied the three floors above the bookshop, and had been abandoned, this being Belfast and not Miami where brothels flourished and bookstores went bankrupt.

The patients (I told him) at the Shaftesbury Square Hospital, for alcoholics, used to gather at their common room windows to watch the girls come to work at teatime and now could only witness the bookseller stocking the upper rooms with cheap literature.

"How do you come by all this?" asked curious Liam.

"One of the patients brought me his poems to read."

"Not one of the girls?"

A block from the bookstore Liam turned cocky and far from afraid, for he was in familiar territory, his very own turf. There was the landmark Crown squeezing Liam's favorite betting parlor between its stained-glass window and Robinson's equally venerable public house. Across the street stood the Europa Hotel celebrating its eighty-fourth unsuccessful IRA attempt to remove it from the skyline; no bomb had more than chipped its cornice: the citadel stood intact behind a moat of bunkerlike parking lots and chain link.

No door closes but another opens.

I could have sworn the policewoman orchestrating traffic at Shaftesbury Square winked at me. Twin punksters emerged from the underground gentlemen's where Liam only this morning stumbled upon his first scavenged smoke of the day. Liam's ebullient self-confidence was contagious for it spread to me; Shock had done its worst, Recovery was just across the Square. At that instant the sun broke through the swollen clouds to illuminate the spiked and dyed crests the punksters affected, two startled peacocks squinting into the unexpected light.

Winking truly this time, the policewoman held up her white glove to all traffic along the five-starred intersection to allow poets and peacocks to cross in safety. Not only traffic was halted, but existence itself was for one moment in suspension. The two punksters were as redeemed in their innocence as Liam and me. Liam was free to believe himself crowned bard of the universe and I could recognize my desire-and-pursuit for an adolescent vanity of vanities. All of which follows from the miraculous: we had not been murdered, it did not rain.

13

In the vestibule on the ground floor of King's English, between the doors marked VicStudies and ModBritLit, was a bulletin board festooned with scrappy notices that fluttered with the draft from Fitzwilliams when the door to English opened, notices no one but the Poet in Residence ever read: warnings about bicycle thefts or the imminent publication of Dr. McDonald's *The Pelagian Heresy in the works of Duns Scotus* and the announcement of an organ recital at Ballymurphy Cathedral, security measures in effect: all tickets purchased in advance, photo I.D. required for admission. Today one notice had blown loose from its ill-placed thumbtack and lay on the floor footprinted by a passing herd of students, a found poem:

> *Vacancy*
> *Responsible person please*
> *Mindful of others*
> *Being quite quiet at the times of study*
> *Please contact Muhammed*
> *Magdala Towers*

Within minutes of this discovery I was in touch with the author of the notice, Muhammed himself, for I immediately walked over to Magdala to investigate the latest residential vacancy. As it turned out, the room was the former digs of Liam Sweeney, from which he had only yesterday morning been dispossessed for nonpayment.

The Piss and Garlic Palace was Liam's name for the place, but "Magdala Towers" was chipped in stone over the asymmetric entryway. There was some talk among the tenants who spoke English that Magdala Towers had been fire-bombed and hastily rebuilt, how else account for the splintered beams and sagging floorboards and seasick-making tilted room Muhammed offered me for nine pounds fifty pence per week? Muhammed's smile was a smarmy display of very good teeth and the best intentions: he wore dark sunglasses in sunless Belfast, so I had no way of knowing if his eyes flashed as brilliantly as his teeth when I passed the pound notes and a 50p piece to him.

Magdala was one of that warren of streets with biblical names, a predominantly student ghetto between Botanic Avenue and the Ormeau Road, known as the Holy Land. This was a buffer zone tangential to the Magic Circle where the circle blended into the Golden Triangle around the gasworks on Ormeau. Muhammed, majordomo of the P&G Palace, was an Iraqi who once dealt in rugs imported from Baghdad and now collected rentals on Magdala. He leased principally to tenants from the East, Near and Far, and it occurred to me (though I attempted to obliterate all memory of her) I was entering Saro's realm without Saro.

By noon the mosque was melodious with Arabic and Tamil, birds twittering out the windows of a Tower of Babel, the wordplay clamorous or strident at mealtimes, the mood turned taciturn during long wet afternoons of study, quarrelsome after the pubs closed and finally the troubled silence after Lights Out through the gruesome hour before the dawn. Strangely, the silent times and not the tumult were the most disturbing. During the dark dead hours I became a little desperate for sound.

"I am bereaved," said I the first night, aloud, "of light."

This did not bring forth the Poet. If Liam's shadow's confiscated drums had been in the room with me (they were under deadfall lock and key awaiting ransom in Muhammed's quarters) I would have rapped out a Morse tattoo in my solitude, an SOS to the world. (Now I could understand Mrs. Kakafroni's compulsion to play her flute at night.) A stolen telephone defined my state of incommunicado. It was a phone ripped from some local call box—Liam's work, no doubt—a drunk's trophy set upon a podium of telephone directories, four years old, as part of the room's sense of detachment.

The double bed was perfect for an insomniac (room for two, when I was only one; room for thought, for tossing) ornamented by a coverlet lent by Deirdre, sheets from Mary B, Miss Chaucer's embroidered bloodstained pillow. Muhammed had generously left a rug he had failed to peddle and, on the wall, a poster of Che Guevara: Che, with his jaunty beret and bedraggled beard (why-do-you-people-grow-beards?) dead in Bolivia but resurrected larger than life here in the Holy Land.

Left behind as well was a grease-encrusted gas ring, but the P&G Palace was not supplied with gas, or no longer supplied: there was a gas jet protruding from the baseboard that brought forth nothing, not even a convenient means of suicide.

And what to do with a closet full of egg cartons, empty, a collection of Guinness bottles, also empty—fried-egg sandwiches, with stout, having been Liam's customary sustenance—a broken-off oar to a racing scull, a bicycle pump but no bicycle, and more telephone directories ever more ancient? I looked up Gold in the four-year-old directory and found two.

The sink might empty after a seepage of hours, leaving a scum of soap and toothpaste along its grinning rim. There was no accessible U-band I might have detached to disengage the former tenant's cloacal accumulations—in fact, I could not imagine Liam's lax ablutions, whatever they might have been, blocking a drain so thoroughly. When I went to Muhammed over the state of my sink his smile embraced all that befalleth mankind: he beamed over the strangled drain and promised instant redress in due time.

The student tenants were nonchalant about where they disposed of their leavings on the landings and altogether indifferent about where they urinated in the hallway water closets. Down through the stairwell echoed their thundering din and the incessant syllables of their thousand-and-one tongues, a tree house of myna birds. The odors seemed to wrap themselves around the sounds, each flavoring the other, bird talk and steaming curries on-the-hob blended in a combination of sensual assaults that only reminded me of my recent indecent adolescent fixation on an Indian princess.

(At elevenses I learned that O'Donegal had once attempted to get it on with Saro and received a rough smack for his try: it was suitable enough for him, a small-time troubadour, to languish unrequited in hopeless devotion, but I would not join the ranks of the rejected in anticipatory transports of the waiting game.)

I saw Saro only from a distance at my office window: once, with her wedding-cake spouse (a cuckold unaware), he carrying an open black BHS umbrella identical to my own, she wearing a lime-colored kerchief against the drizzle, no place for her beneath the umbrella, she was taller than he—she could have shared my brolly, and now never would.

For society I shifted back and forth from King's to Magdala, from Virginia Woolf's suicidal eyes to Che Guevara's lean and hungry look. A pretty girl lived across the street from me on Magdala, window facing window, but I never saw her on campus and would have to await a bomb scare to meet her on the street and persuade her whatever her persuasion (Taig or Prod) to share a double bed with me.

I dined alone in dreary cafeterias or tearooms on Botanic where motherly security officers served double time as cashiers and knitted scarves when not checking handbags for firearms. You could get a rubbery omelet or a mush of fried cod with two vegs steamed lifeless lying in a pool. For lunch I lived on ready-made cheese-and-salad sandwiches sold by floury bakery ladies who called me Love and Dear and said, "That's lovely," when I fished up the proper change. (Once Indian Billy's nickel surfaced amongst the pence and 50p pieces and a barmaid said, "Lovely, but we can't accept coins from the South.") I had grown as indifferent to nourishment as the rest of Ireland and subsisted more consistently on drink. I began to agree with absentminded McMichael who some days forgot to eat at all and with Milton who maintained that food was naught but fuel. After all, Ginny had flourished on fast foods, vodka and vitamin C.

You could always risk—the students did, regularly—a newspaper cone of fish and chips at Ptomaine Tom's fish-and-chips van, with a dash of vinegar to cut the grease.

A poisonous blue-green fungus grew inside the community refrigerator like an oozing bruise beside which tomatoes rotted sweetly away and leftover curries congealed into saffron-colored sludge. I stored my own austere rations—cheese and milk and a jar of instant coffee—on the pigeon-splattered windowsill: the odd shapes and labels a fixed part of my view, adjuncts to the chimney pots beyond, like clay pipes in a shooting gallery.

I watched for the colleen across the street to undress in the light but she drew her blinds, always.

When the sink no longer drained at all and I bailed out the stagnant pool with a coffee jar into a chamber pot, and thought I smelled gas from the nonexistent gas supply, I went to Muhammed to test his grin again. But Muhammed had a smile for me over a difficulty of greater consequence.

"The lady police came looking for you. Are your papers in order, my friend?"

I felt this accusation to the bone. I assumed that Arts Council had handled all of this, or that Bannister had arranged for my poet's licence to be here. I explained to Muhammed that I was Poet in Residence but my landlord could only enlarge upon his smile as a comment on my innocence.

"The lady police do not concern themselves with poetry, only that the papers are in order."

I discovered I must put my papers in order at Stormont Castle and submit photographs and digital prints to the RUC at Castlereagh.

"All authorities are on holiday, their offices, dear friend, are being closed of this moment."

The phantasm of a castle was only a troubled mind-trip away, lurking in the grey weather brewed behind Black and Divis mountains, but Muhammed's smile was a not-to-worry one. With his openhanded gesture of largesse and an adjustment of his cuffs to show nothing up his sleeves, Muhammed granted me the weekend in which to brood about my delinquency before making known to the Castle who Gold, I.M., was.

At the drugstore, or the chemist's, I stocked up on antiacid tablets and milk of magnesia to deal with heartburn and constipation, classic factors in the Irish way of life—the other constants being nightmare and bad news, whose antidote was whiskey. I settled for the liter size of Bushmills at the cut-rate Off-Licence on the Lisburn Road.

Why not just abandon ship? All this rinkydink on the way to fulfillment. Travel had its points: learn new ways to stave off the old glooms. Why should the Great Joke perpetrated on these people be a joke on me. Wallowing in my fear and indecision with only Che Guevara's misguided example and a box of saltines and my liter of Bush to buck me up, what I suddenly wanted to be was Indian Billy rolling along the highways of a southern place with somebody else's furniture to unload and Shakespeare on my tapes.

But that was only one lost weekend's withdrawal and panic. With all his free advice, my father had failed to warn me of the infinite pettiness of the counterfeit life. I was utterly free to skip out of a demented poet's unfinished poem, but wherever I would skip to, the authorities would be waiting in castles with papers to sign.

By Monday a crack in the sky revealed a miraculous streak of milk-water blue, a tracking pattern that possibly led to Ireland's timid sun—or maybe just a jet stream passing across Aldergrove. But I took it as a sign, and crawled out of my fallout shelter. I was on my way to Bannister for advice when I heard the horrible news. The Holy Land buzzed and twittered with it.

The girl across the street who so modestly drew her blinds at night had teamed up with another girl at a neutral tavern and picked up a set of soldiers badly disguised in cheap civvies. Everybody knew Brit soldiers for their polished boot tops and short sides-and-back hair. Magdala was the garden path the girls led them down, and into the flat across the way where a contingent of Provos waited behind drawn blinds.

"The blood ran beneath the doorsill," Molly told me, "and downstairs, it was that abundant."

Molly's was the grapevine that ran to the epicenter of events, and her version was sure to be embellished with grace notes the *Telegraph* neglected to tell.

"They may search house-to-house till they drop," declared Molly, "but the devils that done it are long gone across the border South and safe. Nothing left behind in the slaughterhouse but bloody footprints and a bayonet and bodies of two poor lads their throats opened ear to ear."

An Afghani I knew from Byzantine Studies, who also lived at the P&G Palace, warned me that our block of Magdala was cordoned off by police Land Rovers and plastic ribbon while troops went through performing their house-to-house inquiries and personal searches.

Until nightfall I took scrappy meals at the Common Room and drank vodka with orange juice to numb my overwrought thoughts. Best steer clear of the Holy Land until the searches were over, unidentified as I was. When I did dare return to my lodgings I learned from the same Afghani the latest irony in this grim day's toll: Muhammed had been caught up in the police net.

"He was not the owner of the house, my friend. He was not the owner's representative, nor renter of the premises."

Muhammed was but an enterprising squatter, since Magdala Towers had been condemned more than a year ago and due for demolition (in due time)—squatters were we all. Somehow the building's existence had been overlooked (though not by Muhammed) or lost in the archives at City Hall or Stormont Castle. Muhammed had been taken to Crumlin Remand Centre, appropriate eviction notices were nailed to all our doors. I was obliged to abandon ship after all, but was granted a stay of identity.

As I gathered up my travel gear once again I shook off the gruesome images of dead soldiers, the two-poor-lads like the lads buried in shallow graves in Alabama (how petty became my hassles in Belfast when the larger picture loomed), and saw Muhammed's empty grin lingering on the threshold. He had pulled the magic carpet out from under us all.

When Molly met me for the third time moving back to my desk top she took pity and remembered a brother of hers who ran a hotel at Drumlough, an hour's distance from King's but in a safe place. "A change," Liam would say, a line he borrowed from Brendan Behan, "is as good as a rest."

14

MY REMOVAL was complete, to the desolate spaciousness of the Six Counties Hotel, a seaside stopping-place à la mode before the Troubles but now occupied only by Mr. and Mrs. Tasker, their pet canary and me. I had a bathroom all to myself (with a sink that drained instantly, no pantyhose dripping over the tub)—I had the choice, in fact, of sixty bathrooms, empty all. There was a surfeit of steam heat, conscientiously maintained by Mr. Tasker, throughout the downstairs and as far as my room directly over the lobby. Hot-water taps miraculously gushed hot water. The double windows of my room gave onto an uncertain view of fog-blurred Belfast across the lough, and from the remote dignity of the Six Counties, alone on the strand, you might come to believe there was no such realm as Northern Ireland in the misty distance, ever.

The estuary between Drumlough and Belfast was a serious piece of water, whitecapped with death threats in rough weather, and the weather was mostly rough. The channel was just as menacing when becalmed to a flat drain-water grey beneath which floated—the villagers declared—the corpses of drowned sailors never washed ashore. The local story was that prehistoric undersea beasties lurked in these waters awaiting the unwary. You would see their hellish forms breaking the surface at twilight, if you cared to look. (I looked, and saw nothing but the whitecaps.) It was suicide to swim here or go boating alone, but the legend had been suppressed during the spa's golden age so as not to frighten off tourists. But the Troubles had frightened off the tourists all the same, though the Taskers appeared untouched by the isolation and unmoved by tales of horrors beneath the sea.

There was a convenient ferry across Belfast Lough, but I— impressed enough by local legend—did not risk the passage by boat, or go near the water. Instead, I commuted to and from Botanic Station by toy train that dawdled past the shipyards and gasworks—graffiti on the sides of tanks: 6 INTO 26 WON'T GO and GOD GOVERNS IRELAND (but which God?) and billboards displaying the Confidential Number to dial with anonymous information about terrorist activity—to work poetry weekdays, then retire to my seaside digs at night.

A change and a rest it was, a place to contemplate sea creatures and from which direction the weather blows. I came to think this must be the place, the great good place promised to me—but where was the girl?—by a poet with the gift of knowing What Next. Here I might disengage my futile attachment to a Hindu princess; from this private inlet I could find a maiden of my own, discover paradise, meanwhile recuperating from the Irish sickness of lost causes and dead ends.

Mr. Tasker, Tom, attended the temperamental generator and de-manding coal furnace, or he wandered the strand at low tide picking up whatever flawed treasures and new effluvia floated his way. (His latest find was an uprooted call box, missing only its telephone, intact and tight as a floating coffin, with five 5p pieces still lodged in the slot.) His wife piped proudly about the glories of Drumlough's rude rackety sea breeze that swept to shore great quantities of iodine "soothing to a person's nerves," and did seem to soothe mine, my fears and frustrations somehow becalmed in this setting. The long night's wind was incessant, but I slept the sleep of reason through its assault with only a single drink at night to see me off.

My spacious room was mostly furnished with Tom Tasker's gifts from the sea. The ashtrays were shells, of course, but there was a seaborne captain's chair with several spindles missing, a careful crochetwork of butcher's twine to fill the gaps, and a three-legged deal table wedged into a corner to compensate for the missing limb. I had a shelf of waterlogged books to browse, such titles as *Science and Health, Children's Plays for Holidays, Bee-Keeping Made Easy, Ivanhoe, Forty Years a Country Doctor*—the bindings warped and pages glued together with sea damp. I collected dirty laundry in a baby's basinet (the baby lost at sea?) and stored Bushmills in a hollow tubeless television console. There was a French flag hanging over the fireplace, its blue, white and red faded to pastel. The fireplace was a working one and Mr. T supplied me with all the driftwood I could burn in it. At night I took snug pleasure in the song-and-dance of a log fire as I sat becushioned in the captain's chair, with a shot of Bush in a wineglass, no ice.

Whatever did those former tourists find to do in luckless Drumlough, besides drown?

The Taskers were Protestant born and worked with method, or without, but worked without letup according to the Protestant ethic. They worked when there was no work, as Mr. Tasker was working now, tinkering with the antique hydraulic elevator, hoping to make it operate again as it did in the golden age, though there were no passengers for it, and no need. His eyes watered with remembering: "Och, such a grand time, when Drumlough was crawling with couples up from Dublin and over from Liverpool, taking a bathe or a sail, and the dances of a summer night, hardly a wink's sleep the crack so good." A young blade, he had been boots at the hotel, Tillie Tasker told me, and she herself a chambermaid.

Somehow I suffered contentment in the raucous company of seagulls and lacked not for communication more than somber chats with the Taskers. I cruised the windy inlet with trouser cuffs rolled to keep my leaky desert boots out of the tide pools, walking as if I had a rendezvous with a similarly detached soul or was expecting a message in a bottle. I was as lonely as my thoughts allowed, and my thoughts were crowded but serene. As for a place to keep torment at bay, this was it.

From my double-windowed crow's nest I once saw a whole seminary of priests—unless I dreamed them, or they were not priests (for Drumlough was known as Protestant turf)—trooping through no-man's-land in front of the Six Counties each carrying an ice-cream cone. Anything seen from that window, in this mist, could be mirage—like the older woman I saw who looked so much like the woman from Canada I had seen twice before. One deceptive dusk I could have sworn to three horsemen on an apocalyptic gallop along the strand at low tide. Another time, out walking, I spotted a reclining naiad from a respectable distance: she awaited my imminent arrival in her trailing apparel of kelp. Naked she was, and my heart gave a quick little turn before I realized she was but cold promise in plaster.

A draper's dummy had washed ashore, a truncated mermaid missing its detachable lower half. I flung the disappointment back into the depths to be devoured by the beasties lurking and hissing out there—one less useless artifact to be rescued by Tasker. The plaster head had golden hair and the wide staring eyes out of a poem.

Wait, said a voice, so I set about waiting.

Before they departed, Mr. Tasker, eyes forever moist, said to me in his mournful way, "Cheerio."

"A change," I replied, "is as good as a rest."

The Taskers were bound for Port Rush to visit Mrs. T's moribund sister, "the dear heart, down to skin and bone, all eat up with cancer inside."

Mr. T's thermal underwear cuffs extended beyond his undertaker's sleeves as he presented me with a ring of keys. There was a passkey to each of the sixty rooms and keys to the utilitiy rooms in the basement, and he gave me a telephone number to call in case of emergency. There was no telephone, only the floating call box he had propped up against the side porch: I could always ring from the Red Carpet in Drumlough. The tears fell from his eyes as he demonstrated the gauge levels on the hot-water heater and revealed the secrets of the electric generator.

Mrs. T was so fretful about the dread journey ahead—they must travel by car because the train line to Londonderry had been bombed between Ballymoney and Port Rush—that I volunteered to distribute Miles's daily ration of birdseed and keep his little water basin filled. Both Taskers brightened. "It would be a kindness," said she. Otherwise they would have been obliged to leave their canary at the Red Carpet exposed to all the undoings of a public house. Would I remember to cover his wee cage at night? I would.

The Taskers drove off in a Mini, a vehicle bleached colorless by the elements, scoured thoroughly by the salt air, as if Saro's identical model in scarlet had been bled. I had kept myself from thinking of Saro until now.

I jangled the keys in the wake of the Taskers, caretaker now to their abandoned castle, stranded alone on this empty strand. My only company was Miles, the canary who never sang. ("No birds, you know, sing in Belfast," said Liam, explaining the line "And no birds sing" from one of his poems, and from John Keats.)

"Saro," I told Miles, "once asked me if I sang."

Only minutes after being left alone I found myself talking to a canary, a dangerous sign. I fled solitary confinement into a white swirl of feathery snow, headed for the Red Carpet in Drumlough. It was a brisk twenty-minute hike across the snowy dunes, and I made it in fifteen, but no sooner at the entrance than two brawlers flung themselves in my path from inside the pub, thrown out, or burst out of doors by their own exertions, fists still flying, and I tangled between them barely missed getting hit from both sides. It took the two a moment to realize in their violence a third man had stumbled between, no part of the quarrel, and immediately they ceased. I was even briefly brushed and adjusted and set safely aside in the sober calm of a common truce—then they were back at it, beating one another bloody in the drifting snow. They ran off in the same direction at the sound of a police siren.

No one in the Red Carpet knew I was a poet—their great good fortune not to know, just as it was mine not to know their troubles— and I was known to the barmaid only as Dear. They knew I lived at the Six Counties Hotel and spoke with a Yank accent, so I could be what I liked—Taig or Prod (it was a Protestant pub)—as long as I was a foreign one. They were serious drinkers here, even the dart players and football fans—no wonder the pubs were separated by beliefs, drink was communion itself.

By the time I started for home, the white plumes were still blowing across the Irish Sea, a white shroud covered the lough, and a woman walked ahead of me with a dog as big as she was. Big girl and big dog walked ahead of me all the way to the Six Counties; they walked past and I walked in: not once did she turn to see who shadowed her track. But I had taken drink enough and seen enough hallucinations not to take a strange woman in this strange place seriously. She may have been the shadow and I but real.

"Your Mother was always a fanatic for wine, being French, and my Mother (your precious Grandmother) drank Southern Comfort for her nerves, but there was never to my knowledge an alcoholic in the family. Let this confession be a lesson to you, Son. Dr. B was aware of the way I was drinking whiskey and took it upon himself (we were partners) to warn me my liver was at risk. You can lose a kidney or a lung, but when the liver goes, as the saying goes, 'that's all she wrote.' I switched to 3.2 beer instanter, and have never touched a drop of hard stuff since.

"(Breathwaite himself passed away with cirrhosis while serving time in the Atlanta State pen. He was a drunk, and knew it, and a disgrace to his profession. Though your Mother always thought he was a top-notch diagnostician and doted on him as a doctor. What your

Mother did not know and I never had the heart to tell her was that Dr. B was banned for life by the AMA from entering an operating room, ever. He once went into surgery after a drinking spree and performed a hysterectomy on a woman with appendicitis. You can imagine what that malpractice suit did to his career, even the scrub nurses testified against him.)

"What I am getting at is that sailors have a long-standing reputation as heavy drinkers, and all I ask is that you make it beer, and light beer at that, and think twice with every sip. You can tell your shipmates, 'Sorry, boys, but I promised my old Dad.' "

Damn, I had stepped in that dog's defecation. At least I could be pleased with myself for having thought to carry my ring of keys. Immediately I sensed a depressing emptiness in the other pocket, for I had left my bottle of Bush at the Off-Licence in Drumlough, closed now, my bottle to see me through the weekend.

I whistled in the dark till I touched the light switch (*No, Father—Dad?—I am not yet the family alcoholic*) but the ring of keys rattled in my fist, I was trembling from the oversight of having left behind a bottle. Dr. B may have diagnosed me otherwise, detecting the primary symptoms, and handed down an indictment.

I burglared the Taskers' tiled and sterile kitchen hoping they were hypocrites and he at least kept a stash of something against runny nose and eyes, but only Mrs. T's cooking sherry turned up in the realm of teetotal—and not much of that. Miles cocked a cold eye upon me as I swigged the dregs directly from the bottle.

"Yes," I said to him, "I drink."

Do you now?

"And drink, and drink. Like them, these people. I'm blessed and cursed. With the gift to remember."

Come off it, you self-indulgent clown.

"But I collect. I'm the clown who collects. Secrets."

Come off it, Critic. Fake poet and petty thief.

"Look at Tasker. What else is there but to collect? And remember."

That's history, come off it, you've got none. Desire and pursuit is your game.

"That's a detour, that's a dead end, that's the Big Joke."

Wait, said the bird.

I roughly covered his cage to escape the Poet's beady eye.

Saturday morn broke clear and bright, as if there had been no snow the night before, wet sand where the white had been. I took a peep at the world through Tasker's spyglass at what appeared to be an outing, or an invasion, of wee schoolgirls, aged seven to nine, and their tall brisk teacher, with dog. The dog was the largest canine in Christendom, an Irish wolfhound, loping faithfully behind his mistress and her troops: the woman and dog from last night, no doubt, turned from shadow to substance. The girls were in uniform—Girl Guides or Scouts or Brownies—the uniforms not brown but beige, set off cunningly with orange neckerchiefs: perhaps they were Daughters of the Orange Order. Teacher wore the adult size of same, with a dog whistle attached to her neckerchief.

It was a sight to lighten any hangover morning, so I went out to review the troops. Teacher was walking backwards—in step, as were they all, to an unseen drummer—and didn't see me at first.

"Nice day," said I, "for a march."

Teacher nearly stepped on me, and blew her whistle for a halt. The girls turned their flower faces in my direction, delighted I had upset the military for an instant, but the teacher-leader gave me a look my idiot observation deserved. Her reply was a civil enough "That it is."

She was a big woman, but handsome, as they said here. Her face was pretty (the female complection nourished by the damp), but the look in it was hard. I wanted to know her and she knew it. I attempted to view the scene from her end of the spyglass: bearded stranger on the way to a drink gives asinine weather report to a team of colleens on parade. She had dark hair drawn back by a clasp at the back of her neck so tight it made her narrow eyes Oriental. I had to remember she was the one with the whistle, and might sic the dog on me.

"You're the poet," she finally said.

Everything was known in Belfast and environs except what I was personally Not to Know.

"Gold," I reminded her. The advantage had swung round my way. "I live in the Six Counties."

"Don't we all?" said she—the colleens were known for their wit.

Her expression softened by a shade and she made the troops say Good-day to me, a capella—or was it Good-bye? for she was calling them to order again.

I quickly asked her if she would join me for a drink at the Red Carpet, "When the parade is over. That is." It was foolish of me to speak of drink so early—the pubs not open till eleven—and in front of the girls. I received another hard look.

"Not today, Mr. Gold," she replied coldly, the only reply appropriate to twelve wide-eyed witnesses.

She blew the whistle on our brief encounter and, with her dozen Daughters, was on the march again. I watched the drill squad sadly over the next dune, the big dog's ragged tail the last over. Alone again, in my Arabia Deserta.

My forgotten bottle was safe with the brick-faced barmaid, wrapped in its original brown bag, but the Red Carpet was overrun with football fanatics urging the TV screen to exert its utmost. I lunched on the barmaid's shepherd's pie washed down with a half-lager and suffered the sports fans their shrill victory before scooping up yesterday's bottle and turning back.

The enchanted dune had been wiped clean by the wind, not even a footprint to remember the Daughters by. During the football match I had dreamed up a thousand better things to say than before, greetings to suppress a whistle and break up a parade, but nobody to say them to.

O sweet teacher with cat's eyes and dog whistle, you will never know what you could have meant.

There was the Six Counties perched precisely where I had left it, but going shadowy, for the light was going out of the day early. Dusk descended spookily by midafternoon. The generator had turned cranky, and I would have to resort to candles. Also I felt a cold coming on, or my shepherd's pie coming up. Not even the promise of my recovered bottle could restore this misbegotten day.

I stepped outdoors with a flashlight for a breath of salt air and to vomit the meat pie into a tide pool, then walked back through the swill washed up on that night's shore: lager bottle caps and some infant's sodden eyeless Teddy and creepy coils of toilet paper coming in with the tide. I stumbled over a tar-stained starfish and a dead seagull, bad signs both.

Something out there was watching me, so I hurried back to light candles. No sooner had I festooned the lobby with candlelight, than the front door blew open—I had forgotten to lock it—and half my candles went out. Yes, there was something out there.

"About that drink," she said, and stepped in followed by the dog of all dogs.

I could expect to be put bloody well under arrest, for she had changed into her police uniform, but she carried a poem in her purse instead of handcuffs.

15

THE MIRACLE after shipwreck is to find yourself in your own bed badly cramped but only slightly seasick, a policewoman out of uniform in your arms. We had drunk well into my bottle of Bush analyzing her poem—which I gallantly declared was the very spirit of Ulster (as patriotic as the color orange)—and so, without preliminary grope or the ghost of a kiss, we tumbled into bed together. This thing with the Irish about physical contact would forever escape my understanding.

"Och, we're as warm-blooded as they come when the wind is right."

She was in Traffic Control, Maureen Dowell, one of the spider women with white gloves in charge of Shaftesbury Square, and used to giving directions.

That's right, up and over. Steady, a little higher, nice, wait, back a little, there, ah, now.

I expected a whistle blast to signal our finale, but she trembled and sighed in satisfaction, then went into a fit of the giggles.

"Did you think now a Prod couldn't kick her heels up neat and sweet as a Taig?"

I didn't think anything but pleasure, I let her do the thinking.

"Have you taken up with a Catholic lass as yet, all tangled up in their beads and beatitudes and it takes a Pope's say-so to get between sheets with their young man.

Was Bridey of Irish Studies Catholic or Protestant? I saw no beads, I never asked—which only went to show how removed from their world was I.

"I had you spotted, Goldy, the day you crossed my intersection with that student that's got it on with every girl in Belfast, headed for the Crown, there's two of a kind, said I. I've been on to you for many a week. I'm a leg up out of Traffic into Aliens and you'd best be carrying proper identity next time I nip in: name, photo and digital prints."

The authority of one weighty breast rested on me as she lectured, a muscled leg thrust between mine. Maureen was a tall handsome armful—all there, built to last. I wondered if her black-mail meant I must swive her out of turning me in.

"I'm stiff," I complained.

"I'll see to your stiff, I'll see it confined to Castlereagh Barracks."

Instead she confined my stiffness to barracks of her own. From her superior height and topside position, she was all the more in charge. We took longer at our maneuvers this time around, but came to the same conclusion: I was pleasured out of my mind and Maureen giggled herself silly. Having made love like banshees, we slept like the dead.

By morning the candles had burnt down to wax puddles but I woke up aglow. Maureen was already up twisting her hair back into its plastic catch to make her eyes Chinese again. She allowed me a moment to admire the robust undraped form before she fastened herself into underthings. The black triangle was a bushy marvel she snapped a pair of panties over—knickers, she called them—her breasts hung lower than I liked, or thought I liked, but I was disappointed to see them put away for church. (It was Sunday morning, and the girleens on yesterday's march were also in her Sunday School class.)

"You and your notions of Protestants."

I protested that I had no notions of Protestants, except her—and of Catholics none at all.

"You Yanks are all alike."

"You and your notions of Yanks."

"I showed you, did I not?"

"You did." I patted the place beside me where she had lain. "All of Ireland's problems could be solved right here."

"They could, could they? Little you know."

"I know more after last night than I ever knew before."

She thought I meant all I had learned from her poem. She was back in uniform now, Daughter of the Orange Order again.

"I've more poems than that."

She had more to teach me and I was eager to learn.

"When?"

"Little you know of history."

"History is made," and I patted the place, "right here."

"Little you know."

She hinted we would make more history after church and Sunday dinner with Mum. I was not invited to either event, being a Jew, a lecher and a poet.

"I used to dance here," she said suddenly, thinking of the history of Tasker's time, "in the old days."

Faithful Drum, the wolfhound, had slept the night in the lobby with its transient ghosts, and I could hear his nails clicking on the parquet as he heaved his shaggy weight upright. She was away with Drum to Drumlough and services ᴀt the Church of Ireland without even a goodbye kiss and barely a ta-ta.

On the advice of my father I scrubbed the genitalia well (that had been my oversight with Ginny) and went back to bed with a sack of raisins—also on his advice—and an apple. I slept a second time, for the morning was without light; then, when I was up for good, I realized the windows had been covered by a plague of insects. A flying crawling incredible mass of shiny red beetles, black spots lacquered on their cupcake wings, had blown across the Irish Sea in the wake of the freakish snow. The omens did not disturb me, a harmless enough intrusion, having arrived in the company of Maureen.

I missed her.

Ginny's recommendation for sluggish empty mornings-after was *sirshasan,* a headstand meant to place the universe in perspective, so I hoisted my legs aloft wavering uncertainly, blood pounding downward, then scissored my legs together in alignment. I did perceive an odd sensation of accomplishment and something like pleasure, but perhaps they came with a vision of a woman with a dog walking on the roof of the world.

"You're under arrest."

Maureen was back, trying to sound strict in her Sunday School outfit, but I knew she was tickled to come upon her naked lover upside down.

"This is *sirshasan.* Against hangover."

"It's lewd and indecent exposure, and it's against the law."

She paused upside down to brush ladybugs from her hair, and Drum lumbered over to sniff at my crotch.

"If Drum takes a bite of that sausage your lovemaking days are done."

I collapsed at her feet and was awarded a look of tolerant amusement. Her ankles I noticed were a bit thick (she had walked the strand barefoot, carrying her church heels in her hand) and she lacked the tender earlobes the Poet always talked about: ankles and earlobes being two recommended attributes oft overlooked in women. My father, coincidentally, made the same recommendation.

Under her arm was a carton of the season's first strawberries, and along with her shoes she was carrying a fifth of Paddy to make up for the Bush we had just about polished off the night before.

I was anxious to get to the Paddy and to her, see the bottle out of its sack and Maureen out of her powder-blue Sunday suit, but she was for strawberries first then a tour of the ballroom.

"We danced there, the staff, when the season was over."

As a teenage colleen she had waited tables and made beds at the Six Counties. Nothing would do but that I dress and fetch the hotel keys. History and memories were what the Irish were about, and I spoke up for desire and pursuit but she pushed a ripe strawberry between my lips.

So we set off with Tasker's flashlight, or torch, down the corridors of the Six Counties Hotel in search of Maureen's past. In the ballroom behind the lobby the windows were boarded shut behind the rotted draperies. The ceiling extended beyond the level of the next floor, and at the half-level a narrow balcony skirted the ballroom on three sides. The center chandelier was wrapped in burlap like strange fruit attached to the ceiling. The beam from Tasker's electric torch revealed a silent throng of Empire chairs stacked two together in a half-circle of 69s. The rest was regal emptiness.

"That wasn't there."

I played the light on the antique jukebox where a bandstand had been.

"The caretaker finds these things."

The jukebox was an artifact of no functional worth, missing— —like the television cabinet in my room—its insides.

"Like that call box outside? I wanted to call Mum from there before I saw it was useless."

"He collects. To keep busy. Mainly what doesn't work."

"That's our thing here, that's what we do."

Like collecting poets.

She was humming in my ear, as if to music coming from the worthless jukebox, a popular song blown over from America with the ladybugs, "Settle In, Sister." We danced a step or two together, the torch in my hand hanging down her back illuminating the muscular derrière. She felt me grow hard against her and said, "Enough of that," for she was in another mood. She disengaged from our dancer's clasp when she knew I knew her cheek was damp. She had danced here with someone, for there's always another man.

Wanting to share something with her in this haunted dance hall I said, "We have our history too. I have mine."

"You, you've only been nicked by history." She wiped her eyes in the dark. "With us it's an open wound."

So I said nothing. We left the sea-damp ballroom, and locked, then walked back to my room with Drum trailing after us, sniffing at the bottoms of the doors for rats. She took the keys and unlocked here and there to assess the empty rooms. There was a tale behind every numbered door, how a housemaid keeps her fanny from being pinched by MPs and drummers alike. The mood had lifted, and her cheeks were dry, though one of her tales was tragic enough. A clergyman had died in the room assigned to me.

"Suicide?"

"Now why should you think that? What notions have you of the church? It was apoplexy, and I was the one that found him dead. The manager gave me a brandy to help me over the shock and I drank it straight down but I wasn't half shocked."

What shocks had turned a teenage chambermaid into a cop, I was not to know.

"What shocks me," she said, "is how death hangs over. The Six Counties is haunted, don't you know?"

"All of Ireland is."

"You've come to that have you?"

We had come to that haunted room, my own. The door was left open and the beetles had got in, and on the bed. Maureen, a chambermaid again, brushed the sheets clean with a swipe of her arm.

"In this very bed," she said, the image of a corpse still with her, "with the Book of Common Prayer lying open on his breast."

I needed to unfix her from her Irish wake and into that bed where other things are done besides dying. I patted the place where she had spent the night.

"Love is what makes sense of all our sadness."

"And don't be quoting poetry at me."

It wasn't poetry, it was "Settle In, Sister." I chatted her up till she put Drum into the hall and closed us in together with strawberries and Paddy for starters. She let me help her undress and I was the one who took her hair out of the plastic clasp. She went to work again to prove she was no puritan, to herself more than to me—I never said she was.

"You call that dour?" she asked me. "Is that dour, that?"

"I never said that."

We worked up a satisfying sweat defiling a clergyman's deathbed.

16

THE LADYBUGS vanished as mysteriously as they had appeared, and now that the windows admitted what light Ireland offered I brought Miles up to my room for company. The canary did not consider a change as good as a rest, and still did not sing. Maureen popped in when it pleased her to come, or when she walked Drum, but that was only on off-duty Traffic nights and only when there was no football match on the telly. The Army had requisitioned the Six Counties Hotel, and it was depressing to know I would be out of digs again by Easter. Mrs. Tasker's sister-in-law was taking longer to die than anticipated and my solitude increased to the next almost unbearable degree.

On Ash Wednesday you could tell who was who: the priest's charcoal fingerprint marked Catholic foreheads while the Protestant brows—Maureen's, all of Drumlough—were untouched. No sign of Saro's forehead (my obsession with her was cyclical, according to Maureen's neglect), but I saw the detestable bald pate of Boethius often enough, here and there, circling the Magic Circle. I was unhappily reconciled to being denied the sight of Saro for all of Lent.

Boethius Singh now nodded to me on campus, with a heavy-lidded look of suspicion. Did he intuit my former fondness of his wife?

On April Fool's Day I caught a flash of lime green in the street, but it was a scarf worn by Belle Lovely and not Saro's fetching kerchief. Belle, wife to Clive, the Welsh Composer in Residence, was posted at the corner of Holyrood to inform passersby like me that Clive was sawing only the tree limbs of the mighty oak lying prostrate nearby, and had not cut down the tree.

"Belfast Power and Light has done. We're only carving firewood from it, ask Clive."

"Tell him," called out Clive over the shattering buzz of his chain saw, "the electric company cut the bloody thing down."

"Just told him," his wife shouted back, then to me: "I stand here warning people off. A tree cut down across the road, they think it's a barricade. I pray Clive doesn't have an accident with that chain saw. Can you picture him conducting an orchestra with only one arm? Actually he loves the roar of the thing, thinks it's music. He's the same about police sirens. Composers go a bit bonkers about sound.

He says there's an urgency to a telephone ringing that his Ulster Concerto lacks, so he wrote in a telephone. Airplane motors, dentist drill, fire alarm—all musical instruments to Clive's ear. Those pneumatic hammers for tearing up sidewalks, that's just lovely percussion to him. Do you want a puppy?"

"I've got no place. For a puppy. I'm being evicted."

"They can't evict in months with an *r* in them, it's like oysters. The bailiffs in Cardiff have been to our door, and I read them the law. You never saw bailiffs set back so. When bailiffs come knocking I answer the door and Clive hides. Our neurotic Dalmatian has just had pups and we can't keep them."

"I'm afraid I can't. Keep one either."

Without shutting off the chain saw Clive called out: "Ask him if he wants a pup."

"I just did," Belle yelled back, then to me, "Are you being put out for arrears? That's where they're always onto us."

"It's the Army. They're taking over the place where I stay."

"The bloody Army, they're everywhere. But they can't put you out without notice. April has an *r* in it."

"The Army can. It seems. Martial law or something."

Clive turned off the chain saw and put the machine into a musical case meant for a French horn.

"What's this about digs?"

"He's been put out."

"By Easter," I said.

"There's the gatehouse," said Clive, "now that Jameson's flown."

Jameson the sculptor had quit Belfast to be Sculptor in Residence at Liverpool Polytechnic.

"He was getting anonymous calls," said Clive, and Belle said, "He feared for his life."

Jameson was a Protestant who had sculpted a Saint Thomas for St. Thomas's in Dunmurry.

"For a cathedral, it has to be a Catholic sculptor to sculpt saints," said Clive.

"They gave it to Jameson not knowing," said Belle.

"After that the calls started."

"Don't get a telephone," Belle warned me. "We had a telephone but it was cut off for arrears." Belle and Clive Lovely had lived in the gatehouse before Jameson. "Then came the bailiffs and it wasn't a month with a *r* in it so I told them I was preggies. They can't even the

Army put you out if you're preggies—actually Guinness our Dalmatian was but that doesn't count. How is it that girls that don't want to get pregnant in novels always do and Clive and I who are dying for a babe can't?"

"Dee did," said Clive, "and not in a novel."

"Oh Dee," said Belle, "oh dear."

Deirdre of the Sorrows lived in the second gatehouse or the half of the gatehouse separated by a drive. I thought Belle meant to tell me about Dee's long sleeves or the mystery of her fatherless wean, but she did not.

"We got a stay or a delay or a remand or whatever and I had to remember to put a pillow under my wrapper when I went to the door. Everybody knows everything in Belfast, even the bailiffs, so when my nine months were up we had to remove to dreadful digs on McAuley in the Golden Triangle on the other side of the Ormeau Road and out of the Magic Circle beside the gasworks. Clive and I are heathens from Wales, the neighbors think we're gypsies or tinkers the way we dress and really all they want is for me to tell their fortune, so we're safe enough. We have another lovely fireplace like the one at the gatehouse—smoky but lovely. And Clive adores the racket from the firehouse down the road. You'll like the gatehouse. It had this lovely fireplace where you can burn tree limbs and save on coal as we do. Give him some tree limbs, Clive. Clive will share his tree limbs with you. Do you want a goat? A man from Fermanagh gave us this goat that plays hell with our neurotic Dalmatian. You could have goat's milk on your porridge in the morning if you had a place to tie her. They say goat's milk is lovely in tea but I wouldn't. You could tie her to a tree. A tree would do nicely. We've got no trees around the gasworks and the goat eats Guinness's Ken-L-Ration if she's not tied but there's trees to your heart's desire in the cemetery behind the gatehouse."

I caught another flash of lime green going into the cut-rate Off-Licence on the Lisburn Road, but that was not Saro either.

17

"Do you want to know how I killed my Da?"

Not really. Not after reading Maureen's ballad about the CID man strung up with piano wire by a band of women at Turf Lodge (the man called Da in the poem, so I assumed that was her Da), nor after hearing her tell in detail how her brother was shot in the buttocks (escorting the Lord Chief Justice to Aldergrove Airport), and especially not now after our Olympic stunts in bed and out, beginning with her spine-bending rendition of a chiropractic exercise, back-to-back, arms hooked together praying mantis fashion, then tipping one another's weight backwards until the spine responded with a satisfactory snap—this followed by a wrestling hold demonstrated on the tatty rug until our twisted intimacy aroused us both and led to something else. (Maureen taught karate at the Rape Centre in the Students Union, and had given private classes in judo defense to the Seven Sisters, including Deirdre, who at the time was seven months' pregnant.) But "Do you want to know how I killed my Da?" was not a question to say no to.

"In Armagh, at the horse fair, the spring I turned eight."

I listened closely to her pronunciation of the word eight.

We were lying in bed catching the breath knocked out of us by combat and coitus, eating peanuts, Maureen confessing to history. The peanut shells and pages from her poem were scattered between the sheets where I would lie with them instead of her tonight—but she determined to confess to murder before she left.

"A thousand times have I asked myself" (but she was asking her Da), "why ever did you give me that bloody torch my eighth birthday?" She had prayed for an air rifle, but her mother drew the line at weaponry no matter how much a tomboy was the daughter—an electric torch was tomboy enough, the kind used by gas-meter readers. And on that anniversary of eight years she was taken by her father to Armagh's horse fair where she would gorge on strawberry ice and have a fling on the carrousel.

"I naturally chose the fiercest stallion they could carve in wood, to spin around on, and even that one too tame for me at eight. Och but I sat up ladylike and stiff and sidesaddle (since Mum allowed no trousers on a birthday), melted strawberry dripping into the carved mane of a wooden horse, my cavorting mechanical beast well in sight of the open-air auction tent where Da went to inspect dray horses, the side canvases drawn up like ladies' skirts, like my own, so you could see half-man half-horse and hear an auctioneer sing out bids the men were making."

So much more poetic was the tale than the poem she wrote. While she talked I conjured up a parallel tale; rather, a birthday story written by my father:

"Steamboats plied the Ohio in those days and I can see the mighty *Island Queen* with you and your old Dad aboard to this day, the way you waved your new Teddy bear (never let your Mother—no matter how beloved—tell you I never gave you anything) at the tollbooth keeper on the Suspension Bridge, but darned if the calliope didn't blast on just at that golden moment, so shrill and loud you could hear the echo from the Kentucky bank, and you put your little hands over your ears and dropped poor Teddy into a churning paddle wheel that made one gruesome turn before drowning your Teddy bear in the muddy deep for all time and left your old Dad with a tearful birthday boy the rest of that day."

Birthday stories have a way of turning tragic, as did Maureen's.

"Kept flashing my beam on and off in the light of day with no bloody effect until I took a notion I had burnt the batteries out. Slipped out of the saddle at the end of the next go-round to go in search of someplace dark enough to see if my torch might light up properly—never go looking for dark places in Ulster." True enough: our driftwood fire was out, with barely enough light at dusk to see one another by. "What demon I'll never know though I may ask a thousand times that whispered in my ear to toss the useless batteries (they were brand new) into a trash fire beside the auctioneer's tent. Wouldn't you know? They exploded like the world's end—my world, anyway, the end of it—and one battery came flying forth like a bullet to pierce the sweet man's heart."

She finished with a tearless shiver. I shared her chill in the shadowy room: a peanut unswallowed lingered on my tongue like the undissolved host.

"Did you hear," she suddenly asked me, "about those two Brit soldiers foolish enough to chat up a couple of Taig chippies getting their throats slit for their trouble?"

I told her I had lived across the street from where it happened. Her did-you-now? was missing the usual sarcasm and sounded a faint note of respect for my having been brushed—even to that extent, and a street between—by history. Her "Did you get a poem out of it?" was less respectful.

"There's more cause than the Troubles that people get hurt here, but try getting a poem out of it. Try being poetical about summer drownings off Drumlough Pier or your Mum's jaundice or a barmaid strangling on a fishbone. Cancer and accidents trot along with all else but don't fit into stanzas or turn out the way you want them on the page. Take me for instance." I had her. "What happened to me was actually because of the Troubles, but try as I might I saw no poetry in it."

She wanted me to ask, so I did: "What happened to you?"

"Struck by a rubber bullet." She pulled the sheet down to show me the lump at the base of her spine I already knew by touch. "Struck in the back by a soldier shooting wild. Accidental as you please, could have happened to you yourself. I was crossing an intersection, a march going on a block away. Stones got thrown, then tear-gas grenades were smoking up the streets. Me, paralyzed from the waist down and doctors doubted I would ever walk again. Our neighbors passed the hat (my Da was dead a year, we were on Supplementary Benefits) to buy me a wheelchair. Not me, says I, when I saw the bloody thing. Can you see this one in a wheelchair? I had a hurt spine but I wasn't spineless. O the irony of it, soldier boy scared to get stoned fires wild at a crowd and see who he hits. It was no march of mine, Taigs wanting free status and free bread—status if you ask me is standing on your own two feet and bread is got by working for it. But I was the accident. A rubber bullet meant for them, and the Taig it was meant for would have mucked about in a wheelchair for life, but not me. I had the grit. Suit yourself, said the doctor, meaning rot in bed for all he cared. Rot nothing. I wiggled my toes in secret, one toe at a time, and got a leg over the side of the bed before a fortnight. The knees took forever. Two years. I had a trained nurse from National Health helping, and she said she never saw such grit. (She was Catholic.) Two bloody years it took me, but I walked. Talk about your status, there it was. The nurse said Mother Mary and the Saints be praised, but no thanks to beads and doctors and status and saints—it was pure and simple grit."

I caressed the lump where the bullet had struck until she lost the narrative thread of her preteen ordeals and commenced to purr. To demonstrate what grit can do and show how far removed from paralysis she was, she clipped me neatly into her anaconda hammer-lock just as we lay, side by side: her leg up, my leg under; and she could have constricted the breath out of me except that my cock rose between us like a referee caught in a clinch, then joined us together in a tenderer splice. Soon enough we were that Real Life couplet again: cock in, cock out, easy-does-it trochee strokes until we synchronized at iambic, both breathing a-a, b-b, a-a. When I shot from the hip she was still moaning dactyls, so I rode the carrousel till she got off humming, "Lovely."

If it was grit I wanted Maureen had grit to spare, but did I want this tough cookie and unbreakable, built to last, however pleasurable to bed? She was no part of a suicide pact, only a poet's whisper: "These detours, Critic, will help fill that empty noodle of yours," and a father's advice: "Women, Son, appear in 57 varieties, but each is only a variation on Eve."

Whatever Maureen's easy allure, it faded in the afterglow and did not stand up to light. The Poet promised me a girl with eyes as wide as oysters and Maureen's eyes were only that wide when her hair was pulled into a tight bun at the back of her neck. The mustache of sweat on her upper lip was what Real Life was about—her hair a tangle of kelp, face an angry flush from our exertions. The flattened nose suggested a potential bully when what I wanted (I thought) was a woman of dream and magic and all mine. Maureen I liked best in uniform, with Chinese eyes, accompanied by Drum. So I allowed the fire to turn cold and the light to die so I could not see the kelp and sweat—and fed her peanuts in the dark.

If the poems were appalling, I could be grateful for her gifts in bed with fond recall. And, after all, it was Maureen who blithely lifted the curtain for me (if but the side canvas of a tent) to a glimpse of Out There, or a figment of it.

She confessed to "a leg up" to come—her leg up, at the moment, and mine under (but my slippery member already sliding to independence)—a promotion to Scotland Yard's AntiTerror training, across the water: "Not to tell, mind." Whom would I tell?

The night turned out to be our last together, so in complicit co-conspiracy I was to share a secret in return for hers. What about *my* Da, what was he like? I stalled. I had letters from him, and once a Teddy bear, and that was all. What did the letters say?

"I was conceived, my father said, on the shores of Lake Okeechobee."

I now owned a suitcase I found at a rummage shop called War-on-Want, to go with my Goodwill Gladstone: my luggage made a snug fit alongside Miles & cage in Tasker's wheelbarrow. My last official act before leaving the room at the Six Counties was to take down the faded flag from above the fireplace, a souvenir, and fold it into a compact triangle. The British Army would have no use for a French flag.

The sergeant major who relieved me of the ring of keys appeared far too young for his rank—about Liam's age, I would have thought, though his hair, unlike Liam's rock-star tresses, was cut regulation short-sides-and-back. A pair of field glasses hung by a strap around his neck through which he would occasionally survey the horizon while a platoon clad in camouflage was engaged in stringing barbed wire across the strand and policing the area for cigarette packets and Drum's turds. Tasker would have been made happy to observe the metal detectors minesweeping the shoreline: what treasure they might have turned up. I was offered a man to push my barrow but declined with thanks all the same. Our ceremony was a curious ritual played out under Drumlough's leaden sky: keys passed across a wheelbarrow, as if we were enacting formal surrender. The flag was down, folded under my arm, and the sergeant major may have wondered whether to salute. Instead, we wished one another cheerio, he with thumbs up, and went off at his bantamweight stride with toes turned out in case of quicksand.

The barmaid at the Red Carpet hung Miles's cage beside the cash register well out of range of stray darts flung across the pub, safe from drunks and the resident cat. I left the wheelbarrow behind, so a dart player helped me to the train station across the road. As we departed from the Red Carpet, a shaft of light fell upon the birdcage, and Miles suddenly, for the first time, began singing his heart out. The song was as startling as if the bird had croaked Nevermore—for this was not the place and never would be.

18

DEIRDRE WAS as desperate for company as I was. The day I moved into the gatehouse across from hers she appeared at my door with a gift scuttle of coal, a box of fire lighters—also she carried a bottle of potchin, to housewarm one way or another. Her infant's name was Bobby, I was to call her Dee. Jameson, the sculptor who had lived here before me, had left behind a larger-than-life wax Saint Thomas in the kitchen, and two teacups stained the same caramel color as Doubting Thomas. I poured potchin into the cups and we toasted my new hearth. "*Slíante*" was the word I would hear most often from Dee henceforth.

I suppressed a cough at the first reckless sip. As Dee bent down to work up a coal fire, the liquid fire lingered on my tongue, an unwelcome singing of raw home brew behind my ears. I tried to think where to empty my cup without her knowing, but even in secret the gesture would be offensive. No, I would drink the stuff—was it not the essence of Ireland?—but drink with prudence.

She had set her toddler down, a careless bundle of babe on the bare floor, a wean of some twenty months. Dee's chapped workaday hands were soon black with coal dust: she was so fierce and dedicated about the fire, instructing me in the mystery of it as she took swift nips of potchin that left her teacup quaintly fingerprinted with soot.

"In the west it's easy and lovely to light peat and O the smell but coal is coal and peat is dear—in Belfast, if you can find it."

Bobby spoke not, neither did he move. The large light eyes filled his face: if he blinked, I did not catch him at it. His name was a misfortune, mumbled Dee, because of a Bobby on the blanket in his nineteenth day of a hunger strike at the Maze.

"Who was ever to know a man with the same name as this one would starve to death, the terrible luck hanging the name of a dead man on a wee thing."

"Maybe he won't." I was thinking of the hunger-striker. "Die, that is."

Dee squinted up at me with the look I received here when the Yank in me spoke up.

"The man's to die, why else starve himself? He's gone, never to return to the living except to harrow us all—and my Bobby named for him."

Her implication was that I did not know the way of death here, nor ever would, and she was right.

Miniature Bobby sat in his diapers and a transparent T-shirt immobile and as solemn as Saint Thomas in wax. His unblinking eyes followed the elaborate construction his mother built of pages of the *Belfast Telegraph* rolled tight and twisted into paper knots intermingled with splinters of smashed crate wood. A scree of small coals lay against the outer slope of the construction: she struck a match to this edifice and my small dark mausoleum blazed to life. The spectacle was reflected in Bobby's unwavering gaze, but his face remained expressionless.

With ritual awe we three stared together for some minutes while the more resistant coals accepted flame, then Dee redistributed the pyrotechnics with a poker, saying, "To live in Belfast, if you must, peace is what you want, and a cemetery is lovely for that, and the scenery suits whatever legend goes on about you."

What legend was attached to Dee I did not yet know, but rumors trailed in her wake: "Go on, was a wart she had removed." "Had two removed then." "Wax, hot wax, an accident." "That sculptor." "Hot something, they say. Jameson?" "Hot something else but wax, and not him—I won't go into it." "Wears a tattoo they say." "Go on with you." "Tar. And I tell you I won't go into it."

"What legend," I asked, "is that?"

"Och, that I'm a witch. I'm the witch of Friar's Bush. Did you not know? Have you not heard the talk?"

Her Stranmillis neighbors had determined she was a witch and an outcast, little Bobby was the devil's spawn. But Dee needed no neighbors: she was an intimate of the poets circle at King's and a member of the Seven Sisters. Bobby watched his mum's wounded mouth work queerly in the firelight as if he knew the weight behind every offhand word and read dread messages in the bloated face.

"Now there's a fire that only a witch could conjure for you."

True enough, and I was meant to learn to build a softly glowing miracle in the same way if only I had become a proper student of the ways here. But I lacked the gift, or the stoic patience. Dee came prepared for my failure at fire lighting (and other insufficiencies in the ways of place: the potchin was also a test) for she had brought fire lighter batons of a combustionable something I might henceforth find at the wee Veegee, a means for the likes of me to light a coal fire that Dee conceived from sorcery. Fire lighters were the fast and loose shortcut to hearth heating, the American way.

As it turned out, there was never another fire in that grate except for this inaugural blaze. The empty parlor was no place a spurious poet could warm himself: my view from the gothic window was too grim to contemplate in solitude: broken tombstones submerged in muck, Irish crosses like the cross sights on rifles, tilted messages to the living to pray for the souls of departed Devlins, Muldoons, Carsons and McCanns. The graveyard was overgrown with weed and ivy, no stone unturned, all cracked, untended and the place abandoned even by the dead.

Also, I was truly spooked by Saint Thomas tilted against the kitchen wall. (There was the beginning of a Christ beside it—the armature or skeleton in copper wire and twisted coat hangers—but not enough sculpted substance to haunt a kitchen yet.) The hollow stare of Saint Thomas was more menacing than any human presence: there was no escaping those eyes, that shrewd doubt. (Bobby's relentless gaze was directed toward Mum only.) As long as I kept out of Saint Thomas's range I might sleep untroubled enough in the smaller of the two bedrooms upstairs with the French flag as a curtain against the vista of cluttered burial below.

Aside from sleep, I lingered only long enough in my mausoleum for the use of its temperamental plumbing. (The plaster had collapsed in the bathroom, the furring and wall studs exposed in the same way as what was once the bathroom in the blasted flat across from my office.) And to stash a cache of Bush beneath the bed.

We shared tentatively warmed pork-and-beans from Veegee and lumpen powdered pea soups from an envelope or Franco-American spaghetti suppers, Dee and I—Bobby watching. I passed the time of drink at her gate lodge instead of mine. (We were two gatehouse keepers, actually—the twin dwellings were attached by an arch of brick over the driveway leading to our backyard burial ground. Dee, if mellowed enough by drink, might sometimes play the game of tour guide to innocents wandering about the cemetery unaware.) Her narrow half-a-lodge was more robustly furnished and redolent of living-in than my leftover sculptor's lair. Her walls were thickly postered with Causes from local slum housing to Solidarity, including that same portrait of Che that had graced the Piss & Garlic Palace. I do not think Dee was so much caught up in Causes as in covering cracked plaster—yet there was something she needed to forget by concentrating on Biafra and boat people: the Irish for all their poetry and drink are blessed and cursed with the gift to remember.

The disorder was perpetual, as was her dismay over the mess. She lived in the careless overflow of charity's offerings and excess baggage, spare parts that might sometime come in handy (but never did), a natural spill and stain and pungent smell of nappies and burnt toast. The welcome to her disarray was blunt and Irish and unconditional. A teakettle forever whistled on the hob for "tay," or to make hot whiskies with if she had thought to buy lemons or I remembered to bring them. Her potchin she kept near at hand not hidden like my Bush, in an unmarked bottle in plain sight on the sideboard, but accepted my offerings of daintier Off-Licence name brands—living on the pig's back, that was—after the rough familiarity of home-brewed potato whiskey. Yes, we drank together, much.

My constant hostess waddle-glided through her littered witch's coven with a dancer's surety of foot for such a pudding of a body and stubs of legs. I cultivated my tediously slow acquaintance with Bobby though my beard was suspect and my role a puzzle to him. I even tried to know Dee's cemetery cat, Cat, as suspicious of me as Bobby. Cat was another castoff denizen of cemeteries, with patchwork markings on its mangy fur, the incarnation of its vagabond tribe, who would never enter either lodge but accepted scraps at Dee's windowsill (leftover spaghetti, cold kidney beans) if proffered by Dee herself. At Dee's hearth with drink at hand and the day fading, Cat crouched on his side of the steamed-up windowpanes casting a wicked eye on our close congregations of three, I was as near my center of gravity as an escapee is allowed. The other sanctuary was a pub, but Dee would never be seen in my company at a pub, because of the talk. (What talk would that be, about a witch, wondered I?) Home was the gate lodge next to mine. I was as desperate for company as Deirdre was.

19

I PLAYED father to Bobby feeding him cornflakes from the overbright box that had come all the way from Battle Creek, Michigan, to embattled Belfast—had my own father ever played father to me? I was forever a lad and tyke and toddler in his letters, fixed in his recall at the age Bobby was now, forever attached to a highchair or wearing a tot's sailor suit. "You were finicky about food," my father wrote—as was Bobby. Dee's wean would take tea but not the milk all Belfast whitened tea with. He had never liked milk, according to his mother—"No more," she declared, "than I ever did." But he did like the crunch and feel of dry cereal between his baby teeth. Bobby stared straight at me throughout the feeding, rather than at the graffiti cartoons on the cereal box or at the flakes he mechanically accepted from the spoon. Outside the window, Cat watched us both.

Earlier—before Cat had pounced onto the sill to verify Dee's absence and this new strange order of things—I was certain I observed a human figure flutter past the window, under an umbrella. It may have been that same stray bit of plastic caught fluttering in the bare limbs of a dead oak that yesterday appeared so like a hanged bride, today detached by the wind. Or it could have been the Wraith, the legendary woman in white, with a candle, said to haunt Friar's Bush, a ghost or banshee Dee incorporated into her spiel as she steered tourists round the cemetery. It could have been Liam going by to inspect his plantation: he (Sweeney or Keene) was thought to have sown marijuana seeds, a plot of pot, somewhere below the jungle growth covering the cracked headstones—but Liam had never in his life affected a brolly.

(I was rather certain the apparition was a woman, possibly the same woman I had seen on the strand at Drumlough, the maple-leaf woman who had been on the same flight with me from London to Belfast and I had bumped into in City Centre—as if she were following me, a fixed configuration in my paranoia.)

Dee had left us a pot of strong tea—a fly, she said, could walk the surface of it without drowning—before she went out to do her washing at the laundromat in the Students Union, then to see a wee man who knew a wee man who supplied her with potchin. One laundry errand reminded her of the other, for the wee man kept his merchandise under mounds of bloodstained sheets in the hospital laundry at Musgrave Park. I poured black tea into Bobby's plastic cereal bowl obliterating the painted Mickey Mouse at the bottom of the bowl. I volunteered to keep Bobby, glad of the company, however mute. Dee sometimes left him completely alone, watched over only by Cat.

"He never cries," I told Dee. "How can he be a real baby?"

"He's real enough. Take a sniff of his nappie if you don't think him real."

"But he never. I mean I've never heard him. Cry."

"It's the ones with most to cry about that don't."

Bobby was garbed in the smallest Aran sweater in Eire, tea-spotted, with bits of cornflakes caught in the turtleneck. I spoke to him as I would have spoken to Miles the canary, expecting no chirp in return.

"Once upon a time," I said, then wondered what next. Dee told him stories, surely. "Once upon a time," I said again, "there was this man. Who left."

I awaited Bobby's reaction to this but received no acknowledgment, not even a blink. The thick upper lids of Bobby's eyes were said by doctors to be a sign of Down's syndrome, the ophthalmic flap that indicated Mongolism—all nonsense, said Dee, who had the same flap (as did Cookie, I recalled): "You'd be surprised as the doctor was to know my I.Q."

"Left his wife," I told Bobby. "His wife was sick."

Bobby swallowed this with his tea. I was spared a reply.

"Went on-the-road, as his Da used to say. On the wing. With his wife left behind, sick. Now what do you think?"

Nothing.

"He was a nothing and nothing he did was right. What would he do? Next."

Maybe I thought the suspense would make a storyteller of me. To all appearances, Bobby was intent on hearing what I had to say. I had brought a bottle of cheap brandy with me, and now poured a splash of it into my tea, no help to the vile taste on my tongue. There being no conclusion to my tale, nowhere to go from here, I told Bobby the end to a poem: "A casket," I said, "fell out of an airplane. Onto somebody's greenhouse."

Bobby already knew that poem.

"Son, it is amazing what women will squirrel away. Mrs. G keeps a veritable treasure chest of antiques in the attic and a safe you could open with a screwdriver containing every IRS form ever filed and every Christmas card received in a lifetime. (She possesses personal letters from the governor of Florida signed by the governor himself, that being the type of person she hobnobs with.) I had no business in her garage—but what in the world, I asked myself, does a widow lady that can't drive want with a garage? I was a week trying various keys on that garage door while she was out at Piggly Wiggly or playing canasta and shuffleboard (I am no sport, like her) with the local retirees until, Eureka! There it was, a rusted key to her dark secret—a sight to set an oldster's heart to palpitating. (I had to light matches to see by, since the light bulb was burnt out.)

"A rose-colored Cadillac was stored out there, up on blocks, a pink dream, pining away for lack of action. It must have been the late Mr. Greenleaf's. Mrs. G was holding onto it for sentimental reasons (since she does not drive), a memento so to speak—sans battery, of course, and with the tires removed, but a potential chariot to the stars!"

In an empty sugar bowl on the sideboard I found a cracked Kodachrome of Dee herself when an adolescent in modest-dowdy swimming costume—no beach hat or rubber cap: a mass of Degas pastel hair over one shoulder—slim, with sharper features than now, and a chin not puddled in avoirdupois but smartly uptilted all confidence. Dee was no beauty, even in her teens, but the snapshot showed her as a sweet young coltish thing of juice and spirit—unless it was a photo of her twin.

In a drawer full of cutlery from Boots and odd bits of twine and thumbtacks, receipts for Supplementary Benefits, a schoolgirl book of recipes (including "How to Make Lemonade") and entry forms for slogan contests (*Win Trip for Two to Honolulu!*) was another snapshot, this one of four soldiers connected arm-and-shoulders in a daisy chain of khaki and camaraderie. They sat in a pub booth without removing their berets, more pints on the table than soldiers—one young unhandsome face circled in ball-point with a fallen halo. (A column of soldiers came to mind—soldiers being clones of one another, to a sailor's eye—the two Tommies murdered on Magdala, the sergeant major to whom I surrendered the Six Counties, Ginny's martyred brother, even Major Ward, all.)

Yes, and after settling Bobby in his Thrift Shop playpen—there was hurt in his eyes but no tears at being thus confined (Ezra Pound, penned in an open-air military cage at Pisa)—I persisted in my violation of Dee's privacy, but safely out of Bobby's all-knowing stare. In the bedroom I had still to deal with the accusatory gaze of death's heads starving in Ethiopia, but I turned my back on the CARE poster and went prying through Dee's underthings in a bureau drawer where, inevitably, the lonely hide their poems.

Beauties and dogs alike write rotten verse, the Poet warned me—referring no doubt to his wife as the beauty. "The girlies are never cold-blooded enough to cut through to the bone." And the Old

Poet had delivered himself of similar sentiments, a sharp insult to Maureen at nineteen (just out of paralysis and writing first poems), by saying to her: "Young women should not write poems, a young woman *is* a poem."

As a poem, "Tar" may have been no better or worse than Mary Bannister's artificial revelations in the sonnet form—I suspended my persona as Critic when I read it. The girl in the poem was Ginger, and may not have been Dee at all, but of course it was Dee and that was why I should not have read it.

I read it quickly—guiltily, with Ethiopia watching—yet certain lines lingered in my memory in the way of stray phrases from my father's letters that I had read more than once. There was "fear e'en for the flowers he brought me," for flowers were too bright to conceal against the drab. And there was that about Belfast being "all eyes and ears" (even we aliens could confirm), so that you could never wear love on your face in secret nor hide it in a hotel room for long.

Ginger called her man Mabrinogron who made up a wife out of flowers though his name was Rob and she was never a wife. She was three-and-twenty when they met and he a tender two years younger. He was a Shropshire lad (the poet took liberties here: Rob was from Shropshire in one stanza and Yorkshire in another), a volunteer, for the Army sent none but volunteers to Northern Ireland: "It wouldn't," said Rob, "be fair otherwise."

No Catholic girl from the ghetto would say two civil words to a British oppressor, but Ginger did, her civility not altogether conditioned in the Short Strand, and one thing led to another, the grandest thing of all. It was love, was it not? Rob was never slow and dozy like the boys she grew up with but quick-witted and clever with his hands, too clever with the buttons at the back of a girl's blouse. He would take her to California when the Troubles were done.

"Tar" was written in free verse, so free I wondered if it was verse at all except for the lines being broken in the style of a poem. ("Amateur poets," the Poet said, "are really writing prose, but on a narrow typewriter.") Never was written "ne'er" and even "e'en" and thees and thous abounded—but perhaps these archaic forms were closer to the Irish, and anyway I was no poet, nor even a critic here.

> Each hungry meeting in our secret place
> Was the closer we came to California.

Someone was knocking on my gate lodge door next door.

Jehovah's Witnesses were still on my trail, all the way from Texas: two women, two men—perfectly matched and possibly married sets. They carried their Bibles and pamphlets under umbrellas in this climate.

"Would you happen, sir, to know the resident of this gate lodge," one of the women in a plastic mackintosh addressed me. "We haven't called on this house yet, though I believe we have called on yours."

"Not this gentleman," said one of the men. "We called on the lady of the house at that house."

"Would you happen to know—?"

"Man named Thomas," said I, dropping the title Saint, "lives there. I think."

I think, therefore I am.

"We get no answer from Mr. Thomas."

"He's away. He had his doubts, about the place. Across the water now."

"Wonder, sir, if you yourself might have a moment—"

"Didn't we already speak to this gentleman, Beryl?"

"That was the lady of the house at his house, I think this gentleman must have been out."

The Bibles were not green so they could not have been Jehovah's Witnesses—and the pamphlets did not say *Awake!* Possibly they were Plymouth Brethren (a sect originating in Dublin, not Plymouth—I had been reading in one of the vivid-covered paperbacks about an acid-bath mass murderer who hailed from the Plymouth Brethren), but didn't they realize the danger, carrying Bibles openly in this city, spreading sectarian sentiments door to door? Did this come under martyrdom, could women be Brethren?

"Afraid not," said I.

" 'The Lord,' " said the first woman in the mackintosh, " 'is the strength of my life; of whom shall I be afraid?' "

That was a good question, and one a paranoid might ask—was I paranoid?

"Afraid," said I—of whom?—"I'm in the middle of. I have a little boy."

" 'The Lord shall increase you more and more, you and your children.' "

My children? Any other time I might have been curious—especially curious to know how a son of the Plymouth Brethren had become an acid-bath murderer—but I was in the middle of prying into a poem called "Tar," I was curious about Dee.

What saved me from receiving their psalms and assurances was the sudden appearance of the Wraith at the end of the driveway: she had been studying our tombstones, and carried an umbrella far more stylish than any carried by the Brethren. She came up to us, rather heavily perfumed for the weather, a well-dressed woman in her late fifties who was, indeed, the woman I had deplaned with at Aldergrove, and may have seen at Caesar's Palace in City Centre and at Drumlough, on the strand. She spoke with the sharp authority of someone used to having her way.

"Are you the gatekeeper?" she asked me.

"Afraid not."

She had the hard, clear eyes of an auctioneer: "Then who is?"

One of the male Brethren informed her that the cemetery was a relic, no longer functional—as if a cemetery could go out of business, or out of style—and when the Wraith turned to the quartet for enlightenment, I made my escape.

Inside this graceless carapace (Dee, slumped in her Morris chair in numb resignation) once dwelt a fair colleen, beloved of Mabrinogron. I pictured her in her bathing suit and not as the relic she was now.

"Women are the worst," she said, "or so they say, or believe, for the transport of explosives—so I was stopped."

On her way with laundry in Bobby's secondhand pram with the plastic shields (a two-sweater, built for twins) Dee had been searched and interrogated.

The women are the worst was a line from her poem.

She unbundled the half-dry load of wash to excavate the bottle of potchin secreted in its depths: "If they had found this they would have called it a Molotov cocktail." But the clandestine bottle had been purchased during the long cycles at the washeteria, the search took place when Dee was en route for the Students Union, before the transaction at Musgrave Park.

Later she would hang the damp things on the backs of chairs and across a bamboo pole she propped from fridge to cooker in the kitchen for just such expediency (she would put no more coins into an automatic dryer than for one spin, so short of cash was she)—but would hang later, or tomorrow, or never—now was the time of drink. Vespers it was, or the witching hour: the light going fast and the traffic on Stranmillis down to whispers.

Dee was even less attractive seated than on her woebegone pegs. Her all-wrong proportions were all the more distorted by the ruined chair she favored. I tried to think of her only those few years ago embracing a bouquet of flowers from Smithfield's Market (before it was bombed), a flower herself, where now one fat hand fondled a bottle of home brew and she removed the cork with her teeth. Then, the cork still between her lips, she bade me search glasses from the kitchen.

No, Dee, for I promised my old Dad.

I had brought liquid offering of my own, the brandy, but Dee was hostess in her own gate lodge, abiding by the hospitality of an unwed Welfare mother just that day having collected her benefits check, eager to pour out her own witch's potion.

"*Slíante.*"

"*Slíante.*"

She was quickly into her drink, greedy for the instant effect, Bobby's eyes devouring his Mum now, no move of mine was of interest.

In a little while I was at peace, at a distant remove from Dee's troubling poem. Even Cat was under the spell of the hour and lingered late at the window attending his wet fur with a langorous tongue.

"I finally saw the Wraith. Close up."

"Did you now? Is she wraithlike?"

"Carried an umbrella, not a candle. Canadian, from the accent, and sounds bossy. I think I've seen her around Belfast. Before."

The poster over Dee's head was taped crookedly to the wall: a cartoon Teddy weeping over the devastation of a forest fire. Were there ever such forests in Ireland, dry enough to burn? The first night drinking with Dee I had wanted to straighten that poster, but the impulse passed. I did not even inquire about forest fires in Ireland. The edges of posters were softened and inquiries were answered by drink.

O, the women are the worst.

"O, them," she replied when I asked about the Seven Sisters. "There's more now than seven, more than you can count. I went for the chat (things you can say amongst women you wouldn't want to in mixed company) and it's true, as they say, men will muck you about."

> Granny stood betwixt them and her Ginger,
> But the boyos pushed Granny away.

There was a crate-wood fire in the alley (in the poem) amidst the bricks and broken glass and a politico's poster in shreds on a board fence—a black kettle of tar bubbling on the fire.

Here, the gas oven to the cooker was on, the door open to heat the kitchen so that Dee, in due time, could hang her soggy laundry there. But the parlor grew chill. Dee heaved herself up with a sigh without letting go of the glass of potchin. She put her dead Granny's shawl over the long sleeves that hid her history: there was a fire, and toast and tea to be made.

She had lived with her grandmother in the Short Strand during Rob's time and to the end of her confinement and the baby's first month. Loved the old lady, she once told me, so fiercely it hurt, but never even kissed her grandmother, it wasn't done.

Dee began rolling sheets of *Belfast Telegraph* into paper knots and selecting lumps of coal from a tin bucket. At one point she held up her rough hands made black with coal soot, and said, "Like a fool I painted these fingernails black, waiting at my Granny's to birth this one here." The black fingernails were not in the poem, but that was all she would say of that—though Bobby stared as if he understood. "Granny used to say," she said, "that a baby's as easy got as a wet foot."

There was nothing about babies in the poem "Tar," only the shorn crown of hair coiled underfoot (a girl Ginger knew from St. Theresa's Schools, they baked a cake together in Home Ec, was the one that had the scissors), and after the shearing nothing hurt, her blouse—the one that unbuttoned down the back—torn where Rob had been so deft with the buttons; she was spat upon and slapped— *the women were the worst*—and though the tar seared her flesh it was nothing to what they had done to her hair.

"A policewoman once came to show us how to smash a brick in half with the side of your hand." Dee referred again to the Seven Sisters. "Lovely, if you're on for breaking bricks. What you miss most, for all their wayward deceit and insufferable pride, is a man."

When the potchin bottle was down to half I was away, Dee wishing me safe-home though home was only the other side of the drive.

"In Belfast," she said, "there can be danger across a wee space."

20

MARY BANNISTER stopped by my office, not with a sonnet this time, but a summons. Dr. McDonald would see me in his office.

"When it's convenient, but some time before noon."

Which meant now, for it was eleven-thirty—half-eleven as they said in Belfast. I sensed an ominous note to Mary stopping at my office without a sonnet for me to read. Whatever the trouble was, Mary wasn't telling, not even in sonnet form (her last sonnet had been about marital troubles with Rupert), so I went into the ruddy Scot's office unawares. Dr. McDonald was adjusting a sober necktie to his tight collar, a formal note to what Mary assured me was but a formality.

The view from McDonald's office approximated mine but was more extensive, from a floor higher, and was neatly shielded from the sight of the blown-apart apartment by a stand of elms between his window and the wreckage. My office was only a walk-in closet to his, and the surface of his desk would easily sleep four.

On his desk top was a sun lamp only just now switched off and losing its incandescence. Dr. McDonald's mahogany complection was accomplished by ultraviolet rays, he had just come from a sunning. Also on the desk top was a framed photograph of his son, the chairman's slender incarnation, with a saxophone at his lips instead of bagpipes. There was the smell of cocoa butter in the air, the suntan lotion still glistening on Dr. McDonald's forehead like furniture polish.

The chairman offered me a chair: I obeyed the gesture, for I understood not a word. He might have been speaking about his son now, or the weather—I caught either the word "sonny" or "sunny"— something about son Donalbain or sun-now-but-might-rain.

My reply was politely banal and as inane and incomprehensible as the remark uttered to me. We went back and forth about talcum and Malcolm and King's and things and while I waited for him to get around to his verse (for I assumed he was a poet, and that was what this conference was about) I watched across his shoulder out the wide-lens window a lecturer—probably McMichael—crossing University Avenue talking to himself, unaware that the beeping wee green man on the signal post had turned red, traffic skidding around him as he recited from his lecture notes. Dr. McDonald was talking to himself too.

Spring was on, out there. Tree leaves were beginning to unscroll from their buds, and today in the exceptional sunlight the toasted Scot might have basked open-shirted at his window instead of facing the artificial rays.

From the scaffolding around Wormwood Hall lighthearted steeplejacks called down their provocative remarks to the colleens astroll below. I could not hear the banter from this distance (nor over the sound of the chairman's drone), but from the way the girls tilted back their heads—lips and teeth exposed to the boyos above—I knew the comebacks were in the tradition of Belfast sass.

Then something statistically impossible (or ten million to one) took place before my dozy gaze: three separate couples walking from separate points of the compass (Elmhurst, Fitzwilliams, and along University Place) touched hands as if on signal from the traffic lamp at their center—the boy taking the girl's hand in his, all three boys touching all three girls in a display of miraculous coincidence.

"Take my wife," I almost distinctly heard Dr. McDonald say, or say, "Take my life." His wife for the life of her could not, before they met, play a note of music but before she died was capable of turning the pages of music for their musical son and identify a false note with perfect pitch.

"Something-something musical yourself, Mr. Gold?"

I had always been Professor Gold to him before this, and wondered if the Mr. was significant.

"More of a listener I'm afraid. Than a performer."

Something he said then escaped me altogether. I wanted him to say what a wonderful job I was doing with the poets, and he may have said it, but I would never know.

The view from the chairman's office also included roof, façade and columned entryway to the Antrim Museum, and my eye wandered to the stainless steel effigy of Cuchulain, Jameson's best-known piece of sculpture, said to vibrate in a high wind and, if one listened close, sing.

"Singh," said the Scot. "Professor Singh something-something says it's you."

One of the Singhs—if I understood, but I did not understand which—had been good enough to pass along to our chairman the latest issue of *Ars Poetica*, an international literary journal, which contained text and photograph that would undoubtedly be of keen interest to me, since the photograph was of me. If I understood correctly.

Dr. McDonald in all his ruddy heartiness and goodwill reached like Major Ward into a drawer and brought forth not a .45 pistol (he too was an Army man, the Highland Fusiliers or some such brigade whose banner hung above the chairman's bricked-in fireplace) but *Ars Poetica* folded back to the photograph one Professor Singh or the other had been good enough to pass along.

The quality of the picture was of startlingly incriminating clarity. It was an enlargement or extension of a snapshot I had seen thrice before in its abridged version, but never an inkling of this half. So far I had come across only the photo (beneath a hospital pillow, in an underground fallout shelter, on the sci-fi shelf of a mobile home in Texas) of Ginny, windblown, holding the bridle to her brown-and-white steed. Just beyond the frame had been a poet all along.

The complete triad, as I saw it now, was: pretty girl, dun horse, pale rider; the Poet with a jaunty baseball cap pressing down his wild wiry locks, was perched in the saddle clinging miserably to the saddle horn with both hands. His expression was one of suffering acquiescence to a child bride's request. She had asked him to pose for one humiliating moment on her beloved Rascal. Below the photograph was a paragraph of text having to do with I.M. Gold's demise in a U.S. hospital (the date of death underlined by Singh, or somebody)—but that part I only scanned in passing, since it was cold news to me now.

I might keep the journal, Dr. McDonald said, I think, but I kept my cool instead. Graciously I waved aside *Ars Poetica* as if waving aside its intimations and implications and all else. Dr. McDonald was chuckling to himself over the absurdity. He waited for me to join him over the grand joke, but I offered only the driest of smiles, a display of amazing aplomb my father would have been proud of, if not the Poet.

"Says suicide," said the chairman, chuckling the more, tucking *Ars Poetica* into the drawer scrolled like a sheet of music he intended to ask Donalbain to play. Score settled, he then went to mumbling in his cryptic Highlands monologue to spare either of us the awkwardness of explanation, his trigger finger itching for the switch to the sun lamp.

As statistically unlikely as three loving couples instantaneously inclined to intimacy in public, was that I should have a second trauma that same day.

I was walking down the staircase to King's English for the last time, it would seem, somewhat stunned by revelations but lightheadedly uncaring, even lighthearted (as when I had recuperated from the flu, or collected winnings at the pay window at Calder) when I noticed a thin-haired young man with a silk scarf at his Adam's apple pacing the landing in front of my office.

"Professor Gold?" he whispered.

"I am," said I—the last time I would say it.

Mary Bannister had forgotten to advise me of a second appointment that day. The Whisperer had been kept waiting, and would-I-mind?

"Mind what?"

"Coming along."

I was still too light-headed to be alarmed. I thought of the encounter as drawing a card in a Monopoly game: I had waved away the draw from *Ars Poetica*, and now must take a card from Chance. (Go to Jail. Go directly to Jail. Do not pass Go. Do not collect $200.)

"Roundup," he whispered.

He was either a plainclothes officer here to arrest me for impersonating a poet or the advance man of a Provo kidnap team with a commandeered black taxi waiting.

He did indeed have a taxi waiting, and the roundup was scheduled for half-one. (The word "scheduled" was whispered without sounding the *c*.) *Roundup* was the name of his program.

"Didn't the secretary inform you?"

There was just time for me to turn off my electric radiator, for the last time, so that it would not burn through the floor into Miss Chaucer's office below, and to snatch up—what? There on the desk lay Liam's poem, dedicated to a namesake; on the wall, safety regulations; in the drawer, the Old Poet's pornography. No, none of that. I took only what in all sincerity was addressed to me. And in a moment I was being rather forcefully led (by so soft-spoken an escort) down the remaining stairs, the last descent, down through AngloSax and MidEng, past ElizDrama, Jacobean, and finally to VicStudies and ModBritLit on the ground floor.

Parked under the waxen spring blossoms of the only magnolia this side of the Botanic Gardens was a black taxi, meter running, chauffeured by the same driver who had barely missed hitting a black cat on the Malone Road when I was being evicted from the Bellingham Arms.

We drove to the heavily fortified BBC Tower surrounded with concrete abutments designed as shrubbery tubs ranged alongside the curb, or kerb, against kamikaze squads. There was a team of three guards behind the reinforced door, and after a wait before a two-way mirror one of the guards asked us, "Can he?" but actually he was greeting the Whisperer as Kenny.

We were buzzed into a vestibule and allowed past a receptionist reading *Queen* and into a freight elevator with a *Personnel Only* tag on the door. We got off at a floor lined with sound studios lettered A to L and watched at the soundproof window of Studio C until two men had finished their wordless dialogue into a microphone. Watching their mouths move and making no sense of the words, I recalled my interview with Dr. McDonald.

This interview, the Whisperer informed me, was with a CID man telling of his off-duty hours devoted to evangelical work among the prisoners at Long Kesh, trying to bring them to an understanding of Jesus Christ. If this were television, said the Whisperer, the CID man would have had to wear a hood.

We were next.

The microphone hung from the low soundboard ceiling as if from the end of a spider's web. We sat at the same small round table used in the previous interview, my chair still warm from the interviewer or the CID man. When the red signal light in the center of the table flashed on, the Whisperer introduced me at some embarrassing length, rolling his vowels around like mints into the mike that hung between us like a noose. While waiting, I was reminded of a Yeoman I had known in the Navy who spoke in the same strained vocal range as the Whisperer, and by virtue of his knowing how to change a typewriter ribbon had become Chief Petty Officer and possibly a line officer by now. (The Whisperer's radio voice was more robust than his conversational volume.) The red light went off and the Whisperer touched my wrist, a finger to his lips. When the red light came on again, I began to read into the microphone.

Dear Son. Wherever you may be,

My bowels growled, and I wondered if the sound was being broadcast. I had skipped lunch—I should have carried raisins in my pocket, or an apple.

Mea culpa, I admit, but women are a mystery, My Boy,
That only gets deeper
The more you think about them,
What I am getting at, Son,
Is that you have not answered
A single one

Of my many letters
Sent to you out on the high seas yet.

Poetry without risk, said the Poet, is only garden-variety verse.
So I finished with:

Remember,
We may not pass this way again.

21

"WE DO LOVE a chancer," said Dee, both hands off the iron in a gesture embracing all of Ireland, including me. "A fellow I once knew, never you mind who (so long back it was) was a chancer deluxe, a chancer in camouflage. We still have a joint account at Ulster Bank and not a shilling in it and a . . . never you mind. They all wear camouflage, chancers do."

I had my wristwatch out of my pocket, winding it—for party time was past due. Here it was half-nine and Dee dozily ironing a set of lavender sheets Jameson had left behind when he left.

"Not to worry," warned Dee. "They won't come till the pubs shut. Eight?" (She had a Taig way of saying "eight.") "That's just the time said. A party starts late and the good ones never end."

She was ironing with an antique steam iron that might have come from a Chinese laundry or the rummage shop called War-on-Want. The sheets were too posh to sleep on and she intended them as tablecloths. Dee was the hostess, but I was the restless uneasy one worried for the outcome of the occasion. Without it being said, the party was for me: I was the chancer leaving town. (Dee knew what was what without letting on.) What did the eyes and ears of Belfast think of me now?

Dee had been imbibing since dusk, her tumbler of drink trembling at the end of the ironing board, but the sharp odor of potchin was all but obliterated by an application of furniture polish to the sideboard and table legs. There was still the bare lingering ammoniac smell of Bobby's nappies thrust into a plastic bag stuffed behind the fridge. Dee now spread the ironed bedsheet over the table and together we arranged beverages on the fresh lavender surface.

"O you darling you," said Dee blessing each sealed fifth of whiskey she slid from its narrow sack.

I had presented her with half a dozen bottles of vodka, Irish, Scotch—two of each—and a crate of Guinness, though true Guinness drinkers preferred their stout on tap ("Not to worry," said Dee, "they'd drink it from a garden hose when the thirst is on"). There was Fanta for the nondrinkers, for I had heard of a strict teetotal clan in Ireland called Pioneers, but Dee assured me she had invited no such clan, and the Fanta would serve to mix with the vodka, no ice of course: "Whatever for? Yanks are a caution with their cocktails and calories and heaps of ice." I lined up the bottles of stout and ale military style, ranked according to label.

Dee's delight was childlike (the true child, Bobby, abed early and out of sight), lighting candles the better to reflect the sparkle of amber glass. She burnt a finger when the match burnt down, sighed, brought an unopened bottle of Bush to her lips and kissed it on the neck. When she went to attend her neglected and dangerously explosive steam iron, I went to the door. Someone was banging on the shutters.

Liam was there, the first guest, with the unmistakable shape of a half-pint molded to his hip, but the bottle was not a contribution to the collection on the bedsheet, as was the custom, but for himself when the communal drink ran dry, as was his own custom. Liam was accompanied by Liam Keene, the Shadow I had met that night in the loo. The two Liams did indeed resemble one another though Keene's teeth were better, his smell neutral, and he smiled on the other side of his face. The reason they had come early was that Liam Sweeney, for outrages unspecified, had been booted out of the Bot. He was joined in exile by Liam Keene, out of sympathy, and Felim Delaney tagging after his disgraced mates so as not to be left alone. No one wanted to drink alone or show at a party first, before the pubs closed.

"Great," said Liam Sweeney and Liam Keene said, "Grand," as they inspected the presentation of beverages.

"Smashing," said Felim.

Liam Sweeney was growing a beard. This was either a touch of the poet or to distinguish and thus distance himself from Liam Keene. The patchwork adornment modified his angelic look by a sweet gangster's five o'clock shadow but might shade into saintliness when fully grown. He wanted to engage my attention to show me, not the bottle in his pocket, but a secret he had brought along. His two mates diplomatically faded to allow Liam his private moment with me.

"Found your wee book at that shop," said Liam with sly shyness as he drew forth a copy of I.M. Gold's *Selected Poems* from his shirt. He had found the volume, he said (always shy when he lied), at the bookshop on Great Victoria that had been a massage parlor. Would I please to sign it for him? Here was my devil-may-care younger self incarnate, the marginal bard I played at but could never be. We stared into one another's fraudulent eyes for longer than we ever had before, two criminals on the same wavelength at last.

Liam's plaster cast had been removed, no longer a handy jotting pad for poems—had I seen or heard the last of his verse?—but I noted a telephone number written in ball-point, a tattoo on the inside of his wrist. He presented me with perhaps the same ball-point he wrote poems with, and telephone numbers. Here was the punch line to the long-standing joke between us, and I was game. I signed *I.M. Gold* on the page that bore the library imprimatur from Tompkins Square, New York.

Dee was restored to her social self by the welcome appearance of guests. She beamed over the trio and merrily poured Irish into two jelly glasses for the Liams and stout, carefully, into a paper cup for Felim.

While Dee performed the rites of hostess, I carried the damp duffel coats (it was raining out) upstairs to Bobby's room. The wean was awake of course. He lay on his back peering at me through the sidebars of his crib, wrapped like a miniature mummy in a thin blanket, immobile. There was a band of light across his face from the streetlamp below the window, never a smile for me, his neighbor from next door.

You don't diddle me, said his look. Liam Sweeney might have said the same. *I knew you, Mr. Bogus, from the first.*

His gaze was too steady for me to stay with, that open look of Ireland I could never meet. I greatly wanted to kiss the infant farewell, but—dry-eyed and sober as he—I no more than placed two fingers to his cool forehead, an itinerant swindler's blessing on the innocent.

Jameson's advice to one and all was not to open Dee's door unless the knocker identified himself as Friend. We were bloody liable to get a grenade rolled across the doorsill for our hospitality. If a fire bomb were flung into the room, we could best escape into the cemetery—a cemetery our fate in any case—through the kitchen window. Jameson was back from Liverpool to collect Saint Thomas, and his commission—to have the saint cast at last at a foundry in Dublin.

A third hunger-striker had died this night, and the staccato doloroso of bin lids rattled across the Lagan. "My luck," said Dee, "to lay a party on the night he dies." When the conversation waned (it never abated) I heard what sounded like rifle fire at some distance, and even above the talk the sirens shrieked, though nobody seemed to notice but me. To Clive Lovely it was all music.

"We were actually stoned," said Belle, and I thought she meant drunk, but she was describing a mob of men and boys throwing stones at their Volkswagen as they drove down the Ormeau Road. "Stoned, like in the Bible. We thought at first it was the firemen throwing stones at us." Their neurotic Dalmatian had bit a fireman at the firehouse in the Golden Triangle.

"I thought," said Mary Bannister, "Dalmatians were the fireman's friend."

"Not Guinness," said Clive.

Mary and Rupert Bannister, who were getting divorced, had come to the party together. Belfast was choosy about talk of any fall from grace: while no one dared mention my impending departure, everyone—especially the Bannisters—discussed the divorce.

"Rupert can't even be his own solicitor," said Mary, "or mine, for that matter. He's barred from the bar in Northern Ireland."

"Thank your lucky stars," said a poet up from Dublin, "you can untie the knot at all. There's no divorce in the Republic, it's till-death-do-you-part in those parts."

"Another bloody reason," said someone, "that six into twenty-six won't go."

"No politics please," said McMichael drunkenly shushing the drunken.

"Divorce," said the maple-leaf woman Dee called the Wraith. (She had lately fed and befriended Cat, and seemed to have wandered into the party on the basis of that acquaintance.) "It's the worst thing that can happen to a woman."

"The worst thing that can happen to a woman—" began one of the three Seven Sisters present, but the Whisperer finished for her: "Is to die a virgin."

While the Seven Sisters were all three at once indignantly contesting this blatant statement, Liam Sweeney called out, "Nothing sexual please."

"Lauxes gnihton," said Liam Keene in what I thought might be Latin, but the Shadow had the trick of repeating any phrase up to ten words backwards.

The Whisperer had come with a pretty girl who had brought a substantial wheel of Ulster Munster, and those of us around the lavender-spread table were eating cheese with soda crackers and drinking up while Liam Keene performed a recital of his own verses in reverse.

"Say something to him," said the pretty girl who had brought cheese, her eyes wide as oysters in the candlelight, so I said, "Eyes wide as oysters."

"Sretsyo," said Liam Keene in instant echo, "sa ediw seye."

"How the deuce does he do it?" asked Fiona, Felim's twin, "Tell us, do."

"Od sullet," said the Shadow.

"Sounds like Irish," said O'Donegal tuning his lute. O'Donegal was prepared to play and sing as soon as Liam Keene completed his gig.

At that moment, and only for a flash of illumination, the windows flared with stage lighting. Somebody said, "Police helicopters."

The coughing sound of motor-and-blades hovered suspended over the cemetery—then O'Donegal was playing his harp.

Soon-to-be-wed Mildred Chaucer had come without her fiancé, who was across the water, but with a shopping net of bread—for the bakeries would shut down if the Troubles kept up—and Dee had placed the net of bread on her Morris chair, kept empty otherwise in memory of the Old Poet. Now Arts Council—who had been distantly circling me throughout the night, avoiding eye contact with his good eye—made his way to the chair and was about to remove the bread when Dee intercepted him and whispered in his ear. Arts Council nodded heavily and remained standing.

It came to me with unexpected regret that no chair in Ireland, ever, would be left empty in my honor.

"How does a person get a taxi home?" asked the Wraith, whose name was Rappaport.

"Hold your hour and have another."

Somebody attempted to pour for her, but Mrs. Rappaport waved alcohol away. Dee would be undone to learn she had allowed a Pioneer to crash her party, but the blitzlike conditions of this night promoted an exceptional conviviality and even Mrs. Rappaport relaxed her reserve and was part of the general enchantment. The gathering had evolved into what was known as a good crack. In the moil of Prod and Taig poets, lecturers and students and one disgraced Yank with a dawning sense of detachment, Mrs. Rappaport, Canadian and newcomer, was being made to feel warmly at home. Those who spoke to her hung on her Canadian cadences with apparent fascination. At a handsome fifty-nine or sixty, expensively dressed— a white gown more bridal than wraithlike—she discovered herself a success. She floated from guest to guest the center of whatever group she penetrated: she was mannered and brittle-smiling and sure of herself without condescension; she assumed poses, but charming ones, asked blunt but forgivable questions and replied to questions put to her as if being received by the Press.

"And how do you find us?" asked McMichael gently.

"Like family," said Mrs. Rappaport.

Rappaport was her late husband's name, but she was a Connelly of Irish extraction and had come here to search out ancestors long buried under the old sod. She had already combed Glasnevin and the graveyards of the Republic for kin and had now attached herself to this party in search of living connections.

"And what do you think," Arts Council asked, "of our wee divided Emerald Isle?"

Having principally explored only the burial grounds of Ireland, she tried to think what she thought. Then she struck a pose, made an offhand gesture, and said, "I saw sheep."

"Peehs was I," said Liam Keene.

"On the way in from your airport I saw these sheep in the dark, grazing behind barbed wire."

Before someone could say the sheep weren't sheep, McMichael shushed him, saying, "No politics please."

Lightning at the windows had by this time turned orange, bells were mixed with the sirens, and O'Donegal was singing "Under the Green Tree." There was a rattling of the gate-lodge shutters.

"If they're firemen, don't allow them in," said Belle Lovely, "or we'll only be stoned."

"Pissed as we are," whispered the Whisperer.

Lean cadaverous Jameson had stationed himself security officer at the door, still wearing his loden coat with the toggles undone, as if to remove it might reveal he was but wire armature like his beginning Christ in my kitchen. He called out to the shutter rattler to identify himself or fuck off. Someone from outside called back, "They've fire-bombed the Belly."

Jameson asked Ulster's eternal question: "What are you?" Then, "Not the bloody bombers, I hope."

There were three musicians out there in the black rain: two men and a girl, one flute and two fiddlers. They named names saying they had just fled the conflagration at the Bellingham Arms.

"Tell them," said Liam Sweeney, "we're short of drink here," and Liam Keene called out that we were short of knird.

Clive Lovely recognized the musicians' names and Dee said, "Do let them in." Dee could only anticipate the crack getting better the more who joined.

Jameson opened a narrow space to the drenched musicians and held a candle to their faces. The flute was carrying a wet sack of pints of lager saved from the fire. Jameson made certain to check their music cases for hand grenades and Dee helped them out of their wet duffels. Soon the trio was drinking Flute's lager from paper cups and eating cheese and telling through a spray of soda crackers how bad the Belly was burning. In a little while they were tuning up for playing reels with O'Donegal.

True, the drink was running low. But the party feeling was that drink would pour down from the tumultuous sky or the magic of crack would provide but until that miracle transpired we would drown in what liquid was left whatever the label. Some were drinking potchin with Fanta, others sober enough to reflect on O'Donegal's spare Paddy in the lute case. McMichael was good enough though half-cut to light candles for a reconnaissance mission to my next-door gatehouse for the cache of port the sculptor, if he remembered rightly, had secreted in the hollow bathroom wall before leaving for Liverpool. I had lived there all this empty while unaware of port stashed in the plumbing.

Some there were who did not believe in Jameson's cache or that crack would provide and fished the Paddy out of O'Donegal's unguarded lute case and got Liam Sweeney's half-pint from him more by strength than stealth. Dee wandered about collecting empty paper cups in careless beatitude thinking to wring drink from stone and occasionally touching her hair the way it once was, the knobby hand of course touching nothing. The poet up from Dublin with Tasker's same tragic look and wet eyes cornered me and asked: "Poet in Residence, are you not?"

It was a question like what-are-you? not to answer without reflection.

"Heard you," he said, "on Radio Ulster. The job would've gone to me but for politics."

"The reading?"

"The Residence."

"The residence is a myth. A metaphor, for digs. Everywhere and nowhere, known and unknowable."

"Would have been mine, but for politics."

"Right now, the residence. It's next door."

"Does the loo work? Dee's doesn't."

"Did. When last I flushed."

The poet up from Dublin went in the wake of the search party in search of a working loo with a candle to light his way and Belle said, "Why all the candles? They can't shut off the lights in a month with an *r* in it."

In his wake I reflected on the poet up from Dublin, his beard off-white and Old Testament and silken hair a disorder of snowy plumes, freckled hands—candle in one, paper cup in the other—attached to genuine poet's wrists. I designated him the new poet in town and the Canadian wraith as the new woman in white.

Mrs. Rappaport for all her Canadian age, a camouflaged sixty for certain, did attract men, three of them circling her, Arts Council for one, listening to her sober report on Irish cemeteries.

The drink was in Liam Sweeney's eye as he went up to Liam Keene after the latter's last backwards recall of the lyrics to "Under the Green Tree" and kissed him on the ear. Music wound through every discourse under way, fiddler dribbling his drink and spittle into the fiddle hole sounding much like the Nashville sound that jigged through Miss Ryan's earphones at the Sans Souci: airy-fairy airs Liam Keene called them, forwards, as if they had been played backwards.

"You were the Prophet," said I. "Were you not? In the stall."

"That I was. Liam's doppelganger."

"Full-time job."

"Overtime. Gets put out of pubs on account of me. Got put out of the Bot tonight on my account—both of us poets, you see, and look-alikes. I told you we were all poets here, did I not?"

"You did. You also told me. To fuck off."

"Did I now? That was the drink speaking."

Fred Kinley or Kindly joined us, bringing the Printmaker in Residence for me to meet, she in a printed dress with printed headband, perfumed. I found paper cups for them but nothing to fill the cups with. Fred K was the Keeper of Art at the Antrim Museum and when Liam Keene said we were all poets here Fred said not himself, proud to announce he was the only soul this side of the grave and north of the border never to have written a deliberate line of verse.

"I," confessed the Printmaker, "write them."

I would never have to read them. She was discussing the New Poet's poems and politics when the New Poet himself joined us, back from the loo with his fly unbuttoned, so the talk about him went dead while the Printmaker asked if he would read her verses. I need only study the prints across her breasts and imbibe her perfume wafting through the odor of Dee's potchin and furniture polish.

"If not for politics," the New Poet told her, "I would be him." He meant me.

Bannister took me aside to say how lovely the adieu was working out. Did he mean my parting from Belfast or his from Mary?

"Been asking about you," said Bannister.

"Who?" I thought it might be Mary but was hoping for the Printmaker or the pretty girl with the Whisperer.

"The lady in white. She is quite extraordinary. I told her to take it from me, you come highly recommended."

I frowned on being bandied about and thus passed on.

"Highly."

Mary Bannister came up to us in a state of grace—forever on Bannister's heels, now they were separated—to inform me and for her husband's information that she had changed the locks on their summer house in Sligo until the decree became final. Rupert nodded, as contented as she at how lovely the adieu was working out.

Liam Sweeney was writing on his free wrist the telephone number of a young girl who was telling him he used to steal Fanta from her Mum's wee shop. The Whisperer was rounding up talent for *Roundup*—O'Donegal to sing "Under the Green Tree" and Liam Keene to recite poems backwards—while behind the Whisperer's back Felim, who lately affected one gold earring (which only drew attention to his large red ears), was chatting up the Whisperer's pretty girl about a mate of his shot in the buttocks when a soldier's bullet ricocheted.

For an instant I thought I saw Sarojinni Singh float through the vestibule in silk and thongs, a sight that slightly altered my heartbeat but it was only the woman in white gliding by. Saro I heard was being kept in purdah on Utility Street by Boethius who may have heard Liam's love poem about her. Surely Boethius was my betrayer not she, but whichever . . .

"Forgive and forget," McMichael was saying, referring to the

New Poet's broadcasts from Berlin when Ireland was neutral during the war.

Mrs. Rappaport was having her fortune read by Belle Lovely who claimed to be half tinker on the distaff side and was reading people's palms. The woman looked over Belle's shoulder at me, only half-hearing what Belle was telling.

"A poet," said Belle, "and a gentleman."

Mrs. Rappaport was looking at me.

The stronger stuff was out for those who drank with passion but Pioneers could sip Fanta and there was still sweet port and Flute's lager left. Arts Council deliberately or in his cups popped his glass eye into the cup of port Jameson held and came close to causing a brawl except that Arts Council had got the sculptor his commission for Saint Thomas and the post in Liverpool and Miss Chaucer came between them and fished the eye out with a teaspoon. The New Poet staggered to the Old Poet's memorial chair, picked up the net of bread, and to Dee's dismay sat down and was eating the bread.

"That's bad luck," said Belle looking up from Mrs. Rappaport's palm.

"Isn't it smashing," said Mary B, "how calm we are about it. I still jog, Rupert translates. We're acting as if everything is normal except for changing the locks."

There was no escaping the bold appraisal of Mrs. Rappaport's eyes. She kept staring at me over Belle's shoulder.

"An unknown drunk," said McMichael.

An unknown drunk had followed the search party next door to my digs and had fallen into my bed unconscious.

"There's a pulse," said Bannister, speaking of the drunk, "but no I.D."

"No idea," said somebody, "who he is."

Dee was next door to identify the guest and use my loo.

"Does he have a beard?" I asked.

"Does, as a matter of fact," said McMichael.

"Great tangled black beard," said Bannister, "and a great tangled heap of hair."

"Does he look, a little. Like Mahatma Gandhi?"

"Does, as a matter of fact. Gandhi, yes, now as you speak of it."

"I know him. I think."

You know you think-o, therefore you are. Stinko.

"Nobody else does. Did Dee invite him? We were calling the poor devil the Corpse, he's out so stiff."

"Bad luck," said Belle, "calling your man that."

"That's no corpse, that's my Saint Thomas."

"Not the saint in the kitchen but the corpse on the cot."

Bannister took me aside to confide: "Since you yourself went splits as you say with your wife, you know the drill. I feel like leaving the party and so does Mary but we don't know whether to leave with one another or not. What will people say knowing she's changing the locks and all if we leave the party together?"

"Not to worry," was my advice.

Arts Council came up saying, "She's been asking after you," nodding in Mrs. Rappaport's direction, and winking, I thought, but that was only his missing eye. "Told her you were smashing, tops in your field. Gave you a sterling send-off, highest recommendation. You're a loss to us, Gold, an irreplaceable loss." And he went looking about for his missing eye.

Still called me Gold, a sign of something. Or other.

"In Grasse," said the New Poet, "after the war." The New Poet was telling Mrs. Rappaport about the time he was imprisoned in France, and now included me as if I were the missing side of his triangle. "Every poet should at some time do time in a prison or time in a mental institution."

Time, gentlemen, poets.

"I'm going," said Mrs. Rappaport, "to France."

"Perfume center of the world," said the New Poet, as the perfumed Printmaker turned our triangle into a square. He was speaking of Grasse. "In particular the village of Ys, not far from Grasse, where the prison is, where I spent the happiest summer of my poet's life." He began writing something on the back of a loser's betting slip. "If I had it to do again, and politics were different, I'd—or would I?"

"I'll be going to France," said Mrs. Rappaport, and the Printmaker said, "I'd dearly love to go," but the New Poet passed the betting slip to me. On the back of it was a poem:

> If
> I had it to do again,
> Ys,
> Not far from Grasse.

At a party, which was why parties took place, was the constant anticipation of anything-can-happen, and what would happen was that the New Poet despite politics must surely become the Poet in

Residence meant for Belfast all along. At a party, all tricks of words and verses reversed, prophecy and postponed regret, fiddler-and-fortune's sleight of hand—anything can happen. Was I not a ghost at my own table, already away to France? The Liams knew. I watched the way Liam Sweeney leanly hungrily took in the New Poet's vast beard, a metaphor for his resonant history, while thoughtfully pinching at his own tentative growth. I watched Liam Keene watch Liam Sweeney watch the New Poet from Dublin as I watched the endless wheel.

"Are you a betting man by any chance?" the New Poet asked me.

"Only once," said I. "As a matter of fact."

Belle Lovely was analyzing the handwriting on Liam Sweeney's wrist: "I'm half tinker," she said, "on the distaff side." She had once analyzed handwriting of job applicants for an employer who believed Catholics could be distinguished from Protestants by their handwriting. (From there she had gone on to reading palms.) "Write down something for me," she asked me, "do."

Liam showed her the inscription I had written in the copy of *Selected Poems.*

"Lovely racecourse not far from Grasse," the New Poet informed me, "at Juan-les-Pins."

I wondered, and asked, "Have you ever heard of a horse. Named Naiad?"

"Nameless," said somebody referring to the Corpse, "known but to God."

"Dead soldier," said the Keeper of Art looking into his empty paper cup.

"Bad luck," said Belle, "to call him that." They were calling him the Corpse and the Unknown Soldier.

"Naiad? Not to know of, not—that is—to bet on."

"Well I have come to collect him for my commission."

"Not the wax statue but the dead soldier."

"The saint," said Jameson. "He's to be cast in Dublin in the morning."

"It is morning," said somebody, "or was."

"We'll get your man a taxi," said Dee, meaning the Corpse, "in due time."

I had taken my wristwatch out of my pocket and was winding it, for time was running out. We were out of drink and candles down to stubs and Jameson and McMichael were opening shutters to what appeared to be the aurora borealis. The storm had blown over and the only rub was a smear of black smoke from the smoldering ruins of the Bellingham Arms against a pastel sky.

Black taxis had braved the streets of seige to pull up at the gate-lodge drive, the drivers calling out the names of those who had called for cabs—but how had they been called without a telephone to ring from? The first had been summoned for Arts Council who was delayed answering the horn because he'd lost his glass eye in the wad of nappies stuffed behind Dee's fridge. Mrs. Rappaport autocratically commandeered his taxi. I had my chance to study her without being stared at as she stepped into the taxi, and I saw her in a new light, the tight unnatural shiny look of her sixty-year-old baby skin, a profile in granite, the cowl to her white winding sheet drawn over her wig against the rain though it was no longer raining out.

Those pledging "I'm away" had first to step over Liam Sweeney lying in the vestibule on the musicians' wet coats, his eighteenth-century curls framed in the Fanta girl's lap. She was holding Liam's wrist where her telephone number was written, feeling for a pulse. While the Whisperer appealed to the New Poet to broadcast his politics on *Roundup*, Felim Delaney slipped off in the taxi meant for him and in company with the pretty girl who had brought the cheese he had come with.

McMichael had a broad but absent lecturer's smile for me and a "Best of luck, Professor," but the Lovelys, who had also wished me luck, were back, perhaps to wish me more. Belle stepped over Liam and announced that they had forgotten where the Volkswagen with the smashed windscreen, from being stoned, was parked.

"No one would dare steal it for it's been stoned and smells of goat."

The quartet playing Irish music without letup now played on as if to slow or take a break meant time and tide and life itself was played out, the tempo the pulse of the party. I stumbled back across Liam from saying goodbye and receiving luck's blessing from Beowulf and Kinley and a kiss imprinted on my brow by the Printmaker, on the cheek by cheeky Mary pecking at me with her chicken's beak. "Not to worry," Mary said and Bannister said, "You've been taken on, by Canada."

My thoughts reeled to the Irish music, made me think O lackadaisy as the jig goes, O I was fading now the jig was up but let's not get maudlin over their lovely music this late date.

Belle Lovely was reading the New Poet's palm since having forgotten where the Volkswagen was parked.

"Read your own palm," said Clive, "to see where we parked the bloody car."

"Read Gold's palm," somebody suggested.

But I would not have my future fiddled or past revealed and was already as per Jameson's instructions out the kitchen exit as if a grenade had been tossed across the threshold, to play safe.

22

DEE WAS out back in the cemetery with the beheaded stone lambs and broken angels. She was tying a goat to a tree with a dog chain.

"The creature chewed through the rope I tied him with but this article is British made." The Lovelys had presented Dee with a goat. "Bobby would never touch milk from a cow, maybe he'll want to take this creature's milk. Speak of drink, I never trusted a person wouldn't drink, but you can trust her for what you need."

"What do I need?"

"If you don't know, nobody does."

How homely she was in the new light of day, grotesque and touching, inviting hurt, but with a hard enough center to endure.

"We've talked to her on your account. Wants a ghost to write her life."

"And I'm the ghost?"

"She's had this life, you see."

"Haven't we all."

"Special, hers is. So she says."

"So's mine, and yours."

"Mine you wouldn't know about or care a fig if you did."

"More than you think."

"Hers will sell."

"Ah."

"You see? You're a practicing ghost already."

Dee smiled and showed terrible teeth. Ireland loves a joke like me.

"Just a guesser. I guess. Second-guessing."

"A chancer, too. You resemble a lad I once knew, but without a beard."

"Dead?"

Through the driveway arch we could see Lawrence and McMichael helping Jameson carry Doubting Thomas wrapped in the French flag into a lorry—or was it the Corpse they were disposing of?

"Who knows? The chancers men are, who knows where they might turn up next."

"Desire," said I, "and pursuit." I spoke with drunken gravity. "As somebody said, desire and pursuit. Is all it is. Dog chases tail, goat chews rope."

Cat was delicately bridging the narrow arch over the driveway. Beyond, at the corner of Chlorine and the Stranmillis Road the two fiddles and a flute were playing again, trying to attract the attention of a swiftly passing taxi. Dee had emptied an ashtray into the trash pile near enough that the goat was contentedly chewing fag ends at the end of its tether.

Dee said something in Irish, a blessing I hoped and not the word of a witch, probably something about wishing goat's milk would not taste of nicotine.

The rain had ceased but droplets still fell from the cemetery trees. If I kissed her would she turn from a toad into a princess? None of that, I might taste salt on her cheeks instead of raindrops. We did not even touch hands farewell.

"I'm away."

"Safe home," she said, as if home were a little distance.

Ghosts

1

THERE WAS no First Class cabin on the BA shuttle to London, so Mrs. Rappaport submitted to Tourist. I was indifferent to the accommodations, but I did miss the ambulant bar. Mrs. Rappaport no longer stared at me, now that she had acquired me, but I was just as self-conscious in having been acquired as when I was being appraised. A drink, without ice, might have broken the ice. Instead of a chariot bearing bottles to our seats, the crisp blue stewardess pushed a portable cash drawer down the aisle, collecting late fares. Mrs. Rappaport paid for both our tickets.

My employer made no in-flight conversation except to mumble, more to herself than to me, the word "arrangements." She did not specify what arrangements—hers, mine, hers and mine—were under consideration. As we landed at Heathrow she spoke of legal people as if to distinguish them from illegal people, like me—though she did not yet know how illegal I was.

"There's legal people I want to see here."

In London we were to see her representative in the United Kingdom, a legal person called Parsons, on Blackfriars Road. Parsons was a solicitor (not a barrister, like Bannister)—a solicitor in miniature. He wore a hunting jacket, for some odd reason, with a leather patch to protect the tweed shoulder from a rifle stock: a small man, but one prepared to bear arms. His head came barely to Mrs. Rappaport's breasts; she and I stared down at the long strands of grey hair at the back of his head brushed forward to camouflage the balding center. He spoke with a British accent, but I discovered he was from

263

Chicago, and he wanted to talk to me about a team called the Bears, and to inquire about scores.

"I'm afraid I don't follow—"

"What about the contract?" Mrs. Rappaport broke in.

"I think you will find this agreement—"

"So let's see it."

"Precisely," said Parsons.

Without any noticeable signal from Parsons, a trim secretary glided into the room (this was Parson's private residence, not a law office—though the Law Courts were only a reassuring block away) bearing coffee in a silver jug and a leather binder under her arm. There was an excess of leather about. We sat in leather armchairs that deflated with our weight; I was faced with a wall of leather book bindings, Mrs. Rappaport with crowded hunting scenes in leather frames. The secretary wore a leather skirt. She was aware of Mrs. Rappaport's preference for coffee, knew that she took it black; for Parsons and me the secretary poured from a decanter of sherry.

"Read it aloud, shall I?" asked Parsons.

"He can read," said Mrs. Rappaport crisply, a way she had, I noticed, with people she paid.

"And can *write*, I daresay," said Parsons. He turned to me: "Something I've always wondered. Where do you writers get your ideas?"

Writer, not poet: I was out of the poetry fiddle now, and into prose. With a look of unbearable annoyance, Mrs. Rappaport looked up from her copy of the contract. I pretended to be too engrossed in the legal paragraphs of my copy to reply.

"Ideas," said Parsons, retracting his original question. "I would suppose the ideas will in this case be supplied by Mrs. Rappaport."

"Right," said Mrs. Rappaport.

"Naturally," said Parsons. "And you, sir, will be the wordsmith, so to speak."

"Right," said Mrs. Rappaport.

"I think you will find this little agreement a document both parties can live with, mutually binding but with exclusive advantages to each signatory."

The term "mutually binding" went down smoothly enough, with drink. The secretary's hair, I noticed in my detachment, was the color of our sherry.

Mrs. Rappaport assumed an expression of unbearable annoyance as Parsons rubbed his hands together flylike and launched a summing-up.

"You agree herein to a straight fifty-fifty division of monies generated from publication of said work—"

"Binding, you said," said Mrs. Rappaport. "All over? France too?"

"All over," said Parsons, lifting his little arms to embrace the world. "First North American serial rights and all rights in the United Kingdom, translation and foreign publication rights including subsequent rights such as dramatization for film or television, et cetera, et cetera."

Mrs. Rappaport repeated the words "film, television" with the first evidence of satisfaction she had shown so far. Parsons droned on about the name Teresa Rappaport appearing on the title page as sole author, no secondary by-line necessary, "Since you, sir, I understand, waive the right to an 'as told to' credit line or any public acknowledgment of your role as collaborator on said work."

"This we discussed already," said Mrs. Rappaport, and I nodded.

"—but will receive the stipulated half-share of any and all monies generated by publication of said work."

"We discussed all that."

"We did," I recalled.

Mrs. Rappaport removed her owl-rimmed rose-tinted glasses, having terminated her review of the contract. She inquired vaguely about somebody named Sylvester, in Chicago. Sylvester happened to have been Mrs. Rappaport's divorce lawyer, and Parsons' former law partner, before Parsons, for reasons unspecified, settled in London.

"Miss Thayer, please, if you will."

The secretary was a British national and could serve as witness to a document signed on British soil.

Miss Thayer bent beside me, her leather skirt pressed to my leather chair, her electric hair brushing my cheek, as I signed "I.M. Gold," and she bore witness to its contractual legality.

"All Celestine asks is that people be nice to her," Mrs. Rappaport warned me.

"By all means."

We were to have preluncheon drinks together—celery tonic for Mrs. Rappaport—in the hotel bar. Summoned from Hampstead, Celestine Innocenti appeared to us, pale as a vision but substantial in flesh, dressed simply in tasteful mourning: a black widow with blue stockings.

I touched Mrs. Innocenti's hand how-d'you-do? and spoke only

of weather and wine. There was a telephone booth in the bar, and my
eye kept wandering self-consciously to it. Mr. Innocenti had been
shot to death in a telephone booth in Queens. This happened six years
ago and Celestine, according to Mrs. Rappaport, had never recovered
from the loss. I ordered a Campari apéritif for her, and discreetly
attended to my own Campari as Mrs. Innocenti appraised me closely
and at length. I tried to look away from her stare, and tried not to look
at the telephone booth. Her conversation with Mrs. Rappaport was
clipped and cryptic.

"Is he?"

"You know me, strictly."

"When?"

"A week what difference, I don't know."

"Alfredo, when I think."

"Don't, you live with it."

"Sometimes. Or not."

"That's life, who doesn't."

"Me he was calling, is what gets me."

"Guilt is for the birds."

After a pause the subject seemed to have changed.

"Jewel?"

"Couldn't come in."

"That's right rabies."

"England."

"They take care."

"Wouldn't live here."

"They're polite."

"Look what they did to my hair."

"It's the rain, for skin it moisturizes."

"Couldn't pay me."

"They're politer than New York. Is he?"

"American."

"When I think."

"Strictly, like I said."

"I know. So do I."

Mrs. Rappaport had brought a Vuitton attaché case from her
room, vaultlike in its trimmings, combination lock with shrill alarm
when tampered with—it had gone off at Customs, Heathrow. While I
ordered a second Campari for myself (Mrs. Innocenti was having no
more than one), Mrs. Rappaport drew the case to her lap and flipped
it open. Our contract was on the top of the stack of papers, so I looked

discreetly away—saw the telephone booth, and looked in a different direction. When my gaze returned to the table, Mrs. Innocenti was putting an envelope into her purse.

"When I think."

"The rain you couldn't pay me."

We took a taxi in the rain to a restaurant in the West End. Mrs. Rappaport adhered to the theory that the best food to be eaten in London was Italian, French or Eastern.

What startled me the moment we entered the restaurant was the beaming face that greeted me at the door. The maître d' was Muhammed of the Piss and Garlic Palace in Belfast. His smile only expanded as he examined my face, but in no other way did he or I betray our former acquaintance. He simply bowed to us with no wink or gesture to express a conceivable liaison—do we not all, dear friend, travel devious paths and accept unlikely labor?—then led us through a miasma of incense to a corner of Damascus where he presented us with menus in the form of scrolls, written in imitation Persian script.

2

I DID NOT KNOW we were flying to Brussels until we were at Heathrow again, engaging two porters to attend to Mrs. Rappaport's twelve pieces of matching luggage with maple-leaf labels. She carried the Vuitton case herself, and I tagged after her with the Poet's travel-dented attaché case full of my father's letters.

Mrs. Rappaport knew legal people in Brussels, and a Canadian dentist she trusted. She had teeth and legal affairs to attend to: she was not in the habit of discussing her arrangements in detail. She was in the habit of knowing what she wanted—or if not, acting on the strongest impulse of the moment. She invariably stepped out ahead of me with purposeful stride and barely a glance backwards to see if I followed at her heels. I opened the doors of hotels, taxis and restaurants for her; she, with cash and checks and credit cards, opened all the doors that mattered.

At times I was troubled by the prospect of writing her life story. How was I to write about someone who so seldom addressed her ghost? Assuming Mrs. Rappaport's autobiography would be more complicated to write than a hospital chart, I would need, at least, a chart of facts to draw from. Did I really intend to write this book? Did she?

Meanwhile I followed her lead, slept alone, and patiently awaited the intervals of refreshment. Drinks were served on this flight, and I managed to put away three miniatures of bourbon before we got across the channel. Mrs. Rappaport was oblivious to my indulgence in drink, assuming perhaps all poets, and biographers, drank. When she ordered tomato juice for herself in French, I remembered she was Canadian. We flew First Class.

Fastening her seat belt for landing, Mrs. Rappaport spoke as if thinking aloud: "My father is buried in Belgium."

I wondered if she meant by this announcement that I should be taking notes. This was the first item of personal importance she had offered, and with scant elaboration. Her father was killed in a hospital shelled by the Germans, only three days prior to the Armistice. I attempted to recalculate Mrs. Rappaport's age to accommodate a father killed in World War I, but the mathematics, and factors unknown, were beyond my calculations.

"He volunteered," she said. "Never volunteer."

As the plane taxied along the runway, Mrs. Rappaport retired into her customary silence and I made the mental note: *volunteer father dead in Flanders Fields.* It crossed my mind that our collaboration was going to be frustrating. But I had volunteered.

From the airport I was dispatched to the hotel alone, along with the luggage (I, the thirteenth piece) while Mrs. Rappaport took a separate taxi to her dentist in the suburb of Uccle. The hotel was another neutral three-star establishment like the hotel in London, also fashionably placed, a short stroll from the Grande Place. Mrs. Rappaport had not specified which of the adjoining rooms was to be hers: the rooms were identical size and equally overfurnished, so I chose for her the one with the larger chandelier. But we stayed in Brussels only overnight, and she had no occasion to examine my bedroom and compare chandeliers.

Ostend she called the deadest town outside Toronto, but we were obliged to go there to pick up her French poodle, Jewel, left with a legal friend because of the animal quarantine laws in the United Kingdom.

The reunion between mistress and dog was a study in ecstacy—
repressed on Mrs. Rappaport's part, but she too would have wiggled
her hindquarters in delight if not for restrictive corset and conditioning. The affection for her pet was displayed in her expression: the
only true pleasure her face had showed so far, except over the word
from Parsons about film, television.

Jewel was a miniature black French poodle with eyes, like
Tasker's, forever moist. She wore a collar of rhinestones, and the
nails of her paws were lacquered the same beige shade as Mrs.
Rappaport's fingernails. Mrs. Rappaport held the quivering animal to
her bosom, transported to raptures of infantile talk incomprehensible
to any but the affectionate two. It occurred to me that neither dog nor
mistress was complete without the other, the idealized soul-mating to
which the rest of us can only aspire.

Mrs. Rappaport spoke French to the couple who had kept Jewel
in her absence. It was a language both Vanderwallers understood
perfectly, but they replied in English, perhaps for my benefit, or
because they were Flemish and did not want to express themselves in
French.

"High-toned," said Mÿnheer Vanderwaller. "Will not never
touch scraps."

"Behaving like a princess, snappy with intruders, knows what
she wants," said Madame Vanderwaller, addressing me. She was
speaking of the dog, not the mistress.

A hired car would take us to the border, the driver of absolute
trustworthiness and "of the family." By way of their broken conversation, I learned that our intermediate destination was a military
cemetery near the Franco-Belgian border, to visit the grave of Mrs.
Rappaport's father.

While we waited for the car, Mÿnheer served me a beer, a thick
dark beverage with the three-inch foam familiar to my father's
nostalgias. Mÿnheer had been in the Congo during the crisis of
independence.

"The nuns," said Mÿnheer, "they raped." As an afterthought he
informed me that the beer I drank was brewed by monks. He then
directed his conversation exclusively to Mrs. Rappaport.

"He is?"

"*Américain.*" Mrs. Rappaport gave the shortest possible answers
to questions of a personal nature.

"Of the family?"

Mrs. Rappaport said something in French of which I caught only
the word *ami*. (The poet used to call me *mon ami*.) Mÿnheer

Vanderwaller then said something to Madame Vanderwaller in Flemish, of which I caught nothing.

Meanwhile the driver arrived—also named Vanderwaller, who had also been in the Congo—a middle-aged Flemish chauffeur in a dark business suit and sober necktie, with a billed military cap as a concession to his trade. He carried a wreath of flowers like the horseshoe wreaths placed around the necks of winning racehorses. When he removed his cap to greet Mrs. Rappaport I saw that his head had been shaved or become completely bald in the style of Eric von Stroheim.

Since we could not stay for lunch, Madame Vanderwaller presented us with a picnic basket. The picnic and wreath had been ordered in advance by Mrs. Rappaport, whose impulsive acts may have been hasty but whose arrangements were thorough. I was relieved to see the neck of a bottle of wine protruding from the basket.

The limousine was a highly polished black Mercedes-Benz that easily swallowed the remaining luggage (several suitcases had been sent on to Paris), including wreath, picnic basket and Jewel's wicker bed with satin pillow. The Mercedes was hearselike in its accoutrements and proportions—especially the accommodations for a wreath in the trunk that might have taken on a small coffin.

"The dog, he does not do pi-pi?"

"*She*," said Mrs. Rappaport sharply, "knows how to behave in a person's car." Her eyes flattened and became as hard as the rhinestones on Jewel's collar.

From the Vuitton case she took a white envelope for the original Mÿnheer Vanderwaller that disappeared inside his claret-colored cardigan. Before we stepped into the car, the chauffeur made the tactical error of spreading a plastic coverlet over the backseat. He immediately earned Mrs. Rappaport's unreserved animosity, and I could imagine behind the rhinestone eyes a recalculation of his gratuity. Before placing Jewel on the seat between us, Mrs. Rappaport snatched up the plastic and roughly stuffed the coverlet under the jump seat behind the driver.

Although the day was overcast, Mrs. Rappaport wore a pair of somber glasses appropriate to mourning. She advised Vanderwaller to drive slowly and be prepared for frequent stops: Jewel was upset by excessive speed and overlong stretches of roadway. The driver, impressed by the incident of the plastic coverlet, submitted himself to his client's directions.

We followed the planet's flattest road through a series of identical seacoast towns, each village seeming smaller than the one before, as if a miniaturist was making tinier and tinier picture postcards of the first, in descending order westward from Ostend.

Every town had its Apoteek with the same thick-haunched woman scrubbing the tiles in front of it with fat chapped arms. *Grootmoederbrood* was featured in the sterile window displays of every *bakerij*. Chrome and diamond-glass cafés had little rugs on the tables and served Stella and Maes-pils on draught with cork coasters to keep the rugs from becoming stained with beer rings. We made the café scene on our halting journey because the Mercedes got stuck behind a streetcar named De Panne clanging its laggard way to the border. The funereal pace suited Mrs. Rappaport's instructions, but the streetcar was preceded by a pressurized locomotive sucking sand from the trolley tracks with a hideous grinding wail.

Deep in her entrails Jewel growled displeasure at the screaming blower. There was no opportunity for the driver to pass, except through a spuming spiral of sand. Mrs. Rappaport lowered her handsome profile (she carried her head high, in a defiantly arrogant manner, as if there could be odd smells in small countries unacceptable to her—yet Belgium was blandly odorless and sanitary) and issued the first command to halt. We would pause at a place called Krokodiel and let the streetcar shriek on ahead of us.

The café in Krokodiel was embellished with a boar's head above the polished bar, and a partridge between the boar's tusks. Perhaps this note of excess in the décor inspired me to order another of the beers I had relished at the Vanderwallers' instead of settling for everyday Stella or Maes-pils. My Orval came in a bowl-shaped glass heavy enough to be held in two hands. Mrs. Rappaport sipped black coffee and Jewel lapped Spa water from a saucer. The chauffeur remained behind with his vehicle and *Het Laatste Nieuws*. We snacked from the picnic basket of Ardennes ham on *grootmoeder-brood* and pâté and tomatoes stuffed with peeled shrimps the size and color of Jewel's painted toenails. No, it was not the décor that inspired me to drink the heavy intoxicant I poured down, but the dead interval in our travels that—had I given the time over to contemplation— would revive the anxiety I was beginning to associate with this newest and most random of itineraries. Drink dulled the edge of angst and allowed me to believe I was en route for the great good place meant for me all along.

In this fashion we advanced through the dark dune country, in stops and starts, taking refreshment at cafés that grew smaller and smaller, the beer in larger and larger steins. I played on the monotony—and indulged my thirst—by testing a new brew by a different monastery every café we stopped in. I tried Chimay, Westmalle, Trappiste en route, and one last lager before reaching De Panne, a beer called Mort Subite, which Mrs. Rappaport translated for me as Sudden Death.

When the Mercedes was under way, Mrs. Rappaport crossed her silken legs in the ample space between seats and removed herself spiritually from all but Jewel's company. The driver attempted to jolly the silence with broken English jokes about French-speaking Belgians, the Walloons. A language war raged between the two cultures. The driver boasted of spray-painting out road signs and directions in French (he carried a spray can in the glove compartment for that purpose) so that Flemish would prevail on the motorways.

Mrs. Rappaport was not amused. Jewel responded to her mistress's mood with faint but sustained growling whenever the chauffeur spoke.

"It is not, Madame, the French of France I go against," declared the driver, "nor yourselfs, the French talkers of Canada."

"Listen, the French in Canada go against the English. It gets them exactly nowhere."

"Nowhere, exactly," echoed the driver, unconvinced.

Under an oppressively low sky of leaden clouds we drove toward a slot of uninspired horizon that promised nothing happier than downpour. Finally we emerged from the wastes of windbown dunes into an even more spectacular emptiness broken by a panorama of white crosses laid out in precisely bisecting limitless rows, a perspective diminishing but unending from here to eternity. The sight was dizzying, and the beers I had drunk made it more so. I was obliged to look away and think instead of another burying ground, the humble tumbledown graveyard of Stranmillis.

The chauffeur parked just outside the cemetery gate that bore the emblems of four nations; a sign in all four languages proclaimed that animals were not permitted on the grounds.

Mrs. Rappaport was the first out of the car, with her dark glasses off, to survey the prospect of so vast and mathematical a collection of graves. Far from being unsettled by the spectacle, she appeared rather inspired by the infinity of identical crosses, or perhaps merely relieved to have reached this grim destination.

She swept ahead of us carrying Jewel against her bosom (thus

the animal was not "on the grounds") and had alrady engaged the
gatekeeper in his files by the time the chauffeur and I arrived carrying
the funeral wreath between us. The gatehouse was nothing like Dee's
or the one I had lived in: the interior was as strictly ordered and
geometrically constituted as the calculated rows of crosses outside.
One entire wall contained file drawers the size of crypt doors,
along with a mobile-trolley ladder to reach the files nearest the
ceiling.

"Regrets, my dear lady." The gatekeeper wore a grey smock and
kept a rigid set of books. "*Personne* of that name interred in this
place."

"Try John-Henry instead of Jean-Henri."

"*Personne* of the surname Grandjacquot, nor of any given name
as you see." The gatekeeper reversed the open volume, like a guest
register, and slid the list of names to Mrs. Rappaport's side of the
counter.

Mrs. Rappaport's eyes turned rhinestone again, traveling down
the page.

"*Personne*, you see," repeated the gatekeeper. File drawer G,
pulled from the wall, had been thoroughly ransacked.

The chauffeur shifted uneasily beneath the wreath of flowers,
then began speaking to the gatekeeper in Flemish, presumably on
Mrs. Rappaport's behalf. A light began to dawn as the gatekeeper
responded to the chauffeur's suggestion. In a moment he was
nodding, obviously inspired. He raised a finger, said to Mrs.
Rappaport, "Perhaps," then leaped nimbly onto the trolley-ladder
and propelled himself along the wall of file drawers with unexpected
animation. At the far corner he pulled open a drawer and found a
Violà! within.

Mrs. Rappaport tipped the gatekeeper for the revelation he
provided. To her gratuity, I added a *merci*, my first word in French.

As we three trekked in silence past a thousand crosses to the
one inscribed 1173—no name, the unknown soldier—I realized how
Mrs. Rappaport meant her determination to be indulged if only by
purchase, and that her beliefs be sustained at any price. We shrouded
the anonymous cross in tuberose and fern, no tears shed, no
reflections expressed.

Yes, the book of her life would be written, would appear in
print—filmed, televised—if that was her wont. We were back in the
chauffeur's hearse making slow but certain passage to Dunkirk on the
French side of the border. I would paint out no road signs (our driver's

technique of defiance), but I had learned one attitude from the bald-domed Belgian: the will and expectations of a patron can only be circumvented, never opposed. This was probably a lesson my father meant to teach me by his example of a lifetime of guile.

3

WHILE MRS. RAPPAPORT had genealogists to consult and cemeteries to visit, I inherited the city of bridges and bookstalls. My tourist's eye was prepared for an impertinent Eiffel Tower and the Opéra of ornate pomposity, and certainly for the Arch at the beginning, or end, of the Champs Élysées (beneath which lay buried the soldier known but to God, perhaps Jean-Henri Grandjacquot)— for we did make all the tourist stops the first week, as if to get them over with—but my picture-postcard familiarity could not accommodate the perfect placement and harmony of those landmarks, nor the perspective of long low lovely bridges.

Pinch yourself, Critic—you're seeing Paris for me.

From the useful but mostly banal bridges of my life—the Suspension Bridge across the Ohio, causeways across Biscayne Bay—I was presented these delicate stone spans crossing not just from Right Bank to Left, but links gracefully suggestive of crossing from one mystery to another. The great grey river had chosen to flood its banks when we were there—menacing, to stare down at it—but flowing confined to its stone passageway beneath each stylish interstice of bridge. I could never select a bridge or make a crossing without some stir of anticipation: someone was waiting for me, the other side of the Seine.

Mrs. Rappaport crossed these bridges in taxis only (and I sometimes with her, the anticipation diminished in her company), eyes hard ahead, pursuing some mystery of her own. She carried pedigree papers in her purse, and notes on French ancestry, and guides to starred restaurants and celebrated cemeteries. (Her attaché case was confined to the hotel safe at the Lutetia: a man with a corrugated forehead, possibly a legal person, had met us in the lobby the first afternoon, and went away with a white envelope that smoothed his brow.) I kept the bridges to myself and shared only the restaurants and cemeteries with my employer—there had to be that much obligation to my role as biographer—but she need never know that this horizontal city was spread out for me only, on either shore. She had a camera somewhere in her luggage, she told me, and asked if I thought I knew how to operate one. I said I thought not, and was spared that indignity.

We had yet to write one word together, although Mrs. Rappaport had purchased an IBM electric typewriter for my use. (She considered my humble Olympia too insubstantial for the weight of our words.) All I knew of my subject was her careful attention to dress and coiffure, her constant rendezvous cut short with envelopes, her dog, her dagger of a nail file and her way with servants. We wrote nothing together, we barely spoke.

I was excused from duty at Denfert Rochereau. The attendant at the gate to the catacombs said something that Mrs. Rappaport translated for me as "Consider these bones." Dogs were not permitted under-ground because the bones and skulls of the deceased of Paris were exposed in ornamental piles in cavern after cavern along the labyrinthine tunnels of this place. "*Jamais,*" he wagged a finger at us, never a tour with dog.

Mrs. Rappaport reached for her tinted glasses in a way that made me know her eyes had gone flat and hard behind them, and before her hard flat French could follow, I offered to dog-walk Jewel during the mistress's tour of necropolis.

While Mrs. Rappaport explored the city of the dead, I wandered the living city with Jewel. A good many of the bookstalls were open along the quais, and here was a stroll I could give over to daydream. I imagined myself from an earlier incarnation as a bookseller beside the Seine, a miracle's remove from the bankrupt proprietor of Just Books, in Miami, with scarf and pipe and a folding chair with pooch (not Jewel, a scruffier breed) lying under the chair, and an April afternoon before me with neither success nor bankruptcy in the balance. *Jamais*, said a voice. So I walked on, working up another game.

The name Gabriel L'Homme had come back to me (in a roundabout way, as I noticed the distinction of genders on WC doors), another remembered utterance of the Poet. I invented a quest I considered legitimate, an excuse for my haphazard presence here. In my slapdash scrappy French, picked up from the opening chapters of *Assimil: French without Toil,* and from eavesdropping on Mrs. Rappaport's comments to chambermaids (and long ago, from the Poet), I went from bookstall to bookstall asking for the poems of Gabriel L'Homme. But that poet was as obscure and forgotten as the Poet had insisted. And the booksellers were annoyed, even indignant, in their sharp suspicious Parisian way, to be asked (in French, without verbs) for a volume unheard of and unavailable for sale. I could now believe the only copy extant had turned up a lucky find for the Poet's purposes only, at a garage sale in Santa Fe.

Another quest obsessed me, this one constant: the need to be stricken by love—or lovelovelove, as the Poet put it. Paris was known for spreading that virus to its visitors, so I rendered myself suscepti- ble: this must be the place. (The popular song that spring beamed in on every cabbie's radio and tourist transistor was called *"Maladie d'Amour."*) Love would have to happen here, on the Pont des Arts.

I needed to be in love as others were, all around me, on that bridge, as I tamely walked Jewel across. But I must have looked, to the lovers, as foolish as I suddenly felt—though I do not think they looked at me—when even Jewel fell in love, straining at her leash to lick the muzzle of a poodle straining at its leash to lick hers. (The woman with the other poodle was, alas, a replica of Mrs. Rappaport.) No one saw me, not even the woman with the other poodle. If a boy looked away from his girl for an instant, or she from him (everyone had a lover on that bridge: men with men as well, or women with women), it was only to gaze at the perfect view of the Pont Neuf where the Seine is magically split at the prow of the Ile de la Cité.

"Not here," someone was saying, "not yet."

When? I was desperate to ask. Where?

This was not to my eyes the loveliest of the bridges (Pont Neuf was that), but you must cross this bridge to see Pont Neuf. And this casual wooden span, so pedestrian and secluded from the frantic traffic, was so central to Paris you felt safe in the city's very heartbeat. There was a lane of double benches down the middle of the bridge, and planters of flowers at the ends of the benches; two benches, two sets of flowers. Where but Paris would flowers be offered to lovers on benches on a bridge?

"Look what else it offers," said the Poet.

I had come to the quai that led to the steps of the Louvre, and at that end of the bridge was a life ring displayed in a glass case. (There was one at the bridge's other end, also—for everything here came in twos.) If someone were to be seen struggling in the treacherous flood waters of the Seine, a life ring could be thrown from either end of the Pont des Arts, a would-be suicide might cling to this last chance. On the glass case was an emergency number to call, as well, though there was no telephone anywhere in the vicinity.

Mrs. Rappaport had engaged a suite of three rooms at the Lutetia, an indication that we were to settle down in Paris. When we checked in, the porter (pleased with his gratuity) let us know that the larger of the two bedrooms had been the honeymoon chamber of Pablo Picasso and his first wife, Olga. The larger of the two bedrooms was, of course, Mrs. Rappaport's. There were two Picasso reproductions hung in the room: one was a classic portrait of black-haired Olga with Spanish shawl and fan; the other represented a mantislike creature with sidelong jaws and feral teeth capable of devouring her mate. As she might have done at the Louvre, Mrs. Rappaport examined the Before and After portraits (the latter, we learned from the porter, was painted when the Picassos were on the verge of divorce) in swift succession, sunshades removed, no comment but for the narrowing of her eyes.

She requested that the sequence of rooms be altered. Two handymen in blue denim aprons arrived with a weighty desk of serious proportions, worthy of a Proust but installed under a chandelier with my new IBM to grace its polished antique inlay. All other furnishings were shifted to create an office—sitting room between two bedchambers, a work space and buffer zone between Picasso's canopied honeymoon bed and my narrower sleeping compartment. As a further prop, or spur to our creation, Mrs. Rappaport purchased a ream of cream-colored bond paper for my use, and a gold pen with red ink for hers. It was understood that our joint endeavor was to take place in the intervening *bureau*, the separate bedrooms as neutral corners.

We began writing Mrs. Rappaport's book on a Tuesday at noon in the second week of our stay in Paris. Mrs. Rappaport sat half-reclining on the plum-colored love seat, with a croissant, coffee and Spearmint gum on a tray—Jewel curled beside her—while I sat at the Louis XV desk uneasily fingering the typewriter keys. Our circumstances and positioning suggested a persistent image of patient (side of jaw visible only, set in motion by the swallowing of coffee, the chewing of gum, or an occasional spoken word) free-associating from her love seat to the bored therapist slightly out of range but within listening distance. The therapist, when looking up at the jaw working at its Spearmint, had a peripheral view of the jawline and exposed teeth of Picasso's *Femme assize au bord de la mer*.

"He died," she said. This was about Mr. Rappaport at last, Sy. "He was winning, too."

We had a double-window view of the Bon Marché department store, not in itself inspiring, and the pocket park at the intersection of Boulevard Raspail and Sèvres-Babylone where I walked Jewel in the morning before Mrs. Rappaport left her bed. She was still in nightdress and slippers, as she often was this time of day, an angora sweater draped loosely over her shoulders, hair thrust hastily into a headband, but lipstick and morning mascara in place.

"A gambler?"

"I'm speaking divorce, Sy was ahead in the courtroom, I was going to end up with peanuts." Jewel nuzzled into the warmth of her mistress's crotch. "He had the money, it's that simple. Let's face it, he had better legal people."

Her legal people failed her, but luck did not. Just before a settlement was to be decided by the judge, Seymour Rappaport became so overwrought during testimony he frothed at the mouth, choked, fell forward and died of apoplexy on the floor of the Domestic Relations Court.

"That temper of his, I always told him."

Died in rage, I wrote, *before divorce*.

"The money thing, forget it. I'd just as soon not talk about how it turned out. I ended up paying his legal people as well as my own, but I came out on top. Only I don't want the divorce coming out in the book." She was chewing croissant, or gum, with grim ferocity. "He was no bed of roses, believe me."

"Any children?"

She turned my way and threw me one of her looks: "It's nobody's business we never had kids."

The IBM hummed impatiently during a long thoughtful interval, so I switched it off.

"Do you want to start," I asked, "with your childhood?"

She winced and took an easier position on the love seat, shifting Jewel higher, against her bosom.

"Often," I said, "this kind of book begins. With childhood."

"So I heard."

"But if you'd rather. Rather not, that is."

For minutes she gazed out the window at Bon Marché. She

sipped coffee and stroked Jewel on the frizzy black crown between her ears.

"I never had it easy as a kid. Just say that in so many words."

I switched the typewriter back on and wrote: *Had it hard as a child.*

The sound of typing reassured her: "Just write that I went through the school of hard knocks and came out on top. What the public cares about is how you came out. My life is this story of rags to riches, only I don't want to go into the rags part. It's nobody's business. Who cares what it was like when I was a kid?"

I waited, with the IBM humming.

"You can skip the details," she announced. "The story of my life is very unique and I don't want to fill it up with ordinary details. That's why most people's lives will never be best-sellers like mine, they fill it up with all the details."

It was my turn to gaze out at Bon Marché. The IBM hummed in the silence until I switched it off again.

"Just remember," she snapped, "I came out on top."

I switched on the IBM and typed: *Came out on top.*

"Could we say," I ventured, "something, say. About your birth?"

"What about it?"

"Well. Where you were born, for example. And when."

"When is nobody's business. As for where, O.K., I was born at home as a matter of fact, with a midwife doing it—only don't say that, it sounds cheap."

"Where was home?"

"It was on a lake." Mrs. Rappaport's eyes were seeing beyond Bon Marché now. "On a Canadian lake in a town you or nobody else ever heard of. In Ontario." She was looking at the lake now. "A lake called Lac Seul."

I typed this out, assuming she had granted permission for the lake to be named in her autobiography.

"How about saying," I said, " 'I was born on the shores of Lac Seul, Ontario.' "

Mrs. Rappaport came back into the room with the hint of a smile on her frosted lips.

"I like that," she said. "How does it go again?"

"I was born. On the shores of Lac Seul, Ontario."

"Make it Ontario, Canada, in case somebody doesn't know where Ontario is."

" 'I was born on the shores of Lac Seul, Ontario. Canada.' "

"Great. I like it."

Jewel was due for a shampoo and visit to the vet, so I was free for the remainder of the day to make of Paris what I would.

4

MY MOTHER was born in France, but that fact did not, for her son, grant automatic entree to Paris. But I did seek a way in. I somehow belonged here, a poet told me so. I was his ambassador to France. Yet Paris continued to elude me, as phantom an idea as the idea of love. That was the Poet's word, love. Love had not yet been done in, love was still possible. He was saying that to me now—but sometimes he would begin a sentence with the word Love and not finish.

These were my thoughts walking past Bon Marché on the Rue de Babylone—no one ever walked there, in its upper reaches, but Jewel and I and occasional nuns from the Missions Etrangères—where I passed the restaurant at Rue Vaneau, nestled among minor consulates, where Mrs. Rappaport had taken us to dinner the night before. (The restaurant possessed a star, and appeared in a guide Mrs. Rappaport carried with her everywhere.) Neither guidebook nor *Assimil* was a key to the city. Mrs. Rappaport spoke French, but the French of Paris visibly winced at her accent, then pretended not to understand.

The way into Paris was to be in love here: that, of course, was what the Poet had in mind. There was neither possibility nor evidence of love along this empty thoroughfare, and even less evidence of it as I turned on the wide thriving Boulevard des Invalides. I was headed in the direction of the Seine: there was always a certain romance attached to its banks. At Invalides I could either cross the pastry chef's Pont Alexandre III, Mrs. Rappaport's favorite bridge, or visit Napoleon's tomb (she had checked out his florid memorial in porphyry), but instead I plunged underground—not Mrs. Rappaport's underground, for she never took the Métro—and made my way by subway beneath the Seine to Châtelet.

There was always a great spill of life in this district, from the bird market to Beaubourg, that must have been even livelier in my mother's day when the market sheds still covered the area around St. Eustache instead of a flashy contemporary shopping mall spiraling several layers underground.

At Rue St. Denis the younger girls displayed along that street were beautiful enough to make you stop, to make you wonder. The Poet might have come by shopping and picked out Ginny here—there were poignant duplicates of her, passively available, all but tagged with the price in francs. You looked up from the street (dreamers, poets did) and saw stone Medusa heads at the cornices of buildings, Gorgons supporting the windowsills. It was still the eighteenth century up there, but here at street level the fast food counters and Sex Shops, American style, cast the working girls in garish light.

Down side streets called Impasses, where the crowds thinned and the light was poor, grotesque variations on the trade continued. Meaty types with black bangs dressed in leather smirked beside the *boucheries*, aged veterans padded their strippers' necklines with pink plastic, marginal offerings were painted and costumed so ingeniously as to disguise all gender and intent.

Slim pimps sipped espresso in narrow cafés between Sex Shop and hotel doorway, a necessary penalty to pleasure for sale. That other penalty, the newer and nastier venereal plagues (I would think of that, having worked in a hospital—and how little distance I had traveled from that work) dissuaded little trade nor dampened ardor of those true customers who detached themselves from the mere window-shoppers and entered a hotel with the merchandise of choice. I was then thinking of my father and Dr. Breathwaite, those two specialists in scourge, with their carnival-tent cure of venereal infection, might have set up and in my father's words "made a killing" in this benighted quarter.

As an artery of desire and pursuit, Rue St. Denis was a desperate sidetrack. Later, wandering the Marais, I was granted a thoughtful flash of legitimate quest. I was becoming a more sophisticated connoisseur of streets named Impasses, and backed out of one of these quaint cul-de-sacs into an open park framed to perfection on four identical timeless sides. It was from a café table under the arcades around the Place des Vosges I saw her.

She was not of Paris: she leaned against one of those crude blue backpacks that accompany the young across Europe. We were fellow travelers. Her features were indistinct, she sat cross-legged playing a flute in the park opposite, while a kitten on a leash ate scraps of *boudin* from a sheet of newsprint. Here was a vision, possibly a signal. I was overcome by an impulse to talk with her—what would her language be? I could invite her for a drink at the café.

Just then a top-heavy green-and-white tour bus came wallowing around the square, a drunken boat, loaded with a crew of Scandinavians listening to their nasal language broadcast back at them through the guide's microphone. Among the plump and greying passengers were at least three young women staring blue-eyed with interest at me instead of Victor Hugo's house, and I was momentarily flattered and distracted. (Under other circumstances I might have waved at them, and hoped the bus might park nearby where I could meet one or all three of them.) But I was impatient for the bus to stagger by. By the time the tedious bus passed between me and this vision, there was an empty place in the park where she had been.

I got up and walked to the spot where she had been sitting, but she was truly gone. The square was open and flat, the park had few trees and was thinly populated, but I found no trace of the girl with the flute and unmistakable backpack, nor even the soiled newspaper where the kitten had fed. I could not accept the mystery. Did I really see her?

I came back to earth when the waiter pursued me across the street from the café: I had forgotten to pay for my *demi* of beer.

5

I SAT numbly at the IBM with a blank sheet of paper rolled into place while Mrs. Rappaport finished a long-distance call.

"Twenty-five percent of nothing," she said into the antique French telephone, "is nothing." I could see her rather fine legs through the open door to her bedroom, crossed under her nearly sheer dressing gown, the top leg kicking out nervously at the knee when she meant to emphasize a point. "Tell Lionel from me I want the place renovated to look like what it was in the first place."

She hung up, but immediately put through another call while I watched the antlike activity out the window, the crowds at the Sèvres-Babylone Métro entrance, shoppers pouring in and out of Bon Marché.

"Maury?" she said into the telephone. She got up and closed the door between us to talk with Maury in confidence. Then she opened the door, on second thought and called to me: "Has the dog been out for her walk yet?"

"This morning, early."

"Take her out again, will you? She needs the exercise."

I took the dog to the Jardin des Plantes. Here was a reminder of the Botanic Gardens in Belfast, but with a zoo. I took no interest in caged animals—having landed in something of a cage, however gilded, myself—and anyway, Jewel was forbidden entry to the zoo by one of those pictographs that substituted for language: a dachshund with a large red X through its sausage body.

Paris, whether it rained (it was drizzling now) or the sun illuminated the city, seldom failed to stir some nervous center in me. Love. Maybe the girl with the flute and kitten would turn up. Jewel and the kitten would have to be kept apart, and that encounter would trigger an opening, a friendly comment. But the girl did not appear.

After a brandy at a café opposite the Salpetrière, I felt better. I felt again the nervous surge Paris brought on. Nurses in capes flowed in and out of the gates and along the graveled paths of the hospital grounds. Surely one chosen nurse would come to this *terrasse* for her coffee break out of the rain, sit at the empty table next to mine, be charmed first by Jewel and then by me. But no nurse came to my rescue, no cool hand touched my fevered cheek.

When I got back to the hotel, the two porters in denim aprons who had brought the desk were moving Mrs. Rappaport's luggage into the corridor. I went into the suite by way of the *bureau* and found the IBM machine packed into its case. The door to my room was open, the maid was in there taking shirts out of a drawer. (These were shirts by Charvet, purchased for me by Mrs. Rappaport; and seeing them carefully laid out on the bed, I felt the same shameful feeling as when I was being measured for the shirts.) I should not have taken a third brandy so early in the day. The packed suitcases, the typewriter prepared to travel, brought on another sense of déjà vu, a disembodied state from the time I was evicted from the Bellingham Arms.

6

JEWEL COULD NOT ENDURE air travel, Mrs. Rappaport could not abide trains. Because of this I was alone at the Gare de Lyon—but with the dog in tow—too dismayed and disoriented to savor the frantic animation of a train station at night, or anticipate a journey to the Riviera with anything like pleasure. Not even the romance associated with the famous *train bleu* could lift my spirits or alleviate the bitterness. The Gare de Lyon was another point of departure, no longer Paris.

To Mrs. Rappaport the city had been no more than a shopping stop and cemetery tour (all cities were cities of the dead to her, or places to pass out envelopes and make arrangements for the next stop). Sullenly I pushed along one of those supermarket shopping carts that have replaced porters, loaded with my cracked and disabled Gladstone, the Poet's attaché case full of my father's letters, and now, a single page (one sentence) of Mrs. Rappaport's manuscript. Jewel, in rhinestone grandeur, rode trembling in the pilot rack. I had refused to carry the diplomatic courier case Mrs. Rappaport had bought me at Hermès—a chain attached to the handle went up the courier's sleeve—my one gesture of rebellion: the diplomatic case went along with her baggage via Air France.

I had barely glanced at the ticket in the envelope Mrs. Rappaport handed me, and now, distracted, I boarded the wrong coach, the second-class sleeper. Eurail pass travelers with wine bottles and backpacks lounged and sprawled in the narrow passage-way while the six-bunk berths were being let down. I stepped over their long American legs, tried not to bump some bumpkin's guitar. I should have been here with them, in proletarian discomfort where I belonged, broke, without this ridiculous poodle dangling from my forearm. Easy enough to see myself a fool, but I would be a fool in comfort.

Tell me the truth, Critic, didn't you always want to travel to the South of France?

I found the compartment in the next car, First Class of course. I put Jewel's basket on the second of the SNCF beds: there was a stainless steel basin between us, thin towels, paper cups. Jewel gratefully leapt into her satin-lined basket and curled herself into a tiny trembling ball. The echo and clamor of the train station unnerved her. (I had grown fond of the pooch—but *this*.) Overwrought, depressed, I accepted solitary confinement, complete with poodle. Rich cuisine and too much wine had affected my metabolism: in Paris I had passed through a near-clinical state of passivity and surrender. Traveling First Class, I had finally reached bottom.

I had prepared myself for despair with a bottle of Dee's cheap potchin in the Gladstone. Jewel, with watery eye, watched me sip from my paper cup. The fiery stuff only set off chest pains, gave me heartache. Dee had written her poem, Liam was writing his—the way to begin is to begin.

When I lay down, bile rose to my throat instead of poetry, so I sat up again. I had Jewel's vitamins in the attaché case. ("Earning a living, Son, is essentially a trivial enterprise.") To earn a living I opened a can of Cadillac with the Swiss army knife, mixed the pellucid pellets of vitamin E into a mound of dog food I spread upon the pages of the *Paris Herald-Tribune*, but Jewel, as unhappy as her paid companion, had no appetite.

I did not sleep until long after the train click-clacked deep into the French blackness far from Paris. One image that tormented me was of a dead dog in the trunk of a car beneath the Florida expressway. I could also see Mrs. Rappaport's contorted face, the flat mask torn away, if the dead dog had been Jewel. I was even enjoying the thought of my employer horribly deprived of her pet—say, the little animal thrown beneath the wheels of *le train bleu*. Fond of the animal or not—this grim thought was another indictment of my low character, or vile state of mind.

Then I slept. I woke again at a grinding halt in Lyon, and before the train got under way once more I looked out the window to see two men with wine bottles each, standing under a street lamp back to back, urinating in opposite directions. Instead of finding some comic relief in the drunken duet with their arcs of piss catching the light, I fell back into a spirit of vitriol, playing variations on the theme of revenge. I was thinking of Mrs. Rappaport vulnerable only behind her armor of corset. The mingy grudge I bore was a distortion of the offense, and the offense was self-produced—I was here because I chose to be. Nevertheless, I was consumed with rage against my patron. I wanted her humiliated, and—repelled as I was by the woman at this moment—the only diminishment I could imagine was to seduce her. I would reduce her to the human wallow, screw her into submission and tears. I had not until now so strongly associated the

element of hate in the act of love. Lovemaking was the only
conceivable harm I could bring to her to satisfy some demented
frustration our liaison had brought about. On that train, during the
long night, I shared with the rapist a common impulse. It was
necessary to my self-esteem to reduce Mrs. Rappaport to Teresa: she
must feel a man move above her, if only to endure the weight of a
ghost against her flesh.

"I was dying to let the top down, Son—it was a convertible, and this
was Florida—but Priscilla (we were first names to one another by
then) put her foot down. She had been to the beauty parlor and was
afraid the wind would blow her permanent wave to pieces. Dear sweet
precious Priscilla. I have always had mixed feelings about the women
in my life (your beloved Mother included) but for the nonce was
pleased as punch at the Lady Fair beside me in her Alice-blue
business suit and spanking white pumps with white gloves to match.
She was even wearing nylons and nail polish for a change. She kept
her Bible and checkbook on the seat beside her. It took me forever to
talk her into this trip, but when she went for it (the night of her
seventy-something birthday) she went All Out.

"I give myself credit for being bright enough to think of charging
champagne, to her account at Stop & Shop, and buying her a gardenia
corsage. My argument was: 'What are two good-looking lovebirds like
us doing sitting around slow-pokey Sunshine City for? If we were on
our last legs and confined to the rocking chair, without motor
transport, I could understand.' 'What motor transport?' she asked
dumbfounded (she had been drinking champagne). 'Your *car* darn it,
out there in the garage.' 'You know,' she said distracted (it is difficult
as the dickens to keep a woman's mind on track), 'I think I could take
a liking to this wine.' (Your Mother and I, Son, drank champagne on
the shores of Lake Okeechobee the night you were conceived.) Seeing
at how effective the bubbly was, I poured her another glass and said,
'Here's to health and wealth and happy journeys.' 'Health and wealth,
fine,' she toasted back, 'I don't know about any journey.' "

I must have been talking to myself in my sleep, asking questions of
the Poet: sometimes in the night I heard the reply, "You're getting
warm."

But the statement might have come from the compartment next
door; when next I awoke I heard the comment, "Fabulous," outside in
the corridor. Americans were the first up, and bearing witness.

I opened the window blinds to a watery reflection of pale blue and bright green. A little spit of land extended like a finger into the misty blue of the Mediterranean: two children, a boy and a girl, stood on the balcony of a tiled cream-stucco villa; they were waving together, at the blue train or at me. The sun broke directly behind them, shadow and gold. I was granted the gratuitous insight that rebirth is forever possible. From my vengeful intentions of the night before I was absolved. This was the place the Poet had dreamt of all along.

7

THE JOURNALISTS and photographers had moved in from Belfast, now that the news had cooled there and the celebrities were in Cannes. The Film Festival was on, and the men in multipocketed denim jackets—the uniform for film crews this year—poured off the train as I did. I was jostled by the same mobile camera equipment and men tangled in wires as in the media invasion of the Bellingham Arms. This hive of hyperactivity gave Jewel the usual case of tremors, and I had to hold the little poodle close.

At the top of the stairs to the *Sortie* there was a ring of emissaries with hand-printed cardboard signs, and one sign said GOLD. It took me a moment to remember who Gold was, then I went up to the man with the sign and said, "I'm Gold."

"The writer?" He had a pirate's skull crushed in at the temples: he wore a beret, no socks in his mocassins, like one of the racing touts at Calder.

"That's right."

"Name's Maury." He held out a hand and let the cardboard fall to the floor. "Teresa said to meet you. That your dog?"

"It's hers."

Maury took us to his rented sports car: the interior matched his patent leather sports coat. He carried the Gladstone and Jewel's sleeping basket. Jewel nestled close to my chest, trembling as if she might never recover from the confusion of the station and the trauma of not being met by her mistress.

In the tight one-way streets of Cannes the traffic was as dense as on the boulevards of Paris and there was the same free-for-all attitude among drivers, especially Maury's attitude. The belt of cars moved only micromillimeters apart in a solid swift mass of togetherness, no quarter offered or given. I was unable to take in the look of the city for fear of being crushed flat in the death seat.

"I guess she told you about me," said Maury, assuming I was in Mrs. Rappaport's confidence. "I knew Teresa in Cicero when she was sixteen, what a doll. She could have been Miss Illinois if she hadn't been a Canuck. Sy finally got papers for her to be a citizen. You know Sy, before he kicked? That divorce I could never understand, but I never was married myself. He got her a screen test too but when they got legal Sy didn't want for her to work. He was something. Who would've thought up organizing dry cleaners? He always used to say—Sy was a witty guy—'I'm the one took the cleaners to the cleaners.' In Chi, he bought Teresa her own bulletproof Packard. He used to call her Greatjakes, she was French, her maiden name was Grand-jackoo or something, she can speak the French language like a native."

"Is Teresa. At the hotel?"

"Didn't she tell you? She's in Zurich."

"No. I've been on the train. All night."

"She didn't tell you? Well, she didn't know herself until she got here. There was a telegram from this doctor in Zurich, he only takes appointments for a year in advance and when he's got an opening, that's it. Take it or leave it. Teresa would've had to wait another year if she didn't take it. This guy's the greatest."

"Is it serious?"

"Didn't she tell you? Maybe it's a surprise. It's O.K. though. She left you an envelope."

Across from a park and the sea, Maury turned into the drive of a large starkly modern hotel with its own grounds and a doorman with a plume in his top hat.

"My ex-girlfriend went through the same thing," said Maury, as he got out of the car. "It takes about ten years off a person's face." Maury opened the trunk for the top-hatted doorman who removed my Gladstone and Jewel's basket. "They sand the skin down, but it's all done under anaesthetic, so don't worry. My ex-girlfriend did the same thing and came out fine. I didn't recognize her."

"In Zurich?"

"The guy in Zurich, he's the greatest. You know Teresa, only the best. They slice a little alongside the scalp and draw the skin up or something. They give shots made out of lamb embryos to make you even younger—you won't know her, I swear."

He took an envelope from his leather pocket and extended it to me.

"Ten days, you say?"

"Ten days, two weeks, more or less." We were both holding on to the envelope. "You won't know her. She's going to miss the best of the Fest. Tells me you're doing her life."

"That's what. I'm doing."

"Some life she's had, the script'll be terrific."

He let go of the envelope and backed off, tipping his beret jauntily. I did not open the envelope with Maury looking on, but stuffed it into my pocket.

Mister Gold was expected. The staff at the Mediterranean (or was it the Baltic?) spoke English during the Film Festival, the only word in French I heard at the hotel desk was *"mignon"* referring to Jewel. There were Californians in the lobby dressed in the same style as Maury, and Italian film posters and booths where hostesses sat behind stacks of *Variety* and cinema brochures.

Mrs. Rappaport's presence still haunted the suite, however fleeting her occupation of the place. She had, in her urgent haste, forgotten the black sleeping mask on the night table beside a canopied bed in her room. The maid had not yet cleaned the room: two rubber earplugs lay in an ashtray, along with a wad of chewed chewing gum. The silver-glowing Samsonite bags lined the far wall, unpacked—she had taken only one suitcase with her to Switzerland. The IBM typewriter was in my room. Jewel leapt upon Mrs. Rappaport's bed sniffing for traces of her missing mistress. The bed was unmade, a mosquito net drawn into a crown above the regal pillow mold.

"Well," I said to the indented pillow, "I'm here."

Jewel whimpered something in reply.

The view from the balcony was of formal gardens, a brown patch of sand dotted with footprints, a yacht basin full of varnished craft tied to finger piers. A large inspiring three-masted schooner lay at anchor farther out in the bay: I was reminded of a tale told by Indian Billy, Native American member of the Teamsters, about a gig with his guitar aboard a yacht like the one out there now, perhaps the very ship.

Beyond the sailing ship were two green and gleaming islands, a little apart yet still in France.

"I'm here," I said to myself.

Here you are, said the Poet.

The hostess at the *Variety* booth (the one who had said *"mignon"* when we passed) was only too willing to dog-sit Jewel while I took the noon ferry to the Iles de Lérins. No sooner had I arrived in Cannes than I wanted out, the restless Rappaport syndrome: but what I wanted out of was the busy-buzzing show-biz ambience of a film festival.

Most of the boat passengers were headed with their *pique-niques* and fishing poles to the Ile Ste. Marguerite—the first stop, or last stop for the Man in the Iron Mask, said to have been imprisoned there—but I bore my own iron mask to the next island, St. Honorat, where St. Patrick lived the cloistered life before he ventured to rid Ireland of its serpents.

The deep restful green had not been illusion: there was a sheltering canopy of umbrella pines against a naked midday sun. The walk along a worn earthen path was an aimless relief after the relentlessly driven circulation on the mainland. This was the realm of Cistercian monks (nowhere in sight, of course) who tended lavender, made liqueurs and perfume for the tourists, cut off from the world by stone fortifications, a moat of Mediterranean and a vow of silence.

For all the aimlessness of the path, we did, a scattering of passengers, move forward in the same direction as if following signs saying *One Way*. Ahead of me walked a girl, alone—rather, unaccompanied—with a book under her arm. She wore a simple blue jersey with jeans, an Art Deco *M* embroidered on the hip pocket of her jeans. I was attracted to her long hair, plain and brown and untended except for the luster from brushing. Valerie had longed for such hair, hanging wind-teased and free. When the path diverged, I followed hers, attracted by the way her hips moved, the beckoning embroidered *M*.

No one else was going that way, and in a moment she turned and said, *"Bonjour."*

"Do you speak English?"

"Sure," she said, "I'm American." She was the girl. "Aren't you going to visit the monastery?"

"Isn't this the way?"

"No. This is my way."

"Aren't you? Going to visit the monastery?"

"They don't let women in."

"Oh. Yes. I understand."

She did not walk on but lingered, facing me, close enough to touch.

"Are you," she asked, "at the Festival?"

"I'm trying not to be."

"It's fabulous if you're a film freak, like me. You can see ten films a day, I did already—or more—but too much is too much. This is my secret place, to get away from it."

She carried a paperback copy of *The Oxford Book of English Verse*.

"It's no longer, a secret now."

"That's O.K. I don't own it. I saw you on the boat. Are you a celebrity or somebody?"

"No. Nobody. *Personne*, as they say here."

"I knew you were different. Everybody that wants to swim or picnic gets off at Ste. Marguerite. The beaches there are fabulous. Anybody that comes here comes to see the monastery. But the other side of the cloister is a private beach nobody goes to. It could be the monks' own beach, it must be, but I've never seen any monks there—you never see them, the Cistercians is a strict order. If they don't use the beach, why shouldn't I use it? In a way I consider it mine. Like being a star and having this private beach in the South of France and to escape my fame hide out and swim and read poems."

"Do you have a kitten?" I was remembering a premonition. "Do you play the flute?"

"Not me. I love cats, but my cat's home."

"Where's home?"

She hesitated, as if trying to remember, or decide, then shrugged and said, "Cleveland." After a moment she asked, "Where's yours?"

It was my turn to hesitate. "Here. For now."

"That's what I wanted to answer when you asked me. But I can't make up my mind. I mean, what's home? Cleveland's a drag, it's totally unromantic to be from there. I want to be, you know, a person of the world."

I was unsure of what I was seeing or hearing. The silence in this removed part of the island was profound, the sun through the pines gave the girl the unearthly aura of those children I had seen at daybreak. We were walking together, she slightly ahead of me with her undulant unselfconscious stride, a book of poems swinging in rhythm. We passed in and out of sun spots and shade; she shifted in and out of focus. She was taking me to her private beach.

"Aren't you," I asked, "afraid. Of taking up with a stranger. In this empty place. With a beard."

"I like beards. It makes a man mysterious. You always wonder why he grew it. I was already making up stories about you when I saw you on the boat."

Unable to believe in this moment, I turned back to the tile roofs of the cloister visible through the trees, and a tall primitive tower built to keep pirates at bay. I could have taken her hand as we walked and she would not have cared—I knew this, but she kept me wondering.

There was another smaller path through underbrush and scrub pine, the soil mixed with sand and pine needles. The path ran gradually downslope, then opened to the sea. It was a glorious opening: an ancient tree with gnarled limbs hung over a miniature cove. There was no one, not even a boat on the water. And the water was so clear you could see brown stones and tangled sea growth for some distance out.

"You can skinny-dip here. Who cares? Come on."

I looked back along the path again to see if we had been followed or observed. When I turned back to her she was out of her jersey, braless, and peeling down her jeans.

Whatever else occurs to us at the magic moment, the certainty is this: desire and pursuit have come to an end. It is the everlastingness of love that washes over us like the warm waters of a southern cove.

"Pretend you're a monk," she said, already a part of the translucent water, "and all that time you could only imagine what a girl looked like."

It was during our impromtu swim or after that I lost forever my wristwatch, somewhere in the scrub undergrowth, somewhere in the sand. The moment was fixed, the Mediterranean has no tide.

8

MY LOVELY NAIVE LIAR had decided to confess. We sat on a café
terrace near the Palais des Festivals, with a view of the island where
we met.

"I'm not who I pretend to be."

"Neither am I."

"Who did I say I was?"

On the island she told me she was a student journalist, and that
her father was in the diplomatic service.

"Did I say that?" she asked unblinking, as if she could not
remember that lie among so many. "Sometimes I say Dad is a senator
in the U.S. Senate. He's not. There's a real senator named Hughes,
and when people know my name is Hughes they think I'm the
daughter of Senator Hughes. I'm not."

I asked then what she expected me to ask: "Are you related to
the late Howard Hughes?"

"I've told people that, too. I said he was my uncle—but that was
before he died and looked so awful and they revealed how weird he
was. We've got everything else, but there's no insanity in the family.
So I stopped saying that. Mostly, over here, I say I'm the daughter of
an ambassador, and if people ask what country he's ambassador in I
say he's an ambassador-at-large."

At barely twenty (if that was her age) she still defined herself by
way of inventing a parent. My age might have cast me in the role of
one of her fictitious fathers, but I kept this disturbing conjecture to
myself.

"What does your father do? Really."

"He's dead."

"I'm sorry."

"Don't be. He died a long time ago." (How long a time could
a-long-time-ago be to a twenty-year-old?) "I don't know what he did
before he died because he was already divorced from my mother and
she didn't want to talk about him. Maybe that's why I make up stories
about who my father is." On second thought she added to this: "But I
make up stories about everybody, myself included."

I also lied to her. When she asked my age—so innocently,
seeming indifferent to any answer—I dropped a lucky seven from the

thirty-nine. She was perfectly satisfied with that number and might have been just as accepting of the true one. I was afraid of not being youthful enough for this child. (Don't be afraid, said the Poet.) I realized now that the truth would not have placed me at a disadvantage, but it was too late to rid myself of the lie as easily as she shed hers. (Just as she so easily shed her clothing only hours ago, on the island: this, in the childishly direct way she did everything, gracefully crossed her legs, explained to the waiter in her college French what a spritzer was, and now, telling what was meant to be the truth about herself with less than a shrug of self-awareness.)

The chapel tower of St. Honorat was still visible from here. It occurred to me the monks could have observed us through the pines, but of course the monks were at their prayers or cultivating fields of jasmine and lavender on the opposite side of the island. No such strictures entered my thoughts once Marybeth had appeared naked—besides, I was called upon to play the only monk in our film. In her company, in our embrace, I was aware neither of witnesses nor the gap in generations.

I had come to accept that this girl had strayed into my orbit through no accident nor act of will, but as the tag line of a prophetic joke.

"I told them at the Festival I wrote for *Harper's Bazaar*."

"Do you?"

"I tried to get a job there as a receptionist once, but I didn't get it because I can't type. I've done a lot of other stuff, though, but never for very long. I went to New York just to get out of Cleveland but my first job I was a summer camp counselor one summer but got homesick—can you believe it?—and went back home before the summer got started. New York was O.K. but slightly weird, I interviewed people at the tollgate to the Holland Tunnel asking them where they were coming from and where they were going, for the Port Authority, and a lot of them were very neurotic about being asked. You could tell some of them never thought about where they were coming from and where they were going so they could stay sane. You can picture how uptight they were over my questionnaire."

"I can."

"What I always wanted to do even in high school was write. I wrote letters to the editor of the Cleveland *Plain Dealer* but the editor wouldn't publish them. I guess they were too controversial. Actually I've never really written film criticism before, for *Harper's Bazaar* or anyplace, but to get a press pass to the Festival you have to say that.

My father always said say anything that will help you get ahead, then later live up to it."

"I thought. He was dead."

"He died, yes. That's what he used to say, my mother said, before he died."

By now it seemed her father was as much a phantom as mine.

"Does it work? Your father's advice."

"Like magic." She showed me a press pass for the Cannes Film Festival, a striped seal across the card that could have been our American red-white-and-blue, but reversed in the order of the French tricolor. A photograph of her tanned pleased face was attached (the name was May Hughes, not Marybeth). "It's only good for one person or I'd try to get you into the Palais."

She could not have been more obliging or engaging or decorative had she been created by a poet. The description of a sea creature— eyes wide as oysters, hair down to here—had come to life. (You don't rub lamps, Critic, for that type miracle—just keep your peepers open.) Exactly.

"Thanks. For the thought. I'm not much into movies."

"What are you into?"

"I'm finishing a poem."

"God, you're a poet!"

"The poem is by someone else. No, I'm no poet. My credentials are as bogus as yours. Listen."

For a time the Poet himself occupied the third, but manifestly empty, chair at our café table. He was considerate in his silence, but he was there. I was uncertain of Marybeth's attention span—the sea creature was sipping a second spritzer and checking the café for celebrities— but the Poet wanted to hear about himself, all ears.

I told her about Monopoly games and smuggled matches and how the other patients refused to play Scrabble with him because he made up words. This last caught Marybeth's interest, for she too was inventive, and in conflict with the world of regulations.

"What was he in for?" She made the hospital sound like a prison.

"He jumped from a tour boat into Biscayne Bay."

She considered this smiling and must have come to some private conclusion about jumping from a tour boat—she might have thought it was a stunt, or a joke—suicide, I assumed, having so little relevance to her young and happy life.

"I tried once," she confessed. "In college, the peer pressure was too much. I didn't try very hard, but I tried."

Her wrists were unmarked, but she might have tried some other way. From the next table a woman with bared shoulders and glitter on her eyelids said she had known Beirut when it was beautiful. The woman with her said she had tried to adopt an Egyptian child but the father kept asking for money after the adoption was final and the embassy told her she would have no peace, so she gave the baby back. "Anyway, I don't think I was cut out to be a mother."

I heard only this much, and was not really listening except to wonder if Marybeth and I could be overheard. No one, I concluded, was listening. The café was crowded with mostly Americans, a trio nearby argued about which credit card went farthest in Europe: Visa or American Express or MasterCharge. People were looking around to be looked at, and I was looking too, but mostly at Marybeth, as if to memorize her.

"He missed his wife," I said, to explain the Poet's act. "He missed her. Very much."

The smile flickered out, she could relate to missing.

The café was in the very heart of the Festival and as turbulent and disturbing as the hotel lobby had been. The pop song at festival time was "Little Girl Blue," the theme from one of the films, and the insidious melody ran through the babble of conversation, projected by a Muzak speaker hidden behind palms. At the table in front of us somebody was signing something for somebody, an autograph, a contract. No, in this crowd we were safe from prying eyes and ears and almost as alone as on the island. Only the Poet shared our secrets, sitting in the third chair.

"You were into mental health, then."

"That's right. I worked at a psychiatric clinic. Called the Sans Souci."

"In Cleveland there's a funeral parlor chain called Sans Souci."

"I can believe it."

By then I had grown light-headed, spinning my tale, from a cloudy yellow apéritif called *pastis*, while my enchanted companion in her childlike way (for she was a child) extracted an ice cube from her Perrier-and-wine, popped it into her mouth, and allowed it to melt there, the lump showing tongue-in-cheek. This too she enacted with complete American aplomb, or cool, as her generation called it.

"This poet doesn't sound all that weird." (The Poet grinned at this.) "After Howard Hughes died the way he did I started wondering if he wouldn't have been better off broke. I mean, he would have been better off committed to an institution instead of hiding out in penthouses wearing Kleenex boxes on his feet—you know what I mean?"

"I do. You may be right. But some of us, rich or poor. Have a way of, well, committing ourselves. To long-term personal hells."

The Poet nodded. I had come around to his cockeyed way of the world.

"I was into Transcendental Meditation once—would you believe it?"

"I would," I said, "I do."

"Did his wife leave him or did she die?"

"Inevitably, she left him." I did not go into inevitability, or differences in ages—the news might suggest unhappy parallels.

"My father's not really dead," she suddenly confessed. "Why did I tell you that?"

It was Marybeth who took my hand, not I hers, leaving the café. We strolled through the flower market at the foot of a steep winding street leading to the cathedral and ramparts of an older Cannes. The Poet, with a respectful discretion he had never shown in life, bowed out. He tilted an imaginary glass *santé-bonheur* in our direction, and made no move to leave with us. He was resigned to the Festival set, listening to "Little Girl Blue."

We were on our way to her hotel (perhaps it was not the Baltic, but that name seemed to fit) so that she might change for the gala soirée at the Palais des Festivals. Fishermen in blue undershirts played *boules* in the dust alongside the yacht basin: they did not look up from their measurements as a biplane flew quite low over their game trailing a banner that announced tonight's film. (The sound and sight of the plane caught my attention obliquely, but I did not register the name of the film—only was I reminded that Cannes was film capital for fifteen days, and other movies were being screened than island fantasies.) A flower vendor thrust a bouquet of carnations at us. I exchanged a twenty-franc note for the bouquet so that Marybeth could dip her flower face into the flowers and I could be Mabrinogron for a day. In the next instant she unclasped her hand from mine to count the blossoms.

"Thirteen," she announced, a shadow across the oyster eyes.

"Are you superstitious?"

"I don't know. For some things, yes. A black umbrella brings bad luck—if you open it indoors."

"But not thirteen carnations. If you counted them saying 'He loves me, he loves me not,' a dozen would have been the unhappy number."

The reward for having thought of this was to see her smile again.

"I'm not totally superstitious. But I shouldn't have told you my father was dead. How would I feel if he really did die?"

"What does your father do? Really."

"Oh, he's got an office somewhere, where he makes money. He gives me money. He gave me the money to come over here. Look."

She put the book of poems under her arm and maneuvered around the carnations to extract a booklet of traveler's checks from the pocket with the *M* on it. The checks were in one-hundred-dollar denominations, but I did not count them as she did the flowers. The book of checks was to prove that her father existed.

Satisfied that our relationship had now been launched on a course of strict candor, Marybeth put the checks back into her pocket where they bulged provocatively against her derrière. She took my hand again—her child's hand grasping two fingers of mine—as we resumed our stroll. The late sun eased behind a range of red cliffs called l'Estérel, and she tilted her head to catch the last glimpse, or warmth, of it.

"I don't feel guilty about taking money from him. He ran out on Mom and me, didn't he?"

A breeze from the sea swept a strand of hair across the lower part of her face. I was reminded of a face in a photograph, but she did not resemble the girl the Poet loved, only the girl he invented.

It was Marybeth's idea to leave the curtain open so that I might watch her at her shower. How right the Poet was (among other things) about the ideal complement of sexes in the *salle de bain*. I studied her body avidly, but I did not search for scars.

"If it was a movie," she said through the water spray, "the horse would have to win."

My delight in her was constant and without limit. I had been telling her about the Poet's tip, my day at Calder, a horse named Naiad. She listened to the story with exceptional interest: a tale of easy money, American style. I would have told this to no other person, ever—but the story was part of the enchantment. I told her about the Ten-Percenter, even about Uncle Sam, the broken-down ex-hood.

"Gambling turns me on," she said. "We could go to the Casino sometime."

Whatever she said, however juvenile, made her all the more perfect. I could never predict what she might say or do next, yet she was part of my life I had known all along. I knew her in jeans and in the nude and would soon see her in evening dress, but for now I watched fascinated this girl-woman gleaming wet under the shower—water was her element—and just as the Poet promised: a heartbreaker, perfect ankles, hair down to here.

"What movie," I asked, "are you seeing tonight?"

"A Western. Only it was made in Yugoslavia."

I would be waiting for her on the steps of the Palais. When she emerged from the dark into the overbright glitter of the illuminated Croisette, I would know from the look in her wide eyes if the ending was happy or not.

"What did she say," said Marybeth, referring to my wife, "when you said you were taking off?"

"Said?" I paused before making the uncomfortable switch to fiction. "She didn't say. Anything." I had been living an elaborate lie for so long that invention came to my lips as if prerecorded. "The Poet was right about her, too." Marybeth had shut off the water and I was shouting into an unexpected silence. "He said that women, he said she was probably. Seeing someone. There's always, the Poet said, another man."

All candor was on Marybeth's side now—I was the freewheeling double-dealing liar-at-large.

"But did he win?"

"The Poet? The horse, yes. The horse was a winner from the moment the Poet circled a name. With his Magic Marker."

Guilt did not appear in the indictment against the Poet, but guilt—now that I had the leisure to brood on my cowardice—was one of a number of indictments against me. The Poet promised me a place, and a girl in that place—he did not name the price I would pay for an escape from Passive City.

But I desperately wanted the girl in this place to take her childish pleasure in the moment—just as I, however selfishly, took my pleasure in her. I wanted not to think about paying, I wanted her to have happy endings.

"How much?"

"Do I pay?" I could not shake the indictment. "You mean. How much did we win."

Her accountant's mind for worldly concerns spared me the other accounting. I could, for purposes of a happy ending, recite the number of hundreds of our winnings (I had won only half as much as the Poet, having only half his faith in luck and circumstance) without carrying the tale to its conclusion. For all Marybeth knew, the Poet was a living winner still.

9

MARYBETH'S HOTEL was on a narrow side street at the foot of the old city where the spill from the Festival was rare: the cars of the film makers were too wide to pass. We invariably went to her hotel to make love, and not mine—but I did not stay the night. She was strangely incurious about where I lived; she never asked, content to accept that I too lived in tiny third-rate accommodations. I said nothing about my employer, of course, nor about the three-star Hôtel Méditerranée. My flight from Miami was all she knew about me, and that I was finishing a poem. She could invent the rest.

We ate at small uncrowded seafood restaurants or simple bistros around the market sheds in her quarter. During the day we took rations of bread and cheese and wine to the Ile St. Honorat to sustain us on Marybeth's private beach. She brought *The Oxford Book of English Verse* along, but we did not read the poems in it.

"Pretend," she said, draping herself provocatively against the sandbank, "I'm like the sole survivor of a shipwreck and you're a sailor that's been stranded on this island for years, and you haven't seen a woman the whole time, and then there's me, all naked, my clothes got washed away in the sea. I'm unconscious but not drowned. And you can't help yourself. I'm this vision you had all the time you were stranded, so you throw yourself on my body and like really get carried away."

And so I did.

In the small room at her hotel on the street named for a date in French history, she would turn out the lights and burn candles and incense and play mood music on her transistor to drown the sounds of traffic.

"Pretend," she said, "I'm this real young prostitute you picked up on the Croisette just to *baiser* for the night (that's French for fuck, a taxi driver told me) but when you get me to the hotel room I remind you of somebody you once loved and lost and you're real tender and don't really want to *baiser* anymore but I go ahead and give head and you let me but you're real disillusioned afterward to realize I was only a prostitute after all."

And so I did. When I started to undress her, she said, "First, the money," so I passed money to her to make the game real. She accepted the French bank notes and I tenderly held her head between my hands as she knelt beside the bed and took me in her mouth. I pretended to be disillusioned afterward.

"I told you," she said, "I was a movie freak."

10

FROM LA FONTAINE DE LA JEUNESSE in Zurich (or the Springbrunnen von Jungen) Mrs. Rappaport mailed to me a thick packet of research material, including two volumes she had found at Brentano's in Paris: *Burke's Peerage* and *You and the Stars*. (I thought *You and the Stars* might have to do with film stars, since Mrs. Rappaport had once taken a screen test, but it was a compendium of character traits according to signs of the Zodiac—all references to Mrs. Rappaport's sign, Libra, underlined in red ink.) There were also detailed genealogical charts tracing the Conleys, Connallys, Connolys, Connolays in their infinite variations from the 1690 Battle of the Boyne until the Great Potato Famine of 1840. Mrs. Rappaport had located gravesites of a number of Grandjacquots, and had made notes on their burying grounds and Huguenot origins. As an afterthought she had supplied me with a Xerox copy of Longfellow's "Evangeline" and Jewel's pedigree papers. The note accompanying this collection of curiosa said simply: "Don't give out my return address to *any*body." She was preparing herself for celebrity status. And: "Swiss weather is for the birds. T.R."

The IBM typewriter remained in its case, the bond paper still in my Gladstone.

Like my father, I could never resist an unlocked drawer: the drawers in Mrs. Rappaport's bedroom were empty, but she had left one suitcase unlocked. Inside was a photograph—face down in a layer of lacy underthings—of a short fat man in a white suit and lavender tie, having his shoes shined in some Mediterranean port (not Cannes, the shoeshine boy was barefoot), perhaps Sardinia or Greece, some place from one of Penelope's posters. Here, surely, was the late Seymour Rappaport, frowning disagreeably at Teresa's Instamatic— what a vicious runt he looked. I tried to picture poised cool chin-up Teresa Rappaport in public with this snarling bulldog, then I tried to picture them in bed. There was nothing else of interest in the suitcase: an infinity of blouses, brassieres, and a pocket calculator designed for computing foreign exchange rates.

For a trifling number of franc notes (from Mrs. Rappaport's envelope) a bellboy at the Méditerranée was willing to take my place; that is, my hired substitute took Jewel for walks through the palm-studded formal gardens flanking the Croisette from a public beach to the birthday-cake casino. (What fascinated Marybeth most about the casino was the ornately draped entryway to the Salle de Jeu, not the press conferences she had attended there with Eastern European directors and Italian starlets.) There was a carrousel in the park beside the Casino where Marybeth and I circled side by side, passing from steed to steed a sack of caramelized peanuts purchased from an Arab vendor, while we waited for the ferry to the Iles de Lérins.

One Sunday when the only films being shown at the Palais were *hors competition*, and not worth my sea urchin's professional attention, she announced to me, "I know a place."

I trusted her for places.

The streets of Cannes were full of colored balloons launched from the Carlton pier by a bevy of topless models, a light breeze from the sea swept the balloons inland. The balloons bore the name of a Spanish film entry competing for the Palme d'Or, a film, Marybeth assured me, would never win: "Too intellectual, everybody in it dies."

So we waded through a backwash of balloons to the bus depot opposite the municipal piers. The driver of our bus, with its Art Deco ads for *parfumeries* on the sides, was muttering to himself what must have been curses at the balloons that floated across his itinerary, bounced against the windshield. The only other passesngers were a team of four Japanese in lightweight blue business suits, the suits identical.

During the long transit into the back country behind Cannes I kept wanting to touch the silent creature wedged between me and the window. I tried to keep my caresses discreet, out of consideration for the sober passengers across the aisle. (Because of the uniform suits, they might have been a contingent of Oriental Jehovah's Witnesses.) But I could barely restrain the giddiness of my affection. In public, Marybeth maintained her casual cool: she was flattered, I could tell, by my persistent ardor, but she reacted as if the difference in our ages was the other way around.

We were both so caught up in ourselves we failed to realize that the perfume factories we had planned to visit would be closed on the seventh day. The Japanese were equally unprepared for Sunday, but they at least had brought cameras and could photograph a protest march clogging the main street of the old quarter, blocking our bus in the backup of traffic. Marybeth had French enough to read the posters: she said the marchers were protesting the admission into France of a deposed African dictator, and his several wives, who had settled into a suburban château on the outskirts of Grasse.

These protestors did not seem as organized or funereal as the marchers I had watched in Belfast. Here they were carrying their small hand-printed placards on fragile popsicle sticks; they carried crêpes with jam in their free hands, laughed together as they marched, nibbling crêpes, gesturing to friends at curbside.

With an exasperated shrug that even I could read, the bus driver suggested we leave the bus here, since he could not pass through the crowds to the terminus.

Grasse, of course: flowers, perfume. The New Poet up from Dublin at Dee's party spoke of Grasse, the great good place for him, of all the places he had been imprisoned. He had written out the name of a village I should visit, on a betting slip that had long slipped away, but I remembered the name. It was my turn to say to Marybeth, "I know a place."

Marybeth applied her broken French to an ancient driver whose new taxi would take us to Ys. There was little of the poet about him. His gestures were extravagant and required both hands off the wheel to make a point; his monologue en route was entirely in French, so I did not know if it was poetry. For me the ride was both frightening and exhilarating—the excitement came from being with Marybeth, seeing her face in profile, no matter the danger—as we traversed with unnecessary haste a road known as the Route Napoléon. The name seemed to call for grand-scale catastrophe—true enough there were pictographs at every curve warning of stones that might at any time detach from the rockface hanging precipitiously over the road. (Warnings seemed as useless as the emergency telephone number on the Pont des Arts—there was nothing the driver could have done about falling rock, often enough he was twisted around from the driver's seat addressing us face-to-face.) Far below, in a jungle-tangle of vines and wild fig trees at the bottom of a stony gorge, lay the rusted corpse of a Peugeot that might have been the Peugeot we drove in.

Why, wondered the driver, would anyone want to visit Ys, known only for its two suspect paintings by Rubens in the church, one of which was a copy and the other a fake?

As the road climbed into pine-clad slopes known as the pre-Alps, the rock and greenery closed in on us like walls—indeed, there were man-made walls at distant intervals, marking off private estates, the stone ledges finished off with upright spikes or broken glass imbedded in cement to discourage familiarity. Behind which of these formidable walls, I wondered, lived the deposed African dictator and his harem, guarded by police dogs and machine guns from the crowds who would dismember him, when they finished their crêpes, if they could.

Then the landscape gradually flattened into a tranquil plateau of vineyards and olive groves as we reached the domestic outskirts of the village. Ahead of us lay a flat grassy open park, a backdrop of stone hills, the true Alps rising in the distance. The village itself was built into a cliffside, the ramparts of its broken crumbling château looked out over a vast plain to the distant hazy outline of Cannes, where we had begun our day.

"Fabulous," said Marybeth.

Before we came to the village, the driver pulled up beside an old man walking along the road, white hair in two feathery tufts, tanned but feeble as he eased along with two canes. The driver and the old man were familiars, fellow ancients.

"Let's take him where he's going," Marybeth said to me, and immediately the old man stopped speaking French and addressed us in English: "Are you American? Are you going to the *méchoui?*"

He struggled into the front seat with the driver, arranging his canes between his knees.

I answered yes, meaning we were Americans, but, as it turned out, we were going to the *méchoui* as well.

"Funny you should ask me that. I must be the only person alive who remembers Gabriel L'Homme. He's buried in Ys, you know—have you come to see his grave?"

"No. Not at all." (The cemetery with its graveled grave plots was just across the road we had come in on, but I had my fill of cemeteries.) "I was, I've been. Curious about him."

I had helped the old man to a picnic bench out of range of the smoke blowing from an open pit where a sheep was being roasted whole. He indicated the cemetery with one of his canes. I had taken the other cane from him as I helped him to the bench, and now stood foolishly holding it, attentive, steadfast, listening to his rusty English—he was American, but had spent sixty years in France— like the patient wedding guest from Coleridge's "Rime."

I may have been dupe to the myth that the aged know the secret of the universe, for I allowed the old man to attach himself to me as I listened for the word—and at the same time doggedly watched Marybeth move away. Also, I was bound to him out of our mutual circumstances. One of his stories began, "My mother was French."

Meanwhile Marybeth offered her conviviality to the crowd. They were mostly French, but of mixed nationalities (many spoke English), and she circled the picnic grounds meeting and greeting these multilingual strangers with unabashed American openness and, in her case, charm. I was too shy to follow in her wake, especially to try to converse with the local French, though I would have delighted in the chauvin's pride of escort, moving from group to group with this young animated nymph at my side. But the old man, whom I thought of as the Expatriate of expatriates, held me with his glittering eye.

The taxi driver had decided to linger in Ys and join the village fête: at the moment he was helping the Algerian chef with the sheep carcass, the two spooning collected drippings over the seared flesh, brushing the roasted sheep with whiskbrooms made of thyme. Between two olive trees a double-plank table was laden with Provençal pizzas, baked onion and tomato slices, and thick sandwiches of tuna and olive known as *pain bagnat*. On a plinth made of stones reposed three casks of wine with dripping spigots marked separately *rouge*, *blanc*, and *rosé*. (Dee would have blessed the sight, and called the rows of bottles little darlings.) There were liter bottles of *pastis* and *eau-de-vie* and the light red *piquet* of the Var. A

dark-skinned dwarf with ragged goatee and ropes of black hair came
to us with a wet tray: he and the old man laughed together over the old
man's remark.

"I told him," said the Expatriate, when the dwarf went for our
drinks, "I would have *eau-de-vie*, though my doctor tells me it will be
the death of me."

The jolly dwarf brought me a *pastis* and a tumbler of *eau-de-vie*
for the Expatriate, though we appeared to be the only guests being
served drinks: the custom was to serve one's self and refill at will. I
saw Marybeth walking from group to group with a delicately balanced
glass of *rosé* in her hand.

"I met him," said the Expatriate, referring again to Gabriel
L'Homme, "through the American writer Gertrude Stein—have you
heard of her, or tried to read her work? A curious woman, but hers is
another story. Gabriel was a poet at that time—the Twenties, before
you were born, prehistory as it were—but I fear his way of life
(lifestyle, you say now?) got in the way of his poetry."

"I've never seen. A poem of his."

"As far as I know, he never published any."

"Yes. A volume of his poems turned up. In the States of all
places, Santa Fe."

"Ah. He got as far as Santa Fe?"

"A friend of mine. A poet I knew, was translating the volume.
Into English. They were not—the poems, according to my poet
friend—much good."

The Expatriate had bent forward and was making strange sounds
in his chest and throat. He might have been laughing or sobbing or
both—I think both. His eyes were squeezed shut deep in the tanned
furrows of a face, and he dabbed at the lids with a pocket
handkerchief. When he recovered, instead of picking up on the
poetry of Gabriel L'Homme, he changed—in the way of the
elderly—or forgot the subject.

"One of my canes used to belong to Georges Braque, the French
painter. Braque once struck a dishonest auctioneer over the head with
his cane, but he was not sentenced to jail. He had a distinguished war
record and the war, the First War, was recent enough for the French
to be mindful of the sacrifices. (They even admired Americans at that
time!) He had a plate in his head, Braque, from the war—did you
know that? But the plate as far as I know had no effect on his painting,
for better or worse." This time he chuckled but without the strangling
sound of before. "Braque, Gertrude Stein, Hemingway—I am speak-

ing not of the French now, for only Braque was French (and Picasso, he was Spanish), I am speaking of the Twenties, and the artists of that time. They were our successes—dead, all dead. Picasso lived not far from here—did you know that?"

"No. Did you know him?"

"I did not have the pleasure, or the strain, of his acquaintance. He was said to be an unreliable and disagreeable friend, and he was, of course, the very devil with the women."

"I didn't know."

"No reason you should. Dead, all dead. For the rest of us a plenitude of sun and wine and a little repose before the last repose across the road." He pointed his cane again at the cypresses that bordered that mournful garden. "Even our cypresses are dying, spared the long wait of a natural end, diagnosed by the doctor (trees have their confounded doctors too) as incurable. A microscopic worm eats at their vitals. The plague was imported by us foreigners—we are unaware of our guilt, of course, but that does not make the French any happier with us."

Indeed, every third-or-so cypress had turned a burnt brown, needles fell from the skeletal branches, resinous tearlike streaks ran down the slim diseased trunks.

"What there is to do here in the way of occupation is harvest the olives, pick flowers and grapes, and wait. That is why our young people leave us, and why our young visitors—like yourselves—do not stay on. Did you not think, as you came upon our picturesque village with its spectacular view, that this could be the place?"

I was only half-listening to him, the way I had done with garrulous patients at the Sans Souci, but I clearly heard his question. I was watching the way the underside of leaves from the olive trees rippled silvery in the light when stirred by the breeze. The air was heavily perfumed from the jasmine fields and wild *genêt*, slightly spiked with the thyme-flavored fumes from the brazier where the sheep roasted. Old men, their *pastis* carefully laid by, played *boules* with the élan of youth in the middle of the dirt road, so that traffic—an occasional vehicle—respectfully detoured around their game by driving on the grass. Picnic guests were eating the oily *pains bagnats* and drinking wine, spitting olive pits into the grass, waiting for the sheep to be roasted. And there was Marybeth. She was engaged in a game of Ping-Pong on a wobbly table with a homemade net; when the breeze caught the Ping-Pong ball and blew it into the fire where it popped and melted in the red coals, Marybeth put the green paddle to her mouth making an O of mock horror (it was the one and only Ping-Pong ball), then laughed and danced over to her opponent, the village baker, to shake hands good-game. I had heard his question and was asking myself if this was, truly, the place.

"Yes," I confessed.

"The village," he was saying, "existed five hundred years after Christ. It was abandoned by the populace in time of plague, surrendered to marauders when rebuilt, destroyed by war, rebuilt, put under seige, ransomed, captured, always rebuilt. And here it is still."

"And here we are."

Time, since I had known Marybeth, had been outmaneuvered by mind. These surroundings appeared to me as some sad sweet abiding déjà vu, a place I had known all along, a coming home from that sense of loss I had felt since birth. That was why I had said yes to the Expatriate's question, and why Marybeth said, as she brought us each a *pain bagnat*, "Isn't this place fabulous?"

As if he had not heard her enthusiastic acceptance of Ys, the Expatriate was saying, "In winter, a rude season for the aged, we endure the grim reminder of a funeral every ten days or so—that is an unhealthy mise-en-scène for the young."

There were young people about, even a few children—but clearly Ys was populated by the elderly and retired. (I wondered if the Expatriate, from the distance of his years, placed me among the young.) Marybeth, with her unaffected Stateside ways and gregarious impulses, had made the acquaintance of everyone present, young and old alike. She was serving a *pain bagnat* to a young blond-bearded cyclist taking apart a powerful-looking motorcycle. The boy stood up from his tools and scattered bike parts to accept with rough graciousness the sandwich in his grease-stained hands. He wore a quasi-military getup of Marine fatigue pants and boots, T-shirt with Eisenhower jacket and a Danish cadet's black-billed cap.

"Gerhardt," said the Expatriate, following my gaze. "Yes, but he is leaving us soon. He will return to the Black Forest and Rhinemaidens of his origins. (There is a shortfall of available female companionship in these parts.) He will roar off into the horizon, I would expect, as soon as he puts his two-wheeled machine in working order. Look how anxiously his mother watches him."

The Expatriate swung his cane around and I saw, at a distant table, a heavy woman with a plait of blond hair twisted into a bun at the back of her thick neck. She did not take her avid eyes from the two young people, even as she munched at her onion pizza.

"Emissaries from Germany. We have a mixture of nationalities here, the Common Market in microcosm. Gerhardt's mother left Germany at the end of the Second War, at the very moment the Russians swarmed over her part of Berlin. The Germans, an indomitable people. Antipathetic, alas (Gertrude Stein would not suffer Germans in her intimate circle, except for Kahnweiler the art dealer), but indomitable. In those final apocalyptic days of the Third Reich, Gerhardt's mother got her harpsichord, along with her infant son, out of Germany. Her husband was, I believe, the Commandant of a concentration camp in Holland, and died there defending it. (But you can see how *méchant* we can be with our nasty gossip of one another!) She now lives on the same hillside as that Jewish gentleman playing *boules*, near neighbors and wary friends. He makes lamp-shades for a living." The Expatriate bent forward laughing-crying, and said "lampshades" again. He screwed his knotted handkerchief into the deep sockets of his eyes.

Nearby, I heard Marybeth telling Gerhardt that Amsterdam had been fabulous. Gerhardt in his lispy accent said that he hated cops.

"You see him only in semiformal attire at the moment, the Expatriate explained. "He is without his medallions, today being the Sabbath. He wears the German Iron Cross on his cap, and the American Purple Heart. If you look closely at his belt buckle—though I do not see why you should—you will read there *Gott Mit Uns*, a sentiment the SS in Hitler's Germany lived by, and the Jihad Islamique—in another language, and another God—believes in today. Their victims, alas, believed that God is with them also. But I do not take Gerhardt's plumage too seriously—there are young people calling themselves Punks who dress as outrageously."

Gerhardt had taken off the earphones to his Walkman, and was pressing one receptor to Marybeth's seashell ear. If his formidable motorcycle had been intact, I was certain he would have taken her for a spin. It was a relief that the machine was in pieces.

Though the Expatriate's mind and memory might wander, his ramblings were shrewd, sometimes droll, but often derogatory in a *méchant* (which I learned meant mean) way. The only swimming pool in town was owned by the Communist shopkeeper Pierrot. The gypsy dwarf had furnished his stone *cabanon* with trinkets he swiped from the Monoprix in Grasse. Gerhardt's mother had had an affair not with the baker but with the baker's wife. I liked hearing the old man run on, but listened with only one ear (as Marybeth was doing) since the village scandal held no relevance for me. It was the magic village itself that engaged my attention. I gazed once again at the outcropping of tiled houses built into stone and the town's vestigial château knowing that if I did return here—and I never would—the mirage would have evaporated.

"As for the rest of us," said the Expatriate summing up, "we are for the most part life's failures, narrow failures, but failing even to recognize ourselves as the almost-were in their twilight years, misplaced, too late, in somebody else's Eden. Our Gabriel, for instance. He brought a young sailor here, was vilified and deceived by him, robbed, beaten almost to death. He did not die, and might have gone on to love again, but there was a too-convenient hoard of pills he had saved. (The doctors in France are profligate with their *ordonnances*—prescriptions, that is—I myself have a collection of capsules that could very well come in handy one day soon.) An incurable romantic, Gabriel had put a disc of Mozart's *Requiem* on the record player to ease him through the long night, and it was playing still when the man who delivers eggs to the door found his body."

Since I had asked after Gabriel L'Homme, and now the strange coincidence of his life and death in Ys had come to light, the Expatriate insisted on showing me the very gravesite. He had already heaved himself upright on one of his canes before I could insist no, and he took hold of my arm in place of the other cane, to draw me alongside him (while I glanced unhappily backwards, searching for Marybeth) to the cemetery across the road from the picnic grounds. We shuffled along a narrow graveled path to a plain stone slab, among so many others (some with photographs of the departed) crowded close, like the living crowd we had walked away from at the *méchoui*. There was no photograph on Gabriel L'Homme's slab, only the stark carving of his name and dates, the proof of his existence the Expatriate wanted me to see. Proof indeed, but I had believed without seeing. I was thinking of other deaths: my mother's, no confirmed burial place (only a death notice among my father's letters); the Poet's father buried in Salt Lake City; the Poet himself, last seen between death and disposal in his shroud-pac at the Sans Souci morgue—no grave I would ever know of.

Three short sharp bugle blasts startled me out of my morbid revery. The bugler was a tubercular-looking old fellow with the ravaged face of a wino—the town crier, the Expatriate informed me—barking out an announcement that the *méchoui* had officially begun, the sheep was roasted and ready to be served. It was I who led the Expatriate away, or we might have continued our gloomy graveside contemplations past any appropriate interval of mourning. The celebration of the living took place across the road.

As we crossed, the old man told me of the *trouvères*—the troubadours—who wandered this region seeking they knew not what, writing delightful verses in Provençal (the village still spoke a dialect of that ancient tongue), strumming their lutes and languishing for love of the unattainable.

"Life," mused the Expatriate, "might have been worth living in their century."

Back at the feast, the rotund mayor, with his *boules* still in hand, was saying a few words over the succulent carcass—though the priest was also present, but not asked to offer his blessing.

The Expatriate let go of my arm as he lowered himself to the log bench and took up his other cane. For a moment he looked from one cane to the other as if to solve his life's greatest puzzle.

"I did tell you, did I not, that one of my canes belonged to Georges Braque?"

I refrained from saying yes.

"But I bought myself a second cane as my infirmity progressed. And now," this time he laughed easily and deep, "I don't know Braque's cane from my own."

The tablecloths flapped agitatedly with the late breeze as the evening swallows silently scoured the atmosphere for insect life. Gerhardt's panzer profile was turned my way: he was still blitzing Marybeth with Teutonic charm, and he released her to me with reluctance. Our taxi driver was too intoxicated to drive us back to Grasse, but a young black-eyed Breton offered us a lift in his windowless *deux-chevaux*. There was room for the Expatriate and his canes in the canvas seat beside the driver.

Loic was a fugitive from the Free Brittany movement in the northwest, according to one of the Expatriate's stories, and had been implicated in the blowing-up of an EDF high-tension pylon. He was presumably hiding out in Ys, waiting for a second breath before another assault on the repressive government in Paris, but he spoke not about the problems of the Bretons—he had been picking jasmine and *genêt* for the perfume factories in Grasse. "You pick the blossoms early," Marybeth translated for me, "before sunup, while the dew is still on the petals, for the weight. They pay by the weight, and the jasmine blooms again every morning."

This somehow reminded the Expatriate to inform us that one could see Corsica from the ramparts of Ys: "At dawn, on certain cloudless December mornings, when the mistral has blown away the traffic pollution along the coast. Corsica—the Little General's island—they too have a grudge against the government in Paris." He translated this last into French, for Loic's benefit.

It suddenly occurred to me to wonder what the *méchoui* had been about.

"Was it a wedding?" I had not seen the bride and groom. "Or something?"

We had reached the ancient *mas* where the old man lived, and as Loic helped him from the car, he was not—in another of his moods—inclined to give a straight answer.

"It was a fête, perhaps, to honor your visit—you and your charming young companion."

Loic kept the headlights beamed on the drive for as long as the Expatriate limped homeward.

When Marybeth and I got back to Cannes the night streets were empty of life but still afloat with balloons.

11

"NEXT DOOR there's always some scene going, like constant movies."

The Mimosa Apartments were next to her hotel, a *boucherie-charcuterie* on the ground floor, alongside a corner bar that resounded long and late with pinball bells and buzzers. From Marybeth's narrow balcony we could see stairwell windows of the upper floors to the apartment building. Explosive French oaths erupted across the little distance between buildings, the timed *minuterie* lights flashed on then off as the combatants descended the stairs, hurling their bitter insults from top to bottom of the building, their night-shattering bellicose passage alternately illuminated, then in dark.

"I keep thinking," said she, "some Italian director will step out of the butcher shop downstairs and yell, 'Cut!' or whatever Italian directors yell."

The scenes next door were explosive but brief, nothing like Marybeth's elaborate mind-trip scenarios.

We left the balcony and Marybeth folded herself legs crossed Indian style onto the floor beside the low coffee table. The table was filled with cinema brochures and promotional film stills spilling from manila envelopes. She went back to rolling thin joints on the paper cover of *The Oxford Book of English Verse*, with French cigarette paper, from the dried leaves of marijuana Gerhardt had given her. (Gerhardt had harvested a small crop of pot in his mother's herb garden.) She lit up from the flame of a candle beside her on the floor. Her reference to Italian directors may have prompted the suggestion, "Pretend you're the Mafia and kidnapped me and while you're waiting for the ransom money . . ." She was drawing deep of the joint, her moist eyelids fluttering with the effort, and soon the odor of marijuana was mixed with the incense smoldering in an ashtray. Next door doors were slamming, the obscenities moving from ground floor upward now—a film run backwards—until somewhere mid-stairwell a scream turned to a whimper.

"No," she said. She passed the joint to me with her baby fingers, then settled back on her elbows, legs still crossed, exhaling slowly ceilingward. "Pretend you're this Japanese." (She was probably remembering the Japanese on the bus to Grasse sneaking businessmen's guarded glances at her haltered breasts and bare midriff.) "And it's wartime, on one of those islands in the Pacific the Japs invaded, and you just captured this American nurse." She dreamed this screenplay over for several more tokes.

When the joint was down to a thin ring of paper and a bit of weed, Marybeth took a pair of tweezers from her makeup bag and tweezed the roach to her lips for its last essence, a final concentrated hit. In a moment she got up dizzily and stood near me, eyes wide and frightened, holding her arms above her head as if she had been arrested.

"Pretend," she said, "you're a German—the SS or somebody at some camp or the police station where you're totally in charge. I'm Jewish or something, and I'm your prisoner. You can send me to the gas chambers or whatever you want. You can have me killed if you want. But that's not what you want."

She lowered her hands and—trembling, head tilted back and eyelids half closed—she began pulling down her halter as if I had barked the command to do so in German.

12

JEWEL WAS MISSING from her basket at the foot of my bed. I wrapped myself in a terrycloth robe and opened the drapes to the balcony: the morning light was not yet bright enough to be painful, a curtain of fog had settled over the yacht basin. As the mist lifted, the park was transformed into a Japanese garden. A gardener working alone poked his spiked stick among the formal shrubs—like the stick Gretta used, to tidy the Botanic Gardens—dragging a burlap sack (Gretta's same bag) like something attached to him. The islands— Eden, Marybeth called our island—were fogbound. Jewel was not on the balcony, either.

In the street below, yellow trucks moved in formation with a team of utility men riding the crane lifts to unfasten the frames to the giant ads lined along the Croisette, removing the blown-up images frame by frame and letting the stripped posters fall to the street. Behind the trucks a squadron of street cleaners with willow brooms swept together the poster shreds and skins of burst balloons for the groaning sanitation pickup, and hosed down the gutters. Jewel was making excited dog noises in the room next door.

Mrs. Rappaport was in her bedroom, standing amidst a turbulence of opened luggage, Jewel skipping frantic circles around her ankles in a delirium of joy.

You won't know her, Maury warned—and I did not.

Mrs. Rappaport's face was shiny-swollen, the eyes bruised as if she had been pummeled by a man's fist. Below the turban appeared the edges of adhesive strips, covering what I assumed was scar tissue. There was another strip of adhesive, like a prizefighter's trophy, across the bridge of her nose, and her ears must have been taped to her head, the bandaged lobes showing outside the turban. When she saw me at the glass door, she swiftly donned a pair of dark glasses. Her hands were bandaged in half-gloves of gauze, the finger joints showing: she beckoned to me with one bandaged hand. I fastened the belt to my robe and entered.

"I took a night flight." Her voice had turned nasal because of the taped nose. "I can't go out in daylight like this."

"Maury said—"

"Maury said he saw you on a merry-go-round with some kid.

Eating peanuts, he said. What is this? Is that what I'm supposed to be paying for?"

Maury was a watcher, a witness with a long memory.

She sat, and Jewel scrambled into her lap, licking at the swollen face. I stood waiting in silence, but Mrs. Rappaport did not pursue the indictment. She might even have been smiling, at the dog: she and Jewel were enacting their reunion.

"I met a girl," I said.

Mrs. Rappaport took up her stiletto nail file and went working at a set of bloodless fingernails.

"Nice for you. She's a kid, I hear. What about the book we're writing?"

"I don't have enough material."

"I left you stuff, plenty—all that background."

"None of it is about you."

"It's about my family, my ancestors, it's great background."

There was no answer to that.

"Anyway," she said abruptly, nasally, "I changed my mind about the book. Maury said it would make a terrific movie. He said my life is like a ready-made movie script. So instead of a book I've got this screenplay in mind. I know somebody who knows somebody and with the right legal people I might sign a contract. I could play myself in it."

The rich, Son, do not dream the same dreams you or I dream.

"We've got a contract, remember."

I remembered.

For a moment she was elated, and the tight bright skin glowed. Then she lowered her head (this was the first time I had seen her head bowed) and covered her face with the gauze hands: she was crying behind the dark glasses. She turned away, her face in her hands, and broke into racking sobs—the little dog whimpering in counterpoint. I went to her. The gauze bindings on her hands were spotted with blood, her nose was bleeding.

I got a towel from the bathroom and brought it to her, then took off the sunglasses and pressed a knot of toweling to her face. She was sobbing still, and saying something through the sobs, but the words were muffled by the towel. Her bloody hands reached up and pressed against mine while I held the towel to her nose.

After a frozen moment holding her I put her hands on the towel and disengaged myself to call Room Service for ice.

The ice came in a champagne bucket: I wrapped cubes of ice in

a facecloth and applied the cloth to her lip and bandaged nose. The
loud sobbing had ceased, but her breasts heaved spasmodically and
the words she blubbered into the damp facecloth were full of tears.
Eventually the bleeding stopped. She pushed away the stained cloth
from her black nostrils and put the dark glasses back on her bruised
face. When I started for the bathroom with the bloody facecloth, she
caught my wrists, took a breath, and said in a hiss just this side of
hysteria, "Stay with me."

I stayed with her. We sat opposite one another in low tube-and-
canvas chairs facing the sea in silence until her breakfast tray came. I
poured warm milk from the creamer into a saucer for Jewel, but the
dog was too distraught to lap at it. Mrs. Rappaport trembled as she
brought the coffee cup to her lips. When she had finished her coffee
she was steady enough to take up her nail file again.

I excused myself to shower and dress. From the shower I could
hear Mrs. Rappaport on the phone: I thought she might be calling for
a doctor, but she must have been speaking to Maury, her voice flat
and without affect, fully recovered.

"Why Viareggio when I've already got people in San Remo?
Who? When I talked to him he said three people and San Remo and
now you say Viareggio and four. I can count. What I want to know is
what's so hot about Viareggio all of a sudden?"

She got the hotel operator and put through another call: "Today,
tomorrow, as soon as it sails, I don't care. Someplace near the top of
the boat. A suite, if they've got one, I've got somebody with me. With
portholes that open, I've got a dog that gets motion sickness."

I went out without waiting for her to finish on the telephone. I
was meeting Marybeth at noon at the carrousel: we were going to the
Ile St. Honorat, we had the whole day, the Festival had ended and the
movies were over.

She was late. Watching the carrousel spin around and around was
making me dizzy, so I concentrated on the solitary gardener spiking
cigarette packs from the plots of oleander, pulling his burlap sack
past me like some deformity. The Arab vendor balanced his tray of
caramelized peanuts on his head, selling to the children who were
back; the Croisette had reverted to its out-of-season routine.

It was nearly one (we had missed the twelve-thirty ferry, but
could always take a motor launch—it was only money) when I went
looking for her at her hotel. She had left, the hotel clerk told me.

The Festival was over, and the hotel staff was speaking French
again. I had trouble with the words *sortie* and *partie. Elle est partie*

was the information; *sortie* would have meant she had gone out, *partie* meant she was gone. "Are you sure—*pas sortie?*" "*Partie*," he repeated. He took the key from the pigeonhole with her room number on it, the key dangling from its tag like an earring. Marybeth had checked out of her room. There was no message in the pigeonhole for Mr. Gold.

Why had she not called me at the Mediterranean? Alas, I remembered, she did not know I lived there.

Traffic was moderate on the Rue d'Antibes, and slow paced, but my own pedestrian's stride was somewhat desperate. An uncanny premonition tortured me as I reached the carrousel again—only children, the gardener, the peanut vendor. She would be at the Press Room, surely, at the Palais des Festivals, some final conference at festival's end. We had sometimes met there, in front of the teletype office.

There were still tourists on the Croisette, few, but I felt they lingered along the way only to obstruct my passage.

The mirrored lobby of the Palais echoed with the sound of invisible hammers from the mezzanine. The only soul in sight was a woman on her knees with a scrubbing rag wiping the terrazzo of every footprint. As I hurried up the circular stairs of the stars, I was careful not to see myself in the series of mirrors without end.

The Press Room was empty of course. It was lunchtime, and the carpenters had left the pigeonhole units in the mail room half-dismantled. There was nothing in the pigeonhole marked *Hughes*, I even searched the *M* section for the name *Marybeth*. Paper cups of cold coffee stood on the mail room table, and scattered ashtrays full of butts. The grille was down over the wire service desk. The clock behind the grille had stopped, and I had no watch.

On the bulletin board—she might have tacked a message there—was a petition in English and French protesting the imprisonment of a Czech film director: there were only three signatures, one in pencil, none Marybeth's. FOR SALE: *Canon 16mm camera, Reasonable Offer.* Another notice also in English only: *Wanted, Ride to Paris, Share Expenses.* It was typed, Marybeth did not type.

"You want to know what her price was—you really want to know?"

I did not want to know.

Mrs. Rappaport stood on the balcony at the open glass door to my room, watching me pack. Her arms were tightly crossed so that the bandaged hands were hidden in her armpits.

"What would you say if I said her price was a measly five

hundred?" Mrs. Rappaport was determined I would know the price. "I could have laughed out loud. Five hundred, that's how much she thought it was worth. I offered her four, just to see if she would go that low. She took it."

I did not speak or turn to her. I was careful to pack only my own things into the Gladstone, nothing she had bought for me on Jermyn Street or on the Place Vendôme.

"Went out of here like a bat out of hell, on some kid's motorcycle." I could not see Mrs. Rappaport's distorted face, but I could read the loathing in her voice. "A blond German kid with medals on his T-shirt. He looked at the money like it was a million bucks, that's how hungry he looked, the both of them, kids, hippies, no-goods from the word go."

Once again, in flat contractual terms now, she outlined the plan. We'd get started again, this time on the right foot. We would write the script together aboard the *Michelangelo*, sailing in three days. It would be a nostalgia trip for her—most of the port cities she had already seen with Sy: Naples, Portofino, Piraeus, Alexandria—Alex, she called it. First Class, you use the ship as a hotel, we could write in the cabin while the ship was at sea and still see the sights at every Mediterranean port of any importance. Seeing these cities again would be a refresher course for her, would be great background for the script. We had a contract.

I took off the Cardin silk shirt she had given me, with a fleur-de-lys on the pocket, and changed for one of my own.

Maury drove me to Nice airport in his low-slung bullet-shaped sports car. He was silent the entire drive until we parked underground and he handed me a last envelope.

"You're making the biggest mistake of your life, Buddy." He was still holding on to his end of the envelope. "This woman has been written up in *Time* and *Newsweek* both, her divorce was. I'm telling you, you ought to have your head examined."

He only let go of the envelope when I said, "Just one of my mistakes."

There was a brownish-yellow cloud hanging over the airfield, over the sea—the coastal air pollution the Expatriate mentioned, or an accumulation of jet-engine exhaust—but the Midi sun still blazed through the shameful streak. Between the sea and the layer of pollution was a thin blue line at the horizon, only that much leeway to remind me I had run out of crawl space.

I presented myself—or I.M. Gold—at passport control, then

the attaché case full of my father's letters went through the scanner at the gate. I looked back one more time to see if Marybeth's flower face might miraculously have blossomed in the bon-voyage crowd, but there was only Maury's pirate skull to see me off, a cigarette clenched in the grin, waiting, taking a last look, with orders from his employer to make certain I did not linger in paradise.

Survivors

1

"YOUR REAL NAME I don't want to know," said Schine. The old man sat naked in a canvas chair on the so-called sun deck of his Miami Beach hotel. (No one used the sun deck but the owner, no way to walk on the tar-and-gravel surface without getting melted tar on your feet: Schine wore shower clogs to and from his canvas chair.) We were alone up there in the breathless white heat of noon, so he sat easy in his nakedness, gleaming with suntan oil, slightly ghostly and insubstantial behind the heat waves given off by the roof. His thick white hair was marcelled in measured waves and held in place by a woman's hairnet; his ropey penis, also gleaming, lay half-coiled in a white nest of pubic hair. Even through the veil of heat reflection he appeared in remarkable condition for a man of seventy-something: chesty, hairy, burnished brown, survivor of the Holocaust and many a season in hell since.

"Forget the Frank, Frank's too frank for the Ventura, to me you're Buddy Whatever no-last-names-please so later somebody with a badge comes asking I know from nothing. For all I know you got a record—keep it, I don't want to know. You look straight enough to keep the petty cash straight and I'm a terrific judge of character— where I'm concerned you're sincere enough looking for nights at my hotel, eighty a week and a *room* remember. Don't go whining Minimum Wage at me like the last guy. Now he's out on his ass looking for wage one. That's eighty *net* remember, no Withholding, no Social Security and that crap, keep our government's nose out of it, you look like a person—and I'm a number-one judge of character, so

323

don't disappoint me—that don't want the government's nose in your business. I know you free swingers, no strings attached, O.K. by me (I'm a free swinger myself, but I don't go overboard), just watch how you swing at the Ventura. Here you're watching my lobby nights. Remember, there's seven nights in a week before you collect your eighty, and that means eight P.M. each and every night, you don't show and I myself got to stay on after being on all day, so show. You got your days to yourself. If you got union on your mind I got news for you, there's no unions south of Lincoln Road, so take it or leave it. I got takers waiting, Viet vets and ex-cops and Cubanos by the boatload, but you I like. You can shower in the boiler room. Cleveland the *schwarz* showers down there but he's as clean a person as you or me, I promise you. Another thing I can promise, you don't run hot beds on me or bring your girlies in to rent to my guests and in a month I raise you to ninety. That's ninety net, remember, and your tips are your own, extra on top. The petty cash we check out every morning and it's too petty, believe me, to take off with even if you had a couple of check-ins that paid in advance. Don't hassle me, my friend, and you've got a boss that don't hassle the help—ask Cleveland, ask Joy-O. There's me and you and Joy-O the housemaid and Cleveland the porter—he could be Columbus for all I know, he could have a record—I don't want to know. Joy-O the same, from the islands someplace, I couldn't pronounce her name even if I knew it. What do I know if they've got a record or not? The beard you can hang on to, but keep it neat with the scissors, O.K.? These beards all over the place they look like they're in to stay, it's accepted now, so leave it stay. A beard behind the front desk'll impress people, like Europe. Makes you a sincere-looking person like a professor or something. Just don't grow it too long."

I landed at the Ventura Hotel within an hour of my arrival at Miami International Airport. Doped with airline coffee and benumbed from jet lag, I failed to note or altogether register the cabbie who drove me to the Beach except for the black wire at the back of his head and two coin-sized bald spots at the crown. He knew a zombie when he picked one up, so there was no conversation all the way through downtown Miami and across the MacArthur Causeway. It was up to me, no help, to discover if it was possible to live in places, like Belgium and Miami Beach, places without poetry.

The cabbie delivered me to the Ventura—his idea, since I had no hotel in mind—and collected two dollars turkey-money from the night clerk at the time (the man Schine called Minimum Wage) for steering me there. After ten days sweating out a recurrent nightmare (inspired by a shark movie I saw on the lobby television, but the dream was not about sharks) a seven-year-old boy, Denny, asked me out of the blue if I wanted a job.

"You could get a job, Sir. Mr. Schine needs a night man."

Night man—what a perfect persona to assume. Denny must have noticed my sleeplessness, my affinity for nights.

The boy's father had taught him to say Sir, and in other ways—posture, reserve—to maintain a military bearing. The towheaded Denny and his towheaded sister Lee Ann lived with their father in the room two doors down from mine. The kids were a swimming team, the Waterbabies, performers in exhibition swimming-diving shows. The aquashow was presented at the vast swimming pools of swank uptown hotels, stage-managed by their trainer-father rigged out as Neptune.

"Mr. Wage got fired," said Lee Ann, nearly six. "Why don't you be the night man?"

They had sneaked down to the lobby to watch the late-late shark movie while their father (Bludhorn, or "Sarge," but I thought of him as Neptune) was out drinking at the Blarney Stone, the only Irish bar on Miami Beach, beer-bottle caps pressed into the cork walls for atmosphere—you could get bottled Guinness and Smithwicks on draught. (I went there once only, for a nostalgic pint, but encountered Neptune in his cups droning his dreary case history, and never went back.) The Waterbabies were too wired after an aquashow to sleep, and had come down to the lobby to watch the movie with me.

Neptune barged in just as the film was ending. The kids fled, trying to escape him by the front lobby stairs. In spite of Neptune's distended waist and buttocky backside, he was remarkably agile: he was at them before they reached the room. He was beating Denny with his fists when I caught up to them in the hall. I forced my way between the kids and their father—Lee Ann was weeping as if she were being hit, but Denny endured the actual beating without a sound—and got my lip split. Next day Neptune apologized. He was wearing a padded back brace, the neckpiece protruding from his open collar: "When I get worked up my back goes out on me." He apologized, but reminded me, "They're my kids, remember."

"Right."

Mainly he was worried that the bruises would show on Denny, who wore only swim briefs for the water show.

Neptune had taught the kids to stand at attention and say Sir and Mister but he kept them out of school by skipping around from city to city, one school district to another.

"We were in California last winter," said Denny, "all over, Sir. There's so many pools, some of them Olympic, you can keep moving around and never get traced." For all the beatings, Denny thought his father, who had once swum in the Olympics, was the greatest. He was a willing collaborator in any enterprise his father conceived, the school dodge part of the ingenuity. "Some society turned Dad in in L.A. so we left California. Dad says, Sir, there's just as many showcases in Florida as California and better money in Miami Beach than L.A. any day."

"A bus takes three days," said Lee Ann. When Lee Ann was excited, the words tumbled headlong in breathless exposition. "And you sleep in your seat we crossed the Missus."

"Mississippi," said Denny, lifting Lee Ann's swim cap to speak into her good ear.

Lee Ann was hard-of-hearing in one ear—from a misjudged back flip, according to Denny, but I could only imagine the child's hearing damaged by a blow from Neptune's meaty palm.

Denny, who would be eight this month, could not read or write his name. One Sunday morning when Neptune was too hungover to escort the Waterbabies to the Sandcastle pool for training laps, they sneaked out of their room while their father slept it off. Denny knocked on my door; he had his Dad's *Miami Herald*—would I read the Sunday comics to them?

That next day I took the M bus to Miami to try to find some first readers to get the kids started, at least with the alphabet. (There were no bookstores in Miami Beach.) On an impulse I thought of checking out my old bookshop on the ragged downtown edge of Miami: when Just Books went bust, my lease was taken over by an enterprising chain of booksellers named for Thoreau's woodsy retreat at lakeside.

The neighborhood was Spanish now, a Latin enclave where the reading matter was *revistas* and *libros* to accommodate the shift in population. Still, there might be—and there was, but the store had changed hands again, I did not at first recognize the premises: the display window was painted out, and I stared at a solid blank square of glass painted black. The shingle sign was still in place, and now said ADULT BOOKS. A security door complete with speakeasy peephole barred the way to all but single-minded book collectors: *No Admittance Under Eighteen Years of Age.*

* * *

Eventually I found a set of Edgar Rice Burroughs at a garage sale in Coral Gables—not ideal for a beginning reader, but the books were illustrated, and I recalled reading *Tarzan* at The Children's Home, when I was Denny's age. (Another misbegotten impulse sent me on the excursion to Coral Gables—nothing to do with looking for books.)

By that time I was night man at the Ventura. When the Waterbabies were allowed up, or when Neptune was out, without having established Lights Out—he considered himself fair-minded, on his terms, and our unspoken truce now allowed me a certain leeway with his children, in the late hours—I read to the Waterbabies from *Tarzan and the Forbidden City*. They could now recite the alphabet together, a soprano plainsong of ABC's, Lee Ann rushing pell-mell through WXYZ in a flourish of accomplishment and an attempt to finish ahead of her brother.

After I read a sentence aloud from *Tarzan*, they would stare at the line of text and try to pick out the shorter words they were beginning to recognize—but mostly they were too caught up by the sound of reading to want to pause for lessons. When they were entranced by the story I would wait until a chapter ended before helping them to copy out and then pronounce—again, together—the small inventory of words they had begun to acquire. These words were written on hotel envelopes and scrap sheets from the wastebasket behind the front desk: Lee Ann, I noticed, saved each scrap of writing either of them accomplished, and carried the words away with her to their room.

I could not discern how Neptune felt about these night sessions with *Tarzan and the Forbidden City*. Since the night of Denny's brutal beating, and Neptune's truculent apology next day, the father and I had established touchy tentative diplomatic relations. It was possible he might be grateful for the baby-sitting service. He was their father, he did manifest concern for their welfare, perhaps not just an investor's concern. He may even have loved the kids, so strange are the ways of love. But who knows what a shark feels, or when it is likely to turn and attack?

"Are you really Mr. Frank," asked Lee Ann, "or really Mr. Buddy?"

"Just the night man, you can call me Buddy."

"You used to be Mr. Frank, Sir," said Denny.

"It changes. Like the weather."

"I like Buddy better," said Lee Ann. When she was excited she forgot to say Sir.

"What's in a name anyway? as the Bard once asked," my father wrote—"and why does everybody have to know it, then expect you to sign your John Hancock in blood? Your old Dad has been known over the years as Wadsworth, Wall, Walters, Waltham—and not one monicker with a Social Security number attached, or registered with the Department of Motor Vehicles. (I never had a driver's license in my life, and drove from one end of the country to the other. I was an ace at the steering wheel, if I do say so myself.) When I was younger, and full of the devil, the Abbots and Bakers and Coxes appealed to me, the ABC's so to speak, but as the years run by, you tend to pick a nom de plume nearer the end of the alphabet. There is a certain WASP dignity to the *Wa*'s that appeals to my northern nature (I never gave a darn for Florida or New Orleans, hotbeds of malaria and alligators)— *Wh* is another category I favor. Whitman, Whittier, especially the names of poets—tho I never carried it to extremes (not wanting to draw attention to myself), like Longfellow."

In case anybody should ask, I assumed the surname Willert, but nobody asked. Buddy Willert. The Willert I recalled from a mailbox nameplate in a tenement foyer.

The hours were from eight at night until eight in the morning, no night off. That way, for twelve hours of the twenty-four I knew who I was, and where.

2

THE SOLITARY PALM TREE in front of the Ventura Hotel had suffered damage in last year's hurricane and now was a terminal victim of lethal yellow: the few remaining fronds hung down in fatally folded wings, dried rust-brown beyond hope, ready to drop. Schine could never forget the rich cluster of coconuts and lush green of the great fan of leaves when he bought the place. Now the bare roughshod trunk curved upward, the insulting gesture of a middle finger thrust skyward, before the palm tapered off to its dead end.

"That tree will make a comeback someday," Schine was telling Cleveland, while pigeons cooed mockingly from the next-door Nemo Hotel's dovecote.

Cleveland's African mask registered no such hope.

Each morning before he relieved me at the front desk, Schine sent Cleveland out front with a garden hose to water the earth around the palm tree, even though the leaky clanking air-conditioning units along the hotel's stucco façade sprinkled the ground liberally enough throughout the night.

"What you think, Buddy?" he addressed me through the open lobby door. "You think a dose of fertilizer can pep up the roots?"

I shrugged a who-knows gesture, but my expression surely registered doubt. Schine turned back to Cleveland, he needed confirmation.

"When something die, Mr. Schine, it dead."

"Who says dead?" Schine was wearing his Japanese bathrobe with the yin-and-yang motif, and clogs—for the sun deck later. His nocturnal hairnet was still in place but he would remove it as soon as he stepped behind the front desk. "Never pull a postmortem on Mother Nature. Skeptics I got working for me, no confidence. My own father's father, back in the old country, left his cane stuck in the ground behind the house and went out one day and found leaves growing out the handle."

"Different over here," said Cleveland. "This here a disease, palm trees dying all over Dade County. You water this mother to doomsday you never see no leaves."

Schine reverently bent over the dessicated roots exposed above-ground, and declared, "You guys with no faith in Mother Nature, you're in for a terrific surprise."

Cleveland let the hose run, no surprise showing.

This was the ritual between eight and nine each morning, the vaudeville skit between Schine and Cleveland, and sometimes Schine invited me in as straight man. I didn't know how serious he was about the tree, but he kept it watered. This morning he personally shut off the garden hose and sent Cleveland over to the K&J Drugs for coffee and Danish. Then we tallied the night's telephone calls (two) and counted together the petty cash, enough to cover change from a hundred-dollar bill "some wise guy turns up with a hundred."

"You want coffee?" Schine asked. "I ordered a jumbo, and an extra Danish."

Why did I always decline? It was not coffee that kept me from sleeping, and the lobby was one place I could hear another voice besides my own nagging inside my head.

I turned over the duplicate key to the safe-deposit boxes, then went upstairs to the second-floor closet room that came with the job, to try to sleep.

The room had once been a linen closet: four walls with shelves to the ceiling, even over the door, and a small barred window at one end. The window grille had been put in by Schine when a guest skipped out by way of the linen-closet window owing the Ventura eighty-five dollars.

Of all the rooms of my life and travels, this was the most claustrophobic yet, including the bunk space I occupied aboard ship. Yet the space was suitable, possibly significant—all the rented spaces I had inhabited now shrunken to this closet: a monk's cell.

By some architectural oversight, the linen closet was the only room at the Ventura that gave onto a partial and oblique view of the ocean. Originally the hotel had been named the Oceanview, but Schine changed the name to Ventura when he bought the place. ("False illusions only aggravate your clientele.") He still nourished the hope that the Nemo next door, which blocked the view, would be condemmed and torn down so that the view of the ocean would be restored. He had no fear that another, higher, structure might go up in its place: South Beach had reached the saturation point in the construction of hotels. There were three hundred and sixty-five hotels from one end of the beach to the other: "You could sleep in a different hotel," said Schine, "with a different lady, every night of the year."

The window could be darkened by a set of yellowed Venetian blinds, the door had a lock on the inside. As Schine regularly asked, "What more could a single fellow ask for?"

I locked myself in—why? The lock was important only for the sound of tumbler falling and the safe-home sensation the falling tumbler gave, something like the satisfaction Schine must have felt when the grille was bolted to this window. Closed off was as important a feeling as escape, to or from Out There.

Then I bent apart two slats of the blinds and stared through the space between bars to a narrow slice of transparent blue-green sky-and-water deceptively blended at no defined horizon level. Across the roof of the Nemo Hotel was the open sea. The drill was to acknowledge the Atlantic mornings, reassured that the way was still open, the glorious waterway. Now was the time to play with names: Spain, Corsica, Rome. I was free for that moment by unreckonable dead reckoning to sail forth from the Dodge Island seaport straight through Government Cut to the open sea. The place was out there somewhere—Gibraltar, if you could see it.

"Hello, out there."

(I had taken to talking to myself. Once when I opened the slats I said aloud to all that infinity of sunshine: "I am bereaved of light," without knowing Cleveland was in the hall to hear me. "You-me both, man.")

The Ventura was located on the downbeat side of Lincoln Road at the unfashionable end of Miami Beach. The lower part of the island, where time and weather had worked their worst, was a Jewish-Cuban ghetto known as South Beach. In the grungy hotels with Art Deco façades lived side by side the Cuban stragglers from a captured island and the lost tribes of Israel driven from the lost boroughs of New York. Here was a kingdom of castaways, and I was one of them.

Beyond the leeward side of the Nemo, I could see the prow of the Corsair, the black-greased kitchen vents of the Comidas Latina diner, the roof of the Essex House and one corner of the Sandcastle, with the only private fresh-water swimming pool in the neighborhood.

Looking straight down, closer to home, was the foul alleyway between the viewless backsides of hotels, their garbage cans spilling over with grapefruit rinds, smashed glass and dead flowers. Yesterday there had been two discarded deck chairs from the Corsair down there, the canvas rotted through. Schine had recuperated the frames before the sanitation truck backed into the alley, he was planning to replace the canvas: "Give the *schwarz* something to do in his spare time." This morning there was a fat indolent rat strolling openly along the Surf Hotel's stucco wall, easing in and out of the shadows cast by ragged banana tress. The rodent paused in its promenade to stare back at me, teeth bared, then eased unhurriedly into a nesting place under a harvest of dead palm fronds. Grim portent: a loathsome way to start, or end, my day.

I brushed my teeth in the deep sink where Cleveland rinsed his mops, and spat toothpaste into the grey mop strands smelling of Clorox—also a convenient place to masturbate into. I kept a razor in the room, in case I wanted to shave off my beard, or needed to commit suicide.

The bed was a cot not unlike the cot at Penelope's: to reach my pillow I was obliged to duck low under the loose wire hangers strung overhead on cords. The hangers jangled together playing a different tune each morning, never a melody I wanted to hear.

The cot took the length of a wall of shelves loaded with laundry packs of pillowcases and stacks of bath towels and extra bedspreads with the chenille *V* for Ventura and boxes of miniature playhouse bars of Ivory soap. The shelf just above my pillow was lined with a row of Gideon Bibles, forty-two, as many as the number of rooms at the Ventura Hotel. Since the Bibles contained the Old and New testaments bound together, inappropriate (perhaps even offensive: "Never aggravate your clientele") in a hotel that catered to Jews, many of them Orthodox, and of no earthly use to Cubans who did not read English—Schine had never placed the Bibles in the rooms. Bibles stored in here with me reminded me of the dictionary locked in the Nurses Station at the Sans Souci, as if this were subversive reading. You could not dump Bibles into the cans in the alley. Besides, they were a gift from the Gideons, free, so here they were and would remain.

Beginning with well-meaning matrons at The Children's Home, and my father's frequent admonition ("Son, the miraculous convolutions of your ears as a tiny babe was proof positive to me that Our Heavenly Father is in charge of things and it behooves each and every citizen of His Holy Kingdom to read the official rules laid down in the Testaments"), people had urged me to attend to the Bible. Now, with a library of forty-two of them, I had begun to read from Genesis—first things first—right on. The proselytizing had borne fruit: I was not inspired by the reading, but the swing and force of the words distracted my troubled spirit from a density of sensations. Even the stream of begats I mostly skipped through had a certain monotonously hypnotic power, perhaps something of the effect of a Hindu prayer wheel. The reading was no easement of insomnia but it helped pass the first uptight moments alone in the room. I was looking forward to Exodus, and deliverance into the promised land of milk and honey.

Between the pages of the Bible I kept tens and twenties left from the eighty-a-week Schine counted out to me on Sunday mornings. The stash was perhaps a blasphemous afterthought. (And I expected to come to that part in the Bible about laying up treasure.) I could not spend the money and I did not know what else to do with it—no covetousness involved.

Also, my library contained seven volumes of Edgar Rice Burroughs, a gift for the Waterbabies I feared to bestow outright, since there was no way to predict what gesture of mine would enrage the barbarian in the father and destroy our uneasy truce.

When I had finished reading, and left a twenty to mark my place—"And Abraham sojourned in the Philistines' land many days"—I contemplated sleep as if working out a theorem of possibilities. I took off my shoes, but still lay in the clothes I had worn all night. Sleep was never an easy roll of the dice. Narcosis depended upon a successful supression of thought, a careless letting go, a dose of luck. If I did sleep, there was the predictable headache of reentry, or the heat-fever of anxiety awakening to nightmare. I was already wet with perspiration in the airless room, more than a little desperate about another day.

Think ye not along these lines.

Still lying prone, I began to remove my clothes: there was a way to do this without sitting up, without setting the hangers ajangle again—the horizontal yoga position in which Ginny used to undress. Think not of Ginny, either.

When my clothes were pushed to the bottom of the cot and I lay naked in the dark heat, I took from beneath my pillow the bottle of multivitamins Mr. Bloomfeld had recommended. Beware of vitamin C before bedtime, Bloomfeld warned, C is a stimulant. Later, then, I would eat an orange from the stock of oranges I kept on the shelf with the Gideon Bibles. The smell of orange peel in the room helped make an intolerable confinement tolerable. The only other nourishment in the room was the bright Kellogg's package of Corn Flakes I kept for the Waterbabies, who liked to eat them dry from the box, like Bobby in Belfast.

I took a multivitamin tablet swallowed down with yesterday's glass of water, the glass coated with chlorinated bubbles, without raising my head high enough to derange the tangle of hangers.

The way to sleep is. First close your eyes. Then wait.

Thwack, I heard, then *thwack* again. I heard a child cry out, and jerked upright in bed, the hangers jangling. It was Denny being beaten, I could hear the nearby smack of leather against bare flesh. Lee Ann always cried out for Denny's beatings, but when her father struck her she was frightened into a state of shock. That was when Denny wept.

The beating came to an abrupt merciful end when Joy-O the housemaid thumped on Neptune's door: "Stop that on them kids, you!" The beating stopped, but Lee Ann's subdued whimpering, like the cry of a small animal, went on. I put the pillow over my head to smother the planet's misery, no help. When I came up for a breath of dead air, I turned again to the place marked by a twenty in Genesis: "While the earth remaineth, seedtime and harvest, and cold and heat, and summer and winter, and day and night shall not cease."

It was poetry, after all.

3

IN AN ISLAND CITY where the police patrolled in unmarked cars it was asking for trouble to float around without credit cards, verifiable I.D. Walking openly and unidentified was as risky in Miami Beach as in Belfast. Employees of hotels and restaurants were obliged to register with the police department and carry the registration card at all times, to keep the city safe from crime-in-the-streets. A night job entitled me to a modicum of legitimacy—as for police registration, Schine did not want to know. I had a beard, I did not drive a car—all the more suspect. So I found safety in the lobby of the Ventura Hotel, and in the closet room attached. By working nights, every night, I kept myself out of the way of inquiry and search. All the I.D. I owned was a poet's false passport.

Occasionally I ran errands for the guests at night, as far as Washington Avenue to the K&J Drugs, open-all-nite. In daylight, especially during the sun-hammering heat of afternoon, I might have been anybody, or *personne,* and the danger diminished, but I seldom ventured into the world below the Nemo or beyond the K&J Drugs. Five blocks south of the Ventura was the end of the line, the falling-off place so full of dread for the sailors of the *Santa Maria.*

There was a municipal pier at land's end, but I had never walked that far—nor to the dog track at the end of the island, or to the one good restaurant gourmets from North Beach patronized when slumming south of Lincoln Road, Stone Crab Joe's. My customary tour was the circle from the Ventura to Ocean Front Park to the K&J to the Hebron Nursing Home and back to the Ventura.

Hotels much like the Ventura were wedged for waterfront exposure along Ocean Drive, like hotels crowded onto the narrow properties of a Monopoly board. The porches and terraces were populated with a clientele identical to ours. Old women carrying wicker baskets of knitting and cut pineapple hobbled toward the strand of sand with reed prayer rugs and plastic nose beaks against sunburn. On one portion of the strand a bald-domed little man in a sweatsuit, with a police whistle on a string around his neck, had set off a domain zoned by strips of Day-Glow ribbon—he was directing an exercise session. The elderly bathers—I recognized Miss Berg and Mr. Kolodin from the Ventura among them—took instruction from their miniature gym master. Some (Miss Berg) were too fleshy of arm and leg to function according to the little man's breathless directions; others, whose stringy musculature barely outlined the skeleton, resembled emaciated escapees of Treblinka and Dachau. One turtle-shaped old woman in baggy bathing costume lost her balance and rolled comically in the sand—no one laughed.

They strained on—*and-a-three, and-a-four, and-a-five*—bat-wing flaps of skin extended, stubborn arthritic elbows unbending, attempting to kick the stump pillars of legs. They were a pitiable suffering collection of survivors, the swollen lumps (possibly benign) and bright varicose tracks visible from this distance—a community of castaways marked by the I.D. of infirmity and age. When he had finished with them, the peppy drill instructor took up a collection in a baseball cap.

If the beach was not where I wanted to be, where did I want to be?

I walked against the tide of pedestrian traffic flowing seaward, headed inland to Washington Avenue and the K&J to buy vitamins. I took note of every signboard along my route: Hotel Rooms, Efficiencies, Pulmanettes—Summer Rates, $40 per week!—Special Prices for Veterans (veterans of what?)—façades with gaudy overwrought grillwork, the brothel lobbies painted in baby pink or flat mint green—or the quieter hotels, trying for discretion contrary to the prevailing mode, with beige foyers, a eucalyptus to replace the diseased and recently interred coconut palm, the distinction of a funeral parlor's subdued lighting.

On Espanola Way I came upon Uncle Sam's hard-used convertible bleached unbelievably by the sun, parked well out of sight of the Ventura. The canvas top was shot, chrome stripped away leaving only a line of rust spots like bullet holes along the edges of the car doors. The exposed seats with stringy insulation oozing from cigar-burn holes had accumulated a layer of palm fronds fallen from afflicted trees, roofing for the nests of rodents.

Uncle Sam was the punch-drunk ex-wrestler and self-acclaimed retired hood who had chosen to be my railbird companion at Calder that one memorable afternoon. We had been winners together, that once, but he would not remember. He did not recognize me: Buddy, the night man at the Ventura Hotel, where he was a guest renting by the month. Nor would he remember me as the psychiatric aide who attended him in the Recovery Room at the Sans Souci during a series of seventeen shock treatments meant to jolt him out of a diagnosed paranoia. When Sam could not remember a face or episode out of the past he shook his great shaggy head in sadness, gnawing his knuckles, tortured by a jumble of conflicting recollections.

Schine did not permit Uncle Sam to park his derelict vehicle in the vicinity of the Ventura, an eyesore that would only draw attention to the already disreputable sick palm. Though Sam's reflexes were shot, he could still drive the car to Calder when the tires were not flat and he had gas money. He sold neckties from a cigar box and walked the dogs of the rich on Pinetree Drive. When his Social Security ran out and he had lost heavily at the track, he sold a pint of blood to the Bayshore Blood Bank, but, as Sam himself admitted to me: "You can only s-s-sell so much b-b-blood."

Along Espanola Way the Strictly Kosher cafeterias shared the same block as Cafes Cubanos, and the conversations drifting past the open-air counters could be Yiddish or Spanish here where Jews and Cubans lived overlapping lives without a lingua franca in common. A block past the Hebrew Academy a Havana-style display of fruit and flowers spilled out of the bed of a pickup. I heard no English spoken until I approached Washington. Odd, I did not remember the TV repair shop on the ground floor of the Peter Pan Apartments: a series of television screens all illuminating the same shifty-eyed politico declaiming an empty speech without sound, the black-and-white images bloodless clones of the colored one. The repair shop was new. Landmarks mattered to me, this was my turf.

There were sidewalk tables under the K&J orange awning. I ordered an egg salad sandwich and a malted milk from a waitress with a badge on her breast that said, "Hi!" The first time I sat at one of her tables I said, "Hi," in response to the badge and the waitress replied, "God, am I sick of hearing that."

Next door at the Paris Cinema—all the more Parisian for a neon Eiffel Tower astride the marquee (the neon long extinguished)—the Reverend "John 3:16" Dexter was saying to a police officer, "Why me?" John 3:16 wore a cocoa-colored Cubaverra jacket, huaraches and a priest's white collar: he wanted to know why the policeman was posting condemn notices on the smashed ticket booth of the Paris Cinema. These were the very warnings Schine prayed would be slapped on the front door of the Nemo: UNSAFE BUILDING (*550 Occupants*) SHALL BE VACATED. (Put another way, just as biblical an injunction, the notice on the door to the auditorium read: SHALL NOT BE OCCUPIED.) The sign on the marquee said JESUS SAVES, all caps, and in lower case, *Solo Cristo Salva.* "John 3:16" Dexter had been running

revival meetings at the Paris Cinema after converting the film palace
into a skid row tabernacle. After a healing campaign with rumored
cures by laying-on-of-hands, the draw had become noticeable to the
authorities. The Reverend was a victim of his own success.

The other side of the Paris Cinema was Irish Mike's Blarney
Stone Bar & Grill, "Blarney Spoken Here."

On the strength of half a sandwich and most of a protein-rich
malted milk, I continued north on Washington, a deviation from the
circular. Then, operating by the numbers, responding to some gym
instructor's whistle or mere vagrant impulse, I boarded the M bus for
Miami. It was just that an M came along opportunely, its flexible
doors snapped open in front of me as if demanding decision. *Pourquoi
pas?* as the Poet used to say when I steered him out of the Dayroom in
his bathrobe.

A parking lot. Could I have been so disoriented, was this the bay side
of the Bacardi Tower? It might have happened overnight: a runaway
bulldozer had passed this way, a fire bomb had gone off and left a
stark inexplicable gap in the low skyline along Biscayne Bay.

There were ruts and craters in the hasty paving: the quarter acre
of bright baking autos was maintained by an indifferent car jockey in
T-shirt that said WHO SAYS? and a cap with crossed anchors on the
visor. I approached his sentry box, an upright coffin of unpainted
plywood, to ask what had become of the place and where in God's
name were the patients.

"What hospital?"

An insurance company had bought the space for an office
building. No less than a skyscraper of blue glass would soon arise on
the site: the property, right on the bay, was a gold mine. The parking
lot was only a transitional enterprise until the hard hats with a new
team of bulldozers came through.

"This town, Buddy, nothing stays still."

Everybody in town called me Buddy.

In front of the cool limestone library in Bayfront Park I caught the C
bus for Coral Gables. I knew better than to take that bus, to travel that
route, but the numbing Miami lassitude engenders such ventures. I
would have to learn to reason with the climate, to keep these impulses
toward total folly, reckless exploit, in check.

Coral Gables was unexpectedly intact, as if I expected more
sudden parking lots or blasted-out housing, the Belfast gaps. (Only

one residential home lay under a cloud, undergoing commercial fumigation: the dwelling was completely enshrouded in a sealed tent, toxic gas pumped into the enclosure to exterminate termites and other vermin; the tent bore warning pictographs of skull-and-crossbones, a television antenna pierced the top of the tent like an afterthought.) Otherwise I had penetrated sundrenched suburbia, shadowless and without alleys or bomb shelters. Apocalypse would have no dominion here.

But this was no easy neighborhood for a bearded stray shuffling down Miracle Mile. I was trying to locate a candy-box cottage behind a hedge of pink and white oleander on Carioca Drive. The neighborhood, according to the signs at street corners, was under the protective surveillance of radar patrols.

There it was—now to hover, now to watch.

I did not have to breach the surveillance warning at Carioca, I could linger behind a grandad banyan at the corner of Ponce de Leon Boulevard and still see the lacy dollhouse curtains at the window, but not into the candy box. Never mind, life in Coral Gables was free-form and openair that sparkling afternoon. A carefree postman in shorts and knee socks was delivering mail by motor scooter. A gentleman in swimming briefs was shaving his hedge into mushroom shapes. Both Valerie and Miss Pike (I could never believe in her as Evelyn) maneuvered up and down the cement-treaded driveway playfully washing the Oldsmobile together.

Miss Pike sudsed, and Valerie rinsed the blue-and-silver surface with a garden hose and a Sarasota sponge—the chariot gleamed. I could not hear their voices, but whatever comment Miss Pike had uttered, it was happy-making. Valerie grinned in the way of an adolescent as she hosed. Miss Pike's next statement made her laugh openly.

Miss Pike had thinned appreciably, her hair a shorter grey bristle cut she no longer bothered to tint. From a distance she was a handsomer woman than I remembered, on better terms with herself, from the comfortable way she sudsed and bantered. As for Valerie, she reflected the auto's glow but apparently glowed as well from within. She had acquired the therapeutic pounds Miss Pike had lost, the inverse of the other's shape-up: there was a new curve to her hips, her blouse bulged. Again contrary to Miss Pike's new look, Valerie had allowed her hair to grow longer.

I stayed until the final glimmering rinse. When Miss Pike shut off the water, then released the punch line to her comic monologue,

Valerie tossed her hair, threw her shoulders back and laughed into the light, teeth flashing for all the world, as if she would never stop. Still holding the hose, Valerie stooped and folded herself sharply at the waist, bent double by a long trill of laughter that carried all the way to my banyan.

She was squatting like a child doubled up against the car door, the nozzle from the hose dribbling out the last sparkling car-wash water, her head bent low and her hand on the car-door handle for support—as if she were in pain, but it was not pain.

4

I ENTERED my night's confinement. The little swing door admitted me into the hollowed-out niche behind the front desk: cash drawer and safe-deposit boxes under the counter; calendar on the wall compliments of Dade Trust, the moon-faced clock, switchboard with its pretzel-twist ice-cream parlor chair. At one end of the lobby an eerily lit aquarium glowed; the illuminated color-box TV screen competed at the other end. There was a water cooler at the foot of the lobby stairs: you could hear the cooler humming when the TV was turned off. The furniture was wicker, south-of-the-border, except for the sofa, upholstered in sea-green. I kept the ashtrays empty. The one piece of artwork (besides the calendar, portraying Dade Trust) was Kresge's painting of a palm tree that may have depicted the Ventura's own glorious coconut palm, when living, in a plastic bamboo frame. I was the night man, responsible for rooms 1–21 on the first floor, 22–42 on 2. Here was my Passive City restored.

Schine had brought back from Bob's Hobbyland another of those Chinese takeout containers of tropical fish—a couple, "boy and girl," he hoped—to add to the school of striped and spotted miniatures already in perpetual motion behind the glass panels of the lighted tank.

"Notice," he reminded me, "how I buy all the same size, otherwise the big fish eat the little fish."

This got a laugh from the Prophets on the aquarium side of the lobby. The Prophets were waiting for Schine to sit in on their review and analysis of the *World News Roundup*, just past.

Alone, Uncle Sam watched a gangster film on the TV screen. Sam was home early from dog-walking a set of Afghans in Sunny Isles; he had his shoe box of neckties on the sofa beside him. When he wasn't walking dogs, Sam sold neckties in the driveways of three-star hotels uptown; he collared unsuspecting guests stepping out of Le Barons and stuttered his stories of knowing gangland figures and heavyweight champs. ("I knew the g-g-guy that thought up the name for Joe L-L-Louis, the Brown B-B-Bomber, but I forget the name of the g-g-guy.") The police allowed Sam to operate because of his quaint history and because he was indeed connected to the Mob, their punch-drunk mascot. He could peddle his ties as a cover for panhandling as long as he didn't go overboard, stumble into the North Beach lobbies, or hassle the same guest twice; as long as he parked his derelict automobile out of sight.

The wicker furniture on Sam's side of the lobby was empty but the sagging wicker shapes had taken on the forms of familiar occupants—though these guests were now outside sitting in beach chairs under the *Vacancy* sign beside the afflicted palm tree, in two separate circles. The Jewish women were talking son-in-law/ daughter-in-law; the Cuban women, chattering in Spanish, were perhaps voicing the same praises and complaints.

The Prophets, Jews—the Cuban men were still out at this hour, at card games in the backs of Latin cafés, or at the dog track—dissected world events from the *Miami Herald* and Channel 5, talked money, kibitzed one another's lives.

"Notice," said Schine, "how they kept it under wraps till the papers found out."

"Secret of the confessional," said Kolodin. The talk was about some Vatican scandal

"Take Britain. The Tories know how to keep their mouth shut, they passed a secrecy act that keeps the papers out of it."

"Except with the royal family, then you get leaks."

"B-B-Bunk," said Uncle Sam, but he was talking to himself, to the television screen.

"I read in the *Miami Herald* where L. A. has got maybe two years at the outside before the whole city topples into the San Andreas fault."

"I wouldn't live out there, you couldn't pay me."

"You'd only have to live out there two years."

"You read about that old-time Gold Rush character that had a cabin on a mountaintop out there, in a national park out there, nobody could even get to it except this Gold Rush geezer, but the Forestry Service spotted the cabin from a helicopter and sent the Feds out. They had to go on a regular scouting party to even find the place, it's all wildness out there. When they found him, they told the old boy this was a national park and he was trespassing on government property or something. Two days later the old Gold Rush guy decides there's no place left to escape the bastards and blows himself and his cabin sky high with dynamite."

"It's all politics."

"It's all money. If Howard Hughes built himself a cabin in some national park you think the government's going to evict him?"

"Here's what happens day in and day out," said Bloomfeld, retired from the cut-flower business. "They fade, only on display twenty-four hours and the color goes—it's the fluorescence in your fluorescent lights, I found out—lose their color, lose smell, they depetal all around the edges."

"You talking about flowers or women?" asked Marcus, and got a laugh.

"I'm allergic to the pollen in them."

"The women or the flowers?" asked Bloomfeld, and got a laugh.

"You're retired," Schine reminded Bloomfeld, "you can sleep easy."

"With the President we're stuck with, who can sleep?"

"They're sleeping in L.A. wondering if they're going to drop into some black hole before morning."

"Ninety-five percent of politics is pure bluff."

"So's show business."

"Giants of industry, same thing. The only thing giant about them is the salaries."

"Take show business. Look at these Punk singers, will you? Wiggle his crotch and hump a guitar and they call that music."

"You lose your gimmick," said Shine, "your name is mud." He glanced at the entranced ex-wrestler watching bloody mayhem on TV, Uncle Sam could not hear. (He had worn an American flag in the ring until the American Legion took him to court over the costume.) "Whether it's show business or sports or what-have-you."

The Waterbabies were creeping down the lobby stairs. Lee Ann tugged at one of Denny's fingers: they were dreamy-eyed with imagined pleasure but alert to threat, suspicious of presences. Denny checked out the faces of the Prophets, Uncle Sam (his lower lip hanging in stunned wonderment at the TV film), then glanced quickly at me before allowing Lee Ann to tug him down the next step.

"That's what I'm saying, it's all the same ball game."

"Unless you're Muhammad Ali with an army of Muslims behind you."

"What was his gimmick, when he started out?"

"Poetry. He wrote poems. 'Sing like a bird, sting like a bee.' "

" 'Fly like a bird.' "

"Fly, sing, something. Anyway, he wrote poems about his opponent before he went in the ring and beat the guy's brains out."

The Prophets looked up at Sam, whose brain had been damaged by beatings, aware that he might have heard—but Sam was absorbed by the criminal exploit on the tube. The Waterbabies paused in their descent: they thought the Prophets might have been looking at them.

"You should make what sports figures make. That's where the money goes."

"Yeah but consider the working life in sports. They only make it big when they're young, youth is all they got to offer."

"Here today," said Marcus, "gone tomorrow."

"But while they're here today they make a bundle."

Denny was barefoot and Lee Ann in her bunny slippers—both wore pyjama bottoms only in the heat, the lobby was not air-conditioned. They were treading lightly, thinking themselves small-invisible or out of range. They did not know what instructions their father had left at the desk. I made an O with my thumb and forefinger to put them at their ease, to let them know it was O.K. But they stiffened, and for a moment held back.

"Change the water, rearrange the oldies in the middle so the customer don't notice, and what have you got? Faded flowers."

"Forget the headaches you had, you're retired for crying out loud. You can sleep easy."

"You hear where this guy in Newark, New Jersey, recovered his sight back after his baby daughter hit him over the head with her plastic bucket?"

Earlier, Neptune has swaggered forth in his pressed khakis and polo shirt without the back brace, no instructions. I had a certain leeway when Neptune failed to set strict limits. I could always say I invited them down to the lobby to watch TV when the air-conditioner in their room was temporarily out of order.

But television did not for the moment catch their gaze. After one critical glance, Denny wrote off Uncle Sam's gangland saga. Lee Ann did not even glance, the two children stared straight ahead. They were drawn to the subaqueous light that spookily illuminated the tropical fish. Slowly they lowered themselves to a seat on the stairs, one step apart, Lee Ann seated directly behind Denny with her hand touching his elbow. She touched him often like that, and he often whispered secret replies to questions into her good ear. When they walked together they walked close unless Neptune came between them. Their eyes were fixed on Schine's fish tank watching the slim tropical species dart nervous trajectories behind glass.

"What's retired got to do with it? My heart still bleeds for the retail trade. How can you forget flowers down here where it's so lush? Flowers grow out of the pavement down here, who buys posies in this jungle? You read where this water hyacinth is growing so overabundant it's choking the canals, it's cutting off South Florida's water system."

"In L.A. you get swallowed by the San Andreas fault, so what's a few water lilies?"

"You read where they found another skull in the Everglades?"

On the television screen a mobster held a shotgun to another mobster's ear, Sam studying the scene with his thick lip hanging ever lower.

"How about this Punk rock-and-roller that electrocuted himself onstage with his own guitar at Dinner Key Auditorium?"

"You guys down here make me laugh. We got crime in the streets in Detroit that makes Miami look like Disneyland."

The shotgun on TV went off with shattering effect, as if the victim's blood and brains would splatter forth from the multicolored screen. Only the Waterbabies, for an instant, were startled out of their underwater revery by the murderous blast. Immediately they were back dream-gazing again.

"On TV they announced they're going to recall a whole series of defective pacemakers. Half the things malfunction and people's hearts are stopping left and right."

Abrahams put a pleading finger to his lips warning Stein off the subject. His wife was sitting just outside with the lobby door open, with a pacemaker.

"No mechanical devices for me," said Schine, whose pride was his health and rich tan, tiny feet, thick hair and a regular sex life. "They offer me some spare part off a dead person, with my dying breath I turn thumbs down."

"If you're missing a kidney you'd be only too happy to get one that works."

The mobster with the shotgun was making his escape via urban rooftops, taking the jumps from roof to roof, then through a shadowy jungle of TV antennas and clotheslines, the sirens in the street urging him on.

"No spare parts from fresh corpses, thanks all the same," said Schine, resigned.

"B-B-Bunk," said Uncle Sam, not to Schine but to the shotgun killer's gymnastic getaway across tenement rooftops. Sam's face flushed red with outrage over the cavalier way the networks portrayed the brotherhood. "That's stuff's b-b-bunk."

"Take dialysis, where they recycle your blood when your kidneys fail, I knew a guy went through it, and he didn't have Major Medical. You sit there and get sick all over yourself, he was waiting for a kidney donation. His wife went to work to pay for his dialysis and he's sitting on the machine one day and they pumped the wrong way or something and he was dead before they could get him on the table. Thanks but no thanks."

Mrs. Tannenbaum came in slapping at her bare arms: "That spray plane must be late." Mrs. Tannenbaum led the exodus from the front porch. Summer nights the plane from Opa-Locka airport flew low over Miami Beach spraying insecticide. "Mosquitos are eating me alive."

Mr. Tannenbaum got up from the assembly of the Prophets to walk his wife's way to their room. His wife had thrown out no signal, the Tannenbaums had been married forty-seven years.

Then Mrs. Gold came in. That was when I was to fetch the bottle of nose drops from the refrigerator in the basement. I ministered to Mrs. Gold—mornings, first thing, and at night before she retired—in front of her door in the corridor just off the lobby: drip-drip-drip, three drops per nostril, her head tilted back as far as arthritis allowed. Mrs. Gold was a widow in her eighties. I never administered the drip-drip-drip into her deep black nostrils without thinking this could be the Poet's mother, destination Miami when last seen.

The separate circles were broken now, as the women moved through the lobby first. A husband fell silent sometimes in the middle of a conjecture to join his partner-of-a-lifetime, to help her up the stairs or follow in her weary wake, the summons unspoken. The fish seemed to spin slower figure-eights, wriggling in and out the hollows of their scaled-down plastic hotel. The Spanish women, a heartier breed (or uncertain of their mates)—more resistant to fatigue or maybe immune to insect life—lingered late under the skeletal palm continuing without letup the yip and chirp of puppies and birds.

Schine was the last of the Prophets to leave the lobby: he enjoyed an audience, however thinned out, for his departure. He waved farewell to the world at large and blew a kiss to the ladies on the front porch, reminded me about lighting the *Vacancy* sign and turning down the sound on the TV at midnight. He scored a laugh with the departing Prophets from his farewell remark to me: "Watch the fishes and let me know if they make babies." He stroked the heads of the Waterbabies as he passed them on the stairs. No one climbing to 2 could resist that gesture, with two dreamy miniature Vikings in his path. They were a presence, a sustained miracle.

To myself I said, I never read the Poet's poems, I haven't seen the Waterbabies swim.

Lovelorn Miss Berg timed her bow-out to Mr. Bloomfeld's. She maneuvered her way to the widower's side in the hope of a corridor tête-à-tête, but Bloomfeld nimbly outpaced her, munching his bed-time apple en route. Bloomfeld stroked the two golden heads as he headed upstairs; Miss Berg did the same, as did the Tannenbaums, all neatly avoiding Denny's bare toes and Lee Ann's bunny slippers. Uncle Sam sat immobile on the sofa staring into the disappointing TV screen now animated with ads—the shotgun assassin some minutes ago dispatched to Sing Sing.

"Apple a day," Miss Berg called after Bloomfeld, "that's not what a man like you needs."

Bloomfeld ignored the diagnosis and grunted goodnight without turning to confront the woman who would answer his needs if only he would let her.

No restriction on bathrobes in the lobby of the Ventura. Sam wore his show-business robe, the one he wore when he was a wrestler on TV, styled in a medley of stars and stripes the American Legion condemned as defacement of our nation's flag. ("They got out an inj-j-junction against me and enj-j-joined me not to wear it on T-T-TV.") Now, as he strained upward from the sunken place on the sofa, the flag unfurled around him. Like the Waterbabies, Sam was wearing pyjama bottoms only, and where the robe fell open his chest had turned to women's breasts, the nipples buried in white fuzz. The wrestler's former heft now hung as loose as his banner. He stood unsteadily working himself against gravity, then ape-lunged forward in his ratty slippers. He was always about to trip on himself, yet some inner gyroscope kept him in narrow balance, kept him from crashing to the floor. He was already holding out the key to me even before he reached the desk. You would think he had come for his drug and I the dealer, with his fix at hand—but he only wanted to see and inspect his weapon.

Still playing invisible, the Waterbabies moved softly from the stairs to the now-empty sofa and settled into the hollow Sam had left. They sat close, despite the heat, Lee Ann's furry-faced slippers sticking straight out, Denny on the sea-green edge—both sat erect, the way they had been trained to sit and stand. The flash and jangle of pre-program television advertising challenged the hollow silence of the lobby but did not engage the Waterbabies. They were waiting for me to finish with Sam.

I unlocked the metal panel with both our keys, brought forth Uncle Sam's safe-deposit box and set it upon the front desk for Sam's scrutiny.

"Yeah," said Sam reverently.

I did not like for the Waterbabies to observe the pistol as Sam fondled it, but they had already been witness to the ritual cleaning of the .38 with their father standing by, in approval—the pistol was part of the Real World he intended them to know early. They had watched studiously enough, but had taken no further interest in the deadly looking jewel Sam kept in an oil-stained linen sack.

Uncle Sam took up the blue metal .38 with something like surprise, as if he had just come across a gunsmith's bargain and was eager to buy. Was this a relic from Sam's gangland past? He claimed to have been in the rackets before the rackets packed up and went to Vegas. Hard to believe this ruin had ever been a professional hood and daring driver of getaway cars. I had long meant to ask Sam if he had ever heard of a certain Seymour Rappaport, but questions that taxed Sam's aberrant memory were torture to his twisted nerves.

There was an odd pipelike extension in the sack with the pistol, and only when Sam attached the blunt-capped accessory to the barrel (this he accomplished adroitly, a single act of assured coordination) did he recognize the beauty at last, and nod in passionate approval.

I was relieved when he swiftly detached the silencer and put the two murderous parts into the sack. He stood by in grim certainty to see that I deposited the sack in the metal box and locked the box away with the twin keys, then returned his key to him. Then I took *Tarzan and the Forbidden City* from behind the stack of Greater Miami telephone directories.

No one was watching television, so I turned off the set. Sam lurched away from the desk for the reading: he sat on my right, Lee Ann and Denny wedged together on my left, just room for the four of us on the lobby sofa. Sometimes the Moonlighter would join our quaint seminar, but often he worked nights, or was at the dog track.

Lee Ann innocently asked Uncle Sam if he could read.

"S-S-Sure I can read," said Sam, but he shook his great buffalo's head no when she tried to hand him the book.

Before I read to the end of that chapter, I heard the Moonlighter come by. I knew who it was when the trio of Cuban women began to twitter at a higher pitch. He was witty with the ladies and never failed to pass their way without a dash of Spanish banter. He was as popular with the Cuban matrons as Schine was with the Prophets' wives.

He entered the limelight paunch first, a balding silver-haired Sancho Panza with a carefully tailored mustache stained slightly by the pipe in his teeth. He worked all hours, any hours, with his Mr. Fixit screwdriver and a Swiss Army knife. He preferred to tender his service at night, after the dog track closed down, but first a courtesy stop at the Ventura to chat up the ladies and check in with the Night Man. He did not live at the hotel. He had a telephone number on his bilingual business card, but no known address: his residence, he declared, was Cinco-de-Mayo in Havana and he was going home, first big *quinella* he won.

He flashed his winnings to the Cuban ladies in their canvas chairs, while we students of Tarzan watched through the open window. Then he trotted across the wiry grass lawn to the base of Schine's diseased palm tree and switched on the spotlight mounted there. He pointed out the shape of the tree with his pipestem and made what could only have been a suggestive comment in Spanish, to put the ladies in stitches.

I had stopped reading. The Waterbabies were alert to his presence, and even Uncle Sam—with what passed for a smile on his hung-open mouth—was waiting for the Moonlighter to join us. The Moonlighter intended to improve his English, for obscure reasons of his own: *¿por qué aprender inglés?* he was constantly asked, if he was going back to Cuba? He winked without answering. He called our little gatherings Night School and considered himself a student enrolled. Lee Ann called him Mr. Moon-sir, Denny called him Sir.

In a moment the Moonlighter was mamboing across the lobby tiles to the water cooler humming off beat the tune to "What Have I

Got To Lose?" The twenties between his fingers made a Spanish fan to accompany his dancing jog-trot.

"*Dolares para Fidel,*" sang the Moonlighter as he stuffed his winnings between the pages of the program from the dog track. In English he informed us: "Dollars to spend on communistic womens on Cinco-de-Mayo. Is only money."

He paused to take his ritual evening sip from the fountain spout, and to make his ritual comment: "Too cold. Freeze your bowls, this water here." I did not know if he meant to say balls or bowels.

Then he cha-chaed over to the aquarium and tapped the glass front of the tank with the Mr. Fixit he carried in his Cubaverra pocket. He was counting the fish in Spanish with every tap.

"There's two new ones, Sir," said Denny.

Uncle Sam nodded confirmation, as if he had known.

"Boy and girl," said Lee Ann. "Just like me and Denny."

"Boy-girl, girl-boy, that what makes the whirl go round." The Moonlighter did a pirouette with the screwdriver touching his bald spot.

Then he relit his pipe, put on glasses, turned immediately scholarly as he took the Tarzan book from me. I slid a wicker chair close to our crowded couch, but the Moonlighter preferred to remain standing when he declaimed. He boomed out the first lines of text like a blunderbuss, then stopped and looked at me over his glasses: "What to hell *gal-vantized* mean?"

I accepted the book from him and read the passage aloud: " 'Instantly Tarzan was galvanized into alert watchfulness.' " I paused, then repeated the word *galvanized*.

"Galvanized, Sir," said Denny—he had raised his hand as if he were in school. "That's to coat with metal. You do it with electricity, Dad says."

"Electric, fine," said the Moonlighter. "But what means it here?"

"It means," I began, then wondered, fumbling, dreaming up a meaning. "Here, well. That Tarzan was watchful. As if he were charged, charged up, by electric current."

The Moonlighter blew his lips into a ripple of disbelief, and Uncle Sam did something scornful with his lips as well. We sat, a quartet puzzled by what *galvanized* meant in this instance.

"I read them books in Espanish, I was a kid like them. I never read no electric current out there, in the jungle."

"Not actual current. It's just a figure. Of speech." The

classroom waited with visible impatience. "It's *like* current. Running through Tarzan, and makes him watchful. And alert. They may have translated *galvanized* differently. In your Spanish version."

"What translate? It was Espanish book, this here the American translate."

I allowed the statement to stand, my role as teacher was shaky enough. I handed the book back to the Moonlighter.

"What to hell." The Moonlighter approved of Tarzan all the same. He summed up, to me, to the Waterbabies, to Uncle Sam: "Tarzan, he's alone to his self. He does all, on his own. Animals, fishes, he knows their talk. I go for Tarzan, is full of actions and keeps alive. Nobody to boss him. Only Tarzan is the free man in the jungle, · like me."

With the book sprawled open in his palm like a revivalist's Bible, the Moonlighter began to pace the lobby from the water cooler to the aquarium to the dead television set, reading aloud as he stalked, dodging the wicker chairs in his path without looking up from the page, pausing, bowing for punctuation marks, performing. His delivery was deadpan monotonous but effective for the thespian gestures and sepulchral resonance. Uncle Sam listened with troubled intensity, the Waterbabies were galvanized into alert watchfulness.

" 'For-it-is-only-by-eternal-vigilance-that-a-denizen-of-the-jungle-survives-the-constant-threat-of-the-greatest-of-all-killers—' " and here the Moonlighter stiffened to a halt, drew on his pipe and exploded with the word " 'Man!' " enveloped in smoke and projected with sound and fury.

Sam was shaken by a spasm, and the Waterbabies applauded.

It was painful for Uncle Sam to mount stairs, painful to watch. (Schine had offered him a vacancy on the ground floor but Sam said nothing doing: "There's p-p-people on the street." Sam sometimes wore a shoulder holster under his cabana jacket, but dared not carry his pistol in it: too often he was stopped by the police for selling neckties out-of-bounds; he had no gun permit, he had no cartridges—he stuffed the holster with toilet paper to make it bulge.) Sam still believed there was a contract out on him, he was on some antiquated hit list. From his heavily shaded window on 2 he could mount effective surveillance—ground floor was vulnerable to ambush.

Lee Ann, on the staircase beside him, clung to one of his thick fingers. Denny positioned himself close behind Uncle Sam as if to support the great uncoordinated bulk of the man, a weight that would have crushed Denny flat if Sam ever lost his balance and crashed backwards.

The Moonlighter had left after completing a chapter of Tarzan to repair the bread toaster at the Tinkerbell Deli on Collins Avenue. "Stuff mechanical that break down after midnight, the people need a fix right now or they don't sleep."

People don't sleep anyway.

I was alone in the lobby and could stretch out on the sea-green sofa when I wanted to—if I slept lightly, Schine didn't care, as long as I was instantly available when a check-in drifted in. But the night people wandering into the Ventura that late were not looking for a hotel room. The Prophets and their wives and the Cubans, all, even the sleepless and sickly of the lost tribes, had long retired to their rooms. Neptune was the last in, walking the self-consciously uptight way of a drunk who knew he was drunk but did not want it known.

"Kids bother anybody, they better not?"

"They're asleep. Their air-conditioner went out, the Moon-lighter. Fixed it." I told him I asked the kids down to the lobby while the air-conditioner was being fixed.

"O.K. On your say-so. You're O.K. Buddy you was in the Service, like me. We was both in the Service not like a lot of these yellow bastards. O.K. if they stay up, on your say-so. If they don't bother anybody."

"They never bother. Anybody."

"They better not."

He intended to linger and become friendly; he needed a friend at this hour, in his state. He had the glazed look of a patient at the Sans Souci on heavy sedation, or after shock. In some odd way, under the influence, he came to resemble Uncle Sam. But the little eyes blinked with suspicion, and it occurred to him he was saying O.K. too often. With drunken perception he recognized that his speech was slurred and his cool-sober cover would be blown if he kept talking. He walked off stiffly and with a seriously considered military step marched upstairs.

I was grateful he was as sloshed as he was. He would fall asleep in his clothes without jolting the kids awake—the hard time for them would be postponed.

The walls closed in as I shut off the floor lamps. I kept only the light on behind the front desk. That, and the green underwater lights of the aquarium—with the neon red *Vacancy* sign reflected at the window—cast the lobby in funereal afterglow. Now there were merely the shapes of the wicker chairs sagging from occupants long gone to bed, but the after-image of the guests sitting in their chairs would linger until my eyes adjusted to the lowered light. The television was off, the switchboard silent (no one ever called in or out after midnight) and I was lying on the sofa with a blanket over my legs—the ocean breeze turned cool in the small hours. The lobby door was closed but the wind blew through the louvered windows, the only sound except for the motor hum of the lobby water cooler in counterpoint to the gargling sound of the water filter in the fish tank.

Occasionally a squad car rounded the corner at the Nemo, and I recalled the surveillance helicopters in Belfast. I heard a bicycle come by, a bucket rattling against its fender, and knew the Shipwreck would be coming in.

There he was, trying to open the door the wrong way—he finally got it right.

"I like a place that turns their TV off. I give up drinking on account of bars today."

The Shipwreck and I no longer drank. I had given up drinking, I drank orange juice and malted milks only. I had given up drinking not because of bars today, because of—lassitude.

He called himself the Shipwreck, the only living survivor of the 1935 hurricane that wiped out the CCC camp of railroad workers on Esmeralda Key, "building Flagler's railroad for him. When you've walked off from being through a tidal wave, Son, nothing can wreck you no more." He did resemble a derelict vessel, his ribs showing through a T-shirt like ship's spars, washed ashore at Miami Beach.

He once pulled the T-shirt out of his belt to exhibit a tanned abdomen crisscrossed with hyphenated surgical scars from probe-surgery operations. He wrote letters to Presidents of the Unites States protesting their negligence of down-and-outers like himself, and if he was not satisfied with the official answer—or received no answer at all ("your Republicans got the piss-poorest record in that respect")—he swallowed pieces of broken glass, even a fishhook once, then called the police and the *Miami Herald.*

"If I write the President it ain't just looking to get gravy for yours truly, I write trying to get a flyspeck of attention paid to all us old drifters washed up in the U.S.A. and left behind in the doldrums like me. I'm just a number to them. They don't want to know your name, but they know mine. It aggravates the hell out of them I don't drop dead from what I swallow to get their attention. They assign me a different case worker every swallow and a new suspicious-person number every letter I write, trying to bury me in case numbers and welfare files, but I ain't dead yet."

He was in another mood tonight, devitalized—all the more bloodless in the subdued light—though he had thought to bring a grouper to me in his plastic fishing bucket. He fished nights off the Municipal Pier, transporting his rod and tackle attached to a bicycle that carried him to and from the run-down Checkerboard Apartments on Commerce.

"You still on the graveyard shift, Son?"

"I like nights, it's cooler. An easier time."

"Easier time to be alive? You're working the deadest hotel on the Beach, you know that? But I'm like you, I like it quiet—gets you used to the quiet coming, the long quiet without no TV. You in the Service? Me too, the First War, and that'll get us a flag on our coffin compliments of the VA. Don't go under without your flag, it's coming to you. You like fish? This here's for you, fresh caught, looks long dead like me but that's fish nature, nothing looks deader than a dead fish. I been through a tidal wave and safe out the other end so I don't get rattled by dying no more, death—I got her number. Just like the government got mine. Death is just past time that gets used up and you with it, don't let it rattle you. Keep remembering. I remember when coconuts was to be found in every Miami Beach gutter and you got fifty bucks idemnity from the City if one conked you on the head. Hungry, you could always crack open a coconut and eat and drink of it, that's when you were in the land of milk and honey. Remember oyster crackers? You used to put them in a bowl of soup, but no more. I wrote the President about what happened to the palm trees and you think he'd have the decency to answer but what does that sonofabitch care about coconuts."

Before he rode off on his rusty bike with fishing tackle attached, he left the grouper with me, no polite way for me to refuse. I wrapped the fish in pages of the *Miami Herald* and went down to the refrigerator in the basement. There was barely room for it among the cartons of milk, yogurt, Saran-wrapped slices of kosher rye, hard-boiled eggs of questionable antiquity. The ice machine made ice cubes on a rod. The Waterbabies like to suck on the cubes: there were holes in the ice cubes, and the Waterbabies wore an ice cube each on their fingers, like rings. I wondered if the Moonlighter might like fish.

When I got back a young man in woebegone jeans and Boy Scout shirt was drinking from the water cooler. The boy had stopped by before, I remembered his tangled shoulder-length hair and haunted look, a fellow insomniac. I thought of him as the Beachcomber.

Young men did come into the lobby at night as well as the stray ancients, but the young wanted mainly to borrow enough cash for a few beers or find out if they could bring a girl here later—if they found a girl, and she had no place of her own—or wanted to know if there was a bar open in the vicinity. I warned them off the all-night strip joints where the B-girls worked the clients for overpriced cocktails and the minimum and cover were already more than they bargained for. Gays sometimes failed to find a partner at the Gaytime before it closed at two, and came in to talk and to find out if I were gay. The question was never put to me explicitly, but the suggestion was there that, even if I were straight, I take a walk on the wild side. No, but no hard feelings, and sometimes a gay would stay on, easy, and talk to me anyway.

The first time the Beachcomber came in I thought he might be gay, his manner difficult to assess: a shy delicacy, and the way he hunched his head down into his shoulders. He may have been gay, but he was not looking for a partner. He never told me his name—the name Beachcomber came to me because he said he slept outdoors on the beach.

"Doesn't it get cold. At night?"

"I got an old Army blanket and I sleep in the lifeguard shack that breaks the wind and the police don't see you."

He asked me if I had a Marlboro by any chance. I told him I didn't smoke, but I remembered a cigar Uncle Sam had given me, given to him by a godfather staying at the Roney Plaza. I went behind the desk and passed the cigar to the Beachcomber, then I lit it for him. It was a prime Havana and the Beachcomber smoked it hunching his head down, eyes moving swiftly side to side as if fearful of being caught smoking a good cigar. He went to the louvered window and looked out into the street to make certain nobody was there, listening, then confided in me, both of us standing at the front desk now.

"What's going down somebody asked me yesterday, I know what's going down but I ain't telling. I got a star book at the lifeguard shack full of all the possible constellations of what's going down." The cigar did not overcome the acrid sweat smell of the Beachcomber's clothes, the jeans he slept in and the Boy Scout shirt with the merit badges on one sleeve. "I knew this girl on a bus for Denver—but hers was a different stop from mine. We was talking on the bus, I told her what's going down but she fell asleep on me. Except for getting off at different stops we were like real close before Denver. I should've got off when she did. I still got some shrapnel from Cuba in my skull." He tapped the side of his head with the flat of his hand as if he could knock the shrapnel out through his ear, like water, the cigar smoke trailing from his nostrils. "First I was in the regular Army, next thing I knew I was out, they call it a Section Eight. I was the only American at the Bay of Pigs, they didn't want Americans on account of the publicity, the CIA let us down. All Cubans, and only me. I would've been the Unknown Soldier of the Cuban invasion if I died there. I could've gone down in history, if we won. To cover my tracks after the CIA let us down I had to ditch my uniform off the Huey Long Bridge in New Orleans. You can't get a job with a Section Eight. But I know what's going down, I know where you can get twenty for a pint of blood, I make out O.K. except to run out of cigarettes."

He said he ate a lot of oranges—they were cheap—for vitamin C, and I said so did I. I gave him five singles I happened to have in my pocket, for cigarette money. I could have gone up to my room for more cash, from the Bible, but I did not like to leave him alone in the lobby: he flicked the cigar ash with abandon and might burn the place down, he kept going to the window to check for possible pursuit.

Tarzan and the Forbidden City was lying on the coffee table where the Moonlighter had left it, the place marked with his program from the Miami Beach Kennel Club. The Beachcomber picked up the book, and held it close to his pimpled face.

"I know this here book, I read this book when I was little. This is the one where Tarzan finds out where the elephants go to die."

I did not know the ending, we had not yet read that far.

"Listen, do me a favor, don't tell anybody I was in here. I could go down in history if I can keep my mouth shut. I think I know who killed Kennedy."

I thought of giving him the Shipwreck's fish—but what would he have done with an uncooked fish? When he went out he looked both ways on Avocado Court, head down, his cigar going strong, then gently closed the lobby door behind him. The smell lingered, and the smell of the Shipwreck's fish, but tomorrow morning Cleveland would wipe away all trace of the night's passage with a mop dipped in Mr. Clean.

5

SCHINE AND CLEVELAND were going through their morning vaudeville routine, but this morning they were joined by a professional arboriculturist who had taken over care and treatment. The tree surgeon wore a blue uniform the sky-blue shade of the denim aprons worn by the porters at the Lutetia—a luxuriant royal palm was embroidered on his pocket. He had drilled a hole in the moribund trunk and was now injecting the pulpy aperture with something he called oxytetracycline from a king-size syringe. "You still got a crown," the pro pointed out, meaning the dead growth that still clung to the top of the tree. "And where you got a crown there's a chance of remission."

"See what I tell you," Schine told Cleveland.

Cleveland stood by with the garden hose, unconvinced.

"That's the good news," said the tree surgeon. "The bad news is the injections don't always take. If your tree turns black, it's curtains." Schine shrugged and Cleveland smiled faintly. "What we do, we guarantee if the tree turns black and the crown goes, we substitute you a Malayan dwarf palm, no charge, absolutely guaranteed to resist lethal yellow."

"No dwarfs," said Schine. "That's what the Nemo went for. I want a real palm tree with coconuts back the way it was."

"Where there's a crown there's a chance."

"That's what I keep telling this wise guy," Schine told the pro, referring to Cleveland.

Cleveland watered the exposed roots and kept his smile to himself.

At the same time the tree was receiving its injection, I ministered to Mrs. Gold at the door to her room, three drops drip-drip-drip into each black nostril, her sad strained face lifted in hope to mine. She held her breath during the treatment, then sniffed deeply of the droplets. Each time I administered the drops I thought I might faint from the dizzying close focus. When we finished our ritual, Mrs. Gold whispered a secret request in broken English: would I have a prescription filled for her at the K&J—she put no trust in the *schwarz* for medical errands.

The Waterbabies had gone out earlier for practice laps at the

Sandcastle pool down the block. They carried towels and swim gear in a sausage roll of anorak, goggles dangling from their wrists. Neptune with his back brace showing, his swim trainer's visor shading the bull brow, hustled his charges through the lobby at a pace that allowed for no greetings. He was up early for a change. The kids were in their swim briefs, Denny barefoot, Lee Ann wearing canvas slippers with rubber soles, their slim torsos adult-formed in scaled-down child proportions: they walked stiffly on either side of their trainer-father, already into their workaday personas, faces masked with inner concentration. Despite the bruised moons beneath their eyes, they were radiant with the morning. I saw or thought I saw aureoles around their heads instead of swimming caps. As they passed the desk, only Lee Ann broke through the rigid daybreak setup by tilting her small hand Hi without raising her arm, without turning her head but meeting my eyes out of the corners of hers.

Then they were gone and the morning came down on me with a glare that made me wince, the all-day prospect of implacable heat. I lingered transfixed in the smell of mentholated nosedrops and Cleveland's ammoniac mop water drying on the lobby tiles. My head throbbed already from the rising heat—or from not sleeping, not eating.

Could you get an Ulster Fry at the K&J?

I went to breakfast in a reverse circle, as if to pass through a luckier circuit or alleviate my headache some magic way. That morning I went first past the pink Reform synagogue (and counted the catbirds perched on its dome, three, a good number) and crossed Euclid at the Hebron Institute for the Aged, a substantial half-block of stucco nursing home behind a Star-of-David grillwork fence. At this hour the deteriorating inmates deposited there by children in the northern boroughs began to limp forth into the light. Those who could stand and walk did so with cane or crutches (sometimes two canes, like the Expatriate) or staggered self-propelled in the cage of an aluminum walker. There was evidence of *sans souci* in the unbuttoned flies to the men's pajamas and the women's tatty wigs slightly askew. One shrunken old woman in a wheelchair, her mouth screwed sideways from stroke, came alive in her eyes when she stared into my face and saw son, son-in-law, but then slumped back semicomatose when she saw it was not so. The ancients were being helped to walk or being wheeled down the Institute's ramp by busty Cuban nurses dreaming with dark eyes of islands elsewhere.

It was too early for the sidewalk tables to be set out front of the

K&J on Washington, but the striped awnings were down already and music flowed down the aisles of the notions counters (Japanese mats, caps sporting plastic propellers, nose guards, Italian sunglasses, parasols—cheap needs for the seaside) and out into Washington Avenue. The employees all wore Hi! buttons, even the white-jacketed druggist at the Pharmacy counter where I left Mrs. Gold's prescription to be filled.

As I approached the soda-fountain counter, the smell of eggs sizzling on the short-order grill put me off the intent of a thorough breakfast. I delayed, hoping for restored appetite, by crossing the store to the Weight & Fortune Scale, and for a dime learned I had lost two pounds since last time but the ticket said this was a money day for me: "Trust Your Luck for Twenty-four Hours!"

At the counter I thought, why always an egg salad sandwich to go? There was chicken salad. I could order a tunafish salad sandwich on rye. I could have a malted milk for protein.

"What'll it be, Buddy?" asked Gladys.

"Egg salad. On whole wheat. To go."

Miss Berg came in wearing a blue-green muumuu draped loosely to disguise her bulk. She sat beside me at the counter, her vast buttocks overflowing the stool, and studied the photographs of breakfast specials on the wall. There was also a You-Don't-Have-to-Be-Crazy-to-Work-Here sign and a notice that said *Thank You for Not Smoking*. Miss Berg said hello to me and Hi! to the badge Gladys was wearing; she ordered orange juice, scrambled eggs, an English muffin and coffee.

"What's that one always gabbing to you about in the mornings?"

She was referring to Mr. Bloomfeld who came down to the lobby early, munching his breakfast apple.

"He talks about. Well, flowers, health food."

"Health? In his condition what that one needs is a healthy meal in his stomach for a change."

(That woman, Mr. Bloomfeld informed me about Miss Berg, carries digitalis in her handbag for a heart condition:"—and she's telling me what I have to eat for breakfast.")

"He worries. About cholesterol."

"Cholesterol yet? Him and his apple a day and he's so thin he's fading away like his flowers. What nobody ever told Bloomfeld is that married lives twice as long as single. He ever mention my name?"

I told her yes, and she sparkled. I did not mention that he called her Nice-Berg the Nose.

At the Ventura I had become resident consultant on desire and pursuit in all its forms and multiple frustrations. Cleveland had just loped into the K&J with a paper-wrapped pint bottle in his hip pocket from the package liquors on Espanola Way. He was standing at the Pharmacy counter probably buying the pack of condoms he had promised himself if ever it seemed he was getting to first base with Joy-O. He had large ambitions where she was concerned: he intended to lure her to the boiler room where he maintained a spare hotel bed he used for clandestine catnaps when Schine sunned in the afternoons.

(Joy-O—her name was Joyau in the original—had also confided in me. She was an island mulatto of a shade not much darker than a light tan; Cleveland's black was so intense it gave off light—blacks that black were luckless indigents on the island she was from; the difference in color put her off: "I ain't studying that mon nohow.")

"How come," asked Miss Berg, "he never comes in here for a decent meal like normal?"

"He eats mainly," said I, "at noon."

"Nice. In the worst heat of the day, like a moron, and no breakfast. Ruined his health over flowers without a wife to feed him decent and now he makes it worse with his health food and an apple a day. Health," she said, egg yolk at the corners of her lipstick, "he should live so long."

I collected my wax-paper-wrapped egg-salad sandwich; Miss Berg, by way of gratuity to accompany her request, picked up my check: "Listen, do me a favor sometime and tell Bloomfeld I think he's a living doll."

At the other side of the U-bend counter I spotted a slim familiar figure, her yellow hair cut in the same efficient way, now out of its hospital hairnet. I saw her only from the side, but I knew her. She peeled the paper from a soda-fountain straw as neatly as she would have shaken down a thermometer. The choice here was to turn away and nonchalantly pick up the prescription at Pharmacy, pretend I did not see her—or what? She was tanned. I had always seen her white, white in her white uniform under the hallucinatory fluorescence of Passive City.

I hesitated only for an instant, then got up and went around the counter to sit at the empty stool beside hers.

After a moment she turned coolly toward me, saying, "What's your problem, buddy?"

Everybody called me Buddy. I had been staring at her, waiting to be recognized. Then I remembered the beard: I touched my face to confirm that I was bearded now.

"Sorry," I said. "We used to work together."

She drew slightly back from the counter to confront this revelation. Her face went through stages of puzzlement to half-recall then dazed realization.

"My God." She placed a row of neatly trimmed fingernails to her lip.

"Yes."

Some of her fountain Coke spilled onto the counter.

"My God, it's you, isn't it? I mean my God what happened?"

"I was away."

"*Were* you." She dug into her handbag for something, a cigarette—no, she did not smoke ("Thank You for Not Smoking")—something sedative, and found only a package of Spearmint chewing gum. Flustered, she was peeling down a stick of gum as she had peeled down the straw, then remembered to offer a stick to me. I refused, thanks, no.

I asked, "How are things. With you?"

"O.K. I guess, I mean, I got married. But *you?* What in the world happened? We were well, everybody, totally like stunned."

She was wearing a diamond on the appropriate finger. I remembered her motorcycle boyfriend and asked if she had married JayCee.

Her face went through its memory-puzzle again, trying to ransack the past. JayCee? Then she said, "Oh him, God no. Ralph is my hubby's name, he's a lifeguard. At the Versailles, a real sweetheart," she touched the diamond to be sure of him, "but *you?*"

"I was away. I came back."

"*Did* you, God. I mean, like back from the dead or something. People thought you died or I don't know what. Into the blue, completely, then sitting here at the K&J, just like that."

"Just like that."

"But *you* of all people. I swore I'd never think I had a person sized up and all, never again, not even Ralph, and I'm married to him. You were the *last* person I would've thought." She stopped in the middle of chewing her gum. "I shouldn't have been so surprised, actually. You were a funny guy in a lot of ways."

"What ways?"

"The wristwatch, I don't know." A Country and Western ballad whined through the K&J sound system as if for significant background to Miss Ryan's—Medbh's—recollections. "For one thing," she smiled, "you never made a pass at me."

"Passes, plenty."

"Not really. You never made your move."

"In my heart, plenty. I was married. A married man."

"So you said. I heard, I never met her. Where on earth did you go, by the way?"

I could have told her about Ireland. Miss Ryan—Medbh—had always wanted to go to Ireland, but I did not want to talk about Ireland.

"Do you remember a patient? We called him—maybe only I did—the Poet. His name was Gold, Paranoid Personality. A suicide. He used to tell us, or tell me. He said that people who came to Miami. Really wanted to go to the South of France."

"I remember him, I don't remember that."

"Maybe he only said it. To me."

"God, patients. They were always saying things. They were *crazy*."

"Yes. But he was, well. Different."

"They were *all* different. They were cracked in different ways, that's all. But you? You just up and went to the South of France?"

"No. I just, set myself. Well, adrift. Into the blue, as you said."

She was shaking her head over me. She forgot, and offered me gum again, and I said thanks, no.

"It's unbelievable."

"So was he. The Poet."

"But what actually *happened?*"

"A long story."

It was a long story, she realized, I would not tell, so she said, "O.K, I'm off your case." She got on her own case, she was a private nurse now—I was remembering her in fine white transparent stockings. Her legs were hidden now in pink slacks. "I sit with the terminals, and take their temperature." This reminded me of something we used to say at the Sans Souci: that we sat quietly with the insane, and tucked them in at night. "The case I'm on now is this old retired franchiser with cancer, he's actually dying of it, at the Sunnyside TowneHouse. He promised to leave Ralph and me his ski condo in Vail, but he's got a million relatives so I'm not counting any chickens. (Ralph is, Ralph thinks he's serious.) He's a riot, a real sweetheart, he's had a double bypass, been on cobalt for cancer of the colon, he's blind with only this one kidney and he's on dialysis for that one, the guy's dying and you know what he says to me every time I go off duty?"

She paused for me to ask, "What does he say?"

"He says, 'See you later, alligator.' " She took a nervous sip of her Coke and drew back to check me out once again. She was trying to see past the beard to the psychiatric aide she remembered. "And I'm supposed to say, 'After a while, crocodile.' I mean, he's a riot."

I asked what happened to the Sans Souci.

"God, you've been away, that's right. You probably never heard, over there, but it was in *Time* and *Newsweek*. Dr. K. Remember how I used to say how slack the drug inventory was? How little I knew."

"Yes. We used to drink the medicinal brandy. On our birthdays."

She paused to remember that, and remembered with pleasure.

"Yes," she said. "The drug safe, the inventory, that wasn't the half of it. Dr. K was in deep, real deep. I mean, he was indicted for *dealing*, if you can believe it. Miami—God, have you been away. But this is the pits for drugs. It's Stoned City, did you know?"

"No."

"It's like the port of entry, every drug known. From South America, everywhere. This is the place, I mean it."

"I've been. Out of touch."

"*Are* you. They're building some insurance building where the clinic used to be."

"Yes. I saw that. I saw the parking lot where the Sans Souci used to be."

She was feeling nostalgic in my company, and told me how some of the case histories turned out: "—and the one that drove us out of our minds with the flute all night. She thought there was a worm in her heart or something but she really did have something wrong with her heart and died of it. But you," she drew back from me again, looking at me professionally, "are you sleeping? Maybe it's the beard. But are you getting any sleep—I mean, at *all?*"

"I'm working nights," I confessed, but would say no more. Mrs. Gold's prescription would be ready, so I got up saying, "See you later, alligator," without giving her a sporting chance to say, "After a while, crocodile."

6

WATCH, said the Poet.

From my horizontal watch on the lobby sofa I could memorize the lesson of the eternal wheel: we tropical fish triumphed over stagnation and death only by following our sleepless circular swim around a plastic castle. Watch for what? The Poet had abandoned me since the café table in Cannes, no signal since. Minutes before thinking I heard the word Watch, a tiny lost poodle—not Jewel, but twin to Jewel—strayed into the lobby trailing its disconnected leash, alone. The dog went from wicker chair to wicker chair sniffing at each empty imprint in frantic quest of a missing person. I was about to call Uncle Sam the dog watcher in case this was one of his canine charges gone astray, but the animal took fright at my sudden rearing up from a dark corner, and fled. Sam suffered as much as I from sleeplessness, so it was just as well not to break into his paranoid night.

The dog had pissed a little nervous puddle near the basement stairs, so I went down into Cleveland's cave in search of a mop. If the Poet hovered anywhere in the vicinity of the Ventura it might be belowstairs, so I looked behind the mildewed curtain of the basement shower: *personne*. I listened for the word Watch but the only sound was the methodical rattle of ice cubes falling from the rod in the ice maker. I checked the accumulated treasure of gleaming ice, the pierced cubes sacred to the Waterbabies; I checked the refrigerator for spoilage, but did not throw out the Shipwreck's grouper. There was an orchid mingled with Mr. Bloomfeld's apples, a delicate pink blossom in a plastic box awarded to Señora Echegarray after a son-in-law's winning night at the dog track. Mrs. Gold's bottle of nose drops and Mr. Blumenthal's insulin were in place, as was my plastic net of oranges. The family-size bottle of diet Pepsi belonged to Mrs. Berg. The Poet once asked Miss Ryan to store the first draft of his latest poem in the hospital refrigerator, so that it would not go stale overnight. There were no poems in the Ventura Hotel's refrigerator.

When I got back to the lobby I realized I had forgotten the mop. The Shipwreck was waiting for me. He had had human beings up to here, he said, shading his scowl with a weatherbeaten hand.

Try and ride your bike on the MacArthur Causeway and the law says No, that's why I don't fish there no more and wouldn't be caught dead on no causeway anyway named for the sonofabitch that shot us Vets down on the Bonus March in '24. He missed me, but the government's been taking potshots at me ever since. How was that fish I give you?"

"Good," I said, lying.

"There's no cemeteries in Miami Beach, you notice that?"

"No bookstores. I noticed."

"Potter's Field's on the other side of the bay. Only way across is by way of a hearse, and I never seen a rack on a hearse yet where they could carry a bicycle. I want to be buried with my bike."

After the Shipwreck left, I dozed off for a little part of the night, then came awake with a flashlight shining in my eyes.

They all carried flashlights: plainclothesmen, skip tracers, process servers, private eyes. They came in at odd hours with their flashlights and photographs, they showed me a badge or an I.D. card then a photograph of a missing person, or a mug shot from a Wanted poster. There were so many faces, so many wanted or missing. The wonder was when my own face would turn up wanted or missing some night.

"No," I said automatically, so often did I say it, and still half asleep. But this was a uniformed policeman for a change.

"Says he lives here," said the cop, and I turned the lights up to see who it was.

There were two Miami Beach policemen, one on each side of the Beachcomber: the Beachcomber's hands were handcuffed behind his back and his vacant face had been inhumanly broken.

"You know this asshole?" The first cop beamed his flashlight on the Beachcomber's wounds, though the lobby was alight now.

I wondered if I should know him or not, but the Beachcomber was shaking his battered head no, so I said, "No."

"Says he lives here."

"Not here," warbled the Beachcomber as if he had marbles in his mouth. When he spoke I saw that his teeth had been partially knocked out, then wired together crudely by some Emergency Room interne. He sprayed blood as he spoke: "Some other place, I thought this was it."

"Not registered here," I said, and thought for a moment I was spitting blood myself.

"Why'd you bring us here then?" said the second cop, prodding the Beachcomber in the kidneys with a nightstick.

Both policemen wore dark green glasses as if night lights were too much.

"I know," said the Beachcomber. There was dried blood down the front of his Boy Scout shirt, blood spots on the merit badges. "I know," he warbled, "where the elephants go to die."

This infuriated the two cops, and the first cop did something to the handcuffed arm to make him cringe. "Dragging us over here," said the first cop. "Sorry to wake you, fella, we're checking him out, where he keeps his narcotics."

My mouth still tasted of blood when I said, "He needs help."

"He needs the piss beat out of him," said the second cop.

The Beachcomber lisped whispering, "I know where the elephants go to die."

"You bastard, don't even know what hotel you're staying at."

They spun the Beachcomber around and prodded him double-time through the lobby door so vigorously one cop's sunglasses slid down his nose while the other cop forced the handcuffed hands into his shoulders to speed the Beachcomber along. In a moment the circles of light on the top of the squad car were spinning off in the direction of the precinct house on Commerce.

So if I slept I was subject to unreasonable dreams, unfinished nightmare.

I was never afterward sure if he came into the lobby that night or not. He was a fugitive, he said: he had kidnapped his own son, left his wife.

"She tracked me down, all the way from France. I was in jail, then in a hospital."

He opened his shirt and lowered his shorts and showed me the scar on his groin where his wife had stabbed him with a pair of scissors. Of course, I had administered his Admissions shower, I remembered his case history from the San Souci.

"I wanted to turn myself back in, but when I went over to the hospital it was gone."

He paid for a room for the night, fifteen dollars, ten of it in quarters he must have pried out of the coin slot in some telephone booth.

Next morning while Cleveland was mopping up blood and the place where the dog had pissed, Schine asked, "What's these quarters?" and I showed him the name Swanson in the hotel register, but the bed in the room I had rented had not been slept in; the key was still in the lock, but the guest had disappeared.

7

DEAR SON, so near and yet so far!

Miami Beach may be an old story to you, but to your old Dad (and Priscilla, if she hadn't been sleeping by my side since Ft. Lauderdale) it was a sight for sore eyes. After all those cows and swamps and turpentine pines coming down central Florida, you bet! Three-hundred and sixty-five (count 'em!) first-class hotels lined up along the ocean shore like the Thousand and One Nights. You could lodge at a different inn every night of the year, if so inclined. Hotels galore, all colors of the rainbow—high-class and low alike—named for the capitals of far-flung lands, forgotten song titles, and secret desires—also, precious stones, constellations, sentimental memories, flowers, fairy tales, creatures of the deep, foreign potentates, botanical gardens, signs of the Zodiac, enchanted castles, celebrities, nature's phenomena, Presidents, palatial haunts and all the various treasures a thriving civilization stores up over the years.

"Darn it, Priscilla," I said to her, "if we aren't a striking-looking couple that deserves the very best." But she was getting her beauty rest and had not yet awakened to my excitement. Whichever one of these top-notch hostelries we chose, the guests in the lobby were sure to sit up and take notice.

The hotel that eventually caught *my* eye—and I knew darned well we would end up in—was named for the famed seventh wonder of the world, The Pyramids—a vision right out of the Arabian Nights. Not just one but *three* pyramids stood in a row glowing against the Gold Coast sky. There was a faithful replica of the mysterious Sphinx out front with a mailbox between its paws. The doorman wore a walkie-talkie on his back, and a turban to match the hotel décor. *Exclusive* was their motto, you knew it instanter. I do believe they would accept Cadillacs only, for that was all you saw in their private parking lot.

The driveway was jammed with Caddies and cabs, but I did not hesitate for a moment to make a U-turn in the middle of Collins Avenue (traffic cops are loathe to issue tickets to Cadillacs, never knowing who's a big shot and who isn't) and spun around into that driveway with the instinct of a homing pigeon. Our pink Caddy took its place in line with the Le Barons and so forth, right up there with the stars where we belonged, though a bit dusty from the long drive—but our car was as classy as any vehicle in sight. Car by car crept majestically up the up-to-date ramp with a tropical private lagoon off to one side complete with spouting fountain piece bubbling spa water—though sad to say cigar butts floated in it, and racetrack tickets—out of coral rock, and I hoped the Pyramids people cleaned their lagoon out each and every morning, like their swimming pool.

"Priscilla!" I sang out. "Wake up sweetheart, this is it!"

It was high time Priscilla sat up and took notice. She was in for the biggest surprise of her life.

Something was going on up at the front entrance, and for some unknown reason the line of cars ceased to budge. I hoped and prayed the *No Vacancy* sign would not light up, for naturally we had no reservations. The delay made me uneasy (having been on the qui vive all my life, and no crossword to pass the time) but I massaged my scalp while waiting, then combed my hair back in place via the rearview mirror.

Car horns inevitably began to tune up, but I diplomatically refrained from tooting ours. There is a time and place for everything. I felt a bit dizzy, I admit, and somewhat hollow inside—the same symptoms I felt on Priscilla's lawn that afternoon I fainted, from skipping lunch and standing in the hot sun with my hat off. Son, always carry a package of raisins in your pocket or an apple when "on the road," for meal stops might be few and far between.

"Wake up, Honey," I sang out. "Siesta time is up."

(I am writing this from the so-called lobby of a rooming house in Coconut Grove, the next thing to a flophouse if you ask me—*sic transit gloria* as the Romans said when the Barbarians took over—and literally wondering What Next?)

I soon saw what the holdup was all about. It was a wedding. It looked like a Jewish one, where they step on a wineglass. I knew Priscilla would not want to miss a wedding for the world, so eased her off my shoulder and tweaked one cheek with thumb and middle finger.

"Open those peepers, Sweetheart, Here Comes the Bride!"

Was she playing possum on me? Believe it or not, she did not stir a hair even with the symphony of car horns trumpeting a protest over the bottleneck. Her darling cheek was cold to the touch and I did not like the bloodless look her forehead had.

It was foolish, I now admitted, to drive across the Causeway with the top down, like water-skiers, but there had been no breeze to speak of. Her complexion was definitely off color. I felt for her pulse but for the life of me could not find it! Ditto for the other wrist. When I checked the whites of her glazed-over eyes, I did not like what happened with the lids, one bit! I put my ear to her sweet old-fashioned bosom, trying my utmost to hear a heartbeat or intake of breath, but all was silent in both departments.

A black moment momentarily overwhelmed me and I rested my head on the steering wheel to restore my nerves. I put my hand over my own heart and felt an ugly racket behind the rib cage. Buck Up Old Boy, I said to myself. My adrenals, I sensed, were secreting to beat the band.

She must have passed away that P.M., in transit as it were, quietly in her sleep, without a struggle. If there is a better way to go, I do not know it—but 'tis a shock, Son, to see it happen to a beloved companion and near-fiancée.

Mea culpa, I admit.

Priscilla was no voyager, I should have realized all along. Once out of her House & Gardens home she was literally a fish out of water. That house was a life-supporting oxygen tent to her, air-conditioned throughout. She was preserved there in her cocoon, as it were, completely insulated from the hard knocks and rude awakenings of the outside world.

And I thought all along I was opening wide the windows of her life. Now that she was dead, I could have kicked myself for being so dense. My conscience would have to answer for that, for life.

The next question was What Next? What if some cop would stroll by, Cadillac or not, and tap me on the shoulder asking questions? Where was my driver's license, for instance?

Son, I darned near wept in spite of myself.

Meanwhile, what to do? I noticed the car behind ours was empty—the driver had taken his Polaroid halfway up the first pyramid to photograph the bride and groom. I thanked my lucky stars for that. Then I slid out of the car and propped Priscilla up in my place behind the steering wheel, looking, for all the world, like the bona fide driver.

The effort made me see stars again, and I was obliged to lean a moment on our Cadillac's rose-colored hood. When my head stopped spinning I closed the car door as softly as I could. Sentimental memories swept over me, aplenty, but I was darned if I would be caught crying in a hotel driveway.

The only way out was right through the wedding. I pulled the brim of my Panama down so as not to show up in anybody's photos. The bride, I'm bound to say, was pretty as a picture. As for the groom he had the look of a man of means but sad to say you could see he favored an oil-base hair lotion he would regret later in life. The rice was sticking to his hair. But God-Bless-Them, thought I, in passing, the newlyweds, Mr. and Mrs. Wineglass both.

Just then the glass door to the lobby swung open and a party of bridesmaids and best men poured out of the pyramid. I had to buck the crowd, the rice drumming against my hat brim, going against the tide so to speak, as I have done all my life.

8

"**W**HAT TO HELL who knows what go round in the brain of a race hound or these fishes. Or us."

The Moonlighter was in, but on his way out with a toaster under his arm. He had met a client at the dog track. "Bad luck," said he, "talking fixit business at the track. We turn up losers, the toaster man and me both."

No Tarzan tonight, the Waterbabies were performing a night show at the Treasure Isle Olympic pool. The Moonlighter tapped the aquarium with his screwdriver counting in Spanish, no new fish. He was impatient to return to Cuba ("*¿Por qué aprender inglés?*" the Cuban ladies wanted to know—and he answered their question with a question: Who knows what goes on in the head of a greyhound-fish-or-man?)

He stuck his dog-track program full of losers into the bread slot of the toaster to free his hands for refilling his pipe. *Manos de plata*, with his gifted fingers the Moonlighter was said to have played the concert guitar—but who had ever heard him play? Also, he was said to remain faithful to Fidel (he had suffered the long watch with him in the Sierra Maestra only to be betrayed after the revolution), but that was only what was said, there were no witnesses.

(He did not fancy hijacking a plane to get back to Havana, Arabs had given skyjacking a bad name. With a winning *quinella* in his pocket he could travel anywhere, even home. "You be surprised where money take you to, even Communism.")

He was on his way out, restless—disappointed not to have an audience of Waterbabies—with a toaster to repair. Nights he spent probing the tangled intestines of television sets and broken toasters with his *manos de plata*, tinkering with the leaks in water heaters. He had taken a day job working for the City on a utility truck, lopping the tops off diseased palm trees with a chain saw.

"Daytime I work in the trees, like Tarzan."

"When do you sleep?"

"Me? Like you, I kit-nap."

As the Moonlighter went out, Roxanne was coming in, and the paunchy Cuban performed a shuffling scuffling soft-shoe routine and Don Juan's bow in her honor. (Roxanne knew him: he had repaired an alarm clock for her—I tried to reconcile her professional services with an alarm clock.) Schine had called her for a party. Roxanne clicked her Cuban heels together (she was not Cuban) and responded to the Moonlighter's courtesy with a flip salute to her painted eyebrow.

"Buddy-boy don't you go bonkers sitting around this mortuary all night?"

Roxanne was all movement and rapid-fire exchange, as restless and gesturing as the Moonlighter. Time-is-money she might be saying—which may have explained the alarm clock: Roxanne's meter ran ceaselessly.

"I keep the lights on. Outside, and in the lobby. People come in. And talk."

"Talk? The creeps that would come into this place? Talk is cheap, this is Nowheresville. I picture a bright guy like you in a live town like Denver, where the action is."

"I sort of fit in. Here, with the people who can't sleep."

"Sleep?" Roxanne flashed an armload of bracelets, the hoops of her earrings joggled. "Under the sod, Buddy, sleep is cheap."

True, *the grave's a fine and private place.*

"What's keeping Casanova?" she asked, when I called Schine's room to tell him Roxanne was waiting and he said to give him a minute. I told her he was getting dressed.

"Dressed? He's only going to undress in about three seconds. I'm the one supposed to be dolled up. How do you like this outfit?"

Roxanne wore expensive clothes tailored to attract attention to her hipline. The makeup, jewelry and Cuban heels offset the expensive effect.

While Schine was brushing his thick white hair and donning the dressing gown he wore for his rendezvous with Roxanne—with the Chinese dragon embroidered on the back—Roxanne restlessly recounted the story of her last party, last night.

"You won't believe this, Buddy, if I told you his name, but that's life, you meet all kinds. I met him at the Monkey Bar and there was nothing kinky in sight except God was he cute, so Why Me? I ask myself. A kid, practically, good-looking as hell, so why pay for it? He took me to the Roney of all places, he was living at the Roney Plaza and looks like a movie star or somebody and he has to get his rocks off with Roxie at the going rate—I *mean*. Then it hit me who he was. I mean he looked like him, like the record-jacket pictures of him, but that's who he actually was. I mean it. I can't tell you who. We never tell, it's not professional, it's like doctors and priests. But I just want to give you an example of how you meet all kinds. So we're up in his room—it was a whole suite, in fact, with ocean view, naturally—me with a gin-and-tonic and him with one of those fishbowls of cognac, both of us like an ad on TV playing it so sophisticated you'd think the cameras were rolling. I started to say something to break the ice and he says, 'Don't say anything,' so I shut up. I mean, he's paying, so? 'Don't say anything,' he says, 'please. Don't make a sound, don't be surprised what I do, don't even think about it.' O. K., so he's paying, so I just sit there like a dummy. When he unbuttons his shirt I naturally reach around and start unzipping my blouse—I mean, what else?—and the kid, this great-looking TV type, he says, 'No, don't. Don't do anything, don't take anything off. Just sit there, perfectly quiet. Sit there and listen and don't be surprised.' I'm getting mucho intrigued, I *mean*. Off comes the pants, down come the shorts—he's got his shoes off, socks, everything—and when he was bareass and slightly goose-pimply from the air conditioning he stands right in front of me, not looking at me, right? I mean, he's facing me but looking right through me as if I wasn't even in the room. I mean, this one was something else. Young—nice build, great face, he's well hung. He could have had fabulous girls right off the TV screen, stars, groupies must have been crawling all over him—Why Me? Next thing I know he's getting a healthy hard-on. Without even touching it, and me nowhere near it, his eyes are closed now and I'm sitting like a dummy doing nothing. This is some party says I, but not out loud (he wants me quiet). Then, with his eyes still shut, standing there in his birthday suit, he starts *singing*. I mean it. Guess what he sings? I can't tell you, it's not professional, you never identify your John. If you knew what he sang you'd know who he was. It's at the top of the pops, you hear it all over, it's *his* song, he's known by it. He was singing it to me, I mean it. With the cock up and out as far as it'll go, he's *singing*. And that's the way he got his rocks off. Talk about kinks. At the end I didn't know whether I was supposed to clap or what."

Just then Neptune came in, still in costume, with the kids in tow, the Waterbabies wearing terry cloth robes and their rubber caps smelling of chlorine from the pool. Their eyes were overbright from the white lights they had swum through, small bodies still wired tight from the tension of performance and display. Neptune steered them to the stairs, having to gather his white robe like skirts at the foot of the staircase to keep from stumbling. The Waterbabies had this instant for a ritual soprano "Night-Sir," from Denny and "Night-night, Mr. Buddy" from Lee Ann showing a small palm with wrinkled fingers from the long spell in water.

When later Schine called down to say, "Send Roxie up," Neptune was just coming downstairs again, changed into his chino pants and Western belt, his Service dog tags spilling out of the open V of his linen shirt, the shirt unbuttoned to accommodate the protruding back brace.

Crossing him on the stairs, Roxanne pretended she didn't recognize Neptune with his hair greased back, minus crown and cotton beard.

"Are you the same guy that just went by in drag, with the pitchfork and the kids?"

"Trident, Cunt. It's called a trident."

Neptune avoided her eyes and Roxanne floated past him as if savoring the crude pejorative in her broad smile, earrings jauntily abob, bracelets jangling.

Neptune came over to the desk to say to me, "In the Marines I used to believe you treated a lady like a whore and a whore like a lady but I learned different when I got married."

He lingered at the front desk his small eyes brilliant with malice. He needed to sound off, and he was not yet ready to install himself at the Blarney Stone and sound off to Irish Mike. He needed a night man to hear his philosophy of life, he needed a confidant.

"Whores," said Neptune. "Listen, there's two kinds of women in the world, one's professional and one's amateur and they all start out amateurs first. My ex-wife was an amateur but she didn't lose no time turning pro. You know who took care of the kids when they were little? Me, that's who." He took a photograph out of his billfold

(maybe he loved them, I kept telling myself): Denny and Lee Ann in
diapers instead of swimsuits—babies but Vikings already in a stoic
pose at the cage bars of a gruesome green playpen, stunned by the
unexpected flash of an Instamatic, but standing without recoil.
"That's them when their momma was out playing around on me. I
trained them from day one. I threw water in their face as soon as I got
them out of Maternity. A baby, they're born natural swimmers like a
porpoise, you know that? Kids of mine, there's nothing genetic in it,
they wouldn't've been any exceptional swimmers more than anybody
else except I trained them up. I filled the bathtub up and had them
swimming two weeks old, they loved it. Water's their fucking
element, for Christ sake—babies, they're just out of their momma's
fish tank. So I ducked them in the bathtub, over their head, sink or
swim I taught them—that's life. I trained them up to an early
start—listen, how many kids their age get that kind of experience?"

He put the photograph away after a second look at it himself.
"They were great tonight, the both of them. Denny, he's going to win
gold medals all over the place when he gets to the Olympics. I myself
picked up a bronze medal in freestyle in T⸴kyo, did I tell you? I
should've concentrated on my swimming but ⸴. ⸴t age you want to play
football, high school, that's your glory sport, and I got my cervical
vertebraes messed up in a fucking off-sides tackle.

"You was in the Service, right? I was in the Marines. I thought
you was in the Service, except for the beard. I taught swimming on the
recruit-training team on Parris Island and let me tell you I was the
roughest toughest sonofabitch on the island. I teach my kids the same
as I did Marine recruits, sink-or-swim-buddy. I don't know. My back
was acting up, I left the Service before I got my twenty years in. I
could be retired today, sitting on my ass on a military pension and not
have to hustle hotels in that flaky getup, but the kids are getting the
experience of a lifetime. My ex-wife was who messed up my military
career. When I got transferred to Norfolk she started screwing every
sailor on East Main—I went AWOL trying to catch her in the act. I beat
this Machinist Mate about to death I caught her with, right out in the
middle of East Main. My discharge keeps me from getting a civil
service job or VA benefits. That's what a favor my ex-wife did me.
Anyway, let the kids hustle for a change, see what the Real World is
like, early. What branch of Service was you in?"

"Navy," I said.

He winced. "Jesus H. Christ. My ex-wife married one. Don't
take it personal but I got this thing about swabbies. Pogey-bait, we

used to call them in the Marines. But that's O.K. Buddy, you're still O.K. in my book. You went in the Service at least. At least we both went in the Service not like bastards today that run to Canada to keep from serving their country. I wish I had them in my squad on Parris Island and I kid you not I would've worked the conscientious objections out of their ass."

But I was O.K. in his book—we were both in the Service, weren't we?—and he offered a leathery hand for me to shake before he headed for the Blarney Stone. I allowed his hand to grasp mine and was obliged to return the pressure just to keep my hand from being crushed. He was too bedazzled by tonight's spotlight and high on his case history to feel the vibes of loathing that poured from my reluctant hand to his.

Within thirty minutes Roxanne and Schine—boy-and-girl, girl-and-boy—had finished with one another, and Roxanne returned to the lobby with miniature boy-and-girl escort. The Waterbabies walked with her, Lee Ann in front, Denny immediately behind, both holding Roxie's hands down the stairs, forward and aft. The Waterbabies still wore their aquashow robes, Lee Ann's flapping open to the ruffles at the gills of her one-piece swimsuit, still perfumed with chlorine from tonight's pool time. The radiance of the Waterbabies had infected Roxanne: she glowed with the delight transferred through their hands, while they maintained the sober miens of everyday—nights were their stolen time of wonder, but never could they reveal delight in their expressions (though the bare evidence of a smile sometimes flickered at the corners of Lee Ann's mouth).

"I like the lights," Lee Ann was saying, apropos of night performances, "but it gets shivvy when you come out of the water."

"Shivery," said Denny for Lee Ann. "The pool water was heated."

"Can you believe these kids?" Roxanne asked me as she came down the stairs enchanted. "Their door was open—I mean, how can you resist them?"

They were oblivious of reference to themselves as if they stood forever apart and out of hearing of the crowd's concerns. Praise passed over their heads (though Lee Ann confessed she liked to break the surface of the water to applause) so constantly were they driven to achievement, aware of how much better they must be to survive.

"They're like," Roxanne began, "I don't know what. They're like, so perfect."

"Are you Mr. Schine's sister, Miss?" asked Denny.

"Oh God," said Roxanne, "they're too much." To Denny she explained, "I'm just Roxie, honey. Mr. Schine is a friend."

"We never get kid friends," said Lee Ann.

"Our friends are older like Mr. Buddy," said Denny, "and you Miss."

"You will," Roxie promised.

She settled them on either side of her on the lobby sofa, unaware of their need to sit and be together, unable to resist touching them, patting them into place, stroking the blond down on Lee Ann's thin swimmer's arms. Roxanne crossed her long legs, one Cuban heel bobbing rhythmically with the pleasure of their company.

Schine had called from his room for Roxanne's taxi, but when the cab beeped outside she told me to send it away.

"On second thought," she told me as I started outside, "ask him if he can get a cake someplace. Tell him to get us some ice cream—chocolate-vanilla-strawberry—at the K&J. It's their birthday for crying out loud, did you know?"

"It's Denny's," said Lee Ann. "I'm in January."

I went out to ask the cabdriver (unknown to me) if he could get a cake this late, or ice cream at the K&J.

"This is too much," Roxanne was saying when I came in. "I ask them what flavor ice cream they like and they don't know, they never tasted it."

"Not to remember," said Denny.

"Honey, you'd remember *ice* cream."

"They're on a strict diet," I explained.

"But *ice* cream," she protested, "on their *birth*day."

"It's only Denny's," said Lee Ann.

"We don't get birthdays, Sir," said Denny.

"This is too much," Roxanne said, grimly, as if she would never smile again. "This is not to be believed. You know what they were doing when I saw their door open." She smiled again. "They were sitting together close like two popsicles writing their names over and over on a hotel envelope."

"Mr. Buddy showed us," said Lee Ann. She explained that her name was harder to write because she was Lee Ann Bludhorn, three words, and Denny Bludhorn was only two. She revealed that Tarzan in the movies was an Olympics swimming champion like her father. She also let slip that Denny had been punished during that morning's workout at the Sandcastle, but Denny was quick to remind her of a taboo that bound their narrow lives.

"We don't tell that," he said.

Lee Ann had been overcome by the thrust of her telling, and could not check the flow of words: "— had to keep in the pool after laps and dog-paddle."

"We don't tell that." Denny was watching the lobby door to see if his father might loom large there.

"—with hands up you go under and smother and he was tired you can't dog-paddle with hands up—"

"Tread water," said Denny, "but we don't tell that."

"Because he didn't hold hand-position in a swan he had to keep in the pool."

"My left hand goes out sometimes," explained Denny, forgetting for a moment what-we-don't-tell, "and you have to hold perfect in a true swan."

"And when he got tired and kept going under like you smother he tried to climb out and Dad pushed him under and he swam over the other side and Dad caught him and threw him back in."

"We don't tell that."

"Eddie told Dad if he didn't let that kid out of the pool he was going to throw Dad in."

"That's personal." Denny was watching the door. "Don't tell."

"Denny can stay under three minutes something but I can't only stay two and a half but that's like you smother."

"Dad's a better swimmer than Eddie any day," said Denny defending his father. "He could throw Eddie in."

"Dad's got a gold medal," said Lee Ann.

"Bronze," said Denny, a stickler for veracity. "In the Olympics, in Tokyo."

Roxanne had turned rigid, unable to speak, during the Waterbabies' duet. Her expression was wide-eyed and fierce, she had had enough of Dad, but she softened and was back in control by the time the ice cream came. She scooped out the ice cream into paper cups Denny brought from the dispenser at the water cooler. We ate with plastic spoons Schine kept behind the desk, from his K&J coffee orders. Roxanne could not eat her ice cream: she kept staring from one to the other of the Waterbabies as they ate theirs.

"It's cold," said Lee Ann, shivering to show how cold it was, "but I like it."

"Me too Miss," said Denny. He watched the lobby door as he ate the ice cream.

"Roxie," said Roxie, but Denny, distracted, let the Miss stand.

We began to sing "Happy Birthday" but Denny the stickler said no. He pointed to the clock—he could not read, but he could tell time.

"It was yesterday," he declared. "Tonight after twelve it's a different day."

Lee Ann stopped eating her ice cream as if a deadline had slipped by, so I got up and moved the hands of the lobby clock to a comfortable interval before midnight.

"Daylight Savings," I announced, "I forgot to set the time."

From their expressions there was no way to assess how this make-believe registered with them, but Lee Ann did dip back into her ice cream and Denny made haste to finish his. I found hurricane candles in the cash drawer and lit them and stuck them with melted wax to glass ashtrays.

Roxanne and I softly sang "Happy Birthday" in the candlelight while the Waterbabies sat expressionless, erect and accepting, as if they were listening to the national anthem at an aquashow. Their unnatural poise put them at a strange remove from anything childlike known to me, or to Roxanne: their distance, professionally bred, was affecting and unnerving. Roxanne dabbed at her eyelids with the backs of her hands, I was as suddenly fearful for the Waterbabies as when they were being punished.

"God," said Roxanne, "they're too much." She kept looking from one child to the other, saying, "They're too much."

That was when the Shipwreck came into the lobby carrying his fishing rod and a single boot. We were few enough in number to draw him in, and the lobby perhaps made more inviting by the intimacy of candlelight.

"I've had humanity up to here," he announced, "but when I seen it was kids with candles I figured I'd keep you company."

(The Shipwreck would never enter the lobby when the guests he called the Waxworks were still up.)

He seemed to know Roxanne, and asked her, "What's your fate, lately," but she was so moved by the presence of the Waterbabies she could not speak without betraying a sob, so she opened her palm in the Indian gesture of Peace and rattled her bracelets at the Shipwreck. He turned to me and croaked, "Eleven-thirty? You people are way behind the times."

"It's a birthday, Sir," said Lee Ann.

Distractedly Roxanne, unable to look away from the Waterbabies, offered ice cream to the Shipwreck.

"My stomach can't take the cold. After the glass I swallowed all

I can digest is broken bottles and fishhooks. Anybody missing a boot?"

He held up the trophy of his night's fishing. Roxanne heard nothing the Shipwreck said: she had pressed her hand so hard against her eyes one set of false eyelashes had come off onto the back of her hand, and it seemed as if the tears flowed only from that one naked eye.

The Shipwreck's arrival reminded Denny of the hour.

"It's not the real time," he told us. "Dad will come in."

Lee Ann hastily scooped the last melted drops of cream from the bottom of her paper cup. Neptune might appear at any moment, so I nodded at Denny and he took Lee Ann by the hand.

"Can we take a candle, Mr. Buddy?"

They went upstairs holding a candle together one hand each. In a little while I would follow to make certain the candle was not still burning as they slept. Roxanne, frozen to the sofa, called, "Happy Birthday," after them, her voice too uncertain to carry or they did not, in their novel delight of a candle in hand, hear. As the halo of light disappeared at the top of the stairs, Roxanne abruptly pushed off the sofa and was out of the lobby, heel-clicking down the walk without waiting for a taxi—she could not bear for us to see what was happening to her eyes.

"Them youngsters're the right stuff but'll inherit how we ruint Mother Nature." The Shipwreck's face was a tragic mask of deep creases as graven as the scars on his abdomen. "You can't fish these waters for the pollution. Look at what I hauled up from the scum after all night fishing with a flashlight." He showed me the rubber boot again. "I ever tell you the time I fished up a foot off the Rickenbacker Causeway, a purentame human foot, I swear to Jesus, and turned it over to the police force. They booked me on suspicion of amputating somebody."

I went behind the desk to set the lobby clock back to the correct time.

"I wish you could set that thing back about fifty years, before the '35 hurricane, when all we had was the Depression to get depressed about. The cops by the way never could locate the person that went with the foot, so they had to set me loose. I first tried to get their attention by swallowing a bolt I worked out of the cot in my cell but I just vomited it back up again."

9

As I STEPPED OUT the rear exit into the spill of grapfruit rind in the alley, Cleveland and Joy-O emerged from the basement together. They did not see me in the broken chiaroscuro of banana palms and rusted dumpsters, they were too aware of one another. Cleveland's hand was spread contentedly across Joy-O's calypso hip as they shuffled under the fire escape to her reggae beat, listening to her Walkman one earphone each.

I played again at skip tracing. The second excursion to Coral Gables was meant only to confirm what I thought I had witnessed the time before. I chose the same blind, partly obscured by hibiscus: I leaned against the banyan as if I were a dedicated tree surgeon searching the perfect place to bore and apply a life-element to the tree's core. But the picturesque growth, though gnarled and ancient, was altogether alive and thriving.

A black woman in maid's white uniform sat on the bench at the bus stop opposite. We stared straight at one another with no accountability on either side: when she looked away she might have decided I was taking a leak in public—then her bus came. Minutes went by, and I awaited the squad car that would surely pull up alongside my skulking place, but none did. The day was too innocent to arouse neighborhood concern.

Valerie, when she appeared, was alone. She was wearing a simple cotton dress with a petal-like arrangement at the shoulder, a dress I remembered—which once hung loose, was now filled out—and a hat I did not know, with a wide brim like the beach hat Maureen had worn when I met her in Drumlough.

How quick and confident her movements were—Valerie, who was once lethargy's child—as she turned to lock the door behind her and pop the key into her handbag. At the moment she stepped down from the tiled sun porch she reached out with easy pleasure in what must have been a ritual gesture to stroke the wind chimes hanging from a balustrade. I could not hear the sound they made, but managed to imagine a Celtic jig or the jangle of hangers—trying, in my isolation, to make whatever connections possible across a vacuum.

Valerie was honey-colored from the sun, a golden girl, as settled and assured as the suburb wherein she flourished. She was smiling to herself without letup, a constant smile of well-being and benign content. Against the mirrorlike side of the automobile she had washed the week before, Valerie's own aura was reflected, the very transcendent glow publicists strived for at each television spot, but here there was no artifice in an attempt to convince, Valerie was not trying.

It was inconceivable that I call out to her. I dared not cast my disturbing silhouette between Valerie and the white bright sun. I remained discreetly out of sight, a witness only, a rememberer.

I could hear the motor start—a growl that caught, then purred—an old car but in reasonable condition. Valerie was now capable of venturing forth in whatever direction she chose, she had learned to drive her companion's Oldsmobile.

The auto's easy passage beside my outpost was so close I could clearly make out Valerie's smile, as beatific and private as before. She was a soul at peace, staring blissfully ahead, in perfect rapport with her time, with this place.

Her husband remained invisible behind the banyan. I was confused and undone. Nevertheless, through my tangled feelings and disturbed state of mind I managed to send a silent blessing in the auto's wake.

10

THERE WERE two kinds of guests at the Ventura according to Schine, those who drank directly from the fountain spout and those who wasted paper cups. Schine drank from the fountain spout but this morning the water ran lukewarm instead of cold. He spat the water back into the stainless steel drain.

"Where can I get hold of that Cuban guy that fixes things, works all night, the one the ladies like?"

The Moonlighter had skipped Night School for several nights, the last I had heard he was working for the Sanitation Department clearing the coconut palms from the South Beach streets.

Schine got the Sanitation Department on the phone.

"The fixer, the repair guy, his name I don't know. He's a friend of my night man, he fixes stuff. I got a water cooler on the blink."

Schine was agitated over the water cooler. Cleveland was busy outside: he had attached the suction hose to the vacuum cleaner and was sucking up gum wrappers and eucalyptus leaves on the front porch. So I volunteered to get the Danish and coffee at the K&J that morning.

I was at the K&J when the Waterbabies went out with Neptune, but I saw the three of them getting into a cab as I came past the Hebron Institute. Neptune was in costume and the kids wearing their exhibition swim briefs and carrying their goggles. There was some problem getting the trident into the back of the cab: Lee Ann was holding the door and Denny tugging at the three-pointed staff from inside the taxi. Neptune lifted his robe to step into the taxi, Lee Ann squeezed in, and the cab door slammed shut before I could wave to the Waterbabies and call out Luck. They were doing an aquashow at the King Cole Condominiums, an inaugural gala for the opening of the King Cole's new pool.

When I came into the lobby, Cleveland was down on his knees in front of the water cooler. He had the machine unplugged, the pipes apart—he was trying to fix the motor. Schine had gone to sunbathe: he requested that I bring his coffee to the sun deck, he had asked Cleveland to answer the switchboard.

"Old Moonlighter, look like he headed home."

"He left?"

"That what they say at Sanitation. Went back to Cuba where he come from. I don't see how the man going to get back in. I don't see old Castro wanting moonlighters come back to Havana. You got to be Communist to live down there now."

The Moonlighter gone: the Cuban ladies would be shocked to hear, the Waterbabies would be disappointed. He was gone before I could say goodbye, I kept missing the chance to wish people Luck.

From my closet-room window I could hear the gym master's whistle like a summons, someone calling. Between the slats of the Venetian blind I watched a clean white diesel yacht cut a pale green path through the open waterway, pennants flapping, perhaps a glass bottom through which one might study the depths. Her bearing was due east headed for Gibraltar but she was too small a craft to steam that far. Besides, the crew—just as I had always been—would be fearful of the falling-off place.

*   *   *

I had been reading Pharisees-and-scribes in the Bible, dreaming Phoenicians and telephone booths, when suddenly I was awake and sitting up, the hangers clanging. There was something urgent I must do, a child crying—but the Waterbabies were away. That was Lee Ann crying in the corridor. I thought I heard Miss Berg trying to calm the child, Uncle Sam stuttering something. I dressed and went into the hall. Lee Ann broke from her escorts and plunged stumbling into my knees.

"He vom-vom-vomited," she sobbed. The words poured forth, muffled in my thighs. "To the hos-hos-hos."

Sam managed to say "hospital" without stuttering.

"The kid got hurt," said Miss Berg. "The other one, the little boy." Her plump face had shriveled into worry lines. She had been at the King Cole opening, she had seen Denny dive or fall from thirty feet. "He landed funny."

"Hospital," said Sam, too moved to say more.

Lee Ann lifted her head up, face bathed in tears: "Didn't-break-when-you-should-and-belly—" she gulped for breath, "belly-flopped."

"They had to stop the show," said Miss Berg. "They got the house doctor. The kid's at St. Francis—or is it Mt. Sinai?"

"Mt. S-S-Sinai," said Sam.

Sam had driven Miss Berg and Lee Ann to the Ventura in his broken-down convertible, Neptune was at Mt. Sinai with Denny.

"I mean, thirty *feet*," said Miss Berg. "I couldn't watch, I didn't see it happen. Something with the spleen, the house doctor said."

Miss Berg wanted to put Lee Ann to bed in her room—"She's feverish, poor kid, she should rest herself,"—but Lee Ann would not let go of my legs.

Schine was behind the desk, and said to me, "The kid got hurt." He was pale around the mouth, his hands trembled. Cleveland was standing miserably among the scattered baffling parts of the water cooler, Joy-O close behind him looking grim.

I went behind the desk with Schine and plugged into the trunk line, then dialed Mt. Sinai.

"I already called," said Schine, "they won't give out information this soon."

"Denny Bludhorn," I said to the receptionist at the hospital.

"Are you the father?"

"Yes," I said.

"We've been trying to reach you. He's still in Emergency, he's in a coma."

I went upstairs clutching the key like the mangled bones of a small animal in my fist.

Lee Ann stayed with me in my closet room for the rest of the day. She would not lie down or eat anything, not even the sugar-dusted cornflakes I kept in the room for the Waterbabies. I opened the Venetian blinds so that she could see the Atlantic through the bars and I could watch with her. An airliner left behind a jet stream that might have inscribed a message smeared across the horizon I could not read. The child's spill of words had ceased—she would only nod yes or no to any suggestion of mine. No, she did not want an orange; yes, she wanted to practice writing. Along the borders of the newsprint in the *Miami Herald* she wrote over and over the small words she had learned, but instead of practicing her own name she practiced writing the name Denny.

That night came the first downpour in weeks, and every guest at the Ventura seemed to be in the lobby, out of the rain, waiting. Mt. Sinai called and asked for Mr. Bludhorn, and I said I would take the message.

"Are you a member of the family?"

"Yes," I said.

Denny had been declared dead at 8:47 P.M. and it was requested that the father please come to the hospital to make arrangements. The father, I told the nurse, was not available.

"Some member of the family, then. You yourself, if you're a close relative."

"I'll be in touch," I promised her.

Lee Ann was in the lobby staring into the lighted aquarium. The Prophets were silent, but the television set had been turned up too loudly for Lee Ann to hear me at the switchboard.

According to Schine, Neptune was being held by the police. Miss Berg said she would take Lee Ann to her room to sleep, but Lee Ann did not want to go.

"Later," I said to Miss Berg. "She can stay with me for a while."

Lee Ann stood tapping the side of the aquarium with a ball-point pen, in the way of the Moonlighter counting the fish, but Lee Ann could not count. Miss Berg sat up later than her usual time, but Lee Ann did not want to sleep, so I said I would bring her up to Miss Berg's room later. Lee Ann did not ask about her brother. There was no word from Neptune.

11

THE TELEVISION was off, the *Vacancy* sign on, the switchboard dead—yet, in the tomblike lobby, the tropical fish swam with nervous dervish élan. ("Fishes, O they know better than old Schine's barometer." Cleveland had told how agitated the fish had been before last year's hurricane.) They might have been working up the centrifugal force to fly free of their aquarium.

I had been memorizing the number taped to the switchboard under EMERGENCY when Bludhorn made his way through the rain as Neptune, the cheap orange makeup streaked, the bottom of his toga soaked from the backed-up gutter at the corner of Avocado Court. I watched him wade in from the waiting cab trying to walk on his heels, using the trident like a gondolier's pole.

"They put me in with the fags," he spouted, dribbling rainwater across the lobby tiles. "They stuck me in the queer tank with the pogey-baits."

His rage flared through the clown's bespattered makeup as he jerked around looking for a target. Lee Ann was locked in with Miss Berg, safely out of range.

He lunged over to the front desk saying, "Some mother turned me in." I was standing by the switchboard while Neptune tried to put two and two together. "Somebody called the cops, said I killed my kid."

There had been a *Herald* reporter at the precinct station: now the fuckinaccident would be in the papers.

"They'll say I killed my kid."

As coolly as fever allowed I stood firm behind the desk, ventured nothing, offered no testimony. Neptune was trying to read my empty face or interpret the vibes. He shook off his surly suspicion shaking raindrops from his brush cut: I was a cipher too impassive to accuse.

If it hadn't been for this shyster whose name he remembered from the dog track he'd be in jail still, "In the queer tank, with the pogey-baits." He was out on bail, bound over.

"What I want to know—" his fury came in waves and was building again, "—is the mother that turned me in."

Personne.

He could sense my loathing, smell my fear, and any instant,

acting on animal instinct, might put the indictment to me. But the wave passed over and his eyes went small again, and shrewd. He could work up no immediate case, he had another case pending. He was bound over—but the cab was waiting, he turned away. He vaulted the stairs with his staff in the devil's own haste, and I was left standing holding my breath.

Was it only three heartbeats he was gone and back? He had not taken time to rub off the makeup or throw off his disguise: he was still swinging the trident, enraged.

"Where is she?" he bellowed.

I took in enough breath to say, "Where's who?"

"Don't play no games with me."

Though he looked like a clown with his smeared makeup, there was nothing clownish in the menace he generated.

"Maybe. Maybe she went out. The back."

The switchboard was lit at Schine's room number, the buzzer on (I had already punched the trunk line in, ready to phone outside for him). Schine was calling down for me to call the police: he could hear the tumult in the lobby.

"Don't try and shit me." With deadly deliberation and genuine—to my bogus—cool, Neptune placed the trident on the front desk and took hold of my shirt with a part of my beard caught in his fist. He then leaned sideways, listing heavily, and pulled the trunk line from its slot. "You ain't calling shit. You know damnwell where she is, you're her buddy."

"Sorry," said I.

"Try and shit me going to get your ass busted, Buster."

He pulled me to him by my shirt, his blunt face drawn so close to mine I could feel the heat of his intention. He would have to rip the truth from me. As he drew my collar ever tighter I felt my beard might now come off, felt almost comically faint, curiously weightless and without care as if I might lift off any moment.

Over his shoulder I saw Uncle Sam. Sam wavered at the top of the lobby stairs, aroused from some stupor, looking not at us but reared back, staring at the ceiling to see if the sky might be falling.

"Let the g-g-guy go," said Sam. He had finally focused on Neptune's threatening embrace. Sam was wearing his TV wrestling robe, the vivid cloak of red, white and blue.

Neptune, who referred to Sam as Dumdum, did not even look up. He was saying to me, "You turned me in." My hand touched the trident—if I could turn it to desperate use, but I was smothering, going under.

As if by gravity alone Sam descended on us, his shoulder sliding against the wall to keep him from falling headlong.

Of course she would hear, even with one eardrum damaged. Neptune's obscene bellow raged through every corner of the Ventura and past Miss Berg's locked door. Against the dim Fire Exit lights in the upper hallway, Lee Ann scuttled in her bunny slippers not to safety but directly into range of danger. She had evaded or been released by the frightened Miss Berg: Lee Ann had heard, a conditioned discipline demanded that she heed.

Neptune read my distraught expression, then turned and looked for himself.

Uncle Sam had ponderously descended halfway down the stairwell and Lee Ann drew up behind him, her face a frightened knot of torment. She too was flattened against the wall, pressed so hard against it she seemed imprinted in the plaster. Uncle Sam was unaware of her presence: his bulky shadow only half-sheltered her as the two moved downstairs in tandem.

"Where you been?" Neptune let go of my shirt and swung around to the stairs.

Whatever Lee Ann's rough training engendered, she was now too strangled by fear to reply.

"I said where you been?"

Sam struggled over Neptune's question as if it had been put to him: his tortured expression attempted to wring meaning from it.

At last a barely audible voice squeaked forth, "Upstairs," and Sam glanced heavenward again to discover the source.

"Get over here," Neptune ordered. He indicated with the trident the place beside her father where she was to stand.

Sam must have felt the small thing pressed against his protective wall of flesh, for he could not yet see Lee Ann behind him.

"Leave her," said Sam, without stuttering.

Neptune ignored Dumdum and said, "I said get over here."

Lee Ann pressed all the more desperately into shadow. Clinging to Sam's flag, she tried to make herself small enough to disappear.

Uncle Sam ventured an uncoordinated arm behind him without turning and like a blind man touched the child's head, certain now that she was there.

"L-L-Leave the kid alone."

"Get over here. I got a cab waiting."

"I don't." Lee Ann was swallowing. "Want to."

"Nobody," said Sam, looking blindly for *personne*. Sam was feeling for weight where his shoulder holster should have been, then feeling for the weapon in his bathrobe pocket, and came up with a key.

First Neptune's head sank deeper into the hunched shoulders, then he bulldozed forward with murderous deliberation, the trident aimed for the stars over Uncle Sam's heart, but the rain-soaked toga tripped him up. Immediately after impact the two mastodons were rolling together on the tiles. Sam had simply let his weight fall forward against his assailant, and Lee Ann escaped being crushed in the melee. I moved swiftly unthinking from behind the desk to reach her with my night man's blanket as if to smother an incipient blaze but first to curtain off the shock and horror.

"Nobody," Sam grunted at Neptune exerting inhuman pressure on the body beneath him.

Her father was screaming but the child could not. I swung clear of Neptune's thrashing sandals past the grappling bodies to where she crouched huddled into the wall with her face in the crook of her arm. I swept Lee Ann into my blanket to spare her, to carry her— where?

The weapons had been kicked aside—a key, the trident—and during the grim hand-to-hand combat I could have pulled Sam off, or found help, but I did not consider this as I bundled Lee Ann in the blanket. I sidestepped the wrestlers' bizarre embrace with top-heavy heavyweight Sam topside and Neptune pinned beneath in a grotesque half nelson. Neptune was lying flat on one ear, his streaked face turned outward, turning purple, as I carried the blanketed babe past the frightful tightening of two bodies. When I reached the door I heard bone crack in Neptune's football-damaged shoulder. After the crack of bone there was no sound beyond Sam's animal satisfaction as he did something worse, something final, to Neptune's neck.

"Nobody," grunted Sam, sated.

The echos of all this must surely arouse every soul at the Ventura and I hovered waiting to see guests pouring from their rooms to flood the halls and lobby with outcry—but nothing, and the body beneath Sam was the quietest of all.

It occurred to me that Sam the punch drunk-ruin might now collapse from his dreadful accomplishment, but he sat astride his victim amazingly at ease. There was a thoughtful remembering look on his face as he leaned against the water cooler with no attempt to disengage himself from the body.

The switchboard remained alight with unanswered panic. Even the two outside trunk lines were lit alongside the room numbers as if

Out There wanted in, but our secret was contained. As I opened the lobby door no inner door cracked light in the hallway. I felt Lee Ann squirming, revived, kicking at her confinement or kicking at me. (I was the one, the result of my hate, the passive assassin responsible for the death of her Dad.) The rain had stopped, but water from the leaky air-conditioners sprinkled down on us as we passed beneath the neon *Vacancy* sign. All the street-side window blinds were drawn tight. The doves at the Nemo murmured a last blessing to our exodus just before I splashed across the flooded gutter.

Miss Berg had forfeited all claim—but what about Roxanne, Miss Ryan? (Miss Ryan loved babies before they grow up and go mental.) I did not even know Miss Ryan's, Medbh's, married name. Roxanne, no.

The taxi was still there, the patient driver waiting with the light on inside his cab. A Mercury, the eternal taxi, waiting to take us—where?

Lee Ann said something inside her bundle and I opened a flap for air. The slippers had fallen off her feet, clues as certain as footprints.

Mercury was forever waiting ready to oblige my every directive, accommodate each retreat. The chauffeur's cap rode ridiculously high on his half-Afro, but after all he had not always been a cabbie. For our enlightenment or entertainment he mimed the three wise monkeys by putting his hands to his ears, to his eyes and to his mouth: hear-no-evil, see-no-evil, speak-no-evil—meaning we were safe with him. He was playing to the babe, he seemed to recognize the blanket.

I entered the cab with my curious papoose, Lee Ann too stunned to protest abduction, her small dark eyes staring terrified at the back of the driver's head. The urgency of our flight was so compelling that we were already past GO in my mind's eye. Ahead beamed the Shipwreck's bicycle lights and I was hallucinating my Old Dad's doppelganger beyond the bridge where fathers wait for us to meet them halfway.

In good time we were passing under the WELCOME CHIROPODISTS OF AMERICA banner at the MacArthur Causeway: the siren from the bridge tender's booth meant a boat passing through—or an ambulance siren from Mt. Sinai, or the police speeding across Arthur Godfrey Road. Mercury would understand the need for speed.

What would Valerie do with a child, the only surviving Waterbaby?

There were haunted islands past the first bridge, Palm and

Hibiscus and Star Island, landmarks for tour boats, and beyond, the Isle of Cuba, or Eden, where the Moonlighter was headed when last seen. If we could get past the bridge before it opened, we could outwit pursuit at least as far as Piggly Wiggly on the Miami side.

Lee Ann squirmed inside her insulation but made no sound. It was then I realized that the driver's flag was down, the meter ticking, but the cab sat paralyzed at the curb. There was no falling-off place, only the endless wheel: I would have to name a place, the dreadful beginning again.

"Where to?" asked the Poet.